UP

in the

AIR

BLUE FEATHER BOOKS, LTD.

There is a fine line between friendship and love. To all those who suffer through the course and weather the storms, I dedicate this story.

Up *in the* Air

A BLUE FEATHER BOOK

by

K. Darblyne

This is a work of fiction. All characters, locales and events are either products of the author's imagination or are used fictitiously.

UP IN THE AIR

Cover design by Ann Phillips

A Blue Feather Book
Published by Blue Feather Books, Ltd.
P.O. Box 5867
Atlanta, GA 31107-5967

www.bluefeatherbooks.com

ISBN: 0-9770318-8-8

First edition: June, 2007

Printed in the United States of America and in the United Kingdom.

Acknowledgements

I'd like to thank all those who have come into my life and nurtured my creative side. They have brought me to where I am now, and I hope they will continue to guide me to where I aspire to be. Without their love and understanding, I would not have pushed myself into achieving the goal of becoming an author. Each novel that comes to fruition is a testament to their keen insight.

Prologue

"Trauma in the department!" The frenzied voice crackled over the emergency room loudspeaker. "Trauma in the department!"

Dr. Garrett Trivoli looked up from her charting and down the long hallway. Amidst the hustling staff, she spied the subject of the announcement huddled in a wheelchair, clutching a blood-soaked towel to her groin. Garrett's keen eyes flickered momentarily to the face of the triage nurse pushing the patient toward the trauma area. John's normally lecherous grin had been replaced by a rather grim expression, clearly reflecting the severity of the patient's condition. Before Garrett could react, the nurse and wheelchair whizzed by her. She followed immediately, straining to hear the mumbled ramblings of her newest patient.

"Weak, they said. Never be able to bear the pain. They don't know what real pain is." The patient jerked her head, tossing her long brown hair back from her face and revealing the delicate features of a young woman. "I'll show them."

As the wheelchair crossed the threshold of Trauma Room One, the distraught patient dug down into the bloodied towel with both hands and came up throwing.

The action took Garrett by surprise, as did the sounds of impact that followed.

Splat! Splat!

Blood splattered over two adjacent walls of the room as the projectiles bounced off and skipped across the floor in random patterns.

"I've done it," the patient sobbed loudly. An elongated, bloody mass landed in front of the wheelchair. Garrett stabbed a hand toward the wall receptacle and donned a pair of sterile gloves.

"I'm free," the patient cried out. "I'm finally free."

"Christ, it's a flubbed abortion," John hissed, turning his head to the side. "Another good reason to always have condoms with you."

A stampede of running feet stopped short behind Garrett, and a string of curses filled the air as the scene unfolded before the newest arrivals.

"Oh, shit."

"What the fuck?"

"Fuck you all," the patient spat, glaring at the shocked ER staff. "Leave me alone. You don't know what it's like to live the way I've had to." Her words broke into sobs of desperation. "To love someone and be afraid to express it." She brought her red-stained hands up to her face, tracing the path of her tears. "I just wanted to be loved."

"We can talk about that later." Garrett tried to make eye contact with the patient, but to no avail. "First, let us help you. You're bleeding, and we have to stop it." Garrett turned to search the sea of faces standing in the hallway, hoping that someone would come to her aid. Her prayers were answered as Nurse Danni Bossard hurried over to the patient.

"Hi, my name's Danni. What's yours?"

"Jen... Jennifer," the patient whispered softly.

"Jennifer, I'd like you to meet Dr. Trivoli."

Danni glanced over at Garrett and smiled, then spoke to the patient. "We'd like to help you, if you'll let us."

The compassionate tone of Danni's words was exactly what Garrett was counting on. Five months into her fellowship, it wasn't the job or the training that impressed Garrett, but the people who went out of their way to make her feel as if she were part of the team. She'd learned this firsthand since her arrival at the trauma center. Danni had been the first to extend her friendship, without even asking her name first, and later, when Garrett was seeking a place to live and joking about being homeless, Danni had offered to share her house. In Garrett's opinion, Danni had an unending heart of gold, always caring about others before thinking about herself. For that reason alone, none of the places she'd lived during college, medical school, internship, residency, and her stint in the Navy had a hold on her like this one. Simply stated, this felt like home.

"Right, Dr. Trivoli?"

"She's right, Jennifer. We're only here to help you."

Danni took a step closer to the wheelchair and extended her hand. "Please."

"Help me..." Jennifer's eyes closed, and the upper half of her body slumped over the arm of the wheelchair.

"All right, people, you heard her." Garrett felt for a pulse on the patient's neck. It was weak and thready under her fingertips. "She wants our help. Let's give it to her. She's lost a lot of blood. Let's get her on the stretcher and find out what we have bleeding before we lose her. I want two units—"

"O neg blood coming right up." Rosie finished the thought and took off down the hall.

"Thanks, Rosie." Garrett acknowledged the nurse for jumping into the thick of things. "Okay, people, on my count." Garrett checked to see that everyone was ready. "One, two, lift." As the patient's body was lifted from the wheelchair and placed on the stretcher, Garrett continued to bark out her orders. "I want her typed and cross-matched, two large-bore IVs with Lactated Ringer's running wide open, and notify the OR we might be coming up in a hurry."

A flurry of activity swirled around the patient as Garrett honed in on the site of the bleeding. Armed with a fistful of gauze, she pulled away the towel and swiped at the bloodied area. It was worse than she'd imagined.

"I'm going to need a vaginal speculum to check internally," Garrett said.

"Dr. Trivoli."

"Yes, Danni?"

"I think you'd better take a look at this."

Garrett's gaze flickered from her patient to Danni and back again. "What is it?"

"That's exactly what I was wondering." Danni picked up one of the bloody pieces from the floor and turned it over a time or two before bringing it closer for Garrett to examine.

"Holy shit." John shuddered. "That's a damned big egg there. That baby would have been a giant. No wonder she aborted it."

"Blood's here," Rosie announced, breezing back into the room. She spiked the bag, watched it fill the IV line, and hung it on a rack. Then she peered over John's shoulder. "What are you looking at?"

Garrett took the object in her gloved hand and turned it over. "If I didn't know better, I'd say it was a... ball."

"Ball? You mean like a Ben Wa?" Rosie reached for the item, only to be denied.

"Ben what?" Danni's brow furrowed.

"Sex ball," Rosie stated. "You know, those hard balls that come in a set. You put them in your va—"

"We get the idea, Rosie." Garrett tested the object with a gentle squeeze. It was supple to the touch. "You're wrong, but in another way, I think you're right."

"See?" A smug expression lingered on Rosie's face. "I know what I'm talking about."

"And they say I'm a pervert." John shook his head and backed away from the group.

Rosie stepped up to take his place. "So, what are they, plastic instead of metal?"

Unsure, Garrett stated the obvious as she placed the object on the stretcher beside the patient. "It's lightweight, but definitely not symmetrical."

"Hey, Rosie, if you're so good, then what's this?" John ventured over to the elongated bloody mass on the floor and picked it up for all to see.

"Kind of small." Rosie studied the bloodied form in John's hand. "I'd say that it looks about right for a dildo. Definitely not a fancy one."

Garrett examined the object. "You're close."

"Oh yeah?" John reached for a towel and cleaned away the blood. "I don't know what pleasure women get from one of these. It's kind of... flexible." He lifted it with his fingers and wiggled it. "Kind of like mine when I'm taking a le..." John's face grew pale. "Christ!" He tossed the amputated appendage at the stretcher, ripped his gloves off and wiped his hands with a towel. "Thanks, guys. Why didn't you tell me I was holding some strange man's twinkie?"

"I wouldn't say a strange man's." Garrett's tone was droll. "I'd say this man's." She indicated their patient. "It's not an abortion we're dealing with, but a badly botched sex-change attempt."

"Oh, jeez!" John winced and clutched the front of his groin.

Garrett grabbed another handful of gauze and tried to clear the blood away from the patient's genital area. She examined the tattered spots where the patient's manhood had previously been attached. "Change that OR call to Urology. They're going to need to work on this one."

"I'll get some ice." Danni walked over to retrieve the second projectile from the floor. "Maybe Urology will be able to reattach these."

"Forget it." Garrett worked to control the bleeding. "The only thing they might be able to reattach is the penis. The rest wouldn't be anything more than an attempt for cosmetic effect, at best. I need several trauma dressings and some six-inch elastic bandages." She glanced up to see Danni nod and alter her course. "We're going to have to use a pressure dressing to slow down this bleeding until Urology figures out what they're going to do."

After a few seconds, the bulky pressure dressing between the patient's legs was doing its job. The unit of blood transfusing into the patient's veins was already beginning to reverse the pallor of his complexion.

"That puts a perfect ending to another long holiday weekend. Happy Thanksgiving to you, too," John said. He turned to see several pairs of eyes staring at him. "What? I'm just stating the obvious. I didn't say a single word about how sick someone would have to be to do what she—I mean, he—did."

"I'll thank you to keep your thoughts to yourself in my trauma room." A flash of anger crossed Garrett's face. "The last time I looked, I was the doctor here. I'll be the one making the diagnosis."

The charge nurse's voice cut through the air. "John," Karen said, "triage is backed up. I suggest you get back to your station." Her stare told him not to challenge her authority, and he remained silent. "Rosie, why don't you help John?"

"Sure, Karen." Rosie tore off her gloves. "Come on. They can handle this without us." She brushed past John. "You know the story. A nurse's work is never done."

"Yeah, I know what you mean," John said, and followed her.

It was no wonder Karen was looked upon as the matriarch of the Emergency Room family, Garrett reflected. She had reacted as any good mother would, stopping the conflict before it escalated and separating the two warring parties.

Karen let out an audible breath before turning back to the paperwork in front of her. "Urology is notified, Dr. Trivoli. Is there anything else you'd like me to do?"

"Put a page in for the resident covering Psych. I'd like to talk to him about a consult."

"So," Danni said, "are you thinking along the lines of gender confusion?"

"What I'm thinking is that my patient is going to need some help to deal with this whole situation."

"I see." Danni bit at her lip and looked away.

"I'm not saying that what he did, if he did indeed do it to himself, is wrong. All I'm saying is that I believe he's going to need some support to get through life."

"Because he chose to live outside the mainstream?" Danni's voice was uncertain.

"No. This time, he took his anger out in the form of revenge on his genitals. My concern is for the next time. Unless his anger is managed properly, it could be directed at someone else, or inflicted even more seriously on himself." Garrett's words trailed off and she looked away. "Especially around the holidays," she whispered.

Chapter 1

Sitting in the comfort of her living room, Danni flexed her biceps and smiled, eyeing the muscles she now displayed. "Never thought I could do that one."

"What?" Garrett dropped her duffel at the foot of the stairs.

"I was just thinking about how strong I've become since we started working out together." Danni made a muscle once more and pointed at it. "See?"

Garrett continued up the stairs. "I've got to get my toiletries for the night. I'll be right down."

"I guess that means you're on call tonight." Danni's voice grew softer, and she made a face. Her thoughts were interrupted by the phone.

"I'll get it," she yelled, and made her way to the phone on the hallstand.

"Hello?"

"Oh, Danielle. I'm glad I finally got hold of you."

"You're up awfully early, Brie. What can I do for you?" Danni already knew the phone call was going to be about her missing Thanksgiving dinner with the family. But she had made her choice, and they were going to have to live with it.

"I was wondering why you didn't come home for the holiday. Mother was very disappointed that we weren't all together. You did remember it was Thanksgiving last Thursday, didn't you?" Brie's tone was sharp.

"Danni," Garrett called from the second floor. "I can't find my razor. Do you have one I can borrow?"

"Who's that yelling?"

"Hang on a minute, sis." Danni laid the phone down on the stand, then crossed to the bottom of the staircase. "I have a spare one in the top drawer of my nightstand. Go ahead and take it. I'll get some more at the store later this week."

"Thanks, I owe you one."

I like this new Garrett even better. Danni returned to the phone with a smile on her face.

"Okay, I'm back. Now, what was that question?"

"Never mind the question. I want to know who that was."

"That was Garrett."

"Garrett?" The name lingered in the air for a moment before being replaced by a revised question. "Garrett who?"

"Dr. Trivoli, one of the trauma fellows this year." Danni spoke clearly and without hesitation.

"I guess that's the reason you weren't at dinner. You were spending some time with the doctor, huh?"

"Uh, yeah. Garrett pulled the holiday to be on call, so I volunteered to work, too. That way we ate together, and Gar didn't have to be all alone." Danni was proud of herself for stating the truth and feeling good about it.

"So, you and this doctor are getting pretty friendly."

Garrett came down the stairs. "I'm leaving in two minutes. Are we driving in together?" She stuffed the toiletries into her duffel bag.

"Driving in together?" Breanna's query bordered on an all out interrogation.

"Oh, I guess I forgot to tell you. Gar moved in with me a couple of months ago. Hey, I really have to run now, or I'll be late for work. I promise I'll talk to you soon, okay?"

"Yeah. Get going, but we have to talk soon."

Danni picked up on the urgency in her sister's voice. "As soon as I can. Nothing's wrong, is there? With the pregnancy, I mean."

"No, nothing with the baby. Now hurry, before you're late. Bye."

"Bye," Danni said, feeling better about her sister's call than she'd thought she would, and attributing it to the obvious. Brie must be mellowing with the second pregnancy.

"Danni." Garrett headed outside. "Time's up. I'm leaving."

"Coming." Danni lunged for her coat and ran out the door to catch up. "I'm right behind you." Seeing Garrett getting into the Blazer, Danni hurried along, pushing all thoughts of the phone conversation out of her mind. It was going to be a big day, and she wouldn't let anything overshadow it.

* * *

Garrett fidgeted behind the metal desk in her small, shared office. She was growing nervous about the meeting with Ol' Cutter. Such an appropriate nickname for someone of his medical stature, she thought, smiling for a moment. Every time Dr. John McMurray talked about one of the photographs in his reception area that captured the milestones of his life, marriage, and career, it opened her eyes. In a way, it was like learning from a wise old soul; perhaps even two.

Garrett wondered what she would have someday as similar remembrances of her early days in medicine. As of now, there was little to see or say, and the only things that symbolized her career thus far were her hands.

"Should I have them bronzed?" she asked herself, half-jokingly. "Yeah, right. I can see that conversation becoming pretty boring after the second time, even to my most astute student." She sighed. "I guess they're only good for when you reach out to someone."

She pondered the thought until a knock came on her door. "Come in," she said, and waited to see what needed her attention now.

"Rob." She was relieved to see the face of Dr. Kreger, the chief resident on her service. "What can I do for you?" Rob was a hard worker, and she liked having him on her trauma nights, especially now that he was coming into his own as a surgeon and finally realizing it himself.

"I just stopped in to tell you not to worry about the meeting with Ol' Cutter today. I'll cover the ER while you're in conference."

Garrett let her lower lip extend into a pout. "And I was going to hope for the trauma pager to go off."

"I know how much this project means to you."

"Thanks, I appreciate it."

"Say, if there's anything I can help with—" Just then Danni tapped on the doorway, and Rob acknowledged her presence with a dip of his head. "But I see you probably have all the help you need."

"I'll keep you in mind, Rob," Garrett said, as her eyes fixed on Danni.

"Okay. I'll just go check in on the patient from earlier this morning. Good luck with McMurray."

"Thanks for the offer," both women acknowledged, though slightly out of sync, as he turned to leave.

"Hey, Gar."

"Hey. You're a little early, aren't you?" Garrett looked at her watch.

"Tell it to my stomach. I don't think those butterflies know how to tell time." Danni held on to her midsection and grimaced. "They started getting flighty about twenty minutes ago."

"Would you like me to write you a scrip for some Compazine or Reglan?"

"No. I'll pass, this time." Danni ventured farther into the small office and closed the door. "Do you think they accepted the whole proposal?"

"I guess we'll find out when we get the official rundown from Dr. McMurray." Garrett studied Danni. "This is really worrying you, isn't it?"

"It's just that I've never done anything like this before. I mean, write a proposal and all. I feel a little"—she searched for the right word to use—"overwhelmed by it all."

Garrett smiled at Danni's insecurity. "If I were you, I'd get used to it. I have a feeling that if we pull off this project, McMurray and the Board are going to expect more from us." Garrett's eyes darted around the fixtures of the small room, then back to Danni. "In fact, I'm sure of it. You know how he's into teamwork."

"Let's just see what he has to say first, then maybe I'll feel better." Danni hesitated. "Do you think we could change the subject? I mean, just for a few minutes."

"Sure, what do you want to talk about?" Garrett was curious. Were Danni's nerves just getting to her, or did she have something else on her mind? "Anything in particular?"

Danni hedged for a few seconds before starting. "Have you given any thought as to what you're going to do after your fellowship year is done? I mean, where you want to practice?"

"I'll be honest with you. I've been too busy just getting through this year so far to really give it any serious thought." Garrett noticed the disappointed look on Danni's face. "Why do you ask? Does it make any difference?"

"No. I guess it doesn't. I was wondering if the project would continue without you being here, that's all."

"I think that to give it any chance to do some good, it's going to take more than just a couple of months to even get it off the ground. I hope they won't discontinue their support without giving it a fair shot." Danni might have something there. Maybe she should plant her feet and stay a while, just to get it going.

Garrett thought about her brother. Deep in her soul, she felt it was Lucas who had brought her to this point in her life. What did he think about her staying? What exactly was it that he had planned for her?

Danni took in a deep breath and then let it out. "Maybe we'd better get up to Dr. McMurray's office. We don't want to be late."

"Yes, let's show him how eager we are." Garrett stood up. "Are you walking in with me this time, or do I have to push you?"

"What do you think?" Danni's tone was defensive, and she reacted to the challenge with balled fists resting on her hips. "I was just a little taken aback by how big his office was last time, that's all. You'll see. I'll follow you right in." Danni wrinkled her nose.

"Oh, so that means I'll be pulling you in after me instead, eh?" Seeing the mock glare directed at her, Garrett quickly sidestepped Danni's playful swat.

"You are so bad." Danni tried to keep a straight face, but couldn't.

* * *

John McMurray stood transfixed at the window, but his thoughts were not on the swirling snow outside. Instead, he imagined the excited looks that would be on his new team's faces after he told them the good news

He laughed at himself. They probably thought he ought to have his head examined. The chief of a whole department braving a snow squall just to pass on some news to a nurse and a fellow? Ridiculous.

The intercom buzzer sounded, putting an abrupt end to his thoughts. Irritated, he crossed over to his desk and slammed his finger down on the button. "Yes? What is it?"

"Your ten o'clock appointment is here. Shall I send them in?" The voice broke up, the message barely audible.

"I don't understand why, in the age of computer technology, we can't get a better system installed in this hospital." Glancing over his desk, he saw the note that was jotted on his daily calendar sheet, a reminder of a problem that needed to be addressed if the proposed project was to get off the ground. "Send them in."

"You can go in now, Dr. Trivoli, Nurse Bossard," the voice on the box crackled out.

Like he didn't know the people he was supposed to be meeting with. They must teach that in secretarial school. He quickly picked up some papers and started shuffling them around. He looked up as his door opened.

"Don't stop there. Come in." McMurray laid the papers in a heap on the corner of the desk and strode over to look out his office window.

Garrett and Danni entered and waited for Ol' Cutter to acknowledge them. The first sound they heard was a deep sigh, and then he began to speak.

"Do you believe in fate?" He didn't wait for either of them to answer. "I used to believe that I controlled my own destiny, until I learned a valuable lesson. You're always at someone's mercy. You just have to hope you can satisfy their needs first, and then maybe you can fulfill your own." McMurray turned toward them. "Okay. Enough philosophy. You're here to find out about that proposal."

Garrett caught Danni's sidelong glance, but neither woman spoke. "Let's get down to business, then. Take a seat." He motioned to the two chairs in front of his desk. "We've got some things to discuss."

McMurray eyed them one at a time, then smiled. "The Board liked the idea and commended you both on the proposal. You have their full blessing and authority to proceed with your plan. The other departments in our great institution have been instructed to give you all the support you feel is necessary." He settled into his high-backed chair.

"In other words, you have carte blanche on the project. It's all in your hands. You'll report directly to the Board of Directors."

Danni glanced from him to Garrett and then back again. Slowly, the corners of her lips turned up in a smile. "That's great news. Don't you think, Dr. Trivoli?"

Garrett's eyes narrowed, and she studied Dr. McMurray. Slowly she reached out her hand until it came to rest on Danni's. "I don't think that's all the Board has in mind for us. It's too good to be true. There has to be a catch, somewhere." She and McMurray stared at each other.

"What do you mean?" Danni said. "Come on, we're all on the same team. I don't think this is getting us anywhere. Do you?"

McMurray and Garrett both shifted their stares to Danni.

"Well, is it?" Danni crossed her arms over her chest.

Danni's bold move to mediate seemed to surprise McMurray. "Good God, you've got moxie." He shook his head. "Trivoli, do you think you could work closely with Bossard on a permanent basis?"

"Perhaps I should ask what you mean by 'closely' before I answer that."

McMurray made a sound that was half laugh, half grunt. "You have good reason to ask. It seems the Board likes the numbers you two have when you work together. Ian McCormick may not be an idea man, but he knows his way around the numbers. He's the one who pointed it out to them." McMurray rubbed his chin. "The Board is willing to give you what you want on your proposal, if you do them a favor."

Garrett eyed him cautiously. "What kind of favor would that be?"

McMurray drew a deep breath. "All right. The bottom line is this: The Board wants you out of the OR on a regular basis for the rest of your fellowship."

"Me? Out of the OR? They're idiots." Garrett's eyes felt like crystals of ice as she stared at McMurray. "I'm not cutting off my nose to spite my face."

Danni gasped. "What kind of favor would that be, for either the Board or the patients?"

"I know, but it's not what you're thinking. Although," he said, and paused, "you may think differently about it when it's over and done with. Look at all of the exposure you'll get, working at different hospitals."

"And what exactly do you mean by that?" Garrett asked.

"Yes, what exactly?" Danni's brow furrowed.

"Let's just say that you two," McMurray said, and pointed to them both, "are going to spend more time together than most married couples do."

"I don't understand," Garrett said. "What could that possibly…"

"You're not paid to understand. You're just expected to do your best in the environment we give you." The sound of an incoming helicopter could be heard, and Ol' Cutter swiveled his chair to look out the window. "Perfect timing." The helicopter became clearly visible as he turned back and continued.

"The Board wants to draw some marketable attention to the hospital and what we do here. They feel that their best bet is to capitalize on you and the good PR you can generate. They were kind of excited that you two aren't lacking in the good looks department, either." McMurray glanced outside once more, then turned back to face the women.

"Everybody and his brother was hyped about the new millennium last year. This New Year's is actually the start of the real millennium, with the beginning of 2001. The Board wants to use it to our advantage."

The noise of the spinning rotors grew even louder, and Ol' Cutter raised his voice to speak over it. "You, Dr. Trivoli, are going to be our first flight surgeon on the helicopters, and Nurse Bossard will be your team member." McMurray swung his chair to face the window, just as the helicopter finished its descent to the pad below. "Welcome to the new millennium of health care," he said, with outstretched arms.

The swirling snow gave the helicopter an eerie appearance. Garrett's gaze was riveted on it, her mind in a quandary.

After the noise of the helicopter had died down, she spoke out. "You can't expect me to operate in one of those. There's not enough room to take care of a bad splinter, let alone trauma of any significance."

"So you've been in one, eh?" McMurray's voice was gruff, but teasing.

"Been in one, hell! I rode in them when I was in the Navy, and those were a lot bigger."

"You... You've ridden in helicopters?" Danni stammered.

"Yeah, that's how they got me from ship to ship when I'd have to replace another surgeon. They're not always the safest way to go, but they get the job done." She smiled reminiscently. "It sure beat using a bosun's chair."

"Bosun's chair?" Danni said. "I don't understand. What's so bad about a chair?"

"It's like sitting on a chair dangling from a cable stretched between two race cars. One wrong move and..."

"Oh, my! Gar— Dr. Trivoli, you're scaring me." Danni looked at McMurray. "You're kidding, right?" She blinked several times and waited for an answer. When McMurray shook his head and smiled, her shoulders slumped. "You're not. The Board wants Dr. Trivoli to fly into surgeries. Literally."

"And you, too," Ol' Cutter said. "The Board feels that your presence in the air will be a highly visible marketing tool to the smaller hospitals in the area. You'll be a trauma surgical team flying into their world." He elaborated with a chuckle. "They want your faces to be more recognizable than the presidential candidates."

"That won't be hard," Danni said in a wry tone. "What am I supposed to do? I've never been in a helicopter. In fact, the last time that I was even on an airplane was…" She gulped hard and looked at Garrett.

Danni's pallor concerned Garrett. She slowly turned to face her mentor and studied him for a long moment.

"You want us to fly in and save the day at every little-ass Podunk of a hospital and make the Board look like it's reaching out with its services to every nook and cranny in the area?" Her voice turned angry. "Whose idea was that? Some lame-brained accountant?"

"What's the matter, Trivoli, afraid you might have to interact with more people who don't know your likes and dislikes?" McMurray looked directly at her, challenging her with his stare. "Maybe if you put the patient first, and not your damned need for perfection, then…" He stopped and pressed his lips together.

The office was silent as all three stared at one another. Finally, the silence was broken.

"Come on, Danni. We don't have to listen to this nonsense." Garrett started walking toward the door.

"You do if you want that proposal to become a reality," McMurray said.

With her hand on the doorknob, Garrett hesitated. She saw Danni freeze in mid-step, and they both looked at McMurray.

"You do this for the Board, and they'll guarantee you free rein with your project. It's as simple as that." He got up and circled his high-backed chair. "I know this project means something to you both." He brought his clenched fist down onto the top of the chair. "Damn it! It's that or nothing, as far as the Board's concerned."

Garrett let her hand slide off the doorknob and took a step back in his direction. "I'm not going to have our faces splashed all over the place in some media event. I'm not some publicity-seeking egomaniac, and neither is she." Garrett pointed to Danni before shaking her head in dismay. "We don't need to be high profile in our jobs. Flying in a helicopter is dangerous enough, what with the blades looming overhead and jet fuel onboard. We don't need to be on the lookout for crazed fans, too."

"Is that your concern? Fans? I'll tell the Board the PR is for the hospitals only, and that it's not to go to the general public. Will that help?" McMurray sat down and waited for an answer.

"Gar… er, Dr. Trivoli, maybe we should think about this." Danni looked pleadingly at Garrett. "How bad could it be? We could help a lot of people who are traumatized, both physically and psychologically."

Danni's green eyes were speaking volumes. Garrett pursed her lips and ran her tongue over her teeth as she weighed the pros and cons.

"God, I'm going to regret this." The words seethed out before Garrett turned to face McMurray. "All right!" she snapped, walking back toward the desk. "But first, there'll be some things ironed out right here and now."

"I'm sure we can meet on common ground."

Garrett watched satisfaction settle on McMurray's face. Whatever their demands, he knew he had his team.

Chapter 2

"Ouch." Danni winced as she shucked her coat onto the nearest chair and dropped her gym bag to the floor. "I'm feeling muscles I never knew I had." She rubbed her back with one hand and gingerly rolled the opposite shoulder in an attempt to soothe her aches. "Tell me again why I agreed to this."

"Because it was part of the package you negotiated." Garrett walked past her, obviously unaffected by the rigorous demands of their training regime.

"Don't remind me."

"Thanks, by the way."

"You're welcome, I think." Danni moved toward the stairs. "Do you really think all this conditioning will make a difference?"

"We won't know for sure until we're out there, but from all the EMS people I've talked to, the job can be more physically demanding than most people think."

"Yeah, I can see where some might be enamored with the idea that we're white knights riding to the rescue." Danni smiled weakly.

"Even knights had their training periods," Garrett said. "I'm just glad we don't have to wear chain mail."

"Oh, please." Danni slumped over the banister railing. "I'm worn out doing the Cardiac Rehab circuit and running around the indoor track every other day." She pushed up off the railing. "Speaking of which, I can't believe I'm getting out of my nice warm bed to do that before our full day of classes. And with that thought," she said with a smirk, "I'm headed to take a long, hot soak in the tub, unless you'd like to have it first."

"No, thanks. I'm good." Garrett waved off the offer. "If the hot soak doesn't loosen up those muscles, I could always give you a massage when you're done."

The words caught Danni by surprise. "Uh, thanks," she said, her interest piqued as to what Garrett's skilled hands could do to make her body feel better. She faltered, searching for something more to say. "I'll give it some thought."

*   *   *

Lulled by the effects of her soak, Danni drifted somewhere between consciousness and sleep. Her mind lingered on the proposal Garrett had made. Surely, it had been a simple offer from one friend to another? But what if was something more? Danni imagined the warmth of Garrett's hands starting a gentle kneading action across her shoulders. She could almost feel her flesh moving willingly with the pressure, like clay being molded by an artist's hands—each change of direction sending a rush of electrically-charged particles running rampant throughout her body, driving deep, to her very core. Giving in to her body's silent betrayal, Danni wanted nothing more than to melt at this very moment, never again to feel the need for another's caress. If she let her mind go, she could almost smell the spicy fragrance she had come to recognize as Garrett and hear the sound of her name rolling off inviting lips.

"Danni."

She smiled appreciatively and purred at the gentle stroking of her cheek.

"Danni."

"That was nice," Danni mumbled. "Could we do it again?"

"Sure, anytime you want."

Danni opened her eyes to see a silhouette coming into view. "Gar?" The contented expression on Danni's face turned into one of startled embarrassment.

"Come on, sleepyhead. I think this hot soak has given you just about all it can. Time to dry off before you catch a chill." Garrett held out a towel.

This couldn't be real, could it? Danni averted her eyes from Garrett's. "Massage. Didn't you...?" Danni took in her surroundings. "How long," she struggled to get her words out. "How long have you been—"

"Standing here? Not long."

"Thank you," Danni whispered with a sigh of relief. It was just a dream.

"If you want, I could do you now."

"What?" Danni's eyes opened wide.

"Massage," Garrett said. "I offered you a massage earlier, but it looks like you're pretty relaxed now. Maybe next time I should give you the massage before you bathe."

Instantaneously, Danni felt a blush sweep over her face as she realized that she had been under Garrett's meticulous scrutiny.

"I'll… ah… I'm going to bed."

Garrett hesitated before moving toward the door. "Remember, we've got a photo shoot in the morning."

"Yeah, morning." Danni watched Garrett exit. "It felt so real," she whispered, before hoisting her body out of the tepid bath water. She crossed her arms across her body against the room's cool air. "What the…" She looked down at her nipples, finding them already hard and raised before the rest of her body had time to react. "Girl, you've got it bad." She hung her head and sighed. "Real bad."

* * *

"See what happens when we're not on, Danni?" Garrett sauntered up to the desk with two women behind it.

"I wish some of the nights I worked were like this—just sitting around at the desk." Danni stared directly at Rosie.

Rosie looked up. "Don't look now, Karen, but the prodigal daughters just walked in."

"Huh?" Karen peered over the top of the computer screen. "Hey!"

"Hi, Karen." Danni flashed a warm smile. "Rosie."

"Hi, Karen." Garrett turned, but was cut off before saying anything else.

"What, no quick wave-and-run through the ER? You doing something different today?" Rosie placed her hands on her hips and cocked her head to the side.

Garrett arched an eyebrow. "Like we actually have a choice of what we get to do."

"It's not going to be that bad." Danni patted Garrett's leather-clad arm. "Try to be positive about it."

"I am." Garrett grimaced. "I'm positive I'm not going to enjoy this morning."

"Why? What do they have planned for you today?" Karen asked, looking directly at Garrett.

Garrett coughed and talked at the same time, causing her words to be mumbled and incoherent.

"What?" Karen looked clueless. "Come on, it can't be all that terrible. Just say it and get it over with."

Garrett's voice was slightly more than a whisper. "Publicity shots." Her expression was pained. "We have to get the photos taken today."

"See, it wasn't that hard to say, was it?" Danni rubbed the back of Garrett's jacket.

This was the second time Danni had touched her jacket in the last few minutes. Garrett pondered the action, losing sight of the question directed at her.

"Garrett?" Danni's voice refocused her. "What's so wrong with having our photo taken?"

"I don't see what all the fuss is about. Why can't they just use my hospital ID photo?" Garrett took her wallet out of her pocket and sorted through it until her hospital-issued identification tag was in her hand. "Now tell me, what's wrong with this picture?" She held it out for everyone to see.

"Dr. Trivoli, nothing's wrong with it," Karen said. "That is, if you're already in jail." Her lips twitched as she handed the photo to Rosie.

"If you showed me this, I wouldn't let you anywhere near my drugs," Rosie quipped, all too eagerly. "Yeah, I can see where this would make for a wonderful press release."

"I should have expected as much from you," Garrett retorted.

All attempts to keep from laughing yielded to Karen's contagious belly laugh.

"Ha, ha." Disgusted, Garrett looked over to see a man slowly walking in through the doors. He had no obvious signs of injury, but her instincts told her something was wrong. His steps faltered, and suddenly, he sank to the floor. Without a second thought, Garrett tossed her wallet to Karen and took off to assist the fallen man.

"Hey, you don't have to throw things at me. I was only teasing you." Karen caught the wallet and looked up to see the cause of Garrett's action. "We've got a man down in the waiting room. Danni, Rosie, help her." The charge nurse quickly gathered up the disheveled contents of the wallet and stuffed them inside her lab-jacket pocket.

The two nurses dropped to the cold tile floor and joined Garrett as she assessed the man's ability to breathe. Danni searched for a pulse, while Rosie began to remove his bulky clothing. The only visible sign of trouble was the trickle of blood coming from the corner of his mouth.

"Sir. Sir!" Garrett's commanding voice elicited no response from the man.

"We need a little assistance here." Garrett's words accelerated the staff emerging from every corner of the ER.

When enough of the staff had assembled, they lifted the heavy man onto a stretcher. Seconds later, he was in the trauma room, and the impromptu team worked to find the cause of his worsening condition.

Garrett looked up from pulling on a pair of gloves and saw the familiar face of the X-ray tech across from her. When their eyes met, Garrett nodded her approval and continued with her physical assessment of the patient.

"Clear the chest," the tech bellowed. "X-ray!"

Danni paused for a second, then connected the patient to the monitoring system. "Pulse one-ten, BP a hundred over seventy-six." She turned to double-check the positioning of the finger probe for the pulse oximeter. "Oxygen saturation ninety-four percent."

"Okay, IV is in. Sixteen gauge in the left AC," Rosie announced, placing the last piece of tape to secure the needle.

"No injuries showing on his anterior aspect. Let's roll him and check his back." As the staff opposite her logrolled the patient's body, Garrett's skilled eyes roamed over the entire expanse of the man's posterior surface. There, just below his costophrenic angle on the right, was a small laceration. Garrett gently inserted her gloved finger to learn the extent of its penetration.

Hmm... there was his rib. She moved her finger in the opposite direction. It felt like a downward direction. Looked like she was going to get some surgical time in today, since the team hadn't responded yet.

"Get us an OR room, Karen. He's been stabbed." Garrett removed her finger and motioned for the patient to be placed on his back. "Hang a unit of O-negative blood. Somebody put in a Foley catheter and draw blood for the lab." Garrett stepped back and removed her soiled gloves. "I want him typed and cross-matched for four units, and send them to the OR."

"X-ray's up."

"Good." Garrett strode into the hallway and studied the film hanging on the viewbox.

"Would you like an abdomen film, Doc?" the technician asked.

"Yeah." Garrett continued to examine the image. "Get the film, and we're off to the OR."

"The OR is ready and waiting for you, Dr. Trivoli," Karen said.

Garrett couldn't hide her excitement. She rubbed her hands together in anticipation of holding a scalpel again.

"You miss it, don't you?" Karen asked.

"Yes, I do." Garrett stepped back into the room. "Let's get up to the OR. They have a room waiting for our patient." Garrett fell in step alongside the stretcher as her patient headed for the land of bright lights and cold steel.

* * *

"Now, that's odd." Karen shuffled through the cards in her hand.

"What's odd?" Danni set the portable monitor down on the desk.

"There are no pictures. My wallet is stuffed with pictures of my family and friends." Karen went through them again, finally finding a worn and tattered photo. "Wait a minute, there is one." She squinted. "Darn glasses."

"What are you trying to look at?" Danni moved closer to see.

"Darn bifocals. You'd think they would help." Karen handed the photo to Danni. "Here, see if you can make this out."

Danni recognized Garrett's strong features in the photograph. "Where'd you find this?"

"In her wallet. It must have fallen out when she tossed it at me." Karen craned her neck to see the images. "Who do you think it is?"

"The tall one is definitely Garrett." Danni turned the photo over and looked at its back. The youthful writing on it made her sigh as she ran a finger over it. "It reads, 'Luc and me 1980.' I'll be…" Danni flipped the photograph over and stared at it. "It's her brother." The words came out slowly, almost reverently.

"Tall, dark, and gorgeous has a brother?" Rosie said. "How come she's been keeping him a secret? Let me see." Rosie moved to get a better look from over Danni's shoulder. "Hot damn, he's a cutie." She let out a low whistle. "I wonder where I can find him."

Danni's response was little more than a shrug as she worked out the numbers in her head. Gar had said she was seventeen when the accident happened. This must have been taken the same year. The photo confirmed their closeness. How she must miss him.

The group's attention was diverted by the banging of the fire doors as John walked into the ER. He approached the women and gave them a leering grin. "So, you girls want to be the first Maids of

Desire on my new website?" He held up a shiny pocket camera and pointed to it. "It's digital."

The assembled nurses cringed collectively.

"Come on." John gave Danni a knowing look. "I'll make you and that tall roommate of yours famous on the Internet. What do you say?"

John's camera gave Danni an idea. She looked at the photo in her hands. "So, you want a picture of Dr. Trivoli, huh?" She fanned herself with the photograph and waggled her eyebrows.

* * *

Garrett finished scrubbing her hands, then breezed into the operating room to don her sterile gown and gloves, tugging them into place on her way to join the surgical team at the operating table. She prepped her patient for surgery, then looked up to see her colleague, Dr. Chabot, hurrying into the room.

"Ah, René, you've come to assist me. I was wondering who would be my second." Garrett poised her blade over the patient.

Chabot grabbed a gown and thrust his arms into it.

"McMurray sent me," he gasped, out of breath. "He said you're not to be operating. You have a job to do, and I should send you to do it."

"What?" Garrett said.

"Please, I'm only the messenger." René stood next to her at the operating table, his hands ready to accept the scalpel she was holding.

Garrett wanted to explode at him, but knew it would do no good for any of them, especially her patient. The favor the Board had asked for came dancing back through her head. Closing her eyes for a moment in resignation, she handed him the scalpel and stepped away from the table.

"I'll take good care of him," René assured her.

Garrett pulled off her gloves. "He's got a stab wound in the back, angled down into the abdomen. There's blood trickling out of his mouth, so I'd take a good look at his stomach and esophagus for lacerations."

"Thanks, I will." René grabbed a sterile towel and used it to adjust the overhead light. "Okay, let's do a little exploring, shall we?" He checked his team for readiness and then placed the scalpel to skin.

Left standing on the outside of the circle, Garrett walked to the door, then turned and watched as René guided his team to best serve the patient.

"Suction," René spoke softly to his scrub nurse. "Okay, now give me some retraction."

Garrett pulled open the door and left the operating theater. She wasn't used to walking out before the patient was even worked on. "I'd better not keep my job waiting," she muttered, shedding the gown and stuffing it into the nearest receptacle.

* * *

"I'm strapped for time. Set up for the individual shots," the man with the camera directed his assistants. "You, in the jumpsuit, stand there."

Danni moved to where she was directed and waited as the photographer slowly circled around her.

"Look here."

Flash!

The lights blinded Danni for a few seconds.

"Now, look there," he said, pointing in a new direction.

Flash! Danni blinked.

"Over here." The photographer demanded her attention once more.

Just when Danni thought she knew where to look, he was yelling some other direction at her.

"All right, everyone, take a fifteen-minute break."

The lights dimmed, and Danni was left standing there, alone.

The photographer marched over to a man seated in the corner.

"You want me to give you an excited, accomplished-looking subject for a PR release." He shook his head. "She looks more like a lost child out there." The photographer flopped down next to Dr. McMurray. "Isn't there someone else you can use? I'm never going to get any good shots out of this one."

"She'll be all right," Dr. McMurray said. "Danni's a team player. She'll do better when the other half of the team shows up. Look, here she comes now." McMurray pointed toward Garrett in the doorway. He turned to Danni, and waited for the moment she set eyes on Garrett.

"There," he whispered to the photographer. "That's the image I want you to get."

The man quickly placed his camera to his eye and began to focus on the radiant woman in the light. His face took on a new exuberance as he captured Danni on film.

"So, who's the tall, good-looking one?" The photographer motioned with his head toward Garrett. "I'd like to have her on film. Heck, I'd like to have her myself."

"That, sir, is the other half of the team." McMurray turned to look at the salivating photographer. "And I don't believe you could handle her if you tried."

"A wild one, huh?"

McMurray's lip curled into a smile as he nodded. "Headstrong is more like it."

"What are they, student nurses? Your secretaries?"

"My secretaries? Hardly."

"Let's see how good they are as models." The photographer jumped up. "Break's over. Let's get back to work." He snapped his fingers excitedly. "You, over there. You," he pointed to Garrett, "stand next to her."

The photographer walked around them, letting his stare wash over the entire lengths of their bodies. He snapped his fingers and pointed to Danni, then lifted his finger several inches in the air. Immediately his assistants scurried, rushing back with a small stool.

"Step on it," the photographer directed Danni.

She did his bidding. "I guess I'm coming up in the world," she said as she stepped on the stool.

"Much better. Now you." The photographer pointed to Garrett. "Come just a little closer to the lens."

Garrett complied, then turned to view Danni.

"Look at me, not her," the photographer said. "Okay, now I want you to think of something that would make you very happy to get for Christmas." He positioned himself, watched the women's faces in the viewfinder of the camera, and waited.

"Christmas, huh?" Danni's face lit up.

Garrett's eyes seemed to twinkle as she glanced back at Danni, and the corners of her mouth turned upward.

The photographer began recording their expressions amidst the clicking of the shutter and the flashing of the strobes. Seconds later, his quick hand motions brought the support crew to life. Ladders were positioned and equipment moved to meet his constant directions.

"Hey, Gar, what do you think they're going to do up there?"

Garrett turned a watchful eye to the pair of assistants as they climbed nearly to the top of the ladders. "I'm not sure, but I guess we'll find out."

"Come on, I don't have all day for this shoot. I want it up higher and over more." The photographer waved his hands, then cursed. "Damn it! Not there." He punctuated his words with a piercing clap of his hands. "Over more, Ronnie. Can't you move it any farther?" He turned away with a look of disgust.

The events of the next few seconds seemed to occur in slow motion. Before Danni could shout a warning, Ronnie was falling from the ladder. Her body hit the floor with a thud. Ronnie's limp form lay unmoving, her legs draped over the small stool that Danni had been standing on just moments before.

"Jeez!" The photographer spun around toward the fallen worker. "Don't go bleeding on the backdrop." His hands moved excitedly. "Hurry up, get her off of there."

Garrett and Danni sprang into action, each one sensing what the other would do. Danni went to the phone on the wall to summon additional help and supplies, while Garrett tended to her patient.

"Don't touch her," Garrett warned a young man who was reaching for Ronnie.

The crew backed off, and Garrett knelt beside the injured woman's head. A quick check assured her the patient was still breathing on her own.

"Good, deep inspirations," she said aloud, then examined her further to learn where all the blood was coming from.

Danni made her way over to the scene and crouched beside the patient. "Ronnie, can you hear me? Ronnie?"

Muffled words could be heard as Ronnie began to stir.

"Don't move. You've fallen. We'll take care of you." Danni brushed back the loose hair from the patient's face. "You're going to be all right. Just let us take care of you."

"Did you get us some help, Danni?"

"Yeah, I called the ER and told them we needed a backboard, a hard collar, and a stretcher."

Garrett nodded as she assessed the patient's extremities, carefully checking each of the arms and legs for any sign of deformity or swelling.

"Obvious deformity in the left leg."

The leg was twisted underneath the woman and the lower half of her pant leg was beginning to soak through with blood. Garrett looked toward the people gathered around the outskirts of the lit area. "I need a knife or a pair of scissors."

"Here, will this help?" An older man stepped out of the shadows and produced a pocketknife from his jeans.

"Yes, thanks. That will work." She took the knife and opened it. Using the large blade, she carefully slit Ronnie's jeans up the side of the leg and exposed the injury. Skin was hanging from the avulsion, and jagged ends of the bones were showing. The fracture was nasty, but nothing that couldn't be repaired.

"How's she doing, Danni?"

"She's mumbling some, but nothing really coherent." Danni talked softly as she maintained the position of the patient's head.

"The sooner we get her stabilized, the sooner we can get this fixed." Garrett turned at the sound of the door being thrown open. "And here comes the cavalry now."

Within minutes, under Garrett's direction, the patient was placed in a cervical collar and on a backboard.

Following his initial unconcern, the photographer had stood in shock, not moving a muscle, his eyes riveted on Garrett.

McMurray approached the stricken man. "You okay?"

"She... she..." he stammered. "She's a doctor. I thought she was a secretary."

McMurray wrapped his arm around the man in a fatherly fashion. "Never prejudge a woman, my boy."

* * *

The ER was buzzing with excitement when the group made its way into the trauma room. The full team had been alerted and was assembled there, waiting for the patient. After giving a brief report about the patient, Garret retreated to the hallway.

"That felt funny." She came to stand next to Danni.

"What?"

"Just handing a patient off like that," Garrett said with a sigh. "Guess I'd better get used to it."

As she opened her mouth to reply, Danni felt a tug on her sleeve.

"Hey, nice outfits. Do you know where I can get one?"

"Huh?" She turned to see John standing next to her, a smile on his face.

"Nice try," he said and motioned with his head toward Garrett, "but it still won't get you two on my twins Internet page."

"Knock it off, John. We were doing a photo shoot when one of the crew was injured." Danni pulled at her jumpsuit. "These are the flight suits we'll be wearing."

"You mean you're still going to do that helicopter thing, even after what just happened in North Carolina? I thought you didn't like to fly."

"North Carolina?" Danni looked confused. "What happened in North Carolina?"

John looked at Garrett then back to Danni. "One of the Medevac helicopters went down. It burst into flames, and the pilot got killed."

Garrett's eyes narrowed. "What happened to the crew?"

"They're fine. The pilot got some kind of warning signal or message and put down so they could ground-transport the patient. He thought the problem was fixed. The crash happened on the test flight."

Danni gasped as her hand grabbed at Garrett's sleeve. She tried not to react to the news, but she knew her face had turned pale. How was she ever going to go through with this? But she knew she couldn't pull out now.

"Come on, Danni. We'd better go back to the studio and get our clothes."

"Yeah, right. Our clothes," Danni said in a monotone, her mind preoccupied with images of flaming helicopter bits dropping from the sky.

* * *

McMurray waited at the door for his team to be ready to leave. "You two work well together. You both know your responsibilities, and you do your best."

"Everything just kind of clicked together today," Danni said.

"I know. That's why the Board wants you two for this project." He reached out and touched Garrett's shoulder. "Six months isn't too long. You'll see."

"Yes, sir." Garrett nodded. "Did he make it?"

"Dr. Chabot's patient? Yes, he's doing fine. Said he was Christmas shopping when someone came up and robbed him."

Garrett smiled weakly. "I'm glad he came through all right."

"Come on, Garrett. We need to get to class." Danni stepped around Garrett and nodded to the Chief of Trauma Services. "Dr. McMurray."

"Nurse Bossard." He inclined his head to them and walked away.

"So," Danni said. "Are you hungry? I'm starved. Do you want to grab a bite at the gift shop on the way to class?"

"Yeah, I guess I could use some coffee."

"Okay, but it's my turn to buy." Danni stopped dead in her tracks. "Jeez, I almost forgot. Karen said to give this to you." She dug into her coat pocket, pulled out the thin wallet, and handed it to Garrett.

"Thanks." Garrett placed it in the interior pocket of her leather jacket.

"No need for thanks." Danni wrinkled her nose and smiled. "Now come on, I'm famished."

Chapter 3

Garrett stood with her arms outstretched along the parapet of the hospital roof and stared at the city skyline. The cold, crisp air allowed her to see for miles. She surveyed individual buildings.

Her eyes narrowed as she felt the first twinge of self-doubt to assail her in a long while. She wondered whether the men who had raised these structures ever doubted their efforts. She considered her mission for the last half of her fellowship year. It seemed like it would be no effort at all, except for following McMurray's order to stay out of the operating theater.

The bitter chill of the wind on her face was no match for Garrett's resolve. She closed her eyes, and imagined herself once again out on the deck of the aircraft carrier with the powerful seas rolling beneath her. Everything had its ups and downs, but she'd learned a lot in the Navy. It was simple perseverance that got the ship through.

Garrett opened her eyes and looked down to the busy streets. Suddenly, everything seemed clearer. She was here for a reason, and whatever it was, she wasn't about to give up.

Determined, she took one long, last look at the waning night sky, then walked toward the rooftop portal to the world below. That's when she noticed the door was open, and that a small figure was standing silhouetted against the incandescent light of the stairwell. It was Danni.

"So, you're up here." Danni ventured onto the roof. "I was hoping you weren't trying to sneak into the OR again."

"Hardly. Being thrown out once was humiliating enough. How'd you know where to find me?"

"I thought of where I'd like to be." Danni gazed around at the rooftop scenery. "This is my getaway when the world seems to be crashing in on me. I come up here and let my spirit soar over the rooftops. Sooner or later my mind settles, and I calm down." She brushed past Garrett as she walked out onto the roof, closed her eyes and took in a deep breath. "The air refreshes my mind with its clean, fresh scent." She opened her eyes and became noticeably shy. "I can almost sense the peace and quiet of the forest, even though I can't see many trees from up here. My mother always told me I was a bit of a dreamer."

Garrett took in the innocence of the woman she had come to know. She was beginning to see so much of her brother in Danni that sometimes she thought Lucas was once again physically present.

How could she have been so blind not to see it before? Then, although she was startled by the revelation, Garrett tossed the thought aside. "What do you say we get some breakfast? We've got a full day coming at us."

"Gar..."

Concerned by the trepidation in Danni's voice, Garrett studied her.

"What's on your mind? We're a team. Let's talk about it."

"What if today's the end of our team? I mean..." Danni stared at the ground. "What if I can't do my job up there? I'll never get to work with you again."

"Hey, don't go thinking like that. We work well together. Our numbers prove it. Heck, it's what got us on this team, isn't it?" Garrett lifted Danni's chin with her finger. "We'll do our job. I can always count on you to do that, whether it's in the trauma room or up in the air." Garrett drove home her point. "We're two of a kind. We always do our job. Right?"

"I guess we do." Danni's words were little more than a whisper.

"Enough of this worrying. We've got better things to do." Garrett turned and started down the stairs.

* * *

René Chabot stood silently in the doorway of the small office. The intense look on Garrett's face as she viewed the computer screen concerned him. She hadn't even heard him open the door. At last, Garrett looked up.

"Reading up on some new operation I should know about, or just killing a little time?" The French-Canadian motioned toward the monitor when their eyes met.

"Operation? No, nothing of the sort. I'm keeping abreast of world affairs. If I didn't know better, I'd say the Middle East is gearing up for war."

René thought for a moment. "Surely you don't think your team would be called there to transport. That's a little far for our helicopters to go."

Garrett's steely look unnerved him.

"Hey, I'm Canadian, remember?" Chabot held up his hands in mock surrender. "Why does this upset you so much? I mean, I know you were in the Navy…"

"I'm still in the Navy, René. All they have to do is whistle. I'm at their beck and call, without any choice in the matter."

René pondered the newly acquired information. "I'm sure they won't let it escalate to that."

"I hope not. I'm just concerned about this latest act of terrorist bombing. They made the attack on the USS *Cole* look way too easy. Only a well-organized group could do something like that. I'm sure they have more things planned."

René didn't know what to say. Garrett's outlook on global matters was too ominous for his liking, and it was far from what he wanted to be concentrating on now. He rocked back and forth on his heels as he contemplated his next move.

"Dr. Trivoli?" His voice turned softer. "Garrett, I'd like to thank you for allowing me to spend Christmas with my family." He smiled at her warmly. "You don't know what it will mean for me… for us. Claudette was so upset about being away from the rest of our family members. Now, she's in heaven knowing that we're going to be able to set our own family traditions."

"No thanks necessary. I'm the one who should be thanking you. After all, I'll be able to treat patients again, maybe even get to do a little surgery, if the need arises."

"You miss it, don't you?"

"Yes, but we all do what we have to. I know I'm here for a reason. I just hope whatever the fates have planned for me, I'm able to do it to the best of my ability."

Dr. Chabot smiled. He marveled at the way his colleague was beginning to let down that stoic mask of hers, showing her emotions and feelings.

"So, what are you up to today?" He pointed to her clothing. "A little spin around the city, perhaps?"

"Perhaps." Garrett logged off the computer and stood up, the dark blue jumpsuit accentuating her stunning image. "Enjoy your holiday, and tell your wife I wish her a Merry Christmas." She rounded the desk. "And don't forget to kiss the twins for me, too. Now, I have an appointment with a nurse for a helicopter ride. If you'll excuse me?"

"Good luck," René called out. "Merry Christmas."

Chabot craned his neck to catch her departing words, but a casual wave of her hand and a quick nod were Garrett's only reply.

* * *

The mere sight of the helicopter acted as a catalyst to the butterflies inside Danni's stomach. For weeks she'd hoped that getting in and out of the craft would calm her nerves, but now she wasn't certain it would make any difference at all.

She gently rubbed her abdomen, trying to pacify those wings from bursting into full upward motion. "Please, please, please don't let me do what I've done in the past." Danni turned to see Karen coming out of the conference room.

"Hi." The trepidation was obvious in Danni's voice.

"Know anywhere I could get a suit like that? Sure makes for a nice look." Karen rubbed the material of the flight suit between her thumb and forefinger. "Doesn't feel too bad, either."

Danni looked at the older nurse's face, then back to the helipad.

"What's the matter? Anything I can do to help?"

"Today's..." Danni's voice quivered. "Today's the test flight to see if we..." She swallowed hard. "If *I* can make the team. I don't want to let Garrett down. We've become so close over the last few weeks that I..."

"You've never let me down in all the years I've known you. I'm sure you won't let Garrett down either. Just do your best. Once you get started, you won't even have to think about what needs to be done."

Danni smiled weakly. "That's what I'm hoping for."

Karen embraced Danni. "I'll pray God watches over you. No, better yet, that He watches over both you *and* Garrett." She tightened her grip before slowly releasing it, then stepped back to view Danni's face.

"Thanks, I think I needed that."

"See? I knew staff meetings were good for something."

"Huh?"

"I wouldn't have been here to give you that hug if it wasn't for the mandatory charge nurse meeting with Nan. At least it was good for something."

"Yeah, it was. Thanks." Danni looked down the hall, trying to get a fix on someone in the distance.

"Yep, best staff meeting I've ever attended, and probably the most important one," Karen said. "Someone knew you'd need me." Karen saw Garrett approaching them.

"Anybody know what time the next helicopter comes by?" Garrett asked.

"Hi, Doc."

"Hey." Garrett's attention centered on Danni.

"Oh, my gosh! Look at the time." Karen made a show of glaring at her watch. "I should have been home and in bed by now." She reached out and pulled both Garrett and Danni in for a group hug. "God, I feel like I'm sending you off to your first day of school." Karen sniffed, then dredged up a smile. "Look out for each other." Garrett gave a slight nod.

"I want to hear all about it when I see you on Christmas." Karen released her grip and wiped a tear from her cheek. "Aw, jeez. I'd better get going before I really lose control."

As she left, the last of her good luck wishes were nearly overridden by the hum of the helicopter blades.

Garrett looked at Danni. "Cowboy's here with our helicopter, but if you don't want to go through with this, it's okay. I'll understand."

"No, if I'm not going to be part of this team, it's not going to be because I didn't try." Danni looked out the window to where the wash from the helicopter filled the air with debris. She settled her hand on her stomach.

"Butterflies?"

"Nope. I was… um… just getting the wrinkles out of my suit." Danni tugged at her clothing. She turned away and glanced over her shoulder. "You coming with me, or are *you* giving up?"

"I'm game. Let's go for a ride and put an end to all this talk."

"Sounds like a plan to me." Danni reached for their jackets. Teasingly, she held onto Garrett's until it was tugged from her hand.

"Let's go kick some butt." Garrett gave the thumbs-up sign, and headed for the trauma bay door.

Danni replicated the signal, then gulped hard. "Quiet, down there." She held her stomach in place. "If I'm going for a ride, we're all going for one."

* * *

Ian McCormick sipped his coffee as he waited for the gathered assembly to settle down. It always amazed him how much there was to talk about when ER physicians got together. Couple that with several other hospital executives thrown in for good measure, and he was sure the rumor mill alone could keep a small hospital going for days on end.

From the front of the room, Ian viewed the male-dominated group. If at least one of his flight team had been male, preferably the surgeon, he'd feel better about the new endeavor succeeding. Ian took a breath and readied himself for his speech about how two women were going to lead their hospital into the new millennium. It was imperative to their plan for everyone to know that after today, treating a traumatized patient would never be the same. Glancing at his watch, he leaned toward the hospital PR person.

"Time to get this show on the road, wouldn't you say?"

"Road?" The man gave Ian a sarcastic look. "I thought they were flying." He then moved to the podium and tapped the microphone, capturing everyone's attention.

"Good morning, doctors. We'd like to get the preliminary introduction to today's demonstration underway. Our speaker is one of the co-founders and organizers of our system's newest trauma delivery division, Chief of Emergency Medicine, Dr. Ian McCormick."

During the brief round of polite applause, Ian stepped up to the podium. "Good morning. I bring you greetings for the upcoming New Year with a demonstration of what we consider to be the best our system has to offer. The Departments of Emergency Medicine and Trauma Services have combined forces to establish a groundbreaking first for our region. After much consideration and many hours of planning and development, we present to you the first-ever Trauma Flight Team." Ian basked in the thunder of their applause before continuing. "Flight Surgeon Dr. Garrett Trivoli and Nurse Danielle Bossard are getting ready, as I speak, to make their first flight as part of this morning's presentation. It is our idea that, if a patient's condition is too serious for him to come to the surgeon, we will send the surgeon to the patient. Whether at an outlying hospital such as this one, or in the field, this team will be there to assist in our ongoing commitment to better and more timely intervention for the traumatized patient." He looked at his watch.

"In approximately fifteen minutes, our flight team will land outside, ready for action the second they hit the ground. I've arranged this little demonstration to show you what you can expect each and every time you request them." He glanced again at his watch. "Better make that twelve minutes and counting. Now, if you'd be kind enough to get your coats and assemble outside in the parking lot by the ER, we should be just in time for the show."

* * *

"Dr. Trivoli, Nurse Bossard, we're cleared for liftoff." The voice of Cowboy, their assigned pilot, came over their headsets. "Everyone secured back there?"

Garrett saw Danni make a last tug at the seatbelt. "Belted in and ready to go."

"You know we're just going to get up there and land, right? Your team will go into the hospital, evaluate the mock patient, and decide what needs to be done. After that, load him into the Medevac, and we're off for home. Nothing fancy. You got that?"

"Yeah, they mentioned it." Garrett watched Danni out of her peripheral vision.

"I'm going to increase my revolution speed so we can lift off. It's going to be a little bumpy at first. Just sit tight." He gave a thumbs-up signal.

Garrett glanced over. Danni had closed her eyes, and her lips were moving, but the hum of the rotors drowned out her words.

The engine whined under the strain of lifting the ship off the helipad, and what had started as small tremors escalated into an outright shaking of the helicopter.

Garrett reveled in the adrenaline rush of the moment. Turning back from the window to look at her companion, she was met by lifeless eyes. Danni's sluggish movement in response to the violent bumping of the airship was her only visible motion.

"Danni." Garrett spoke softly. When no answer came, she repeatedly called out Danni's name, increasing the decibels each time until she was yelling at the top of her lungs. "Danni! Danni!"

Garrett waved her hand in front of Danni's face as the ride started to smooth out. Danni's features remained empty of emotion, her skin a sickly white. Garrett fumbled to release her seatbelt. She brought her face within inches of Danni's and searched for some semblance of awareness. Gone was the spark that had flickered and danced with mirth, giving that familiar impish quality to Danni's features.

"I'm right here with you, Danni. Can you see me?" Garrett remained calm. "You're safe here with me. I won't let anything bad happen."

Garrett tapped Cowboy's shoulder and motioned for him to turn his headset controls to monitor the back of the ship. "Danni's having a bad reaction to the flight. How much longer until we set down?"

"One minute to designated landing zone."

Garrett repositioned herself in front of Danni. "We're going to be landing soon. You'll feel some vibrations as the ship descends. There's nothing to be afraid of. Do you hear me?" Garrett detected a slight nod of Danni's head

As soon as the helicopter touched down, Garrett jerked the door open. "Firm ground, that's what you need." She released Danni's seatbelt and scooped her up into her arms, then exited.

Cowboy hopped out, too, a look of concern on his face. "Anything I can do?"

"I'll take care of her, thanks."

He nodded, crossing his arms and leaning against the helicopter while Garrett carried Danni beyond the overhanging blades.

The sting of the cold air against Danni's flesh made her turn into the leather-clad form that carried her. The leather's soft feel against her skin, mixed with the familiar scent, helped to bring her back to reality.

The barely audible mumbles coming from Danni were like music to Garrett's ears. "You're safe, Danni. We're on the ground."

There they remained, oblivious to the world around them, absorbed only in each other.

* * *

"This is certainly action packed," the PR man said with a smirk.

"Cutting edge, Ian." A voice spoke up from the crowd. "Where did you get your idea from?"

"A wax museum," another man answered from the opposite side of the group. "They're not moving a muscle."

"What the hell are they doing?" Ian looked dumbfounded.

"Nothing." The PR man next to him fought to keep a straight face. "That's the problem."

"Hey, McCormick," a voice called out from the edge of the crowd. "Do we need to provide a psychiatric consult each time they come, or will they bring their own shrink?"

Before Ian could address the question, another one was thrown his way.

"Is that all they can do, just stand there, huddled together?"

Another heckler answered in Ian's stead. "Maybe they faint at the sight of blood."

Ian cringed in embarrassment as laughter filled the air.

* * *

"You're safe. I've got you." Garrett held Danni tightly to her. "I've got you."

"I know," Danni whispered faintly, the microcosm of her world expanding to include the lone figure headed toward them. "Gar."

"Hmm?"

Small hands tugged on the leather they were curled around. "I think you better put me down."

"Oh, um… yeah." Garrett stumbled over the words. "Are you able to stand?"

"I think so." Danni looked over Garrett's shoulder. "I think we're in for trouble."

Garrett spun around and saw Ian McCormick headed their way. She lowered Danni to the ground, keeping her hands on her to steady her. Together, they waited for the impending confrontation.

"What the hell do you think you're doing?" Ian called to them as he approached. He sounded menacing. "You look more like a poster for Boys Town than a surgical team. I can't believe you made me look like a fool in front of all those people. Because of you, we're going to be the laughingstock of the entire area." He threw his hands up. "Hell, within a week, it will probably be across the entire nation."

Danni could feel the tension in Garrett's hands. She glanced up to see Garrett straighten to her full height. Danni stood her ground when Garrett tried to position herself between her and Ian. Their eyes met. Each seemed strongly intent on her own plan.

"I'm not hiding behind you, Gar."

"All right, we'll face this together as a team."

McCormick kept advancing until he was within a few feet, his hands moving in emphasis to his spoken thoughts.

"I expected more from you, Trivoli. Goddamned hotshot. I should have known a woman would fall to pieces at the first sign of danger. You were supposed to be our ace in the hole. Now look where you've gotten us. We look like asses. It will take years to live down this fiasco."

Garrett's hands dropped to her sides. Her fists were balled up tightly, waiting for the call to action. The sound of her heavy breathing signified the anger building up in the usually stoic and commanding surgeon.

"You don't even care what happened up there. You're more concerned with how you look to those idiots than you are about your own people." Garrett clenched her jaw. "I have a good mind to—"

"If you had a good mind, you would have been able to complete your mission," Ian snapped. "What's the hell's the matter with you?"

"Nothing," Danni said. "Nothing is the matter with her. I'm the one that zoned out during the flight. Dr. Trivoli was only trying—"

"To do what?" McCormick said. "All you had to do was get off the damned helicopter, come over to the mock patient, assess, treat, and take him for a ride in the helicopter. Plain and simple, nothing fancy. Just a show, that's all." He turned away, took a couple of steps, then spun back in their direction. "And what a show you made it." Ian's arm thrust forward and he pointed at Danni. "Bossard, you're grounded. Better yet, you're out of the program."

Cowboy's movement toward them caught Ian's attention. "There's no pilot needed here right now." Ian waved an arm. "You might as well go inside." Cowboy gave a small salute and headed into the hospital.

Danni looked apologetically at Garrett. "I'm sorry," she said, obviously fighting back tears.

"We'll get you another nurse, Trivoli. Try not to be so soft with the next one," Ian said with a sneer.

"Soft? You call being compassionate and caring 'soft?' I thought doctors were supposed to come to the aid of the sick and injured." Garrett stepped toward Ian until she was within arm's reach of him. Her fist shot up to within inches of his face and her forefinger extended as she brought it down into his bulky, coat-covered chest. "I suppose you would have wanted me to walk away from her while she was in a catatonic state?" With each new point she made, her finger pushed a little harder until finally he began to backpedal. "Would it have been a better show for you? We're a team. Do you know what that means? In the military, it means you take care of your own, first and foremost. If you get rid of Danni, you eliminate me, too. I don't want another partner. I won't *have* another partner." Garrett's eyes narrowed to slits. "Do you understand?" She raised her other hand.

Sensing what was coming, Danni bolted forward and stepped in between them. She caught hold of Garrett's arm, preventing her from slamming a fist into Ian's chest.

"He's not worth it. Nothing is worth that."

They locked gazes, and after a tense moment, Garrett's anger started to dissipate. Danni breathed a sigh of relief.

Ian looked disgusted. "Very well. Have it your way. I'm sure the Board will have a few things to say to you both when you get back." He marched off, never once looking back.

"I'm sorry," Danni said again.

"No need to be sorry. This wasn't why I came here. I'm a surgeon. I never wanted to be riding around in helicopters, doing drop-in surgeries." Garrett looked over to the helicopter "I never wanted you to have to go through that."

"I know. Thanks." Danni gave a forlorn-looking smile. "Come on, Gar." She gave Garrett's sleeve a tug in the direction of the hospital. "Let's go tell Cowboy his crew has been grounded."

* * *

"Mmm… this is good." The man in the flight suit and silver tipped boots savored the warmth of the beverage he held in his hands. "Java," he said with a reverent sigh, then took a sip. "Oh yeah, nothing like a good cup of coffee to keep you warm and out of a fight." A smile tugged at his lips as he inhaled the aroma.

The abrupt opening of the lounge door broke his concentration, and a starched white linen cap stuck out into the doorway. A second later, a harried-looking nurse appeared and peered into the lounge.

"Cowboy! I thought I saw you come in. We've been looking for you. They need a Medevac up at the old logging site. A tree came down wrong, and someone's pinned underneath it." The nurse's face was etched with desperation. "Come on, get up there."

"Can't." Cowboy shook his head. "I don't think I have a surgical team anymore. You better call dispatch and put in your request." He took another sip of coffee and then set the cup down on the table in front of him.

"We already did that. They're all committed. Can't you do anything to help?"

"Sorry. Given what happened on our test flight, the best I can do is check with dispatch and see if they can hurry one along."

The nurse's gaze stayed on him until her pleading eyes and fretful brow began tugging at his heart.

"Damn." Cowboy looked away. "Okay." He drawled the word out, making it last twice as long as it was meant to. "Stop looking at me like a pet shop puppy and show me to your phone. I'll see what I can do."

Chapter 4

The day had gone to hell before it even reached noon. When Garrett slowed her steps, Danni took the lead as they crossed the wide expanse of asphalt-covered parking lot. She heard Garrett snarl, then say a few words under her breath.

"Did you say something?"

"No, I was just thinking out loud." Garrett looked up, and Danni turned away from her.

It wasn't hard to tell what was going on in Garrett's mind. Danni's shoulders slumped, and she stared downward. Her inability to cope with flying had probably ruined everything. She trudged on as she reasoned things out in her mind.

She'd never be able to make this up to Garrett. She considered all the ramifications that the day's botched demonstration would bring. She was sure their privileges on the Survivor project had just gone right down the tubes. She closed her eyes tightly for a moment, then shook her head as if to cast out the thought. But it was over now. She'd never get another chance. "Damn it!" The tip of her boot made contact with a stone and sent it flying.

They entered the door single file, and searched the sparsely populated waiting room for their pilot. Danni spotted the flight suit through the window of the ER doors leading into the treatment area.

"I see him." She tipped her head toward the flight-suited form standing at the desk with his back to them.

"We might as well tell him we're both grounded," Garrett said, "and he's free to go without us."

They pushed open the ER door and strode in together. The reverberating noise echoed down the hall. The ER clerk's head bobbed up, and his mouth dropped open. A nurse fumbled a chart in her hands, dropping it onto the floor.

"Dr. Trivoli," Cowboy said, "that's what I call perfect timing."

Confused, Garrett frowned at him. "What's up?"

"I've got dispatch on the line here. Seems all of the other helicopters are committed to patients, and there's an emergency call for a Medevac up here in this neck of the woods. I told them I'd ask you if you'd take it."

"It's up at the logging site," the nurse behind the desk said. "A man's pinned underneath a tree. Cowboy offered to pilot a helicopter, but we need a surgical team."

By the gleam in her eyes, Danni suspected Garrett felt compelled to help. "What do you think?" she asked softly.

"I'm sorry, but we won't be able to help. We've been officially grounded."

Danni blinked in surprise. Damn! Garrett was doing this because of her. She looked from surgeon to pilot and back again. "Wouldn't it be best for the patient if—"

Garrett cut off Danni's query. "I'm not making you get back on that helicopter."

"We can't *not* help. We could be his only hope."

"Danni…"

"We're wasting time, Doctor." Danni planted her hands on her hips. "Are you coming or not? This could be the only chance I ever get to prove myself. At least let me try."

Hesitantly, Garrett nodded. "Don't just stand there," she said to a grinning Cowboy. "We've got a patient to take care of."

* * *

Danni's face was set with determination as Cowboy signaled his intent to lift off. Fearing for the worst once the vibrations started, Garrett racked her brain for something to keep Danni's mind off the flight.

"Protocols," Garrett blurted out, forgetting the microphone in her helmet. "We have to follow protocols." Danni's knit brow told her the nurse was cognizant of what she was saying. "We're on our way to a real patient, aren't we?"

"Yes."

"Then we need to follow the protocols." Garrett could feel the strain of the engine as the rotors screamed their ascent. "Before every flight, we check our equipment. I'll take the intubation bag. You take the drugs."

"Right." Danni reached for her designated bag and began running through a methodical checklist of their supplies.

Garrett proceeded with her inspection of equipment, stealing glances at Danni whenever she could in order to keep abreast of her condition. Danni seemed unaffected by the change in direction as the helicopter reached the pinnacle of ascent and started its forward thrust. Several minutes later, she could see that Danni still seemed unscathed by the flight. Garrett breathed a sigh of relief when their skids finally settled onto the snow-covered ground.

In the blink of an eye, Danni released her seatbelt and grabbed her assigned satchels while Garrett opened the door. Keeping their heads down and their bodies hunched over, they disembarked.

A hundred feet away from the landing zone, they were met by a burly-looking man. "I'm the foreman, Sam Johnson," he yelled over the noise of the helicopter's slowing blades. "We were taking down one of the big ones." He motioned toward a stand of trees. "Damned thing took off on us and set off a chain reaction."

Garrett scanned the area for victims. "How many are hurt?"

"Only one, and thank the Lord, he's not one of mine."

"Not one of yours? Who else would be up on this site?"

"He belongs to the State." Sam led them closer to the edge of the hillside. "He's one of the road crew. You know, the ones that scrape and salt the roads." Sam's voice waned. "I guess we should have closed the road, but we've never had anything like this happen before." He slowed his steps and pointed down the embankment. "The tree caught him just as he was passing by. Pushed him right over the edge, down the slope, and that's where they came to rest."

They peered down the hillside and saw an upended dump truck with a huge tree resting on top of it.

"Oh boy," Danni said.

"Where's the driver?" Garrett scanned the wreckage.

"He's trapped under the side of the dump. Got his foot pinned beneath the edge of it. We tried, but we can't get him free. His foot is between a ledge of rock and the side of the truck. I think he's either going to lose that foot or stay under that truck bed forever."

Garrett noted a skittering of loose stones from around the wreckage. "Is EMS or the fire department on the way?"

"We usually take care of our own evacs up here. We call for the helicopter to get them out. Takes the locals way too long to get up here to our part of the hill. Besides, their vehicles usually get stuck on our mud roads."

"You got a backboard?"

"Yeah, it's already down there."

"Good. Less for us to carry. We'll take the drugs, surgical tools, and large dressings."

Danni immediately ditched the other bags. "Ready to go."

They walked along the edge of the road until they were parallel to the rear of the dump truck. Garrett evaluated the degree of tilt and the slope of the hill, trying to figure out just how much time would be available to do the necessary procedure, if it was warranted. She didn't like what she was coming up with.

"Give me the bags." She held out her hands. "There's no sense in both of us risking our lives."

Danni held on tightly. "We're a team. Where you go, I'm going. You'll be able to work faster with another set of hands to help you."

Garrett clenched her teeth as she traded glances with Danni. There wasn't time to argue. "Okay. Just make sure you stay right beside me and do what I say."

A subtle smile graced Danni's face as she fell in step with her teammate.

* * *

"Jesus H. Christ! What are they doing, selling tickets up there to this sideshow?" The angry words came from the pinned man.

Garrett took in the scene. A middle-aged male with a cervical collar around his neck lay with half of his body on a backboard. A single belt wrapped around the man's waist held the board in place. The bed of the dump truck pinned the man's ankle into the rock and kept him from sliding farther down the hillside.

"Sir," Garrett said as she made her way toward the man, "we're here to help you. How are you doing?"

"For the love of God," he half yelled. "What the hell are you two going to do to get this damned truck off of me?" He shook his fist. "I should never have come up over that damned hill."

"So much for checking airway and breathing." Danni knelt down next to him. "Just try to stay still. Do you hurt anywhere besides your ankle?"

"Nah, I got a few scrapes and scratches, but they don't bother me like this damned ankle." The man lashed out with his other foot, kicking the side of the dump truck with a resounding thud.

"Hey!" Danni lunged to stabilize the man's head and neck.

"Stop that," Garrett commanded. "You want this whole thing to take us all for a ride? That's not what we came here to do, is it, Nurse Bossard?"

"Not in the least, Dr. Trivoli." Danni spoke firmly as she made eye contact with her patient.

"I'm a goner. This truck isn't budging without taking us all down the hill with it." The man shooed them away. "Go on. Get out of here before it shifts."

"We didn't come here to watch. We came here to help," Danni said.

"Now, that's funny. What are you going to do? Lift this truck off of me?"

Garrett surveyed the damage to the man's ankle. "No, but I may have to amputate that foot to save your life. From what I can see, it's pretty well crushed."

"No kidding." His answer was flippant. "When they told me a surgeon was flying in, I knew it was hopeless." His expression changed to one of intense pain. His eyes widened and he let out a scream as more stones traveled down the hillside, evidence of the instability of the situation.

"Are you allergic to any medications?" Danni opened the drug bag.

He grimaced. "No."

"Start an IV," Garrett said, "and give him five milligrams of morphine."

Danni cut away the sleeve of his jacket and shirt, then found a large vein in his forearm for the IV site. When the task was accomplished, she reached for the pre-filled syringe of the pain-killing drug. "Five of morphine going in. You should feel it starting to work very soon, sir."

"Harry. My name is Harry T. Waterbury."

"Like I told you, Harry, that medicine will kick in very soon." She placed the cap back on the syringe and slipped it into the breast pocket of her flight suit.

Within minutes, the drug took the edge off of Harry's pain. "That's some good stuff, Doc." Then he spoke to Danni. "Thanks, little lady."

"You're welcome. Let me know if the pain worsens again."

Garrett worked to expose the trapped limb from all clothing while, in her mind, she prepared for what she was about to do. "There are no obvious breaks above the ankle. That's good. It's not the ideal place to be doing this, but we're stuck with it." Garrett unrolled her surgical tools next to her.

"Danni, could you give me a hand?"

"Sure." Danni positioned herself. "Tell me what you need." She donned a pair of sterile gloves.

Garrett pulled on her sterile gloves.

"Are you ready, sir?"

"I don't think I'll ever be ready, but go ahead."

Garrett extended her hand. "Scalpel." She wrapped her fingers around the handle and brought the point to flesh. As she prepared to make the first cut, several small stones rolled down from the edge of the wreckage. Their numbers began to multiply, and soon a cascade of shifting stones and dirt prevented her from continuing. Garrett looked up and saw that the dump truck's body was teetering above them. Acting on instinct, she threw the scalpel behind her, dove over the top of the patient, and pulled Danni under her arm.

Amidst shouts and the whine of stressed metal, the three lay huddled, one on top of the other. The rumbling they heard soon escalated into a loud roar as the weight of the tree caused the truck to roll, trapping them in the overturned bed. The slow, agonizing sound of metal being ripped apart preceded the loud snap that followed. In an instant, the tree came shifting over the top of the wreckage, taking the truck with it down the embankment. One loud metallic crash followed another as the mangled vehicle stopped abruptly at the bottom. When the dust settled, the trunk of the tree was clearly visible resting over the cab, nearly crushing it.

Garrett cautiously raised her head to see where the next barrage was coming from. Aside from some shifting stones, the worst was past.

"Everybody all right?" She took stock of her body.

"I'm good," Danni said. "How about you, Harry?"

"Well, that's one way to get the damned thing off me."

"It wasn't exactly what we had planned, but it will do." Garrett leaned back on her haunches. "The truck must have been resting on some other pivot point than your ankle."

Sam yelled from the roadway above. "If you're done playing, we can help you up."

Garrett hastened the logging crew with a wave of her arm. "What are you waiting for? We need to get him loaded onto the helicopter and to a trauma center." She looked down at her patient. "We're going to do everything we can to help you keep that foot."

"I'm sure you will, Doc." Harry yelled to the logging crew coming down the hillside, "Watch where you step. I survived one accident. We don't need another."

* * *

"Dr. Trivoli, Nurse Bossard." René greeted his colleagues as they made their way into the trauma room. "I thought you were only doing a demonstration today. What have you brought us?"

"Tree versus dump truck." Garrett's voice was all business. "Our patient's only serious injury is a crushed ankle."

"His name is Harry." Danni gripped the patient's hand and smiled. "Harry T. Waterbury."

"Thanks, little…" Harry paused. "Danni. See? I remembered."

"I know." She turned her attention to René. "We've given him morphine to ease the pain."

"Hey, Doc," Harry called out rather hoarsely. "Thanks for everything. You two are A-number-one in my book."

"You listen to these fine people now. They'll take good care of you. He's all yours, Dr. Chabot." Garrett officially handed off her patient and left the trauma room.

"Gar."

"Yeah?"

"Thanks for what you did back there." Danni spoke softly. "I realize it could have been a little messy if you hadn't pulled me in."

"We're a team, remember?" A look of concern came to Garrett's face. "Are you okay?"

"Yeah, I'm fine now."

"Danni, Dr. Trivoli. Dr. McMurray wants you in his office. Stat!" Having delivered her message, Nan, the nurse manager, promptly walked away.

"Well," Garrett said, "isn't our day just full of surprises?"

* * *

The Board of Directors filed out of Dr. McMurray's office, each member with a somber look on his face. Bringing up the rear of the line was Ian McCormick. He scowled and cast his eyes downward as he walked past the seated flight crew, who were rumpled, dirty, and stained with road salt.

Danni sat up ramrod straight and nudged Garrett's upper arm with her shoulder. Garrett took in a deep, cleansing breath to calm her nerves.

The feather-light touch of the small hand on hers sent soft tingles of electricity through her body, chasing out the last remnants of anger and apprehension over the upcoming meeting with her mentor. As calmness overtook her, hints of a one-sided smile surfaced. The women glanced at each other and began to chuckle.

"Trivoli! Bossard!" Ol' Cutter stopped in his doorway. "In my office, now." He walked to his desk.

McMurray sat down and motioned for them to do the same as he studied them further before speaking.

"I understand you two have had a pretty rough day. Seems to me all you were supposed to do was go for a little ride in that helicopter of ours, and show your faces at an outlying facility." He paused. "Isn't that correct?"

Danni and Garrett nodded.

"You didn't do that, did you?" He looked from one to the other, his eyes devoid of any emotion.

"Sir," Garrett said, "if you would allow me to explain—"

McMurray threw up his hand to stop her. "When it's your turn to talk, Dr. Trivoli, I'll tell you." He peered at them over the top of his glasses.

"Let me tell you what you *did* manage to do today." He looked directly at Danni. "You, Nurse Bossard, should have told us of your problem with flying. But you didn't, and therefore, you put the entire helicopter crew in a high-risk situation. The confined space of a ship such as that is no place to lose it and go berserk."

"But I didn't go—" Danni started to protest, but then stopped. "Yes, sir."

McMurray turned his attention to Garrett. "Did you know about this phobia of hers?"

"I suspected she might be a little uncomfortable."

"Don't you think it might have been a good idea to let us know about it?" He snorted and then coughed. "I guess not."

"I was looking out for her."

"You are the only two I know of who could totally botch up a simple little exercise to the point of humiliation for the entire hospital. Dr. McCormick wants your heads on a platter, and this situation has the whole Board of Directors in an uproar." McMurray looked at Danni.

"You get grounded." He shifted his glance to Garrett. "Then *you* barge right in and ground yourself along with her. Interesting."

He waved his hand as if to erase the thoughts from his mind. "Then, when an emergency call for a helicopter comes in, you two just up and decide to take it." He paused. "Oh, let me correct that. First you argue about not letting her"—he pointed to Danni—"ride in a helicopter again. Miraculously, she overcomes her phobia of flying and has you"—his finger now pointed at Garrett—"go commandeer an airship."

McMurray looked at each of them in turn. "I've gotten everything right so far, haven't I?" He waited a moment, but neither woman spoke. "I thought so."

He got up and walked behind his chair. "Then, you put yourselves in the middle of a damned-near suicidal rescue, thinking you're going to have to amputate a man's foot to save his life. If that's not enough, things go drastically wrong fairly quickly, and beyond belief, nobody gets any additional injuries. The logging crews are your biggest fans. The media that got wind of the botched-up training flight is now clamoring at our doorstep to do a human-interest piece on the new Trauma Flight Team. A team that is already doing heroic rescues and saving lives, and isn't even fully trained yet." He narrowed his eyes. "Imagine that."

The room became deathly silent.

Danni squirmed in her seat a little before speaking. "We're sorry. I… We didn't…"

"Sorry? Hell!" McMurray walked over to them and smiled. "It was the best damned PR this hospital has ever gotten. All the news stations want to know about the two women who overcame adversity to save a Public Works employee."

Danni looked up at him. "Does that mean you're not mad at us?"

"Damned right."

Garrett's voice was tinged with skepticism. "Not at all?"

McMurray stared at her and slowly shook his head. "No. In fact, I'm very pleased with you both. Now, go and have a Merry Christmas."

"Thanks, sir." Garrett felt befuddled.

"Thanks, Dr. McMurray." Danni beamed.

"Yeah, yeah." Ol' Cutter gave them a wave and focused his attention on some paperwork on his desk. Just as they reached the door, he said, "Oh, Trivoli."

"What, sir?" Garrett turned to face him.

"You *are* allowed in the operating room. I can't have my holiday trauma fellow standing outside looking in, now can I? Your OR privileges are reinstated."

Garrett perked up. "Really, sir?"

"Don't get so excited. It gets pulled again when the holiday is over. Consider it my Christmas present to you for a job well done."

"Thank you, sir." As they left, Garrett cocked her head and returned Danni's beaming smile with one of her own.

The Chief of Trauma Services watched the pair walk out his door. He could hear their soft, friendly bantering as they moved into the next room. The two had shown under fire that they were a strong team.

McMurray eased down into his leather chair. It was going to be a very good Christmas, after all.

Chapter 5

Soft music filtered in under the door as long limbs began to stir beneath the covers. Slowly, Garrett's senses came to life. The smooth, silky touch of the sheets stimulated her, causing her to moan in a low, throaty tone. She turned over and nestled her head into the pillow. Her nose twitched, trying to distinguish the scent that enticed her and caused her mouth to water.

"Nuts." She opened first one eye, then the other before stifling a yawn. "When did you start sleeping in, Trivoli? Maybe McCormick was right. I am getting soft."

Methodically, she reviewed the previous day's events. The image of Danni's lifeless stare haunted her mind.

A searing pain spread in her chest, and Garrett felt as if her life was being drained from her. Her eyes widened as she realized just how close she and Danni had come to being killed. Terror-stricken, Garrett sat up.

"I nearly lost her yesterday." Her whisper magnified the reality of the stark truth.

"Gar?" Danni called from the hallway.

Garrett's heart beat faster upon hearing Danni's voice. She leaned forward, clutched the covers to herself, and tried to steady her breathing. "Yeah?"

"I was wondering if you'd like to join me for breakfast."

Garrett blinked until the digital clock came into focus. "Breakfast sounds good. I'll be down as soon as I'm dressed."

"Don't be long. I still need to trim the tree before I leave."

Leave? Suddenly, Garrett remembered what day it was. Christmas Eve. Damn! She'd better get moving.

* * *

Danni pulled the mitts off her hands and tossed them onto a counter. "I was wondering if you'd changed your mind about breakfast."

"No, breakfast is good." Garrett moved into the room, eyeing the baked goods as she passed by. "Is that something special for the holiday?" She nodded toward the pastry.

"Are you making fun of my artistic expression?"

"No, I think it's interesting."

"Interesting?" Danni bristled. "Okay, tell me what it is." She stood with her hands on her hips. "Be careful what you say, or I'll rope you into helping me with the cookies."

Garrett took a step closer. "Hmm." She stroked the side of her jaw. "A Santa something or other?"

"Good guess."

"You know, I would have volunteered to help decorate anyway. The cookies, I mean. That was always my job when I was…" Garrett let her words trail off. "I haven't thought about stuff like that for years."

"Shaking colored sugar onto cutout cookies is like riding a bike. You don't forget it." Danni pointed at Garrett. "And I'm accepting that offer to help."

Garrett smiled, and Danni looked surprised.

"What do you think of it?" Danni said.

"Smells good." Garrett tipped her head in the direction of the counter where Danni's creation rested on a cooling rack. "Is it an old family recipe?"

"Nope. Old family tradition, although 'contest' is more like it. It's my mother's way of making every holiday gathering a test of culinary skill between my sister and me. She wants to make sure we have what it takes to get and keep a man in our lives. The biggest showdown of all is Christmas. That's when she bestows the Domestic Goddess title on the winner."

Garrett looked appalled. "She actually picks one daughter over the other as more suitable for marriage because of how well she bakes?"

"My mother's idea, not mine."

"That's preposterous. It's archaic."

"I know." Danni's tone was nonchalant.

"I thought you told me your sister was married."

"She is. You would think it was a moot point now that Brie has a family of her own and a second child on the way, but it's not.

Maybe because I'm still trying to find what's right for me, in a sense."

"Well, if that…" Garrett pointed to the pastry on the counter. "Stollen."

"Yeah, Stollen. If it tastes half as good as it smells, you're already the winner, at least in my book." Garrett grew quiet. "I don't know what I'm talking about. I'd do better in judging incision sites or wound drainage." She changed the subject. "Isn't 'Stollen' German? I thought you were French."

"French via the Canadian border." Danni grimaced. "Another of Mother's ideas, making the name Bossard sound aristocratic." Danni raised her pinkie and made a mocking attempt at a curtsy. "My grandfather was Canadian, but all of his sons were born in the United States."

Danni turned to the refrigerator and opened the door. "So what's it going to be, Gar? Eggs and ham, eggs and bacon, or…" Danni looked over her shoulder. Garrett's attention was on the Santa-shaped Stollen.

"Oh, no. I worked all morning to make that, and it's not cool enough to put the icing on, let alone eat. If you're really good at decorating the cookies, maybe I'll let you have a few of those. Deal?"

There was a moment of hesitation on Garrett's part while her eyes lingered on the Stollen. "Deal."

* * *

"Damn, that woman has eyes in the back of her head." Garrett smirked at the thought of Danni's reaction when she had figured out where all the cookies were disappearing to. "She's got my vote for being able to run a family, even if her mother doesn't see it." Garrett turned her gaze into the living room.

There, in front of the window, was the Norfolk pine they had bought yesterday evening on their way home from the hospital. The sparsely branched tree stood with its roots planted firmly in the soil-filled pot, looking like something out of a low-budget movie. Garrett had thought Danni was joking when she picked out the little tree, declaring that it was just what she was looking for. Then she realized it was just like Danni to see beauty in a scraggly tree.

Danni called from the kitchen. "Do you think I could trust you with some popcorn and cranberries to string garlands for the tree? I figure you could use it as practice for surgery later tonight."

"Sure, where's the stuff?" Garrett licked her lips. "I've got a little room left for popcorn. It doesn't take up much space once you chew it."

"Garrett!"

"Gotcha!"

Danni sighed. "I'll pop the corn for you in a minute, as soon as I finish this last pan of cookies. I want some to take with me."

* * *

Danni stood silent, searching for a place to hang the last ornament. It had been so easy to place the other ornaments, but this one was special. The crystal-blue ball in her hand was the color of Garrett's eyes.

She moved closer to the tree and hung the ball near the trunk.

"Is there a reason why you placed it there? I noticed the others went up fairly fast, as if they had a designated place from year to year."

The question startled Danni. Should she tell Garrett that each ornament was someone Danni held dear? Better yet, should she reveal that was Garrett's ornament she'd just given the spot next to her heart?

Danni took a few strands of silver-colored tinsel and carefully placed them on the branches. "Each one is a friend. I remember them as I place their ornament on the tree."

"I don't see any names on them."

"They're here, written on my heart." Danni's voice was barely a whisper as she pointed to her chest. "You think I'm silly, don't you?"

"No. Just caring and filled with more love than you know what to do with, that's all."

Their eyes lingered on each other. The moment seemed almost magical, with the twinkling lights in their peripheral vision reminding them of the holiday season they were in.

"More tinsel?" Garrett broke the spell.

"Sure." Danni put the last of the tinsel on the tree and stood back to admire the symbol of her love. "What do you think?"

"It's nice. The lights really bring it to life."

"Good. Now I can take care of the presents." Danni disappeared from the room, only to reappear a few moments later, her arms laden with packages. She piled them neatly near the door. She felt somewhat pensive making her way to Garrett with a bright red foil-wrapped box, complementary green ribbons edging the corners. "Merry Christmas." Danni held out the box for Garrett to take. "I know you like to travel light, so I…" She took a breath, then let it out. "Just open it, and you'll see."

"Thanks." The word was spoken with much more warmth than the simple syllable indicated.

"You're welcome. Go on, open it."

Garrett set to work, undoing the ribbons and stripping the foil from around the box. She glanced at Danni, then back down at the box as she separated the tissue paper to reveal her gift. Garrett gasped.

Danni let out the breath she had been holding.

"I hope you like it."

Garrett searched Danni's face. "But how?"

"When you tossed your wallet the other day in the ER, things sort of fell out."

"But you gave me everything back intact an hour later." Garrett's eyes were glued to the image of her and her brother, her fingers moving slowly over the scrolled pattern running along the length of the wood frame. "This is way too clear to be a Xerox copy of a wallet-size photograph."

"Believe it or not, John actually helped me."

"John?" Garrett sounded skeptical. "How?"

"He had his new digital camera, and I borrowed it. I hope you don't mind." Danni's eyes searched for any sign of approval and found it in Garrett's smile.

"Thanks, Danni."

"I thought that perhaps with you having an office, you might like to be able to look at it a little more often." Danni wrinkled her nose. "Besides, I saw how you always look around McMurray's office. I figured it could be the first photograph for your desk when you're a chief."

"I'm only a fellow. What's this about being a chief?"

"Don't worry, I know it will happen. It's your destiny."

"I think I piss off too many people for that to happen anytime soon, but if you say so."

Their eyes met, conveying the faith and goodwill that they shared.

"Hey," Garrett said, "I, um… I got you something, too. Why don't you sit down on the couch and I'll get it?"

"Okay." Danni kept her voice soft and reassuring, knowing that Garrett was not in the habit of either giving or receiving gifts.

Within seconds, the sound of footsteps bounding down the steps echoed through the house. Garrett hit the landing at the bottom of the stairs, and Danni looked toward her with a curious expression. Garrett walked into the living room at a seemingly reluctant pace. In her hands was a large box, its gold and silver wrapping shining brightly. She set it on the coffee table and stepped back.

"Merry Christmas, Danni." Garrett's eyes twinkled with excitement.

"You know I'm not going to be able to open it without trying to guess what it is first, don't you?"

"Guess away, you'll never get it." Garrett sounded confident. She watched Danni lift the box and heft it as she tried to judge its weight. "I can tell you…"

Garrett was met with quickly upturned eyes that had a silencing effect on her. "Sorry."

"Hmm." Danni shook the box. "A robe?"

"No."

She flipped the box upside down, watching Garrett's face for clues, and shook it again, only this time more vigorously. "Hip boots for fishing at the cabin," she declared triumphantly.

"Nope." Garrett chuckled. "Good thing it isn't something that's still alive. You'd have traumatized it by now."

"Aha! So it's something dead." Danni reached for the bow and started to undo it. She slid her hand along it to find the tape holding it in place. "Let me think."

"You're not going to give up, are you?"

"Not until it's totally uncovered." Danni smiled rakishly. She pulled off the wrappings and lifted the lid slightly, being careful not to expose the gift. She closed her eyes and sniffed. Her eyes popped open with realization. "A leather knapsack."

"No." Garrett laughed.

"A purse. That's it." Danni opened the box without waiting to hear Garrett's reply. She ripped back the tissue paper and stopped short when the gift came into view.

"I never expected this. I… I don't know what to say."

"A simple 'thanks' will do."

Without warning, Danni sprang up and pulled Garrett in for a hug. It only took a few seconds for Danni to realize she had made Garrett feel awkward. Releasing her grip, Danni eased away.

"Sorry, I tend to get a little emotional at Christmas." Danni looked up, and a stunned Garrett stared back at her.

"That's okay. I just wasn't ready for it."

Danni lifted the gift out of the box and held it in front of her. "I don't deserve this. I almost cost you that project."

"But you didn't. You came through when the chips were down, and I appreciate it." Garrett pointed to the embroidery on the front of the leather jacket. "That's what I consider us, a team."

"Trauma Flight Team, D. Bossard, R.N." Danni read the embroidery on the leather jacket.

"I figure we need something to help them tell us apart in a hurry."

Suddenly, Garrett was wrapped in nurse from head to toe, with Danni resting her cheek on Garrett's chest.

It was only minutes after the first hug, but this time Garrett responded by slowly wrapping her arms around Danni. She rested her cheek on Danni's head and placed a gentle kiss on her hair.

Danni closed her eyes and prayed for the moment to never end.

Chapter 6

The house was quiet without Danni. She had left for her parents' house over an hour earlier, and all Garrett had done since then was sit on the couch and watch the lights twinkling on the tree.

"This tree is so much like her." Garrett spoke the notion aloud, and her words eased the silence.

She looked down at the framed photo of her brother and herself, taken at a memorable time in their lives. "We were so close then, Luc," she said softly. "You were in my every thought of the future. We were going to rule the world, you and I."

The random patterns of twinkling lights caught her eye, and her gaze drifted back to the tree. "Now it seems my thoughts are filled with someone else." Garrett smiled as the image of Danni strolled lazily through her mind. "But you already knew it, didn't you?" She glanced at the boy in the photograph, then settled back into the couch. Absentmindedly, she moved her fingers again over the scrolled pattern on the frame, until her watch alarm pulled her back to reality. It was time to go.

Garrett got up from the couch and placed the gift into the top of her duffel, then pulled on her leather flight jacket. She looked around the house.

"Soft, Trivoli. You're getting soft and mushy with the holiday, just like McCormick said." Garrett chastised herself as she started down the steps. "It's time to buckle down and gear up. You're the trauma surgeon tonight."

At the bottom of the steps, she glanced over her shoulder to see the twinkling lights of the tree, a beacon in the window. "It's going to be a long night without you, Danni."

* * *

"Merry Christmas, Danni!" Henry Bossard wrapped his arms around his daughter and planted a kiss on her cheek. "I've missed you, li'l one."

"Dad, I'm the oldest of your children. You can't keep calling me 'li'l one' forever."

"You'll always be my li'l one. Brie is two inches taller than you, and Matt..." He smiled and chuckled. "He was taller than a wild weed when he was born. Face it, daughter, the title is all yours." He kissed her again, this time on the forehead.

"Here, let me help with those." Henry relieved her of the packages in her arms.

Danni followed his line of sight. "Who are you looking for, Dad?"

"I thought your mother told me you were bringing someone. Maybe I heard her wrong." He quickly changed the subject. "I see you've got a new car. Malibu, eh?"

"Yes. I got a good deal when Garrett needed to buy a car. I traded in mine, and we each got what we wanted."

"We?" He saw the blush come to Danni's face. "So, you finally got one big enough for more than just yourself." A smile flickered across her dad's face. "A sensible around-town car, too, I see."

"Yep, and Gar got the full-size Blazer, with four-wheel drive of course."

"Henry, what are you doing with the door wide open? You're letting all of the..." The voice trailed off as Danni's mother stepped into view. "Oh, Danielle." Antoinette Bossard regarded her oldest child without much enthusiasm. "I'm glad you could make it home for *this* holiday."

"Hello, Mother." Danni's mood chilled. "Merry Christmas to you and Daddy both." She stood dutifully as her mother leaned in to almost touch her with a feigned kiss. "I guess I'm a little early this time."

"Nonsense. It will make up for the time you missed at Thanksgiving." Her mother looked out to the driveway.

The sour expression on her face prompted Danni to speak. "If you're looking for Garrett, Mother, I told you that surgeons have responsibilities to the hospital."

"Humph. I thought you could pull some strings."

"Mother, the only strings Gar will be pulling tonight are suturing material."

"At least I know I can count on the rest of the family being here." She turned and walked away.

Danni let out a long breath before looking at her father.

"Your mother thinks the world should move for her wishes. Come on, let's get these under the tree."

Presents jutted out at every angle from beneath the intricately decorated tree, which was was complete with metallic garland. Gingerly, Danni placed her packages wherever she could. As she took the last one from her father, she saw the front door open and heard the pattering of small feet.

"Auntie Dan! Auntie Dan!" the two-and-a-half-year-old tyke screeched as he leapt into her open arms.

"Hey. Merry Christmas, my little dumpling."

"Berry Chrissmust to you." The boy held on as Danni danced him around. "Hi, Grampa."

"Hello, Gunther," Henry said and waved. "You got a kiss for me?"

Danni held the wide-eyed little boy as he stretched to give his grandfather a kiss on the cheek. "Wuv you." He put his head down onto his aunt's shoulder and hid shyly.

"You're not afraid of Grampa, are you, Gunny?" Danni nuzzled her face in his hair.

"Danni, I wish you would call him by his name." Brie whisked into the room, her coat flapping open to showcase her pregnancy. "Tell Aunt Danni what your name is."

"Gunther," the tyke said, pouting. "My name Gunther."

"And a nice name it is, at that. You know that my name is really Danielle, but everybody calls me Danni. That's why I'm always going to call you Gunny. Okay?"

Gunther nodded eagerly and began giggling. "I wuv you." He kissed Danni's cheek.

Danni smiled as Gunny pulled back, and she touched her forehead to his. "Merry Christmas, Brie. Mark." She greeted her brother-in-law as he came to stand next to his wife.

"Auntie Dan, how come you smell?"

"Gunther!" Brie's voice was sharp.

"It's okay, sis. I think he's referring to my present from Garrett." She tugged at her leather collar pulling it closer to the boy's nose. "Is this what you smell?"

Gunny nodded emphatically.

"So, Garrett got you a leather jacket for Christmas." Brie moved closer. "What's that writing on it?"

Danni shifted her nephew in her arms, and her smile stretched from ear to ear. "It's embroidered *Trauma Flight Team, D. Bossard, R.N.* Garrett and I are a team."

Brie gave her a quizzical look. "You don't fly. You never could." She turned to her father. "You remember, don't you? The time you tried to fly us all down to Disney World and we ended up having to drive instead."

Antoinette breezed back into the room and joined the conversation. "I was never so embarrassed in my life. As soon as we started to taxi away from the gate, she went into a trance. The stewardess stopped the pilot from going any farther and made our whole family get off the plane. She said it wasn't safe for Danielle to go up in the air."

"I did perfectly fine in the helicopter after Garrett helped me through my first time."

"I bet." Brie rolled her eyes.

"Nobody else would have been so loving and kind when I zoned out on the test flight. Anyone else would have walked away from me, but not Gar." Danni shook her head. "Not even when I got grounded. Garrett told Dr. McCormick that we were a team, and if they grounded one of us, they grounded both of us."

"So, your boss lifted the restriction?" Mark's interest was piqued.

"Not really. *I* kind of ungrounded us."

"Danielle, you disobeyed your superior?" Antoinette sounded aghast.

"Actually, Mother, I disobeyed my superior and Gar. You have to understand the circumstances, though. They needed a Medevac for a rescue, and I wasn't going to be the excuse for us not helping a patient. The only thing I can say is when a patient was involved, I had no problem flying." Danni thought about her last statement. "As a matter of fact, I have no problem doing anything when someone's in need."

Gunny tugged Danni's hair. "I need a cookie, Auntie Dan." He leaned back and made a sad face.

"Okay, Gunny. Enough talk of flying. I've got to get something out of my car." Danni began to walk toward the front door with the child still in her arms. "I made some special cutout cookies just for you."

"You're going to spoil his dinner, Danni." Brie nudged her husband. "Mark, take Gunther. He weighs a ton."

Danni shifted her precious cargo to her other arm. "Don't even think I'm giving him up while I'm home. Right, dumpling?" Danni kissed his cheek. "Now, what do you say we go get those cookies?"

"Yeah!" Overjoyed, Gunny clapped his hands.

* * *

"Care for one?" Rosie held up an empty cup. "I'm buying, Dr. Trivoli. I'm afraid coffee's the best I can give on my nurse's salary."

"Sure, why not? Looks like it's going to be a busy night for us." Garrett waited until her cup of coffee was poured. "I see you went all out."

"Nothing but the best. So, how'd you like Danni's version of Christmas so far?"

"Version? What do you mean?"

"You know, all that labor-intensive rigmarole she goes through—baking, decorating, exchanging presents." She studied Garrett intently. "Things like that."

"That rigmarole. It's different." She looked around the cramped quarters of the lounge with its sparsely decorated Christmas tree and a wreath hung on the back of the door. "This is more like what I'm used to." Garrett stopped talking as the first tone came from her trauma pager.

"Trauma page. Trauma page. Two elves fighting over where the last toy from Santa's bag should go. Fisticuffs and a fall, that's all. At your chimney… I mean door in four."

"Ah…" Garrett raised an eyebrow. "A hospital Christmas, complete with drama. What better way to start off Christmas Eve than with two elves fighting?"

"And I thought it would have been a partridge in a pear tree." Rosie looked disappointed. "Someone at Dispatch is really screwing up."

"Or has a wry sense of humor." Garrett drank a mouthful of coffee and discarded the rest before heading to the door. "You coming?"

"Sure, why not? I've got nothing better to do than to keep you company for the rest of my shift."

* * *

"So, how's my baby brother doing?" Danni slid onto the living room sofa next to her sibling.

"Merry Christmas, Danni." Matt flashed a smile.

"And a happy New Year to you, too." Danni kissed his cheek.

Matt pointed toward Brie as she headed up the stairs, Mark and Gunther in tow. "Look who's expecting again."

"A husband and family is all she ever wanted in life," Danni said with a sigh. "You'd think she was mother's clone, wouldn't you?"

"I guess her dream came true before any of ours. Say, you wouldn't have any hot-looking girlfriends with eight or nine kids under their belt? I'm going to need all the help I can get for my dream to come true."

"Still sticking to that hope of a wife and ten kids by the time you're thirty, huh? I would have thought you'd come to your senses by now." Danni's laughter softened as her brother's demeanor became somber. "Matt? You didn't really believe it was possible, did you?"

"At one time I did. I guess we never really know what the future will hold for us, do we?" Matt swirled the eggnog in his glass. "I've spent so much of my time becoming a lawyer that I'd forgotten about my dream until now."

"It can still happen. Maybe not by the time you're thirty, but you can still find someone and settle down. Heck, I expected you to come waltzing in today with a girl on your arm, ready to show her off to the family." Danni watched the expression on her brother's face quickly change. A smile slowly came to her face. "You *have* found someone."

"Shh." His finger quickly went to his lips. Matt started to blush and seemed to find his drink very interesting. "I've been seeing someone I think I'd like to really get to know. But she's not exactly what Mother would think of as wife material."

Danni studied her brother. The astute lawyer now reminded her more of a clumsy young boy. "What gives? Is she some kind of alien? Does she have seventeen kids and four exes?"

"No, nothing like that. It's just that she…" He sipped nervously from his glass until he found the courage to continue. "She wants to make her own way in the world and not rely on anyone else for support. You know for damned sure that it wouldn't sit well with Mother. Taking care of a husband and home is her idea of a woman having a career."

"You can't let Mother rule your heart. You know what it is that makes you happy. If you think she's the one, you have to go for it." Danni's heart went out to her brother. "Let's make a promise to each other right here. Next year, we bring the one person in our lives who makes us happiest, whether we think Mother will like them or not."

A wry smile came to Matt's face. "I guess it couldn't hurt if we both did it. You've got a deal." He reached over and hugged Danni. "I love you, sis. I'm sure someone else does, too." He gave Danni a knowing smile, then downed the last of his eggnog. "It's time for me to head to bed. God knows Gunther will be waking us up early enough, shouting that Santa's been here. G'night, Danni."

"Night, Matt." Danni settled into the sofa as she watched her brother walk away. When he was gone, she saw the only other occupant of the room, her father, half-dozing in his recliner with his face turned toward the dying embers in the fireplace.

Lost in her thoughts of the hospital and Garrett, Matt's words came back to her. *I love you, sis. I'm sure someone else does, too.*

She sure hoped so. Danni looked away from the fireplace and saw her father watching her intently.

"Penny for your thoughts, Danni." Henry's voice was hardly more than a whisper.

"I was just thinking." Danni paused. "How did you know Mother was the one for you?"

"I was wondering how long we were going to sit here before you finally got around to talking about what was on your mind."

"You always could read my moods. So tell me, how did you know?"

"There's no real explanation for it. Love just happens, li'l one. All of a sudden someone walks into your life, and your world changes. Things that were important no longer matter, and all you can think about is that one person."

"But what if it's someone you never expected to love? Someone you don't even know everything about?"

"You never know everything about a person. Why, every day I find out something new about your mother. That's what makes it last. There's always another facet to look at and learn."

"But will I know enough to be sure when it happens?"

"That's assuming your heart doesn't already know. Love's a funny thing. It doesn't always come knocking at the door, announcing itself. Sometimes it comes from places we least expect."

Henry looked his daughter squarely in the eye. "Listen to your heart. That's how you'll know."

Danni opened her mouth to speak but was interrupted by the phone.

"I think you should get that," Henry said. "Anyone who would be calling me this late at night is already here. I'm betting it's for you." He got up from his chair and stretched. "Besides, I'm going to head up to bed."

Danni crossed the room and picked up the phone. "Hello, Bossard Residence."

"Danni, is that you?"

"It's me, Gar." Danni's breath caught, and she felt a warm glow.

Henry's eyes twinkled as he placed a kiss on her forehead. "Night, li'l one. Tell Garrett I said 'Merry Christmas.' Maybe next year I'll get to do it in person."

"Night, Daddy. Gar wishes you a Merry Christmas, too," Danni called out before turning her attention back to the phone. "What's your night been like so far? Did you get into the OR yet?"

"Nathan was kind enough to leave me with a hot appendix in a twenty-year-old. It felt good to be back. Other than that, it's been pretty quiet, except for stitching up two elves. How was your drive today?"

"Fine. I actually got here earlier than I expected. Dad and I were just sitting and watching the fire die out. It was nice being able to talk to him again."

"Good. It sounds like you're enjoying the visit."

"I am. My nephew is a hoot. He's been keeping me busy. I ended up taking a nap with him before church. He said to tell you thanks for decorating his cookies."

"Why would he say that?"

"I told him you helped me."

"Yeah, right," Garrett said and snickered.

"He's so cute. I wish you were here to see him."

"Me, too. He sounds like a lot of fun to be around."

"He is." Danni paused for a moment. "Is there any reason in particular why you called me tonight?"

"I... I..." Garrett began to stammer. "I just wanted... I needed..." The conversation was interrupted by the sound of the trauma pager beeping in the background. "I just called to say Merry Christmas to you and your family. I have to go. Trauma calls, you know."

"I wish I was there with you. Have a Merry Christmas, Gar. I'll see you tomorrow around noon."

"I'll be here. Come find me when you get in. I've really got to go. We've got a Santa coming in who fell off a roof. Bye."

The sound of dead air didn't deter Danni. She held on to the phone, not wanting to lose the connection. She couldn't believe that Garrett had called. How had she even gotten this number? Danni hugged the receiver to her before replacing it. Garrett was just full of surprises.

Chapter 7

"I thought Christmas would be an easy holiday," a young intern stated, too tired to don the lead apron in his hands.

Garrett stared aimlessly into the cup of coffee she held in her hand, its aroma almost obliterating the overpowering antiseptic smell of the hospital around her. "Anytime you involve rooftop sleighs, elves, reindeer, and presents being brought into the house via a chimney, there is always potential for trauma."

"How was I supposed to know that? I'm Jewish. We don't get much trauma from spinning dreidels. In fact, I don't think I've ever heard of any of my friends or relatives coming to a trauma center for a splinter removal."

"I guess that depends on the size of the dreidel, doesn't it?" Garrett shifted her gaze to watch the intern's reaction. "Maybe next year I'll volunteer to cover Hanukkah instead."

"What's that about Hanukkah, Doc?" John rushed by, pulling on his gown and mask. "Did I hear you say you'd do it on a dreidel?" John grinned cheekily until the dire look on Garrett's face told him to do otherwise.

"Come on, cut me a break. It wasn't my idea to be stuck in these trauma rooms all night. Thank God, my relief is coming in at noon."

Relief. An image of Danni flittered through Garrett's mind, only to be disrupted by the blaring crackle of the overhead speaker.

"Trauma is in the department. Trauma is in the department."

"Like it hasn't been all night," the intern said.

"Okay, people," Garrett set her coffee cup on the desk and pulled her mask up into position. "Let's see how long it takes us to make a mess out of the room this time. Maybe if we're really good, they'll let us have a little break."

* * *

"What's that all about?" Antoinette said to Henry. She indicated her elder daughter, who could be seen in the next room staring out the window. "I swear that child is behaving strangely. She passed on her favorite foods last night at dinner, and this morning she doesn't want to eat. That's not like Danielle at all."

"It's not strange for someone in love," Henry said in a hushed voice.

"What? She never said a word to me, and I'm her mother."

"I wouldn't worry about it. I'm not sure she even knows it yet." Henry peeked down the hall to where his daughter was standing, unaware of those around her. "I think this Dr. Trivoli's the one."

"And you know this because?"

Henry turned to his wife and smiled, then walked away without uttering a word.

* * *

Danni silently cursed the body that betrayed her innermost feelings at the mere thought of Garrett. She looked around and wondered if anyone else had noticed it. Seeing the indifference on their faces, she breathed a little easier. She brooded, unsure of her next move until the tug at her pants claimed her attention.

"Auntie Dan, why you sad?" Concern was written all over Gunny's adorable face.

Her heart melted. Danni didn't want to lie to him, but how could she tell him the truth when she wasn't sure of it herself? She knelt and gave him a hug. "I'm sad because I have to leave, and I won't see you for a while." She mustered a weak smile.

Gunny puckered up, then kissed Danni's cheek. "Wuv you."

"Love you, too." Danni hugged him once more before standing. She waved, picked up her overnight bag, and headed for the door.

"Danni!"

"Yes?" She turned to see Brie heading toward her.

"I've packed that last piece of your Stollen for the trip." She handed Danni a bag. "Come, Gunther, your Aunt Danni is too busy to stay."

"Brie, hospitals don't close on holidays. We all deserve a chance to be with our families for part of the day. I'll be taking someone's place so they can be with their family for a while."

"Whatever you say. Have a safe trip."

Danni gave her sister a weak hug. "Thanks, Brie, for everything."

"I'm pregnant, Danni. I won't break."

Danni closed her eyes and waited for her dismissal. Brie leaned in and delivered the ritual kiss that their mother had patented. Danni cringed at the barely brushed cheek and audible smack.

Henry waited patiently until his younger daughter and grandson had gone up the staircase. Finally, he cleared his throat.

"I didn't see you standing there." Danni crossed the vestibule and circled her arms around her father's waist. "I'm headed back to Pittsburgh."

"I know. I asked Brie to pack a little something for you for the drive. I noticed you didn't join the breakfast line earlier. Too much eggnog last night, li'l one?"

"Maybe." Danni smiled sheepishly, then reached up on tiptoes to kiss him. "You know, Dad, I really miss Grampa, but I'm glad you're able to fill his shoes. Thanks for our little talk last night."

"If you ever need to talk, I'm always here."

"I know."

"Have you said goodbye to your mother?"

"Yes, she was the first one."

"Matt," Henry called in a loud voice, "your sister's leaving."

Seconds later a fair-haired blur came sliding to a stop next to her. "Sorry for the abrupt entrance."

"It's good to see you're still the little brother I remember sliding around the house in stocking feet."

"But only when I'm not dressed in my suit." Matt wrapped his arms around Danni. "It was great seeing you again. Let's not make it so long in between visits, though."

"Stop by anytime. You're always welcome at my house." Danni kissed his cheek. "Remember about next year," she whispered, then gave him a quick squeeze.

"I will. Here, let me." He pointed to her stack of packages.

"I've got it, Matt," Henry said, coming to his daughter's aid.

"Thanks, Dad. I really appreciate it." Danni turned to her brother. "Next time, you'll get the honors."

Matt watched as the pair walked out the door. "Somehow, Danni, I don't think so."

* * *

From her position in the second-floor window of her room, Brie could see the tender scene unfolding in the driveway between father and daughter. The sound of his hearty laugh brought back memories.

"Parents..." Brie gently rubbed her belly. "How differently we see things as we grow older. We even seem different, the older we become. Who'd have thought Danni wouldn't be the first one in line for Christmas breakfast, or would refuse her favorite wine at dinner? Imagine both of us drinking grape juice like two children." Brie's eyes widened. "What did Danni say in her pre-dinner prayer? Wasn't it something about thanking God for new life?"

Brie looked down at her own belly, then to Danni getting into her vehicle. "I hope that's not what you're trying to tell us." Brie swung away from the window and reached for her son. "I hope your Aunt Danni knows what she's doing, Gunther. Raising a child is tough work with two parents, but with just one... I sure hope this Garrett is the right man, for Mother's sake."

* * *

"I did say I missed the OR, didn't I?" Garrett muttered as she thought about the time she had spent in surgery, going from one patient to another on the busy trauma service. "I just hope whatever I run into today, only good comes from it." She took a breath then slowly let it out. "Yeah, right."

She picked up half a sandwich and bit into it. Her eyes drifted over to the framed photograph of Luc and her. The soft knock at the door pulled her from her musings. "Come in." The door opened slowly, and the sight of blonde hair made her feel cotton-mouthed.

"Hey, Doc, we're going to eat, and Nan sent me to..." John looked at the food-filled tray on the desk. "Never mind, you're already eating. Would you like some company? They say I make a great dessert."

"Sorry, I gave up dessert a long time ago." Garrett's expression was serious. "Tell Nan I said thanks, but no thanks."

"Just remember, I don't go out of my way for anybody. Hey, I see the photo turned out pretty good."

Garrett's mood shifted with the compliment. "Yes, it did. Thanks for helping Danni with it. It means a lot to me."

"Glad I could help out. I'll let you get back to your food. Merry Christmas."

"Merry Christmas." Garrett returned the greeting, and her gaze went again to the photograph.

At the second sound of knocking, John's image darkened her mind like a rain cloud. When would he learn that she wasn't interested?

Garrett strode to the door and yanked it open. "When are you finally going to..." She stopped short, her eyes growing wide. "Danni?"

"You told me to let you know when I got in. Is this a bad time?"

"No, not at all. Is it noon already?" Garrett looked at the watch pinned to her scrub top.

"I'm early, but I just couldn't wait. I mean, I left early, with all the snow coming down."

"Come in." Garrett opened the door wider and ushered Danni in. "Have you eaten yet? I've got some extra food."

Danni looked at the array of food on the tray. "You starving, or what?"

"I don't think so." Garrett picked up a plate and offered it to Danni. "I'm willing to share."

"Thanks. I didn't feel like eating this morning. I guess I had other things on my mind." Danni took the other half of the sandwich and bit into it. "Good choice."

"I didn't feel much like eating earlier, either."

"Speaking of earlier..." Danni produced a small bag and set it on Garrett's desk. "Brie wrapped up a piece of my Stollen."

"I wondered if I was going to get to taste it." Garrett opened the bag, took a piece, and popped it into her mouth. "Mmm... good."

"Thanks."

"You're welcome."

Danni pointed to the framed photograph. "It looks nice on your desk. I'm glad you like it."

"It's definitely something I'll treasure forever. Thanks again for thinking of it."

"You're welcome." Danni smiled shyly. "That jacket kept me pretty darn warm last night, even against the coldest chills."

"I hoped it would."

"Thanks," Danni said softly.

* * *

Danni watched the snowflakes fall to the ground. It didn't take long before Karen joined her outside. "Look, it's snowing."

"I see." Karen watched as a particularly large snowflake came to rest on Danni. "New coat?" She stroked the material with her fingers. "Leather. Must be nice to get perks like that."

"It's not a perk. Gar gave it to me for Christmas." Danni's face brightened. "I'm glad we're still a team."

"Was there ever any doubt?"

"I really flubbed it Saturday. I froze on the helicopter ride out of here."

"It was a test ride," Karen said, shrugging. "So what?"

"So what?" Danni was surprised. "Garrett had to carry me off the helicopter when we landed. That's when McCormick grounded me. I never thought Garrett could be so protective of anybody except her patients, but I was wrong."

"How were you wrong?"

"She told McCormick that if he grounded me, he grounded her, too. Garrett said she wouldn't be paired with anyone else." Danni lowered her eyes self-consciously. "In her place, I'm not sure I could have been so supportive and understanding."

"You, not supportive?" Karen laughed. "I've seen you support what others would have called a hopeless cause, and Garrett Trivoli was one of them."

"Really?"

"Really." Karen nodded.

"I guess you're right." Danni brushed her cheek against the collar of her jacket. "We really are a team now."

"I've been thinking that for a while. What do you say we go back in and have some fun, since it's all nice and quiet?"

"I'd like that," Danni waved to Garrett, who had appeared on the other side of the plate-glass door. "I think we'd all like that."

The two nurses walked back into the hospital clutching their coats to stave off the frosty weather.

"Merry Christmas, Karen," Garrett greeted the charge nurse. "So, when is the action going to start?"

Danni shook the snowflakes from her arms. "Should be anytime now. She just said the 'Q' word."

"No. Tell me she didn't." Rosie poked her head out of the trauma room and glared at Karen. "You know better than that. I wanted a nice..." She replaced her spoken word with a calming hand motion. "Night," she whispered.

Karen shook her head. "Not going to happen. Nope. No way in hell is it going to happen. Trivoli is on, and you know what that means."

Rosie looked at Garrett, then Karen. "We're doomed. Trauma gravitates to her like iron filings to a magnet." Rosie's shoulders slumped and she cast her gaze to the floor. She stayed that way for the longest of moments before bringing her head up with a devilish grin. "But there's one good thing about tonight. We have Danni back with us."

Without warning, Rosie began to dance around her co-workers. "Dan-ni's trauma nurse, num-ber one."

"Fa-la-la-la-la, la-la-la-la." The somewhat subdued singing from the rest of the staff soon began to snowball as Rosie led them from one chorus to another.

"Trauma time 'til Garrett's done," Rosie sang as the number of staff grew around her.

"Fa-la-la-la-la, la-la-la-la."

"Don we now our trauma-'pparel."

"Fa-la-la-la-la, la-la-la-la."

Rosie opened her mouth to start the next verse only to be beaten to the punch by the shrill tone of the trauma pagers.

"Trauma team page. Trauma team page. Medevac Two is inbound with a twenty-two-year-old male victim of electrocution. Contact made attempting to unscrew a broken light bulb from an outdoor display with a pair of pliers. Patient has burns to right hand and left foot. ETA five minutes."

"There goes that quiet night." Danni laughed at the face Karen was making at her. "Then again, you knew it wouldn't stay quiet for long with both of us here, didn't you?"

"That I did." Karen sighed. "That I did."

Chapter 8

"Argh!" Garrett slammed her hand on her desk in a fit of desperation. All she wanted to do was help those who were now in the same position she had been in for the last twenty-some years: that of Lone Survivor.

"No wonder the Board approved this program. They knew the paperwork would be insurmountable." Garrett looked at her brother's image, perched atop the computer monitor. "But I'm not going to let this get me down after what Danni went through to get us here." She took a cleansing breath and released it. "First, we need a room to meet in." Garrett sifted through the stacks of papers heaped on her desktop, looking for the necessary forms.

She was so focused on her task that she didn't hear René open the office door.

"First coffee cups filled the desk, and now all this does." René held his arms out in emphasis. "My friend, if you wanted to be buried alive in a snowdrift, I could give you the location of several nice ones in Canada. You'd have a better view at least, than in here, eh?" He made a comical face as he tipped his head from side to side giving the impression of an animated marionette.

"Sorry, I didn't mean to take over the office. I'll have this all cleared up by the time I leave today."

He chuckled good-naturedly.

"What? You don't believe me?"

"I know how you are, Dr. Trivoli. You'll get so caught up in everything that you could be here for days and not realize it. I don't even think you would stop for food. Coffee?" He wiggled his fingers in indecision, "Maybe."

"Haven't you heard I'm part of a team now? One thing I've learned this last month is that everything is for the good of the team."

"Speaking of teams, I'm in charge of keeping this one running with a full tank," Danni announced from the doorway.

"Ah, Nurse Bossard," René said.

"Season's greetings to you, Dr. Chabot. Care to join us?" Danni dangled a take-out bag in an enticing manner as she entered the room. "I've got more than enough." She pulled open a desk drawer and placed the package there.

"No, thanks. I'm trying to get rid of all the food my wife stuffed me with on Christmas." René patted his stomach. "I take it you both had a nice holiday?" His eyes darted back and forth between the two women.

"What is this?" Garrett said. "Everybody needs to have a nice holiday? Of course mine was nice. I got to operate for the first time in nearly a month."

Danni's hand came to rest on Garrett's shoulder. "I think he meant with friends and family." She looked to René. "Right?"

René put his hands up in mock defense. "Coming from her, that's more than I expected."

"I, for one, had a nice family holiday." Danni nudged Garrett. "Unlike some people."

"Come on. I had fun, too." Garrett reached for the proffered burger that Danni held playfully just out of her reach. "You're giving me a hard time because I ate most of your sugar cookies."

"Stole is more like it, and from a child, too." Danni handed Garrett her sought-after prize. "Dr. Chabot, you have children. Would you take cookies your wife baked specifically for your twins? Take them before they were even cooled?"

René pondered the question. Finally, a smile began to blossom on his face.

"René." Garrett drew out his name.

He blushed. "Sorry, I was thinking about something else."

"The cookies, René." Garrett directed him back to the question.

"Ah, the cookies. If it were my favorite kind, I might be tempted." He grinned then laughed out loud. "Although I'm sure my wife would probably smack my hand and throw me right out of the kitchen."

"See?" Danni's expression was smug.

"I should leave and let you two get back to more important matters, eh? Like finding the desk so I'll be able to use it later tonight, when I'm on call." René gave them a quick wave and backed out the office door.

His hasty retreat left both women with their mouths agape. Garrett was the first to recover. "Do you think he's serious about finding the desk?"

"Yes!"

"That's what I was afraid of."

* * *

"Yes, Everett, I have everything in place," Dr. McMurray said into the phone. The Chief of Trauma Services swiveled his chair to take in the view through his office windows. "I know we had a little incident on the first flight. I assure you, nothing like that will happen again. She's gotten over it. Nerves." McMurray cleared his throat. "That's all it was."

He listened intently before pulling the receiver away from his ear and looking at it as if it had grown three heads.

"Stupid son of a bitch," McMurray groused under his breath. His adrenaline flowing, he returned the phone to his ear.

"And you never got nervous in your life, right? But then again, you don't have that far to fall when you're pushing numbers around in your ledgers, do you? Being up in a goddamned helicopter for the first time would scare the pants even off of me. Everything is fine. They've been in and out of the helicopter so much they think it's their new home."

Ol' Cutter listened for a few seconds before drawing the conversation to an end.

"I know my staff. I trust them. They'll come through with flying colors." McMurray smiled. "The first official flight will commence minutes before the start of the New Year. Now, until that's done, I don't think we have anything more to say. Goodbye, Everett." McMurray spun his chair around to his desk and replaced the telephone in its cradle.

"Goddamned bean counters. They never want to commit to spending a dime unless they know they can make a dollar. Three days before the New Year, and already they're getting their balls in an uproar."

He glanced at the photo of his wife and reconsidered his words. "Sorry, Mary. I know I shouldn't talk like that, but they just get me mad, sometimes."

McMurray sprang from his chair and began to pace as he wrestled with his thoughts. Bean counters didn't deal in feelings. They dealt in cold, hard, facts. And numbers, lots of numbers. Proof, that's what he needed to show them. But how and when, with so little time left?

Going to the window, he stared into the open expanse of sky. McMurray's focus shifted from one wisp of cloud to another before settling on a moving speck of darkness in the distance. Within seconds, the low hum of the rotor came to his ear, and an idea was born.

"They want proof. By God, we'll give it to them." He slammed his finger down on the button of the antiquated intercom.

"Stella, get me the Trauma Flight Team in my office. Stat."

* * *

When Garrett and Danni entered McMurray's office, they noticed several large manila envelopes on the desk. Danni craned her neck, trying to read the writing on them, while Garrett looked around the office for Ol' Cutter.

"These envelopes are addressed to the hospitals that refer trauma patients on a regular basis." Danni picked one up and examined it. "I wonder what's in them?"

"I wouldn't even have a—"

"You're here." McMurray entered the room, his arms piled high with another stack of envelopes. "What took you so long? Never mind."

He placed the envelopes onto his desk and looked up. "I've got a mission for you, Nurse Bossard. Between the two of you, seems like you're the more personable one." He glanced over and saw the shock on Garrett's face quickly turn to a scowl. "Sorry, Dr. Trivoli, but there was never really any question about it. You're a damned good surgeon, and everybody here knows it. What we need is a person who can get right next to someone and open their arms in a loving embrace."

"I don't understand." Danni's brow furrowed.

"He's saying that I'm not a people person and you are," Garrett said, matter-of-factly. "You're the lead in this next mission, not me."

"Lead? I'm not a surgeon. Hell, I'm not even a doctor." Danni stopped, hearing her own words. "Sorry."

"Forget it. So what if you're not a doctor?" McMurray glared at Garrett as he spoke. "It may be even better that way."

Danni's head turned quickly from one surgeon to the other. "Will somebody please tell me what's going on? I thought we were a team."

"You are!" McMurray boomed. The shocked look on the two women's faces made him hesitate. When he started again, his voice was softer. "We need this program to succeed for everyone's sake. That's why we have these." He gestured to the envelopes on his desk.

"What do you want us to do?" Garrett's voice was tinged with sarcasm. "Hand-deliver them?"

McMurray grinned. "Why, yes. That's it exactly."

"There are so many of them." Danni met his gaze. "That would take days."

McMurray saw the glint of realization in Garrett's eyes.

"Not in the helicopter, it won't," Garrett said.

"What's so important that it has to be hand-delivered?" Danni eyed the stacks of envelopes.

Ol' Cutter picked one up. "A lot of information that physicians will need to know when they utilize our service. And a few other associated things."

"And exactly how long are we going to be playing meet and greet?" There was a marked lack of enthusiasm in Garrett's voice.

"I'd say a day and a half, to be on the safe side. I've already requested the same pilot you had before."

"Cowboy?" Danni said. "Cool."

"I thought you might feel more comfortable with him."

"Great." Garrett added her sentiments.

"You'll leave bright and early tomorrow morning. My secretary will have an itinerary ready for you this evening. Any questions?"

"Dr. McMurray, what exactly are we to do on these little meet and greets?" Danni asked.

"Be yourselves, of course. Let the directors and the physicians in the emergency rooms see who'll be coming when they yell for help."

"That doesn't sound too bad, does it, Gar? I mean, Dr. Trivoli."

After a moment, Garrett zeroed in on her mentor. "I think it sounds like a perfectly good idea."

"Now go on, get a good night's sleep." McMurray shooed them out of his office. "I've got work to do here."

The pair walked out the door. When they were safely out of earshot, Danni spoke. "I wish he had talked about some of his photographs. I like hearing his stories."

"Maybe we've seen them all."

Danni looked back at the gold lettering on McMurray's door. "Somehow, I really doubt that."

*   *   *

"Morning, ladies," Cowboy said.

"Good morning, Cowboy." Danni climbed into the helicopter ahead of Garrett.

"I understand they want us to drop in and visit a few places." Cowboy looked over his shoulder as Garrett took her seat.

"Where are we headed first?" Garrett asked.

"We're going north. Franklin Regional Hospital is the first stop. You ready?"

Danni stuck out her right hand in a thumbs-up signal, but there was no response from Garrett, who was staring out the window.

Danni noticed the pause in their pilot's actions and looked for its cause. She found it when she turned to her team member. Garrett seemed a million miles away. "Gar." When no response came, Danni spoke a little louder. "Gar."

"Huh? Oh, yeah. Sorry." Garrett quickly donned her helmet, then gave a thumbs-up.

"I can already see it's going to be a long day," Cowboy said with a sigh.

*   *   *

With one of the large manila envelopes tucked under her arm, Danni led the way into the last hospital on their itinerary for the day. Her easy smile and pleasant voice greeted the director at his office door, just as she'd greeted the directors at the previous stops. "Hi, I'm Nurse Danni Bossard, and this is Dr. Gar…"

"Well, if it isn't Ian's little girls. Come in, I've heard a lot about you. I've been waiting to see you in the flesh." The director's eyebrows danced as he gave a hearty laugh.

"What?" His words took Danni by surprise.

"Excuse me, sir, but we're the Trauma Flight Team, not 'Ian's little girls.'" Garrett's reply bordered on contemptuous.

Danni's natural ability to mediate took over to calm any possible confrontation. "I believe we have a prearranged meeting with you about the new support program being offered by our Department of Trauma Services. As I said before, I'm Nurse Danni

Bossard." She offered her hand. "And this is Trauma Fellow Dr. Garrett Trivoli."

Garrett reached out to shake his hand. The director studied Garrett's face, then quickly scanned the rest of her body. His smile became a smirk.

"Ian was right. You've got the attitude of a surgeon and the body of a goddess. The pin-up poster doesn't do you justice." He looked at Danni. "Neither of you."

Garrett clamped down hard, then quickly released his hand. "What are you talking about?"

"The poster he sent me the other day."

Garrett glanced at Danni, then back at the director.

He shook out his hand. "You've got a good grip there. I bet you don't lose any tools during surgery." He gave a weak laugh, then pointed to the large envelope in Danni's hand. "Ian said I'd be getting another poster. Do you think that I could get you to sign this one for me? I mean, since you're here and all. Kind of make it a collector's item." He gave a leering smile.

Danni undid the clasp of the envelope and looked inside. Besides several small brochures and a few sheets of paper, there was also a heavier-weight poster, folded over. She opened it. Her expression changed from shocked to intensely interested as she studied her own likeness. Then she blushed. The photographer had captured them with a look of determination on their faces and a gleam in their eyes.

"How did he get this?" Dumbfounded, Danni stayed fixated on their images. "When?"

Garrett moved next to Danni and looked at the poster.

"That could have been when he asked us to think about Christmas…" Garrett's voice trailed off.

"So, will you sign it for me?" The director repeated the question, louder this time, as he eagerly held out his pen.

Danni was the first to break her trance, remembering their mission. She smiled kindly at him as she accepted the proffered pen. "I'd be happy to. How about you, Dr. Trivoli, wouldn't you like to autograph this, too?" Danni nudged Garrett for a response, feeling mischievous. She signed her name, then handed Garrett the pen. "Meet and greet, not kill and eat," she whispered.

"Yeah, right." Garrett scrawled her signature across the poster.

"There you go. It's a real collector's item now." Garrett returned his pen. "I can guarantee you nobody else will have one like that."

"She's right, you know." Danni handed the poster and the manila envelope to him. Glancing at her watch, she made a point of noting the time. "I'm sorry, but we seem to be running a little behind schedule, what with signing the poster and all. Would you mind if we come back on a later date for the tour of your ER? Maybe we could spend more time with you then."

"But I…" He paused for a moment. "If you're running late, I guess that will have to be the case."

"I'm sure the next time we drop in, your staff will make us feel right at home." Danni offered her hand.

He clasped it and nodded vigorously before letting go. "I'll make sure of it. Tell Ian I said he really knows how to pick 'em."

"Oh, it will be my pleasure." Garrett turned to leave, pausing only for a moment to look at Danni, her cold stare bordering on icy.

The shiver that passed through Danni didn't hamper her mission. Without missing a beat, she flashed another dazzling smile. "Thanks for everything." She pivoted and followed Garrett out.

* * *

The blades of the helicopter were still winding down when Garrett entered the ER. Without breaking her stride, she took off her helmet and released her plastered-down hair from its confines. A vigorous shake freed ebony tresses from their loose braid, giving her an untamed appearance.

"Is Dr. McCormick in?" She demanded loudly, of no one in particular. Her gaze locked onto Nan, who was headed her way. "Good. Somebody who has answers. Where's McCormick? I have a bone to pick with him."

"Is there something wrong?" Nan asked.

"Damned right, there's something wrong."

"Please, Dr. Trivoli, there's no need to raise your voice. I can hear you perfectly well, as can the rest of the ER."

Garrett's voice dropped a full octave. "Tell that… that… *man* that I'm waiting for him in his office." Garrett pushed her way past Nan and headed for McCormick's lair.

"What's up with her?" Nan looked at Danni.

"I'd stay out of it if I were you, Nan. You don't even want to know." Danni felt a storm churning inside her as she followed Garrett. Nan hurriedly stepped out of her way.

"Garrett's not letting this drop, and neither am I."

* * *

Garrett paced back and forth, her mind racing with the thoughts and feelings she was holding in. When the door opened, she spun around and watched the smile on Ian's face quickly dissolve.

He barely had time to look from one woman to the other before they battered his ears with a barrage of words.

"You despicable chauvinist." Garrett tossed her helmet toward Danni.

Caught off guard, Danni botched her attempt to catch the helmet and it went bouncing all over the office. Every effort she made to capture it only sent the helmet ricocheting off another surface, until it finally landed on the floor and rolled lazily under a chair. She quickly grabbed it. A moment later, it was tucked neatly under her arm, and Danni's full attention was directed to Garrett.

"Is there something wrong, Trivoli?" Ian positioned himself behind his desk.

"What the hell is wrong with you? Where do you get off thinking every woman is your 'little girl'?" Garrett drew her shoulders up as she placed her hands on her hips, creating a foreboding image. "The only 'little girl' I'll ever be is my father's, and even he knew better than to call me that."

"It was a joke. A pet name, that's all. I didn't mean anything by it."

"Men like you are all the same. You think every female is nothing unless they belong to you." Garrett rested her hands on his desk and thrust her head to within inches of the startled man's face. She stared directly into his eyes. "Ian, let me tell you something. Not every woman wants to be called your 'little girl.'" She turned and walked toward the door. Halting abruptly, she reversed her direction and strode right back to his desk. "If I ever hear of that term used in reference to me, my team, or any female in this hospital, I'll go straight to the Board of Directors with a charge of sexual harassment. And if that happens, buddy boy, you'll be one sorry excuse for a mobile sperm bank."

Ian was speechless as Garrett made a hasty departure. He looked at Danni. "What do you have to say?"

Danni shifted Garrett's helmet so she held it by its chinstrap. Then she folded her arms tight against her chest. "Nothing." Her voice was calm and reserved. "I believe my teammate said it all for both of us." She turned on her heel and left.

Ian wiped perspiration from his balding head, his hand shaking. An image of Garrett's irate face filled his mind. "That woman is going to drive me crazy." He slumped into his chair, and his attention focused on the rising mound in his lap. "One way or another."

Chapter 9

From her vantage point on the helipad, Danni watched as Ian McCormick turned the corner of the building and headed for the ER door. Garrett came through the doorway, meeting Ian's compact body almost head-on.

"Great!" Danni cringed. "As if yesterday wasn't bad enough."

Neither adversary spoke. Garrett's unflappable stare never faltered as Ian sidestepped and Garrett whisked by, completely unaware of the desire written plainly on Ian's face.

Danni sighed.

Cowboy glanced away toward Garrett, then back to Danni. "It's a new day in an almost finished year. Time to look to the future and not to the past."

Danni mulled the comment over. "I like that. I only wish we could get *her*"—Danni tilted her head in Garrett's direction—"to accept it."

"We'll see what we can do," he whispered conspiratorially. As Garrett neared, he greeted her. "Morning, Doc. We all ready to leave?"

"I'm not the one in charge. I'm just along for the ride." Garrett looked at Danni. "What's our plan for today?"

Danni was relieved when a hint of a smile settled on Garrett's lips. "Let me see." Danni squinted and tapped her chin with one finger. "Oh, yeah! More meet and greets."

The sound of laughter rose from the trio, as did the steam from their breath as it met the cold morning air.

* * *

"Coffee, the nectar of the gods. If we could only get it to come out of our mother's breasts instead of milk, we'd be starting life off right." Cowboy savored a mouthful as it warmed him from the inside out.

He leaned back in his seat and stared out the cockpit window. The blue sky on the horizon caught his eye, and he wondered what the night ahead of them would bring.

He brought his cup closer to his lips and blew over the steaming liquid. A noise startled him. "Hey!" He separated his legs just in time for the few drops of coffee that escaped his cup to land on the seat. "Dad-burn it! Don't go sneaking up on me. Can't you see I'm holding a cup of scalding hot coffee? I'm going to start locking the doors if you do it again."

"Sorry, Cowboy." Garrett had opened his door and made a grab for the cup in his hand. "We finished faster than we planned."

He batted at her hand. "Get away from my cup, woman. I'll buy you one at the next hospital."

"Likely story." Garrett stepped back and climbed into the rear compartment after Danni.

"Only one more stop, Cowboy." Danni displayed the last envelope to be delivered. "If you both can wait until we get back to the base, I'll buy."

"A celebration, huh?" Cowboy studied Danni in the mirror.

"You bet. Mission accomplished," Danni said, her voice triumphant. "You should have come in there with us. You would have laughed—they were acting like we were going to steal all their patients."

"Huh? They think I could fit them all in here?" Cowboy swept an arm toward the empty area of the helicopter.

Garrett looked around the cramped quarters with a discriminating eye. "Maybe, if we let them all dehydrate for a while. But only if we could package them up like MREs, the old Meals Ready to Eat."

"You know about MREs?"

"Sure do. I had them in the Navy. They're not the best cuisine, but they're edible in a pinch."

"You're right about that," Cowboy said.

Danni continued her story. "The staff here thought this whole idea of calling us in for severe trauma was about the city hospital needing more patients."

"Increased revenue for here is more likely," Garrett said.

"True, and I'm glad you told them exactly that. I guess they're looking at us differently, knowing they aren't going to lose a lot of money out of their staffing budget."

"We take the chance of upping our hospital's mortality rate," Garrett said, "do all the work trying to patch up the train wrecks when they do survive, and then they're going to take all the credit for sending the patients our way."

Cowboy took one last sip of his coffee, opened the door, and dumped the remaining contents onto the ground. "Now that we got the dynamics of the impact of this program all worked out, what do you say we get this last stop under our belts and head home for some celebratory coffee to warm our bellies?"

"And hands. It's damned cold out here today." Danni blew on her fingers, trying to warm them a little.

"I'll vote for that." Garrett belted herself in. "Besides, I still have some phone calls to make before Saturday."

"*You're* going to make the calls?" Danni looked surprised.

"Sure. We're a team, right? I'll dial the number, then you can talk to them."

Danni burst into laughter. "I should have known better than to think you'd actually be the one inviting people."

Garrett settled back into her seat with a satisfied-looking grin. "You got that right."

* * *

Danni slumped back into the chair, the last of the phone calls made.

"You're done?" Garrett said.

"Yep. I think it's going to be a pretty good turnout on Saturday. Are you getting nervous yet?"

"Why should I be nervous? It's not like I'm going to run the meeting."

"I don't know. Maybe because it's your project?"

"Our project. You're as much a part of this as I am." Garrett studied Danni. "Are you nervous about tonight's flight?"

"Maybe. I've never been up in the helicopter at night. Can Cowboy even see to land in the dark?"

"It's all done by radar. You don't have to see." Garrett laid her hand on Danni's arm. "Don't worry, I'll be right there with you. We're a team, remember?"

"That's what I was hoping for." Danni looked away. "Besides, who would want to be alone on New Year's Eve?"

"You'll have me and Cowboy for company. If that's all right with you."

Danni felt her heart skip a beat at the prospect. She nodded, preferring to keep her thoughts to herself.

"How about we stop in to see Dr. McMurray, then go home? There's not much we can do around here until later tonight. We should both get some sleep before we're on call for the next six months."

"Okay." Danni pulled herself up and took the leather jacket Garrett was holding out to her. "I guess I'll have to give the report."

"Better you than me."

*   *   *

"There's someone here to see you."

Stella's voice interrupted McMurray's thoughts. He leaned across his desk to reach the intercom. "Who is it?"

"Dr. Trivoli and Nurse Bossard."

"Send them in." McMurray looked up, and the pair was standing in his doorway. "Come in. How did the meet and greets go? Anything you couldn't handle?" He observed the subtle shake of Garrett's head and turned his attention to Danni.

"I think we made some fine contacts, and I hope they'll think of us before they're in over their heads."

"Good." He stood and walked over to the window. "Looks like a nice night for being out under the stars. You two will have a front-row seat on that one." Ol' Cutter turned back to them and smiled whimsically. "It's times like these that make me wish I was twenty years younger."

"I think we might be able to squeeze you in for a fly-along tonight, if you really want to go."

"Or you could take my space," Garrett offered.

Chuckling lightly, he shook his head. "I don't think the wife would be too happy with me. She'd be entertaining a whole slew of people by herself. No, that's not the way I want to start off a New Year." McMurray reached out to touch the photograph on his desk. "Maybe some other time. Tonight is just for you young people. Enjoy it."

"Thanks, sir," they said in unison.

"We will," Danni added.

McMurray picked up his coat. "Oh, and, Dr. Trivoli."

"Yes, sir?"

"The next time you have a need to use your helmet for something other than its intended use, make sure your mike is turned off. It does a number on the eardrums when it bounces around a room." He fiddled with a coat button. "Never realized they picked up that well, until yesterday. The dispatcher was quite upset with you. He wanted to file a report about your rough treatment of the equipment." Ol' Cutter raised his hand to ward off any defenses Garrett might muster. "No, not a single word."

He tipped his head to each woman as he spoke. "Happy New Year, ladies." With that said, he went out the door.

* * *

"Maybe they're not home," Danni said to herself. The repeated ringing bolstered her false sense of security.

"Bossard residence, Mrs. Bossard speaking. How may I help you?" The words were uttered with an aristocratic flair.

"Hi, Mother."

"Danielle, I thought you would have been here by now." She paused for effect. "It *is* a holiday. You *are* aware of that, aren't you?"

"Yes, Mother. That's why I'm calling. I wanted to wish you and Daddy a Happy New Year."

"When are you going to learn that holidays are meant to be spent with loved ones? I don't understand why you insist on working under these conditions. I really think it's time you give some thought to your future and settle down. Your sister Breanna understood that early on. I don't know why you can't. Surely, you've made some friends, acquaintances you would like to nurture. A young woman like you shouldn't have to be around all those drunkards tonight."

"But I won't be, Mother. I'll be spending my night with Garrett, and I think we'll both be flying pretty high by midnight. That's why I'm calling now, instead of later. I may be a little too busy to get to a phone."

"Danielle! I suppose your mind is already set on this?"

"Mother, I've been waiting all my life for it."

"I hope you know what you're doing."

"I'm a trained nurse. Of course I know what I'm doing."

"I hope you're right, dear. I wouldn't want to see you get hurt." Antoinette hesitated for a moment. "You will take all the necessary precautions, won't you, Danielle?"

"Yes, Mother. I know how to watch out for the tail rotor, and Gar is pretty good at keeping that head down and protected when the lower hatch opens. You don't have to worry. We've already practiced it to the point that we could do it in our sleep."

"I swear you're not my daughter, Danielle."

"Happy New Year, Mother." Danni didn't wait for an answer. She pulled the receiver from her ear and laid it in its cradle.

"It wasn't the conversation I was hoping for, but at least it's over with for another year."

The figure advancing down the stairs sidetracked Danni's thoughts. "Did you get any sleep?"

"A little," Garrett said. "I think I'm getting excited about being on call for the next six months. How about you?"

"Me, too," Danni's mood turned somber. "I guess."

"Something the matter? You look a little worried."

"It's probably nothing." Danni hesitated. "Did you ever have a conversation with someone, and after it was over, think that you weren't both talking about the same thing?"

"Can't say I have. Why do you ask?"

"It doesn't matter. Gar, look at the time."

"Time to leave. If we're lucky, we'll be back home by 0100 hours."

Danni put on her flight jacket and zipped it. "I have to get lucky sometime. Maybe it will happen this year." Pausing to thrust her hands deep into her jacket pockets, Danni sighed as she watched Garrett head out the door. *Don't I wish!*

Chapter 10

Cowboy was making his last pass around the tail section when he saw his team approaching. "Good evening, ladies. Looks like a fine night for a little flyby of the town. What do you think?"

"You're sure it's not too dark for you to fly?" Danni asked, voicing her insecurity.

"Little lady, you could paint my windows black, and I could still fly this machine. Just like bats, we've got us some good radar here." He winked. "Now, don't you go worrying, I've got everything covered."

"Great. That's all she needs to hear. You'd better show her that the glass in the windows is spotlessly clean," Garrett joked as Danni pushed her in playful retaliation. "How are you doing tonight, Cowboy?"

"A little cold right now, but otherwise, just fine. My checklist is all done. I'm only waiting on you."

"Good. Let's get to work." Garrett waited for Danni to climb in ahead of her, then swiftly followed inside and closed the door behind her.

Cowboy shook his head and spoke quietly to himself as he stomped the snow off his boots. "Those two are just like kids, the way they tease each other. I wonder if they know?" He reached for the door to his compartment. "Nah, it would be too easy to tell them." He pushed back the cloth on the basket wedged next to his seat, checking to make sure everything was as he had planned it.

"Besides, this ride should be real interesting, come midnight."

* * *

"It's nearly midnight," Cowboy said. "They want us high over the Golden Triangle when the New Year comes in. I'm going to buzz around the Point."

"The Point?" Garrett craned her neck to see what Cowboy was referring to. "I don't see any golden triangles. Well, maybe one, on top of the building over there with the red light at the tip."

Danni shook her head, thankful for something to keep her mind distracted from their night flight. "That's the old Gulf Building. It used to be their corporate headquarters. The colored light is a weather forecaster. By the way, it's forecasting fair weather tonight."

"So that's the Point?"

"Not really. The Point is the tip of the land where the Allegheny and the Monongahela Rivers meet to form the Ohio. That's why Pittsburgh is noted for its three rivers."

"So that's where the name Three Rivers Stadium comes from," Garrett said. "I remember that one from the football games during the seventies, when the Steelers were a championship team."

"You remember back that far, huh?"

"Yeah, my dad was a big football fan."

"Hey, so am I. Maybe we can watch some Steelers games together."

"What's that?" Garrett pointed to a half-finished structure.

"The new football field. Three Rivers Stadium will be torn down early in 2001." Danni pointed to an area just past it with a large, lit sign. "And that's the new baseball field, PNC Park."

The helicopter turned on its path around the downtown area, changing the view outside their window. A tall spray of illuminated water was now visible.

"See that?" Danni nodded toward the shimmering golden glow. "That's the fountain at the Point."

"I'd hate to have to pay the water bill."

"Silly." Danni nudged Garrett. "They don't pay for the water. It's kind of fascinating where it does come from, though."

"The river?"

"Yes and no. It's water from a subterranean river, actually, not one of the three you can see. We have a lot of buried treasures around here. You just need to know what you're looking for." Danni searched Garrett's face. "I guess you could say 'still waters run deep.'"

The helicopter took another banking turn. The view of the glistening metropolis had been replaced by one of vast darkness, with two parallel lines of lights stretching up a hillside. One set was yellow and green, while the other, some distance away, glowed white. On the top of the hill was an ornately lit yellow-orange brick building that resembled a church.

"Now what am I looking at? Lighted pathways?"

"No, not exactly. The hillside is Mt. Washington, and those 'lighted pathways' are the Monongahela Incline and the Duquesne Incline. They're cable car systems. They used to be the only way to get up or down Mt. Washington. Now, they're tourist attractions for the city, although some city residents still use them as connections between bus lines."

"I see. What about the building over there?" Garrett pointed to the illuminated building at the top of the cliff.

"That's St. Mary of the Mount Church. It stands as a landmark for the overlooks."

"Okay, I'll bite. What overlooks?"

"It's not real easy to see from up here." Danni edged up on her seat toward the window. "There, the lighted platform with the railing around it. That's one of them."

"Right across the road from the church?"

"Yes, that's it. The circular platforms extend off the hillside to offer the best view of the Point. Supposedly, it was all the rage in the late forties and the fifties to have your picture taken on your wedding day, posed on a platform with the city skyline as your background. I remember my parents' wedding photograph with the city in the background."

"I guess it's one way to always remember the city you were married in."

"Somehow, I think on a special day like that, you'd be able to remember it without the photograph. I know I would." Danni's voice trailed off as the heat of a blush slowly crawled up her neck and over her cheeks.

Cowboy broke the silence. "Two minutes to the real new millennium. Hey, Doc, could you grab these?" He held out two fluted glasses and a bottle.

Garrett handed Danni a glass. "What's this for, Cowboy?"

"I was thinking that since this is the new millennium and all, we should offer a toast to the New Year. You and the Doc, I mean. I'm not allowed to drink while I'm flying. They say I need both hands on the controls. What do they know?"

"Hey, we're on duty, too." Garrett shoved the bottle back into his hand.

"Take a look at the label. It's non-alcoholic. I didn't know what you two liked, so I just got sparkling cider. I hope that's all right."

Garrett appraised the bottle, then offered it for Danni's inspection.

"Thanks, Cowboy. I can see you're a full-service pilot." Danni was all smiles as she spoke.

"You bet. I figured the Doc might want to make a toast to new beginnings at the stroke of midnight. It would only be proper, since this is the first official flight." He looked back long enough to catch their attention. "I'd hurry up and pour if I were you. There's only a minute or so to go."

"How will we know when it's time?" Garrett carefully brought the neck of the bottle to a glass and started to pour.

Danni looked out the window. "The Bayer sign. It's 11:58 and fifty-fi... six seconds right now."

"Here, take this glass and give me yours. Got it?"

"Yes." Danni smiled.

Cowboy cleared his throat. "Ten, nine, eight..."

Danni's gut fluttered with anticipation.

"Seven, six..."

Garrett stowed the bottle and turned to face Danni.

"Five, four, three..."

Glasses were raised in preparation of the toast.

"Two, one. Happy New Year!"

"Here's to dedication and teamwork." Garrett focused on Danni. "It's what brought us to where we are now, and it will carry us into the future. May the year 2001 be a turning point in our lives."

Glasses clinked, and soon afterward, the sweet cider met their lips.

Danni sat mesmerized as an errant drop lingered on Garrett's lower lip. She could feel the attraction reaching out and pulling her closer with each passing second. She willed her body to stay where it was, but it wouldn't. Already it was beginning to lean as Danni watched Garrett lick her lips.

The simple action triggered a series of reactions throughout Danni's body. Her skin tingled with excitement while other parts of her body, long thought to be dead, came to life. Stunned by the sensations, she felt her heart beat wildly within her chest. The distance between the two dwindled to only inches, and suddenly, something felt different. The force that had been drawing her closer to Garrett was being met with resistance.

Without warning, the helicopter shifted. What had been so close for the taking now seemed thousands of miles away.

"Hey!" Danni said indignantly.

"What the…" Garrett turned abruptly toward the pilot. "Are you trying to kill us back here or what? Sound off before going into a hard turn."

"Sorry. I thought you heard. They're requesting us for a scene run."

Danni breathed in short, gasping spurts as she tried to calm her raging soul. She stole a glance at Garrett. The woman looked just as confused as Danni felt. In a single moment of transformation, Danni saw Garrett's demeanor change to one of stoicism.

"What's the nature of our call, and how long before we get there?"

"MVA with entrapment, north of the city on Interstate 79. ETA is approximately ten minutes to LZ. The patient is in hard labor, contractions four minutes apart."

* * *

The tuft of blonde hair made Danni stop dead in her tracks. "Brie?" Panic gripped her. "Gar!"

"Stay here. I'll go see if they know who it is." Turning to leave, Garrett was stopped by Danni's grasp on her sleeve.

"I'm going with you. Whoever it is, she's going to need both of us."

Garrett nodded, and they moved forward together.

The clump of distorted and twisted metal was barely recognizable as two vehicles, and the rescue workers had little to show for their efforts. The deafening drone of hard-pressed hydraulic tools overrode the sounds of the commands being issued by those in charge.

Garrett headed to the ambulance, whose flashing lights acted like a sentinel to the grisly scene. The lone attendant's concentration was glued to the activity on the wreckage.

"Do you know who that is?" Garrett projected her voice over the din of the rescue equipment.

"Huh?" The attendant's gaze switched to Garrett.

"Dr. Trivoli, Flight Surgeon." Garrett offered her hand in greeting. "They requested my team. This is Nurse Danni Bossard."

"Oh, sorry, Doc. I didn't mean to be rude." She clasped the offered hand. "I'm Sandy."

"Do you know the woman's name?"

"It's B… something."

Garrett's heart jumped and she glanced at Danni.

"B-r..." Sandy hesitated. "Brenda, that's it. Brenda Connors."

"Thank God." Danni sighed in relief.

"What do we know about Brenda? When is her due date? Who's her obstetrician?" Garrett fired off her questions as she studied the back of the ambulance.

"Hey, Doc, I'm not a medic or anything. They all left with the people in the other car, who were hurt pretty badly. It's just Ed, over there, and me." She looked at Danni and then at Garrett. "And you two, thank goodness."

Danni edged closer. "What exactly are you and Ed?"

"Ed's in EMT class and I'm a driver."

"What?"

"Heck, we only have two medics in the whole town. Our two EMTs went with the other ambulance. They said they'd send help." She looked toward the helicopter. "I guess you're it."

* * *

Upon reaching the gangly-looking young man in the EMS parka, Garrett tapped him on the shoulder. "Are you Ed?" she shouted.

He nodded.

"I'm the Flight Surgeon, Dr. Trivoli." Garrett pointed at the entrapped woman. "How's she doing?"

"She was on her way to the hospital when the accident happened. They were meeting Dr. Jenkins there. It's her first pregnancy, and she's overdue by a week. We checked in with her doctor, but he's already delivering another baby. Our command hospital figured your team might be a good choice."

"I'll have to thank them for thinking of us. Let me get the other half of my team."

"Hey, Doc." Ed tugged on Garrett's coat. "I need to tell you something else."

"What?"

He pointed to the tarp-covered body on the ground, not far from the wreckage. "That's her husband."

"Does she know?"

Ed nodded.

Garrett gulped hard, tasting bile at the back of her throat. Her gaze darted to the woman in the wreckage. Another lone survivor in the making. She couldn't let that happen to either the mother or the baby.

"Do you know what you're going to do yet?" Danni yelled over the noise of the rescue attempt.

Garrett looked at her. "Whatever it takes."

*　*　*

Garrett hoped the situation would have a satisfactory resolution. Helicopters didn't make good delivery rooms.

Cowboy leaned in to be heard over the whining noise of the hydraulic tools. "Any progress?"

"No." Garrett shook her head. "How about you?"

"Here's the information you wanted." He handed her the notes jotted on a piece of paper. "But we have to lift off within thirty minutes. Weather pattern's changing."

"Thanks." Garrett read the paper and mentally started planning her method of care.

The ear-thumping sounds abruptly stopped and elated voices filled the air. Masses of metal had been peeled away, exposing the trapped victim. Sidelined firefighters and ambulance personnel whooped and hollered. Workers had won the critical battle to free the woman and her unborn child.

"Cowboy, get ready for liftoff. We've got some work to do," Garrett called out, breaking into a brisk run.

Already in the thick of things, Danni helped to stabilize the patient as the firefighters placed her onto the long backboard. With the woman's spine immobilized, Danni was finally able to view and assess the patient. Her left arm was somewhat misshapen, and Ed was applying an inflatable splint. After the boarded woman was lowered onto the stretcher, Garrett put her hands on Brenda's abdomen, checking for the baby's positioning.

Danni produced a stethoscope from her jacket and offered it to Garrett. "Here you go."

"Thanks."

Garrett listened to the heart sounds of the fetus while Danni turned her attention back to the soon-to-be mother. Brenda's panic-stricken eyes and her rushed, staccato breathing were a dead giveaway as to what was happening.

"Contraction?"

"Y-y-yes."

"Squeeze my hand." Danni clasped Brenda's good hand as her eyes searched for any obvious injuries or indications of potential blood loss. Aside from the splinted left arm, there were none. Within a few seconds, the spasm eased and Brenda began to relax.

Danni shook her hand, trying to get her attention. "Hang in there, we're here to help you."

"My baby," Brenda gasped. "Don't let anything happen to my baby." She began to sob, and dropped Danni's hand to clutch at Garrett's arm, drawing her attention. "If you have to choose, save the baby." Brenda's desperation was evident in her eyes.

"I'm going to do everything I can to keep you both safe and alive." Garrett broke her gaze with the woman. "I need a flashlight and another blanket. Now!"

As soon as the items were produced, Danni quickly draped Brenda's lower half with the blanket while Garrett positioned her legs. Under the privacy of the impromptu examination area, Garrett used the flashlight to assess the time left to delivery.

"There's no crowning yet. We've got a little time."

Brenda clamped down on Danni's hand.

"It's another contraction."

"I have to push," Brenda said from between clenched teeth.

"No!" The shout came from nearly every rescuer within earshot.

"It's coming. I can't hold it. Help me," Brenda whimpered. "Please, help me."

Garrett made her decision. "She's delivering. We may be here a while. Let's get her into the ambulance and out of the cold."

"Okay, people. We're moving," Danni said, spouting orders as she took the flashlight from Garrett and handed it to the person next to her. "You, take this and get the ambulance doors open. Everybody ready? On my count of three, you're going to lift and carry. One, two, three."

There was the sound of a joint groan as the stretcher was lifted. Danni hustled the group to the waiting rig, while Garrett moved ahead of them to prepare for her part in the birth.

"Danni, change places with Ed. Brenda can hold his hand just as well as yours. I'll need you with me." Garrett began pulling on her sterile gloves. "Sandy, turn the heat up to high and get some blankets warmed up."

Once the stretcher was locked in place, Danni knelt at Brenda's side while Garrett positioned herself at the foot of the stretcher.

Danni quickly pulled gloves on and assisted Garrett in gently positioning the woman's legs for the impending birth.

"Gar?" Danni's eyes flitted between Garrett and the small butt protruding from Brenda's birth canal.

"I see it." Garrett moved faster to intervene, well aware of the complications a breech delivery entailed. Sliding her gloved fingers gently along the small body, she tried to gain access to the birth canal. Garrett's long fingers finally found what she was searching for, and carefully, she worked to loosen the loop of umbilical cord from around the infant's neck.

"When the contraction comes, I want you to push, and push hard, Brenda. We're going to need your help." Garrett looked at Danni. "Are you ready?"

Danni nodded and turned to Ed. "You ready up there?"

Ed gulped. "R-r-ready."

Sensing the beginning spasms of the upcoming contraction, Garrett alerted her team. "Here it comes." She waited until the muscles started to clamp down before giving the woman her final instruction. "Now, Brenda. Push!"

"Grrraugh!" The strangled scream started deep within the woman's chest, growing louder as it escaped, consuming all of her breath.

The agonized cry, combined with the death-grip Brenda had on his hand, were more than Ed had bargained for. His face turned white and his knees buckled underneath him as he sank onto the bench seat.

"Ed!" Danni yelled to get his attention. "Ed! Lean forward and put your head between your knees. You'll feel better in a minute or two." Danni watched until he complied, before turning her attention back to the patient.

Garrett slipped her fingers under the cord and tented them, allowing air to reach the area around the baby's mouth. "One more push should be all we need."

Tears streamed down Brenda's face as the contraction started.

"Push!" Garrett said. "Push with everything you've got."

Within seconds, another guttural scream heralded the baby's birth. The close quarters reverberated with the excruciating noise as Garrett presented the baby. Hastily, Danni worked to clear the infant's airway.

"Come on, breathe," Danni whispered.

A few heartbeats later, the newborn's silence was broken. A high-pitched screech immediately brought a smile to everyone's face.

Garrett placed two clamps on the umbilical cord, cut between them, and then delivered the afterbirth. Danni wiped the baby's face and wrapped him in a warm blanket. Hospital staff would clean him properly.

"Good work," Garrett said. "You have a beautiful baby boy."

Tears were streaming from Brenda's eyes. "Thank you," she whispered, reaching out as Danni handed her son to her.

Garrett picked up a clean towel. "Now, what do you say we get you both to the hospital?"

*   *   *

Danni leaned against a wall outside the trauma room. "Feels a little funny, huh?"

"You mean standing out here?" Garrett watched the action in the trauma room. "Yeah, it does."

"You think we'll ever get used to not being in there?"

"I'm sure we'll have our moments."

Danni thought back to their midnight toast and the moment shortly thereafter. "God, I hope so."

"Don't look now, but McCormick's here. Wonder what words he'll use to describe us now?"

"Danni, Garrett. How's my team doing?" Danni had come to expect his lecherous smile.

"Dr. McCormick." She returned his greeting.

"Looks like we got off to a quick start." Ian rubbed his hands together.

"Two or three minutes into the New Year," Garrett said.

"Good work, you two. Now, go on home and get some rest. We'll take it from here." His oily grin resurfaced. "You know, you're both on call until the end of June."

Garrett gazed toward Ian as he walked away. "What was that all about?"

Danni shrugged. "I'm not sure."

The newborn's cry filled the air, bringing Garrett's attention back to the trauma room. "Who cares? I'd say hearing *his* cry is all that matters tonight."

Seeing the satisfied look on Garrett's face, Danni smiled. "I guess that's one name we won't be adding to our list of lone survivors."

"You got that right."

Chapter 11

Between the members of the newly formed Lone Survivors Club and the support staff pledged to aid their evolving psyches, the moderately sized conference room was filled to capacity. Standing off to one side, Danni and Garrett watched the two groups mingle after their formal introductions had been made.

"I know the statistics all say that males predominate in trauma patients under twenty-five years of age," Danni said, "but I never truly grasped it until now."

Garrett nodded. "That was a good idea, having them bring a favorite photograph of their deceased loved one."

"Thanks. I feel a little self-conscious without a picture. Maybe I should go."

"Nonsense. You're a co-founder. You belong here."

"But I—" Danni was interrupted by loud tapping on the microphone.

"If everyone would take their seats, we'd like to get on with the second half of the meeting." The man at the podium waited.

"Danni."

"Yes, Gar?"

"I…" Garrett stuck her hands in her lab coat pockets. "I'd like it if you stayed."

Danni studied Garrett for a long moment. "Then I'll stay."

"Thanks." Garrett sounded relieved as she turned her attention to the Master of Ceremonies.

"Good evening, everyone. My name is Dr. Jaffers, and I've been asked to moderate the last half of tonight's meeting. I'm sure you remember me from earlier." He looked around, and a number of people nodded. "For those of you who may not know, I'm a psychiatrist, and a counselor for the Trauma Services workers." He paused for a moment, and smiled. "Yes, even the rescuers need somebody to talk to sometimes." His attempt at humor was met with little more than a chuckle from his audience. "And now I'd like to introduce to you one of this year's trauma fellows, Dr. Garrett Trivoli."

Polite applause filled the air as Garrett slowly walked to the podium. She paused while her eyes swept over the room, and then she began speaking.

"Prior to becoming a surgeon, I was a normal, everyday child, growing up in a typical family. That was until one day, when, out of nowhere, my sense of belonging and family were shattered. You see..." She paused. "I, too, am a lone survivor, just like all of you.

"Dr. Jaffers thought it might be good to have someone talk with you tonight about his or her experiences as a lone survivor. I volunteered, because while we've asked you to attend these meetings, we weren't about to ask you to share your life with the rest of the group just yet. I know each of us has to do that in our own time. Some will take longer to share their experiences, and others will be willing to do so much sooner. I only ask that when you feel ready, you let us know." Many in the group were nodding, but some were showing no signs of emotion at all.

"It was a normal Saturday evening. I was seventeen years old, and out with a group of friends at a movie. My parents and brother were together at one of his baseball games. I came home that night to find the house dark and empty. I didn't think anything was unusual about that, except I remember being jealous that I wasn't sharing in the celebration after one of my brother's games. Win or lose, they would always stop to have ice cream and discuss the game.

"When the phone rang, I hoped it was my father, asking me what flavor of ice cream I wanted him to bring home." Garrett's expression grew deadly serious. "It wasn't. Instead of someone I knew, there was a voice informing me of an accident, and telling me I needed to come to the hospital. I don't remember hanging up the phone or leaving the house. The only thing I do remember was the look of terror on our next-door neighbor's face, right before he reached out to hold me in his arms. He and his wife took me to the hospital, where I was told my parents had been killed in a motor vehicle accident. Their car had been broadsided and pushed into a telephone pole."

The tears welled up in Danni's eyes as she listened to Garrett talk. It hurt to think of that young girl being thrust into an adult world, with little sympathy from the medical community she now embraced as her own.

Garrett paused until the whispering of the audience died down. She cleared her throat, then forged on.

"Then the doctors told me about my brother. They took me into Lucas's room and showed me the array of machines and tubes connected to him. They impressed upon me that there was no way I would be able to care for him, either at that time or in the future. Needless to say, I was shattered. While in that state, I was asked to sign a release for the funeral home to remove the bodies."

A number of gasps arose from the audience.

"Oh, my God!" The words escaped Danni's mouth in a hushed tone before she could stop them.

"I found out a few years later that I had signed for my brother to be taken off life support." Garrett paused and blinked several times.

Danni could see the guilt Garrett had been carrying. Her heart went out not only to the woman she knew, but also to the child Garrett had been when it happened. "She felt his death was her doing," Danni whispered. It nearly broke her heart when she looked up and saw Garrett's blue eyes looking more like a dismal gray.

"I can't tell you the torment and doubt I experienced following that knowledge. I have second-guessed myself so many times over the years since then. If I had known, would I have done it?" Garrett paused and looked down at the podium. She lifted her gaze, squared her shoulders, and met her audience head on.

"Since the accident, I know I've felt isolated, always wondering what would have happened if I had been with the rest of my family that night. Would an extra few minutes to wait for my ice-cream cone have made any difference in the outcome? Or was it fate that I lived on without them? I can admit to you now, thoughts of ending the pain did cross my mind. I had no one to miss me if I were to commit suicide. The memory of my family would be all but wiped from the face of the earth, except for the writing on our tombstones."

Danni's eyes grew wide as she realized Garrett's true inner strength. She'd had nobody but herself to rely on. No wonder she demanded so much more of herself than anybody else would. Danni fought back the urge to run to the podium and wrap her friend in a loving embrace.

"So, you see, I've been where you are. Desolate, alone, and isolated from the rest of the world at times that should be filled with happiness and family. It wasn't until I came here to Pittsburgh that I learned it didn't have to stay that way. There are people out there, without any blood ties to us, who can be just as much our family as the ones who are no longer with us." Garrett stopped and rephrased her statement. "No longer with us physically. It's up to each of us as individuals whether we open our eyes and our hearts to them. I strongly suggest that you do. I have." Garrett made eye contact with Danni. "It's made a world of difference to me."

An eerie stillness settled over the room as Garrett left the podium. Tears rolled down Danni's cheeks, and there wasn't a thing she could do to stop them.

* * *

The group milled around Garrett as she made her way through the room.

"You really know what I'm feeling," a young woman sobbed as she reached out to touch Garrett's hand. "I can see now that there's hope for me. Thank you, Dr. Trivoli."

"That was brave of you, young woman." An elderly man peered deep into Garrett's face. "I could never do what you just did."

"Thanks, but I'm not brave. All of you are the brave ones for coming here today. I just did what I had to do—something we all have to do eventually, if only for ourselves." Garrett wasn't sure whether she was more nervous now or before her talk had begun. She slipped her hand into her pocket, nervously fingering the paperclip she found inside as she scanned the crowd for Danni. When she couldn't find her, Garrett began to worry. "Excuse me," Garrett said to the next person who shook her hand. "I... excuse me." Without giving any reason, she made her way to the door.

Once out in the hall, Garrett looked down one side of the hallway, then turned to look the other way. A wave of relief washed over her. There stood Danni.

"Hey! It looks like the meeting was a success."

"Thanks, Danni. I hope they got something out of it."

"I'm sure it opened a few eyes."

"I hope so. Thanks for—" Garrett's lips were stilled by a finger.

"Not here, Gar." Danni took her hand and led her away. She didn't stop until they were outside Garrett's office door.

"I think this is a better place to continue our discussion, don't you?"

An inkling of a smile came to Garrett's lips. "Thanks."

"There's no need to thank me. I did what any friend would do. I just wish I had been able to do more." Danni paused until they were inside the office and the door was closed. "Why didn't you tell me before?"

"What? That I was so upset about what I had done to my brother that I wanted to end it all? That I had even gone so far as to plan it all out?" Garrett became restless, not wanting to see the empathetic look in Danni's eyes. She stared down at the floor.

"You didn't know what they were going to do," Danni said. "You might have thought about taking your life, but you didn't go through with it. Your nature is to preserve life, not end it."

"It took me a long time before I could stop thinking of myself as a murderer, that I was no better than any one of those criminals on death row. I killed my own brother. I was the one who let them take him off the machines, not someone else." Her eyes clouded with warring emotions, and she fought to get her stoic mask back into place.

"No! Don't even think that. You were a teenager when it happened. You didn't know they were taking advantage of you. You've devoted your life—your career—to being the best surgeon you could be, to make up for it. You've saved so many patients already, and you're nowhere near the end of your career. I don't ever want to hear you talk like that again. Where would all those people be today if it weren't for you? Can you tell me that?" Her small hand traveled up to Garrett's face, and softly touched her cheek. "Your commitment to keeping others from experiencing what you went through makes a difference." Danni's eyes softened. "Can't you see? You make a difference for a lot of us."

"Maybe you're right." Garrett swallowed hard and looked down at the small photograph of her brother that was pinned to her lapel. "I guess I never considered it that way. Thanks."

"What are you thanking me for? I can only point these things out to you. I didn't save those people. You did."

"Yeah?"

"Yeah."

"Danni."

"Yes?"

"Thank you for sticking around long enough to be a friend. I know I'm a pretty arrogant person," Garrett paused at the sound of a snort. "And I demand a lot from those around me."

"Come here." Danni reached out and wrapped her arms around Garrett's waist. "Thank you for asking me to stay."

"Thank you for not leaving." Garrett tightened her embrace, then released it.

"I just wish I could've been there for you back then."

"Me, too," Garrett whispered. "Me, too."

Danni's embrace bolstered Garrett's shaky confidence. Today was the first time she'd ever spoken of her secret, and having done so, it didn't seem as dark as she had imagined it to be. She hugged Danni again and placed a gentle kiss on her golden hair. Inhaling the delicate scent of jasmine, along with the warmth and strength of Danni's hug, she committed this moment of renewed confidence to memory.

Chapter 12

"Hey, Karen." Danni's somber tone reflected her mood.

"What's wrong, no flights today?"

"Not yet. I was just thinking, that's all." Danni stared out the window.

"If you ask me, it looks like you're doing some heavy-duty thinking. Come on, you can tell me. Can't be anything I haven't heard from my own brood when they were growing up."

How could she tell Karen that she thought she might be gay? "It's nothing."

"Nothing?" Karen rubbed Danni's shoulders. "Must be a pretty important nothing. Your back muscles are as tight as knots."

Danni considered her options. She could keep holding everything inside, or she could use Karen as a sounding board. It didn't take her long to come to a decision. "I've been thinking a lot about relationships." The last word was little more than a whisper. "Why can't things be simple?"

From the look on Karen's face, Danni could tell the subject matter wasn't what she had expected.

"Sounds like you've gotten hit with one of Cupid's arrows."

"I wouldn't exactly say I was the one he was aiming for." Danni slumped forward. "I'm not sure I'm ready for this."

"Danni…" Karen hesitated. "Sometimes we don't get to choose who we fall in love with. It just happens, without any rhyme or reason. There's nothing scientific or mathematical about it. One day, out of the blue, our heart tells us, 'This is the one for you.' We only have to accept it."

"That's all well and good, but what if the other person isn't feeling the same thing?" Danni looked up, pleading for understanding. "Could it…" She started over. "What if the other person thought it wasn't right and walked away?"

"Not right? Love is always right. It's the most natural thing on this earth. A person would have to be a fool to walk away from love that was honest and pure, especially if it was coming from someone like you. As I see it, you have two ways to go. You can forge ahead and let your feelings be known, or you can sit tight and hope for the best."

"That's the problem. I'm not sure I can live with the answer, either way." Danni's head fell into her hands. "God, why does life have to be so hard?"

"Sometimes it's not as hard as we make it for ourselves."

Danni looked away and became even more tense. Karen followed Danni's line of sight.

"Garrett?" The name escaped before she could stop it. "I knew you two were getting closer but I..." She stopped abruptly. "I should have known."

Worry gave way to dejection as Danni waited to see a look of disappointment appear on Karen's face. Instead, she was met with a bittersweet smile.

"I'd give her some time. She's just learning what it's like to have a friend." Karen squeezed Danni's shoulder. "The rest might take a while."

"Thanks."

Garrett stopped next to them. "Karen, haven't seen you in a while." Her attention settled on Danni. "So, when's the next outing?"

A rush of air escaped Danni's mouth, as though she had been punched in the gut. Oh, God!

"Outing?" Karen's voice sounded strained and raw.

"Yeah, who's it going to be? Danni, or me?"

"Whoa! Whatever you heard, it wasn't me. I... we..." Karen stuttered.

Rosie came out of a trauma room. "There you are. I've been looking all over for you. Did you hear about the ski trip?"

"Ski trip? Yes. No. Yes." Karen dived right in. "We like ski trips, don't we, Danni? I know how much fun you had on the outing last year with David. I figured you'd want to know as soon as the plans were solidified."

"David?" Garrett's interest was piqued.

"We're booking the lodge for Saturday. February tenth, to be exact." Rosie looked from Danni to Garrett. "Both of you will be able to come, I hope. Won't you?"

Danni shook her head. "Sorry, Rosie. We're on call."

"She's right," Garrett said. "This is one outing we won't be able to be a part of."

"Well, that sucks."

"Yeah, it does." Danni sighed, then looked away.

Garrett gave her shoulder a pat. "Maybe next time."

Karen took a step toward the door. "I've got to get going."

"Yeah, me too." Rosie waved a piece of paper she held. "I've got to get the word out."

"Come on, Rosie, I'll walk with you to the locker room." The two nurses went off down the hall, leaving Danni and Garrett to fend for themselves.

Garrett turned to face Danni. "You want to talk about it?"

"Talk about what?"

Garrett stared out the window, but Danni thought she looked nervous. "The ski trip last year. You and David."

"Oh, that." Danni was relieved it wasn't something else. "David was the chief surgical resident last year. We had a good time trying to learn how to ski, that's all." A pleasant smile crossed her lips as she reminisced. "Neither one of us was any good. We just kept falling into each other. If you ask Rosie, she'll tell you David spent more time with me in his arms trying to get ourselves upright than he did holding onto the ski poles." Danni laughed. "All I know is, after a while, sitting in the snow can make you very cold."

Garrett's face suddenly lost any defining expression. "I see."

Danni noticed the change almost immediately. She wasn't quite sure what had set it off. Had something she said touched a nerve? But what? Danni thought for a moment before finding safer ground. "I guess you have patients to see."

Garrett nodded, although it was evident her mind was elsewhere.

* * *

"So, let me get this straight." Cowboy sipped his coffee and looked off into the distance. "You'd like me to pull in a few favors and get us deployed up to Seven Springs for the weekend of the ski outing. Is that what you're saying?"

"Yes," Garrett said. "You've been in the business for fifteen years, you must have connections. I figure you've flown into just about every hospital or clinic in the tri-state area. You've got to know somebody at the resort, or at least connected to it."

He cast a doubtful glance in her direction. "And you want this done on the QT, right?"

"Quietly. Right."

"Can't promise anything, but I'll give it a try. You think this PR idea of yours will work?"

"It has to. I think McMurray and the Board of Directors will jump on it, given the chance. We have to get someone to request it, though. I'd hate to see Danni miss out on something she likes to do. Right about now, I think a little group activity would be the best medicine for her mood."

"She has been a little quiet lately. Not like her at all," Cowboy said, bringing his cup of coffee to his lips. "I'll see what I can do. No promises, mind you, but I'll give it a try."

"Thanks. That's all I can ask."

With her plan set into motion, all Garrett had to do was sit back and wait until the pieces were in place.

* * *

It wasn't long after Garrett and Danni were called to his office that McMurray bustled into the room.

"I'm glad you're here." He shuffled two business-sized envelopes in his hand. "It seems these are for you." He handed them over, then stepped behind his desk.

Garrett looked at the return address. The name and address were unfamiliar to her. She looked at Danni's, only to find it a near carbon copy of her own. "What's this about?"

Danni opened her envelope, unfolded the enclosed paper, and scanned the page. "These are summonses. We've been subpoenaed as material witnesses."

"What?" Garrett ripped her envelope open and checked over the words, stopping short at a name. "I don't remember treating anyone named Leza McCoy." She looked at her mentor. "Somebody has to be mistaken, here."

McMurray picked up a folder from his desk and flipped it open. "Do you remember working on a..." He looked down the page until he found the name. "Sunshine Doe?"

"I think so," Danni said. "Wasn't she the woman who was assaulted and raped last year? You remember, Gar, the one Jamie—I mean Dr. Potter—had to intubate on the helipad. You hadn't been here long."

"Let me help you, Dr. Trivoli. Think back to the night you chose to banish a medical student and throw Nurse Bossard out of your trauma rooms. Does that bring it to mind any better?" He waited for an answer.

Garrett lowered her head. That night seemed to have taken place a million years ago. She'd learned a lot from that particular night, and by the look of things, she was going to learn even more.

"Yes, I remember it now."

"Good. Then you won't have any problem when you're called to the stand at the Fayette County Courthouse, on March sixth. It seems they've subpoenaed the whole lot of you who gathered evidence for the rape kit. Keep me posted on what happens so we know whether or not you'll be available for flights."

"Yes, sir."

"You too, Nurse Bossard."

"I will, sir."

"Is that all?" Garrett asked.

"Oh, I almost forgot. I've received a special request for a little PR show up at Seven Springs Ski Resort tomorrow. I thought it was rather funny, coming on the exact same day as the ER's ski trip, but who am I to question coincidence?" Ol' Cutter looked from one woman to the other.

Garrett blushed slightly at his insistent stare.

"If I were you two, I'd pack a small bag and take it with you. You never know what storms might sweep through this time of year and ground you for the night. I mean, just to be on the safe side."

"Yes, sir," Danni said. "We'll do that."

"Thanks, sir." Garrett's plan had worked even better than she had hoped.

"Now, go on." He shooed them. "You've got things to do and bags to pack. Don't come back with any broken bones, either of you."

*   *   *

Danni had mixed emotions about whether to be practical when it came to packing. On the one hand, she knew for a fact that sitting in snow was darn cold, but on the other hand, she figured she'd end up sharing a room with Garrett. All kinds of possibilities came rushing through her mind, some of them making her blush just thinking about them.

Hmm. They could be grounded for the night in a ski lodge with a snowstorm raging around them. Her eyes grew wider. Or maybe in a cabin with a fireplace.

Danni's hand brushed across the delicate lace on a pair of thong underwear. "They won't take up that much room." Her smile grew wider. "Besides, didn't McMurray say a small bag?" She giggled like a schoolgirl as she searched for a matching bra.

"Danni?" Garrett called out from the living room.

"Yes?" She could feel her face turning into a blazing showcase of her secret emotions.

"It's going to be cold in those mountains. Don't forget to take something to keep you warm at night."

"Oh, right," Danni said, as images of Garrett wrapping her arms tightly around her proceeded to dance through her mind.

In a matter of seconds, the fire that burned in the pit of her stomach had been turned up another ten degrees. Beads of perspiration formed on Danni's forehead. Silently, she fell back upon her bed and her mind screamed at the top of its imaginary lungs.

Arrggghhh!

* * *

Cowboy smiled when he heard the aircraft's rear door open, and glanced down at his watch. "Right on time," he said. It was exactly 0900.

"Morning, ladies. I trust you had a good night's sleep."

Danni felt the beginnings of a blush creeping up from her chest into the base of her neck, and she struggled to keep it at bay.

"Thanks for the tip about spending the night." Garrett reached out and cupped Cowboy's shoulder.

"Huh? I didn't..." His brow furrowed. "We're staying overnight?"

"Apparently. Didn't you suggest it?"

"Sorry, it wasn't me. I did suggest that we move up the departure time before the storm front was anywhere close."

"Hmm." Garrett's voice rumbled deep within her chest. "I guess Ol' Cutter's giving us a reward."

"It doesn't matter where we are once the storm hits. We'll be grounded. I guess he figured, why have you stuck at home when all of your friends are going to be up there?"

"I'd feel better if he'd warned you, too."

"Don't worry about it. Women will go wild for a uniform." He tugged at his flight suit. "Besides, I'm an old 'Nam vet. We always have an extra pair of socks with us." He patted her arm. "Now get in and buckle up so we can take off, will you?"

* * *

Danni heard the muffled voices, but she had things on her mind. Things that were distracting enough.

Okay, she was a professional. She should try to act like one. There was a whole day to get through before she had to worry about any sleeping arrangements.

"Something wrong?" Garrett climbed into the helicopter.

"No, I was just waiting for you." Danni flashed the thumbs-up sign. "All accounted for and ready for liftoff, Cowboy."

"Doc?"

"Ready when you are."

Cowboy put his hands back on the controls. A moment later, they were up in the air.

"Gar, do you know how to ski?"

"Ski? I'm not an Olympic-caliber skier, but yeah, I can ski, or used to be able to. I haven't been on them in years. Why do you ask?"

"I was hoping… I'm not very good."

"You want a few lessons?"

"Even if you could teach me how to stay on my feet, it would help."

Garrett's grin widened. "Sure, no problem. It'll help me get back in the groove of things, anyway."

Danni struggled with her emotions. She took a deep breath, held it for a few seconds, and let it out. "Thanks, Gar."

* * *

"So, are you ready for this?" Garrett nodded at the ski equipment in her arms.

"No. God, I can't believe I'm this nervous," Danni said.

"Come on, there's nothing to be afraid of. I'm not such a tough instructor." Garrett shifted the equipment in her arms, then proceeded to cross her heart with her finger. "Honest, I swear. I don't bite, not even a little."

"And I was hoping for some nips here and there."

"What's that you said?" There was the gentle sound of laughter in Garrett's voice.

"Tips," Danni blurted out. "I was hoping you could give me some tips about skiing." Internally, she chastised herself for lack of forethought. She knew better than to whisper around Garrett.

* * *

Gracefully, Garrett shifted her feet and her body turned slightly to the right as she skied nearer to where she saw Karen and Rosie waiting. Turning sharply, she came to a stop near Karen, snow spraying in her wake.

"Hi!" Garrett flashed a smile and dug her poles into the packed snow. She turned to follow the progress her protégé was making.

As Danni came closer, Garrett gave encouragement under her breath until she knew that Danni was within earshot.

"Okay, now shift! Lean back with your weight." Garrett held her breath as she watched Danni slide to a stop right in front of her. "See? I knew you could do it."

The beaming smile on Danni's face was priceless. "I did it! I stopped. Karen, Rosie, did you see? I'm still standing. I didn't fall down."

"Yes, it seems like you have a better teacher this year." Karen looked at Garrett. "Great job, Doc."

"I don't know. She's no Picabo Street, by any means." Garrett pulled down her wraparound sunglasses. "But I guess she'll pass."

"Danni, where'd you learn to ski?" Rosie asked. "Is that mandatory for the Trauma Flight Team? I guess you've got to be able to use all sorts of skills to get to where you want to be." Without waiting for an answer, Rosie walked toward the line of skiers waiting at the lift.

Karen looked at Danni. "She's just jealous. What do you say we get out of the cold for a while before we have to do our presentation for the ski patrol?"

Garrett juggled her skis into one hand, then grabbed her poles in the other.

"Yeah." Danni rubbed her arms with her gloved hands. "Maybe some hot chocolate would help defrost my frozen bones."

"Hey, Danni," Rosie called out from the line. "You might want to keep an eye out for some of the others who are coming up. I think you might enjoy seeing one of them in particular."

"Karen?" Danni drew the word out.

"Beats me. I don't know what she's talking about. Honest."

* * *

"Brrr." Danni's teeth chattered as she quickly turned her back to the wind. She grabbed for the door of the helicopter and climbed inside. "Jeez, it's cold." She tried to warm her body by rubbing it. "Hey, Cowboy, are we going to be able to go home, or what?"

Cowboy stroked his chin as he thought for a moment. "I don't really think it would be a good idea. The wind's a little more than I'd like to be flying in. If we ran into some turbulence, we'd be tossed around like a dandelion seed."

"Guess we're spending the night, then." Danni suppressed her smile.

"Looks that way."

A chill swept through the helicopter as Garrett climbed in.

"Whew! It's a little cold out there." Garrett settled into her customary seat and looked around the cockpit. The somber look on Cowboy's face was the direct opposite of Danni's hopeful exuberance. "Stuck for the night, aren't we?"

Danni and Cowboy nodded. Within seconds, the giggling started. Danni reached for her bag. Garrett grabbed her duffel and looked over to the pilot.

"I told you I always have extra socks. What do you think I carry in my flight case?" He pointed to the large bag he carried his maps and navigational tools in. "I don't need much room for a map of the tri-state area. Got to keep them from bouncing around somehow. You ever try reading off of a dog-eared page?"

Garrett shook her head. "Only you, Cowboy. Only you."

"I, for one," Danni said, "vote we get out of these flight suits and relax a little. What do you say?" She looked at her team members. "I wonder if any of the people from work are staying over? I know some of them did last year."

"Speaking of staying over, I think we'd better see about getting some rooms." Garrett patted her pocket and pulled out her ever-present credit card. "Never leave home without one. I'll take care of the rooms." Garrett threw open the door.

"Wait for me." Danni scrambled out the door right behind her. "I'll take a nice, warm ski lodge over a drafty airship any day."

Chapter 13

"What were you able to get? Are we on the same floor?" Danni jumped from question to question with the fervor of a child on Christmas morning. "Did you get us a cabin instead?"

Garrett held the set of keys in her hand and thought for a moment. "A room, yes to the second question, and sorry, none available." Garrett watched the twinkle fade from Danni's eyes as she associated the words to her earlier questions.

"You got us a suite?"

"No, all they had left was a single room. I figured three of us sharing was better than sleeping in the halls or in one of the lounges around a fireplace."

"That wouldn't be so bad." Danni shrugged. "In fact, it sounds romantic."

"It sounds a little crowded to me," Cowboy said as he joined them. "Have you seen all the people here?"

"At least we won't be sleeping in the helicopter. Let's get rid of our bags and get changed, okay?"

"You ladies go on. I'm going to get me a cup of java and warm up a bit over there by the fire."

"You'd better take this." Garrett handed him one of the room keys.

"Thanks, Doc." Cowboy gave her a little nod. "I'll see you both a little later."

* * *

"Mind if I take the bathroom first?" Garrett threw her duffel bag down on the desk along the wall.

"No, go ahead. I'll get my things ready."

Garrett moved into the bathroom and closed the door.

Their room was small, but at least they had one. She wasn't very enthusiastic as she stood looking into the mirror. She'd had to share rooms before. In her adult life, space was all she'd ever shared with anyone.

Garrett scrubbed her hand over her face, trying to rub away the guilt of never being able to let another human get close to her. It had been so simple before. Why wasn't it now? What had changed to make her feel guilty about it? She lingered, trying to feel more at ease with her reflection. With a shake of her head, she finally gave up and exited the bathroom.

She grasped her duffel and quickly untied the flap. With her toiletry bag in hand, she turned and stopped abruptly. Slack-jawed, she stood mesmerized, watching as denim slid up shapely legs, to hug barely covered buttocks. Who would have known that such a simple thing as seeing Danni slip into a pair of tight-fitting jeans could be so… interesting?

Danni hadn't heard the door open, nor had she seen Garrett emerge, until she was tugging her jeans over her hips.

She looked over her shoulder and caught a glimpse of a rather dumbfounded Garrett. Garrett's gaze met her own, and Danni realized she was half undressed in front of the woman who owned a piece of her very soul. Her cheeks flushed crimson and she turned away for modesty's sake. Unfortunately, that ended up in a full frontal show instead.

"Criminy!" Danni hurriedly tugged the denim into place at her waist, fumbled with the button, then grabbed her sweater and held it to her chest. She looked up and saw the bathroom door closing.

Damn it! What was Garrett thinking of her now? Danni crumpled down on the edge of the bed. She pulled on the sweater, then sat with her elbows resting on her knees, her head in her hands. Here she was, slutty nurse at your service. Damn it! She lashed out at the bed with her fist. This wasn't how she had imagined the night would go.

Needing more space than the room allowed her, Danni pushed off the bed and headed for the door.

"I didn't mean to scare you," she whispered as she left the room.

* * *

Garrett's heart was racing at the wave of emotions that barraged her soul. Slowly, she looked at her reflection in the mirror. The clothing was the same, but for some reason, the woman inside of them seemed different. Her mind searched for a word to describe her feelings. Scared was the only one that came to mind. The color drained from her face.

The cool, levelheaded surgeon was nowhere to be found. Jumbled thoughts ran through Garrett's mind as she faced her image in the mirror and tried to find something to bring her back to the world she knew. The world of self-control.

"You're an accomplished surgeon, not some medical student. You've seen hundreds—no, thousands—of human bodies, in all states of undress." Garrett peered deep into the windows of her soul. "What makes this one any different from the rest?" She waited breathlessly, and then it came to her.

"Danni," Garrett murmured. "That's what makes it different. It was Danni."

* * *

Garrett surveyed the stranded skiers crowded into the lounge. The corners of her mouth curled into a slow smile when laughter and taunting jeers erupted from a corner of the room and she saw Rosie preparing to chug a glass of beer. In the meager lighting of the Tiffany-style shades, she made her way over to the boisterous group.

She heard someone mention Danni's name, and looked toward the area where the voice came from. Danni was sitting there.

"Gar, over here." Danni looked away once she was sure Garrett had heard her.

Garrett focused on the man nestled up to Danni's side.

"You remember David, don't you?"

"Dr. Trivoli." David greeted her from across the table. "It's nice to see you again."

"Again?"

"I handed off the trauma beeper to you on your first day here," David said. "Well, at the hospital."

"Yes, I remember you now." Garrett took note of his close proximity to Danni, then casually looked away.

"I don't know about anyone else," Rosie said, "but I say it's time to dance." She jumped up and headed for the small open area. "Who's coming with me? Karen, Danni, come on." When no one complied, Rosie glared at David. "Pull that woman up and bring her out here, will you?"

"I-I-I…" David stuttered. He turned to Danni and offered his hand, hope written all over his face. "Care to dance?"

After a quick glance in Garrett's direction, Danni acquiesced. "Sure, why not?"

Garrett watched as they made their way onto the dance floor. The closer the two got, the more ill at ease Garrett became.

"Thanks for saving a seat for me, Dr. Trivoli."

Distracted, Garrett hadn't noticed Ian McCormick take the seat next to her. He had a leering smile on his face and a tall glass of beer in his hand.

"Could it mean you've decided to thank me for the little weekend I've arranged for your team? I thought maybe you gir— ladies were working a little too hard lately and needed… shall we say… a little fun?" His eyebrows wiggled, and the lines in his forehead followed suit, rippling nearly up to the top of his balding head.

His words caught Garrett off guard, and she turned her attention back to the dance floor to hide the sardonic smile on her lips. So, it was Ian. Two could play at this little game.

Garrett moved her chair a tad closer to Ian. "So, how easy was it to get McMurray to agree to this? You didn't tell him what your agenda was, did you?"

Ian chuckled slyly. "That old man has no idea what's really going on. He doesn't know what we younger people are all about."

Garrett digested the information and casually looked out at the dance floor. She saw Danni's derriere in the distance, and the memory of pale skin and cream-colored lace filled her mind. "You know what the younger bunch is looking for, huh? Tell me, what is it that we need?" A fleeting glance in Ian's direction told Garrett more than she wanted to know.

"We're more cosmopolitan than most. Don't you agree?" Ian was trying too hard to act suave. "Why don't you let me get you a drink? A nice lager? Or would you like something with a little more kick?" He leaned in toward her ear. "You know, you *are* down for the night. Why not let go and enjoy? You do know how to have fun, don't you, Dr. Trivoli?"

"Humor me. I can be relaxed drinking coffee. You wouldn't want me to not remember what fun I've had later, now would you?"

Ian's face lit up. "No. Not at all. Coffee it is, then. Anything special in it?" His eyes were aglow with undoubtedly licentious thoughts.

"Sure, why not?" Garrett's mind turned back to Danni. "I'll have a little cream with that," she purred.

* * *

"What's with those two?" Rosie motioned to where Garrett and Ian were seated together.

"Huh?" Danni and David had stopped dancing and stood alongside the dance floor talking with Rosie.

"Don't look now," Rosie said, "but I think they call it love."

Danni spun around to see Ian leaning in toward Garrett's ear, and Garrett reciprocating. "Maybe she's just being nice in front of everyone."

"I don't know." Rosie shook her head smugly. "They always say the ones that protest too much end up as bedfellows. You think maybe her and McCormick will do the tango under the sheets tonight?"

"No way," Danni said.

"Don't be so sure," Rosie said. "Rumor has it that's why you got grounded up here today. Ian arranged for his girls to have some fun time. He's the one who suggested I invite David. I guess he figured if you were busy, that left Garrett for him to entertain."

"Why, that—" Danni's forward motion was halted by David's tug at her hand.

"May I have another dance? Come on, Garrett's old enough to take care of herself. She can say 'No' as well as anyone." David whispered into her ear. "I've missed being with you. Can't we forget about everyone else and enjoy our time together?"

Torn, Danni sighed. "All right. Let's dance."

David wrapped his arms around Danni's waist and let the music move them. "So, how are things in the ER without me?"

"All right, I guess. I'm not there as much anymore." Danni's eyes strayed in Garrett's direction. "Ever since they teamed Garrett and me together, we've been pretty much out of that area."

"I guess it's different than what you're used to. What we had together." He looked into her eyes. "You have to admit we had some good times together, knee deep in blood."

Danni's expression softened. "We did."

"God, I miss all those times we had over the years. I'd never have made it without you."

Danni didn't comment. She merely followed along, her thoughts nowhere near the dance or the man holding her in his arms.

She had never dreamed that Gar would be the one for her. But then again, maybe she had never really dreamed at all. She had just let herself be guided down the path of her mother's dreams. Until now.

"Hey," David said, "I have an idea. Why don't you stay with me tonight? We could just talk about old times. What do you say? You don't have to decide now. Think about it and let me know. I'm not going anywhere tonight, same as you."

With each turn of their dance, Danni renewed her view of Garrett and Ian at the table. First they were sipping their drinks, next talking, then Ian dangled something in front of Garrett. After the next spin Danni watched as Garrett snatched the object from Ian and held onto it playfully. Was that a key? Danni's eyes grew bigger as the shock settled in. What the hell was Garrett doing?

* * *

"I guess you didn't make it to the room yet." Garrett sat down next to Cowboy.

A slow, toothy grin spread across his face. "Nah, I figured I'd give you two enough time to do whatever it is women do when they change clothes." He looked at her and winked. "So what are the sleeping arrangements, Doc, shifts or floor?"

"I can't have my pilot sleeping on the floor." Garrett flashed him a smile. "It seems that Dr. McCormick arranged this overnight for us." Garrett produced a key for Cowboy to see. "His only implication was that whoever shared his room was someone of higher capabilities. I figured since you were flying all the time, he meant you." She tossed the key in his direction.

Cowboy laughed whole-heartedly. "You expect me to sleep with that idiot so that you don't have to?"

"Sort of. Ian thinks this little girl can't wait to be with him." Garrett made a face at the bitter taste the idea left in her mouth.

"Now, that's a look of lust if ever I saw one." Cowboy paused. "Not!"

"Thanks. You had me worried for a second there."

"Me? Never."

"Anyway, I told him the door would be open for him in about an hour. If I were you, I'd get there first, though, and take the bed. That'll leave him the loveseat or the floor." Garrett flashed another devilish smile.

"Gotcha, Doc." Cowboy got up, digging his room key out of his pocket. "Here, I won't be needing this, then. You and Danni get some rest. I'll see you in the morning."

"G'night." Garrett watched as he started to walk away. "Hey, Cowboy, see if you can snore *really* loud. I'm sure he'll appreciate it come morning, especially with the hangover he's going to have."

"Roger that, Doc." He gave her a thumbs up before resuming his meander through the lobby.

"Okay, McCormick, let's see how you feel about sharing your bed with someone now." Garrett fought off the Cheshire Cat grin that was trying to surface. "I sure hope he doesn't burst in calling Cowboy his little girl."

* * *

"Penny for your thoughts?"

Danni looked up from the barroom table with a half-filled glass in her hand. "Gar, what are you doing here? I thought you left a while ago."

"Call me crazy, but I couldn't sleep until I tucked in all of my crew. Cowboy's taken care of. Are you coming to bed?"

Danni's heart skipped a beat. "Why don't you go ahead? I'll stay up and talk to David."

"David, huh?" Garrett studied Danni.

"I know how you like your space. One less in the room will help."

"What are you saying, Danni?"

"David offered to let me share his room tonight. I just figured that you and Ian…"

"Whoa, wait a minute. The only one I'm sharing a room with tonight is you. Cowboy's sharing a suite with Ian."

"But I thought you were…"

"Yeah, well, so did he. Let me tell you, you're both mistaken." Garrett smiled reassuringly. "Now, what do you say we go sack out? You never know when we might be called on, with that storm out there."

Danni pushed her drink away and rose from the chair. "I hope you got a sled and a team of dogs to go with it, 'cause there ain't nothing else getting through out there tonight."

"Aw, damn. I left them in my other duffel bag."

Danni's pensiveness puzzled Garrett. "You want to let David know where you're going?"

124

"I guess I should."

"What are you going to tell him?"

Danni thought for a moment. "I'll tell him the truth. You go home with the one who brought you."

* * *

Ian tiptoed past the flight suit with its reflective tape aglow in the dimly lit room. Seeing the long form stretched out in the bed, his mind raced in anticipation.

"Shh! Good. She's resting up for the long night ahead," Ian whispered as he eased down onto the bed, his deliberate motions a testament to his alcohol-induced unsteadiness. He started to take off his shoes, only to stop abruptly at the sound of loud snoring that came from the other side of the bed.

"Jeez, we gotta get that septum taken care of." He lifted his foot out of his loafer and smiled. "I wonder if she's as vocal in the heat of passion? Guess I'm just going to have to find out," he murmured as he disrobed.

The thought of sex with Garrett brought a fine sheen of perspiration to his brow. Ian took his shirt off and wiped his forehead. The room spun a little.

"Whew! I think the alcohol is getting to me. Maybe I should catch a little nap before we do anything." He slipped under the covers and fell fast asleep.

* * *

The elevator door opened, allowing Danni to disembark first. "I told you I could sleep on the loveseat."

"Nope, you're small, but not that small. You'll never be able to stretch out and relax."

"I'll sleep on the floor. You can have the bed."

Garrett slid the key into the lock and turned it. "There's more than enough room in a double bed for the two of us. End of discussion." Garrett opened the door and stepped inside.

"Okay, but you pick which side you want." Danni went to her overnight bag and started to rummage through it.

After Garrett closed the door and locked it, she crossed the room to her duffel bag on the desk. "Why don't you take the bathroom first?"

"Okay." Danni gathered up her things and headed into the small room. "Don't worry, it won't take me long." She turned on the light and pulled the door closed.

With the speed and precision of her Navy training, Garrett reached into her duffel bag, pulled out her clothing for the night, and disrobed. "Not my usual, but it'll have to do." She slid a pair of silk boxers up, grabbed the tank top, and pulled it on.

Danni emerged from the bathroom with her jeans and sweater tucked neatly under her arm. As she turned the corner into the larger part of the room, she caught a glimpse of long legs slipping under the covers. Trying to steady her mind, she clutched at her clothing. It took her a while, but finally she was able to get the words out. "I'm done in the bathroom, if you need it."

"No, thanks." Garrett snuggled down under the covers, then looked back at Danni. "You'd better get some rest. Who knows what could happen during the night?"

"Yeah, who knows?" Danni swallowed hard.

Garrett reached from under the covers and turned off the light. "G'night."

"Night, Gar," Danni said, before slipping under the covers. Turning onto her back, she stared into the blackness, realizing just how little sleep she was going to get.

*   *   *

The first rays of light drifted in through the drawn window drapes as Cowboy rolled up on one elbow and looked at the lump of human flesh on the far side of his bed. The skivvies-clad pilot crawled out of bed, put on his boots, and headed into the bathroom with his shaving kit in hand.

The brilliant glow of the lights in the tiny room made him close his eyes for a moment. Slowly he opened them, letting them adjust to the light.

"I have to hand it to her. McCormick is never going to realize he slept with me in place of Garrett." He lathered up his face and took out his razor.

"Hmm... that gives me a little idea of my own." He looked into the mirror and made the first stroke down the side of his cheek.

*   *   *

Not long after the door closed, Ian's sleepy form rolled over to face the now-empty half of the bed. Feeling for the warmth of a long, sensuous body, his hand came up empty. One bloodshot eye opened. He saw the thrown-back covers and rumpled sheets where a warm body had been only moments before.

Then the sound of water running in the shower stimulated his mind. He imagined himself a drop of water rolling over the soft skin and ample curves of Garrett Trivoli. His eyes darted over to the chair he remembered seeing the flight suit on. It was still there. Ian sighed. Life was good. He rolled onto his back and drifted off into his own little world of perverse dreams.

* * *

Cowboy emerged from the bathroom to the sound of loud, rasping snores. He dressed quickly and grabbed his flight bag from under the desk. Then he sat at the desk and picked up a sheet of hotel stationery. Taking a moment to collect his thoughts, he began to scrawl on the paper. Once finished, he folded it in half and laid it on the desk.

"That should do it." He looked over his shoulder to the lump in the bed. "Sweet dreams, big boy." He scribbled a single word on the front of the note then laid the room key next to the note for Ian to find. Cowboy picked up his bag and exited, pulling the door shut as he left.

"Mission accomplished," he said as he marched off down the hall.

* * *

Awakening from the most restful sleep she'd had in ages, Garrett opened her eyes to a blur of blonde. One by one her senses came to life as a familiar floral scent filled her nose. Soft skin lay directly under her fingers and she found that she was encircling another body with her arms. They fit together perfectly, like two pieces of a puzzle.

Lulled by soothing sensations, Garrett lay basking in the warmth of the contact. Seconds later, it was shattered by the ringing of the phone. Startled, she let go of Danni and they separated.

Looking away, Danni rolled to the edge of the mattress, while Garrett grabbed for the phone.

"Hello."

The sound of Garrett's husky voice sent waves of excitement through Danni's body. Before she knew it, her heart was racing. She sat up on the edge of the bed and stole a glance over her shoulder. She couldn't believe that she and Garrett... Danni brought her eyes forward again. They had been lying together, wrapped in an embrace.

Garrett hung up the phone, then rubbed her eyes. "That was Cowboy. The weather's cleared, and we're able to leave."

"Oh. Okay." Danni tried to sound unfazed by the suggestion. She stood up and reached for her flight suit. "I won't be long."

Garrett pondered Danni's aloofness as she watched her enter the bathroom. She got out of bed and started to pace.

"Damn, I don't want to lose this friendship." She knew what she had to do.

As soon as Danni vacated the bathroom, Garrett entered it with her toiletries kit in hand.

Hearing the click of the lock made Danni feel closed off and gasping for air. She could have sworn her heart was ripping in two. Tears welled up and threatened to spill over onto her cheeks.

If only Garrett had let her sleep on the loveseat or the floor. It would have been uncomfortable, but she wouldn't have hurt like this. She wiped at her tears and sniffed.

Danni turned to see Garrett standing in the doorway, watching her. The moment their eyes met, Garrett looked away. She reached for her duffel and started to pack. She put her toiletries kit in the bag and pulled the strings taut.

"I'm sorry for being all over you earlier," Garrett said. "I must have been dreaming. I didn't mean anything by it."

Didn't mean anything by it. It felt like a stake going through her heart each time the words echoed in Danni's head. With her back to Garrett, she closed her eyes and fought to control her tears.

"Don't worry about it. It's forgotten," she lied. Feeling no better for it, she picked up her bag and turned. Their eyes met for a second, and the hurt she felt was more than she had ever imagined. "I'll meet you at the helicopter." She walked out the door, not waiting for a reply.

Stunned, Garrett picked up her bag and followed. When she reached the door, Garrett turned back to view the bed they had shared. What had started out as a warm and inviting awakening now left her feeling cold and alone.

"Fuck!" she said, then closed the door.

* * *

More hung over than he cared to admit, Ian spied the note on the desk. Picking it up, he studied the handwriting.

"You'd think that as well-educated as we are, doctors would be able to write more legibly."

The only word on the page was a strange one at that.

"McDoc?" He thought about it for a minute before the corners of his mouth edged upward into a smile. "God, I love pet names." He opened the sheet and began to read aloud.

"Thanks for letting me rest before taking off to new heights."

"Guess I was good, as usual," he crooned, thrusting his pelvis a time or two as a euphoric expression settled on his face.

Ian was still gloating when the whir of spinning blades drew his attention to the window. He stood with the note still in his hand, watching the helicopter lift off.

"Next time, Garrett, I'm going to remember it all."

* * *

Danni welcomed the background noise of the rotors. She had a lot to think about, and words would only get in the way. Even though she'd spent the previous evening in the company of David and her friends, Garrett was all she could think about.

Chapter 14

"Good morning, Cowboy."

"Morning to you, too, Doc." He smiled at her. "You know of a flight that I don't, or is there something on your mind?"

Stalling for a moment, Garrett wet her lips. "No flight, although I do need to talk to you. But not here. How about letting me buy you a cup of coffee?"

"Me, refuse java? Never."

"I didn't think so."

Garrett opened the door to the ER lounge and looked around the room. Seeing no one there, she sighed in relief. "Come on, the coast is clear."

Quickly crossing to the large urn, she picked up the package of disposable cups and offered Cowboy one. "First pour?"

"Sure, why not?" He accepted the honor and hoisted the pot. Coffee in hand and pot placed back on the warmer, they sipped in silence.

Cowboy was the first to speak. "Good coffee. Thanks."

Garrett didn't answer, her mind obviously elsewhere.

"Doc, is there something going on between you and Danni?"

Garrett's eyes flashed, but she remained silent.

"Stop me if I'm wrong, but you two just aren't acting the same anymore. Like one of you is hurt, or... Hell, I don't know. Call me crazy, but something just doesn't seem right." He looked down at his cup. "I thought you two..." Cowboy stopped short. "It's no business of mine."

"What were you going to say? Don't try to spare my feelings. If you have any ideas, I want to hear them. I'd like to know the reason for the uneasiness myself."

"What I was going to say doesn't have any real bearing on the matter at hand. At least, I don't think so."

"Damn!" Garrett said. "I've got to find out why things aren't right. For the last three weeks, it's like McCormick and Danni somehow changed minds where I'm concerned. Ever since that night at Seven Springs." She paused. "I expected a wild tantrum from McCormick when he found you in the room instead of me. Funny how nothing ever came of that." She gave Cowboy a sidelong glance. "Or did it?"

"Whoa. Hold those horses right there. I stayed on *my* side of that huge bed, and he did the same... only on his side. Jeez, Doc. Give me some credit for at least picking someone better looking than that bald peckerhead. He's not my type. Not enough curves in the right places, if you know what I mean."

"Peckerhead, huh?" Garrett chuckled. "So what did transpire in that room?"

"I hung my flight suit over the back of a chair and crawled into bed. The last thing I remember was pulling those covers up over my head." Cowboy headed toward the urn for a refill. "You know, I don't think I even saw him. Heard him though, with all the snoring. Next thing I knew, it was morning. When I got up, I remember looking at the bed. McCormick was sound asleep, with his clothes at the foot of the bed."

Garrett chewed on her cup. "Interesting. Can you think of anything else that happened?"

"Nope. When I woke up, I did my morning ritual in the bathroom, put my flight suit on, then got my case and left."

"Did you say anything at all? Do anything he could have misconstrued?"

"No. Nothing." Cowboy's eyes widened. "Oh, shit! I left him a note with the room key. I bet he thought it was from you."

"Why do you say that?"

Cowboy cringed. "I didn't sign it."

"What did it say?" Garrett braced for the worst.

"Something about being thankful for the rest." His eyes flicked back and forth. "I wrote: 'Thanks for letting me rest before going off to new heights.'"

Garrett laughed. The mystery of Ian's attitude change was solved. "That's why he's been treating me so nicely. He thinks we had one hell of a good time before I—I mean you—slipped out in the morning."

"That dirty peckerhead." A lazy smile came to Cowboy's face.

"At least one part of the mystery is solved."

"What are you going to do, tell him the truth?"

"All in due time, Cowboy. But I'll tell you this, it will be when I need the advantage." Garrett raised her cup. "Boy, is he ever going to be surprised."

"And Danni?"

"What about Danni?" Garrett sounded distracted.

Cowboy eyed her curiously. "How are you going to get Danni acting like Danni again?"

Garrett stared into space. "I'm not sure, but it's something I'm going to have to think about."

* * *

Alone in her office, Garrett tried to remember what had taken place that could be making such a difference in Danni. They hadn't quarreled or exchanged words. Their only discussion had been about where Danni would sleep. Why would she be upset about sleeping in the bed? Images of waking up with her arms around Danni and spooning her lingered in Garrett's mind.

"We've been tangled up worse than that before. Why would this time stand out? We did nothing but sleep."

So they had slept together. Garrett pondered the phrase and all its implications. Love was something that had always seemed to be out of her reach, until Danni came knocking on her door. Danni's warm and welcoming ways had opened Garrett's mind to the world around her. She had given her a sheltering home in the midst of her inner storm, and had helped lay her demons to rest. Well, at least some of her demons. Garrett released a long breath, realizing that there had been more between them than she cared to admit.

Garrett daydreamed of the woman who had been nestled in her arms. But instead of seeing herself, she saw blonde hair teasing someone else's nose. Images of Danni in David's arms flashed before her eyes.

That was it! Garrett had found the last piece of her puzzle. Danni wanted to be with David. That was an easy fix. First stop would be Rosie.

* * *

"Can I buy you a cup of coffee?" Coming up from behind, Garrett slowed her pace to match Rosie's stride.

"Doc, are you feeling okay?" Rosie eyed her cautiously, then looked around. "Where's she at?"

"Where's who?"

"Danni. You two are usually inseparable. Okay, what's the joke? Where's she hiding?"

Garrett swallowed the lump in her throat, and reaching out for Rosie's arm, directed her off to the side of the hallway. "I need your help. I want you to get in touch with David for me."

"You're interested in David?"

"No! I want to surprise Danni. I thought that seeing David again might help lift her out of the mood she's been in."

"She has been out of sorts lately," Rosie said.

"I thought if David could come up next weekend, it might help her out of it."

"You want to play yenta, huh?"

"If that's what it takes to get Danni back to her old self, then yes."

"They do make a cute couple."

That wasn't exactly what Garrett was thinking, but she mustered a weak smile, if only for show. "Yeah, maybe they do."

Rosie's face lit up. "I'll get David here."

*　*　*

Buried deep in the supply room, Danni focused on the mundane act of stocking supplies. Here, nothing would remind her of Garrett Trivoli, or of the feelings of anxiety she was experiencing over her own awakening sexuality. That was, until she was beckoned out of the closet by a familiar voice.

"Hey, Danni?" Rosie stuck her head in through the door. "I've got someone on the phone who wants to speak to you."

"Can't you see I'm busy?" Danni looked up over an armful of IV tubing. "Take a number, and tell them I'll call back."

"I'm thinking you'll kick yourself silly if you don't grab this now. Who knows? It might be the phone call that changes your life." The intrigued look on Danni's face seemed to encourage Rosie. "I'm betting it may even put a smile on that glum face of yours we've been seeing here lately."

"I'm not glum. I've just had some things on my mind." Danni unloaded her armful of supplies, and then brushed her hands off on her scrub top. "Okay, if it means that much to you, I'll take the phone call." She looked over to see a flash of teeth become a broad smile. "Rosie, I swear if this is some kind of trick…"

"You'll kill me." Rosie ducked the playful slap that was headed her way. "It's on line two at the desk, killer."

Danni made her way to the desk and picked up the phone. "Nurse Bossard."

"How's my favorite trauma nurse?"

"David?" Danni's voice became softer. "Is that you?"

"It's me. I'm going to be in Pittsburgh over the weekend, and I was wondering if we could get together and do something on Friday night?"

"Wow. That's short notice, but I know the rest of the bunch would love to see you again."

"I was thinking maybe we could do something together, just you and me. Kind of like on a date."

Danni was shocked. "I'm flattered, but..."

"Come on, Danni, you name it. Anything you want to do. Think about it and let me know. I won't be leaving here until Friday at noon." David paused. "I've been thinking a lot about you since Seven Springs. Just give me a chance, that's all I'm asking."

"Okay, David, let me see what I can come up with and I'll let you know on Friday morning."

"Sounds good to me. I'll be waiting to hear from you. Bye, Danni."

"Bye." She hung up.

Was it really fair to David to let him believe she was interested? But how could she refuse his invitation after it had taken him this long to ask? Danni sighed and said aloud, "It's only a date."

Karen turned the corner of the desk. "Did I hear you say something about a date?"

"David asked me out."

"I thought you had feelings for..." Karen threw a cautious glance around before she leaned in and looked Danni straight in the eye. "You know who."

"I don't think Garrett is that kind of woman." Her eyes conveyed her pain.

"How do you know? Did you ask her?" Karen directed Danni into a chair and sat next to her. "What? Something happened that I don't know about? Talk to your mother."

"Yeah, right!" Danni snorted. "My mother wouldn't understand. She'd be jumping for joy if she knew David was interested in me."

"I meant me," Karen said sternly. "Now give, young lady. When?"

"The night we stayed at Seven Springs."

"What?"

"We shared a room." Danni's words came out sounding rather bland.

"Who? You and Garrett, or you and David?"

"Me and Gar, of course."

"And?"

Danni wished she could hold her blush at bay. "I—we woke up spooned together, and her arm was wrapped around me."

"So? There's nothing wrong with that."

"I know, but later Gar apologized." Danni tried to quell the tears that threatened to start. "She said it didn't mean anything."

Karen brushed a lock of stray hair from Danni's forehead. "Oh, sweetie, is that the reason for your behavior around her lately? You think you don't mean anything to her?"

"Yes." The word was barely audible.

"If you ask me, Garrett was trying to save you some embarrassment. I see how you both act around each other. Trust me, I think it matters a lot to her." Karen hugged her. "You matter to her."

Danni looked up doubtfully.

"I know what they call her in the operating room. Garrett may be the Ice Queen to them, but when have you ever seen her not care about her patients?"

"Never. Garrett would die for her patients."

"You're darn right, and she doesn't even know those people." Karen leaned in and whispered into Danni's ear. "She probably sensed that you were uncomfortable with what happened and decided to take the blame."

Danni felt a glimmer of hope. "Really?"

"Don't write her off until you find out. You owe her that much. You owe it to yourself."

Could Gar have done that? Danni reflected on the possibility, then looked over her shoulder at Karen's retreating form. Karen was right. She did need to have a talk with Garrett.

*　*　*

Using Garrett's pager or her personal cell phone would have been too easy. Danni did not want to discuss this over the phone.

She needed to see Garrett in person and register her reactions firsthand. After all, her future—their future—was riding on it.

It didn't take long to track Garrett down. Danni found her in the Medical Staff Library, with her back to the far wall, bent over a dusty volume from some long-forgotten medical series.

She wavered for a moment. "Always looking for something to fall back on, aren't you?"

Garrett looked up. "Hey."

"Hey, yourself."

The world around them seemed to vanish, until a muted cough behind them brought the two women back to reality.

Garrett glanced in the direction of the noise, then back to Danni. "Are you here to do some reading?"

Danni shook her head. "We need to talk."

"All right, let's go, then." Garrett pushed her chair back and stood. "We can talk better somewhere else. Rumor has it that librarians don't enjoy conversation as much as you do."

Silently, Danni followed Garrett as she crossed the room and headed into the hall.

"What do you want to talk about?"

Danni sidestepped to allow a group of staff nurses by, and waited for the last person to move out of earshot. "Could we go somewhere else besides a hallway?"

"Okay. Cafeteria, then." Garrett turned toward the elevators. A tug on her sleeve stopped her.

"Gar?" Danni's eyes pleaded her case.

"Then where?"

"Somewhere a little more private. I was thinking more along the lines of your office."

Garrett nodded as visions of David and Danni invaded her mind like the figurines on top of a wedding cake. She felt weak-kneed, and her step faltered.

"Are you all right?" Danni reached out to steady her. "You look a little pale."

"I'm fine." Garrett squared her shoulders in an effort to regroup. "My office, then?"

Danni nodded.

"I'm not sure whether anyone else is using it, but we can have a look." Garrett started down the hall. By the time she dug into her pocket and procured the key, they stood at the door. "After you," Garret said, as she opened the door to the office and flicked on the light switch.

Hesitantly, Danni entered. Nothing ventured, nothing gained. "There's something I have to say." She opened her mouth to continue, but strident tones sliced through the air, interrupting her.

"Dr. Trivoli and Nurse Bossard, please call the Command Desk."

A questioning expression settled on each face. Garrett made the call.

"Trivoli here." She listened intently.

"Thank you. Nurse Bossard's with me," she said, then hung up.

"What is it? Where are we headed?"

"McMurray's office."

"Why?"

"He wants to see us."

"When?"

"Now." Garrett walked toward the door. "You coming?"

"Right behind you." She followed Garrett, thoughts of their talk pushed to the far corners of her mind.

* * *

Ol' Cutter hung up the phone and contemplated the proposal presented to him. He loved the idea of getting recognition for the services his staff provided, but this time he was a little more than concerned about how a particular staff member would take it. There were some parts of Dr. Trivoli he couldn't quite put his finger on. McMurray considered the effect the other member of the team had on his fellow, and was glad Danni would be a part of this, too. Perhaps it would help.

"Trivoli has a long career ahead of her. She's going to have to learn to accept the honors that go along with it. She might as well start now." McMurray swiveled his chair to bring the windows behind him into view. Looking out at the city he called home always helped calm his nerves. With a little luck, he might be able to persuade another talented surgeon to call it home, too.

"If only there was something to anchor her here." His mind drifted to his wife. He stared out the window. Lost in his memories, he didn't hear his office door open.

"Dr. McMurray," his secretary said softly.

"Yes, Stella."

"The flight team is here to see you." Stella motioned for Garrett and Danni to enter, then closed the door.

They stood just inside the door, the silence surrounding them adding to the suspense. The women turned their attention to the chair behind the desk. The contemplative look on McMurray's face gave no clue as to why they had been summoned.

He stopped his chair and leaned forward to rest his arms on the desktop. "Dr. Trivoli, Nurse Bossard, I'm glad you could get here so quickly."

"That's part of our job, a quick response to any call."

"Ease up, Trivoli. I haven't called you onto the carpet for anything. Nothing of the kind." He rose slightly and motioned to the chairs in front of his desk. "Have a seat, ladies."

"Thanks," Danni said.

"Thanks, sir." Garrett tipped her head.

"Relax, you two. It's nothing bad. In fact, it's something very good for both of your careers." He settled back into his chair and studied the women before him. Slowly, the corners of his mouth turned upward into a smile.

Garrett eyed her mentor suspiciously.

"I'm sorry, but you have us at a loss." Danni looked first to Garrett, then to the man behind the desk.

"The Board of Directors would like you to honor them with your presence at a dinner they're hosting on Friday evening." He looked at them, hoping for some kind of pleased response. Seeing none, he continued. "I know there's not much time between now and then, but they'd like you there all the same."

"This Friday? I already have a date." Danni caught the quick turn of Garrett's head in her direction.

"Good. Then you'll have an escort." McMurray beamed his approval. "Anyone we know, Nurse Bossard?" Ol' Cutter turned a curious eye to Garrett's shocked response.

Danni blushed, looking embarrassed. "Dr. Beckman. You remember David."

"Yes, a fine man and a promising surgeon." McMurray disregarded the muted snort that came from Garrett and pushed on. "I thought he was somewhere in West Virginia, though, not around here."

"He is. He'll be in town for the weekend."

"Dr. Trivoli?" McMurray tried to get her attention.

"What?" Garrett seemed embarrassed to have taken so long to answer.

"Dr. McMurray wanted to know if you'd be bringing someone. An escort, maybe?" Danni said.

"Escort?" Garrett looked even more confused than before. "Me? I guess I could find one." Her eyes darted around the room.

"See what you can come up with. Oh, and Dr. Trivoli…" McMurray paused, waiting for her full attention. "I wouldn't raid the School of Medicine's cadaver lab. That style of escort didn't go over very well the last time someone tried it."

Danni wrinkled her nose. "Eww."

"No, sir. I wouldn't think of it."

"So," Danni said and cleared her throat. "This gathering, does it call for formal attire?"

"No tuxedos or gowns will be needed. Suits and whatever is appropriate these days for women will be all that's necessary." He looked directly at Garrett. "No designer original scrub clothing either, Trivoli." He pointed a cautionary finger at her. "You hear?"

"Yes, sir."

Danni's giggle was cut short by Garrett's penetrating stare. "Sorry," she said, properly chastised.

"Now get going, you two. You've got a lot to do before I see you on Friday night." McMurray dismissed them with a wave of his hand. He turned to look out the windows, then spun back again.

"Trivoli!"

Garrett stopped short at the sound of her name. "Yes, sir."

"You'd better have something on your arm other than that flight suit when you walk through the door Friday evening."

Garrett's lip curled and her breathing slowed. Damn!

Chapter 15

Danni hung up the phone and muttered to herself as she walked over to her closet. "That's taken care of. David knows to bring a suit for tonight. Now, what do I wear?"

Reaching into the closet, she pulled out a sleek, black knit dress with a scoop neckline and held it up to her body.

"Oh, so very sexy," she purred, observing her reflection in the mirror. "This could turn some eyes my way." Danni thought of one particular set of blue eyes, and her fantasizing started. It wasn't long before she snapped out of it, though. "I wish! Unfortunately, wearing this tonight would send David the wrong signal."

She tossed it aside and pulled out a dark green suit. "With this I could look presentable for dinner and David. Then, if we get called out, Gar would be the only one to see me without the jacket." She slid the jacket off the hanger to reveal a simple form-fitting shell underneath. A turn to the mirror confirmed her choice, the color bringing out the green of her eyes. A smile spread across her face.

"Oh yeah," she whispered triumphantly. "If that doesn't do it, I don't know what will."

* * *

Garrett sipped her coffee in the surgeon's lounge and surveyed the meager selection of escort possibilities as the candidates regrouped before rounds: a gangly medical student and a few obsessive interns. She eyed them disapprovingly, wondering if she'd have to change her date's diapers during the course of the evening. Why, all of a sudden, was she feeling so old? Garrett let out a long breath. Time was running out, and so were her options.

When the room cleared, she got up and went to the bank of phones on the one wall. She pulled out the business directory and started paging through it.

"Escorts." Garrett flipped through the pages before bringing her efforts to an abrupt halt. "What am I doing? I'm not that desperate, am I?" She pushed the book away, crossed the room, and flopped down on the couch. "It would be so simple if David wasn't here." She settled back into the leather couch and closed her eyes.

Not long afterward, Garrett felt someone sitting down on the couch. She opened one eye and cast a wary glance to see who it was. The glare reflecting off the top of the other person's head was unmistakable.

Damn it! Garrett hurriedly closed her eyes and feigned sleep. Silently, she cursed the headache she knew was imminent.

It was too late. At the first stirring of her eyelashes, the other body had shifted its position.

"Yes?" Garrett drew the word out, her eyebrow edging upward at the person who dared to infringe upon her space. "Something I can do for you, Dr. McCormick?" *Gallbladder need ripping out today, or would you rather I resect your bowel and strangle you with it?*

The man laughed nervously under her icy glare. "Let's cut the crap. We're both adults, and judging from our little tryst at Seven Springs, we both know when to keep our mouths shut." He eyed her approvingly.

"You could say that." A smile surfaced on Garrett's face. "I see no need to feed the rumor mill."

"Right." Ian laughed again. "I understand you haven't given the committee the name of your escort yet for the seating charts. I figure the two of us could attend this dinner tonight, and no one would be the wiser. A busy woman like you doesn't have time to meet a lot of people." He hesitated, and then blurted out the rest of his idea. "I rented a limo for tonight. I thought maybe I could give you a ride. We could walk into dinner together, play the mingle-mingle game, then split after the awards. What do you say?"

Garrett weighed the pros and cons. *It would be an escort, but I'd be with Ian.* Her mood soured. *Danni and her date could come with us in the limo. That way I wouldn't have to amputate Ian's hands for what he'd try to do if we were alone. Besides, I could keep an eye on David, too. Just in case.* Garrett smiled. *Hey, don't they always tell girls that there's safety in numbers?*

"Sounds great. What time can I expect the limo?"

Ian seemed startled by Garrett's quick decision. "Ah, six-thirty, if that's okay with you."

"Sure. Why not?"

"Great!" McCormick jumped up and started for the door. Halfway there, he stopped and turned.

"What?" Garrett snapped.

"Nothing." Ian shook his head, then pinched his own arm and grimaced. In the blink of an eye, his expression turned completely opposite. "God, I love it when dreams come true." He spun on his heel and quickly left the room.

Garrett rubbed her temples. "My headache is starting already." She reached for her coffee, hoping it would rid her of the bitter taste in her mouth. This was definitely one team she wanted no part of. Then she glanced at her watch and frowned.

"Now all I have to do is talk Danni into joining us."

* * *

"Danni?"

"Up in the bedroom." Danni continued to get dressed. She saw Garret standing in the doorway, and greeted her with a smile. "Hey."

"Hey. What time is David coming?"

"He said he'd be here around six o'clock."

"That's good. We can all leave together when the limo gets here."

"Limo?" Danni stopped what she was doing. "I don't remember anything about a limo."

Garrett smacked her forehead with the palm of her hand. "Sorry, I must have forgotten to tell you. They're sending a car with a staff member to pick us up. It'll be here soon."

"I guess we could do that. I don't mind, and I'm sure David won't, either."

She bought it. Garrett breathed easier. It was time to get ready. She looked down at her watch as she made her way across the hall to her room. It was 1740. Throwing open her closet door, Garrett studied her sparse collection of civilian clothing. "Hmm, what to wear?"

* * *

When the doorbell rang, Garrett grabbed the jacket to her navy pinstriped pantsuit and pulled it on. She bounded down the stairs, making a few last minute adjustments to her silk blouse. At the bottom of the steps she headed for the door and opened it.

"David."

"Yes." He searched the room for his date. Not finding her, David stated the obvious. "I'm here for Danni."

"Come on in." Garrett stepped back to allow him to enter. "Make yourself comfortable. Danni should be down any minute. Did Danni tell you that we would all be going together tonight?" She watched his face fall. "They're sending a limo for us." *Top that one, will you?*

"No, she didn't."

Garrett gloated.

Creaking floorboards drew their attention to the stairway. Danni descended the stairs with the grace and poise of a debutante. She looked from one slack-jawed watcher to the other.

"I thought I heard the door." Danni smiled. "David, it's so good to see you again." She crossed the room and took his hand in hers. "I take it Garrett has made you comfortable."

"Yes, she has," he lied.

Garrett cleared her throat. "The limo should be here any minute. Danni, do you have your flight gear?" Garrett walked over to her waiting duffel near the door.

"I left it upstairs."

"I'll get it." Garrett took to the stairs.

David looked to Danni. "You're flying tonight?"

"The weather's fine, and we're not grounded. If they need us, we'll go." Danni watched his expression turn sullen. "It's not like we can refuse. We're the Trauma Flight Team."

He nodded in understanding.

Bounding down the stairs with Danni's bag in hand, Garrett turned the corner at the bottom of the steps and looked out the window. "I think our ride is here." Garrett grabbed her duffel and headed out the door.

"Here, allow me." David reached for the door.

"Thanks."

* * *

Ian McCormick sat on the far side of the leather seat, a smile etched across his face as Garrett climbed inside.

"You look lovely this evening, Dr. Trivoli." Tiny beads of perspiration were already appearing on his forehead.

"Thank you, Ian." She settled their bags on the floor and herself in the curbside seat. "I hope you don't mind, but I thought we could all go together." She motioned toward Danni and David as they closed the door to the house and started for the limo.

Ian glanced out the window and eyed the young couple coming their way. "Afraid we wouldn't make it to the dinner, Garrett?"

"Huh?"

"Come on," McCormick said, smiling. "After Seven Springs, I know you find it hard to keep your hands off me." He reached over and patted her knee. "At least this way we'll have a good dinner and be fueled for later tonight." Ian's chuckle turned somewhat lecherous. "If you know what I mean."

Garrett stared incredulously at him. *Only in your dreams.* The sound of soft banter drew her attention. She turned and watched as David helped Danni into the vehicle, looking to see exactly where he was putting his hands.

* * *

The automatic doors opened into the medical staff dining room, bringing the grandiose decorations into view. At the front of the room, maroon curtains with gold tassels lined the wall, while floral centerpieces added splashes of delicate pastels across the white linen.

"I can't believe I had lunch here this afternoon." Dr. McMurray placed a chaste kiss on his wife's cheek. "They've probably spent a fortune making this look like a ballroom."

"We do our best." Mrs. McMurray smiled as she surveyed the room even further. "I see they put the place cards where we requested. The Society will be pleased."

"Yes, I see." He nodded with approval. "Nice idea having all the honorees and their guests seated closer to the podium. That should save us some time." Ol' Cutter cleared his throat. "Remind me to keep my talk brief and not just ramble on about everything, will you?"

"Don't I always?" Mary turned to her husband. "Anything else you need to be reminded of while I'm at it?"

"There was one small thing, but I think my memory will hold it for another minute or so." McMurray turned to the doorway and looked down the hall as though waiting for something.

"John?"

"Yes, dear."

"You don't have some kind of surprise for me tonight, do you?"

"No." He peeked at his watch. "Well, maybe."

"John." Mary's voice sounded fretful.

"Nothing to worry about. I'd like to introduce you to some of my staff. I want to see if you get the same feeling about them that I do." His eyes brightened as the door started to open. "I'd say this could be them now."

"How are you so sure?"

"Punctuality, my dear. I told Dr. Trivoli I'd see her at seven," McMurray said, tapping his watch. He looked up and scrutinized their attire. "Why in blazes are they carrying duffel bags?"

"That's the trauma fellow you were telling me about?" His wife looked confused.

"Garrett Trivoli, dear. I showed you her pictures."

"I remember the photographs. That woman's name was listed as René."

"Typo." He dismissed it with a wave of his hand. "Though her name is androgynous enough, as it is. Damned good thing, too. It's gotten her more experiences than you could imagine. How many women do you know who have been assigned to a sub, or did tours of duty at sea as a flight surgeon?" Ol' Cutter turned back and beamed at the small group, like a father seeing his children. He puffed out his chest. "Let me introduce you to our Trauma Flight Team." He raised his arm and waved them over. "Dr. Trivoli, Nurse Bossard. I'd like you to meet the guiding force in my life."

"Mary, this is Garrett Trivoli, one of my trauma fellows this year."

"Good evening, ma'am." Garrett inclined her head.

"And this is Danni Bossard, one of our dedicated trauma nurses."

"It's so nice to meet you, Mrs. McMurray." Danni said, smiling. "I think I would have known you even without the introduction, from all the photographs we've seen."

"Why thank you. I've heard a lot about the two of you." She turned to address her husband. "You told me you kept those pictures in your desk drawer."

McMurray cleared his throat nervously. "I think you know the rest of the group here, Mary." He inclined his head in acknowledgement. "David."

"Good evening, Dr. and Mrs. McMurray." David slid his arm around Danni's waist. "I hope you don't mind me escorting Danni this evening."

"Not at all." McMurray glanced at Garrett, then the man at her side. "Ian?"

"Yes?" There was a moment of awkward silence. "Mary, good evening. I…" He took a handkerchief from his pocket and wiped his brow. "It's a little warm in here, isn't it?" McCormick grinned nervously.

"A little, perhaps," Mary said.

"We came together in a limo. I wanted to make sure my g—" Ian stopped short. "I mean, our flight team got here without any problems. I figured there was no sense in all of us driving tonight." He saw the ire in Garrett's eyes fade. "Speaking of which," Ian said, shifting from one foot to the other, "let me get them settled at a table." He reached for Garrett's duffel bag and gave it a little tug. "Danni, why don't I take yours, too?"

Seeing her reluctance, David said, "Come on, Danni. He's not going to steal your gear. Let's mingle before we sit down."

"Someone who can run an emergency room can find name cards, dear." Mary spoke softly to Danni as she pointed at the table to the left of them. "I'm sure David would much rather see some of his old colleagues in the few minutes we have before dinner."

"Sure," Danni said, mustering a wan smile. "I'd love to."

"Dr. Trivoli, let me introduce you to some of the Board members." McMurray let go of his wife's arm. "I'll be right back, dear."

Danni released the bag into Ian's hand. "Thanks, Dr. McCormick." She turned to Mary. "It was nice meeting you, Mrs. McMurray. Perhaps we'll see each other again this evening."

Mary nodded. "Perhaps."

* * *

"Garrett."

Garrett held back the look of disgust. "Dr. McCormick, are you summoning me?"

"Me? Summon? I was only going to suggest we head back to our table. I believe dinner's about to be served."

Garrett turned to her colleagues and smiled politely. "If you'll excuse me?" She started for the assigned table.

"Excuse me." Ian left the group and strode to catch up. "Hey, Garrett." He dodged a chair that accidentally slid into his path and kept on going. "Wait up, will you?"

A step away from the table, Garrett stopped short and pivoted to face him. "What do you want?"

Ian sidled up beside her. "Why, nothing but talk, my dear lady." He looked at the couple approaching the table. "Right, David?"

"I'm not sure. What am I agreeing to?" David reached for a chair, offered it to Danni, and everyone sat down.

Ian said, "I thought we might share some insight on being summoned. I'm sure you've been summoned a few times."

"More than enough," David commented dryly.

"I'm assuming you also got a subpoena for the Sunshine Doe rape case, Garrett. If you ask me, I think we spend more time in courtrooms than anywhere else, anymore. In fact, I have it on good authority that almost half of the ER staff on duty that night got subpoenaed, by one side or the other. I'm curious. Which side summoned you?" Ian turned toward Garrett and waited for an answer.

"The prosecution, I believe. The summons mentioned something about being material witnesses."

David rolled his eyes heavenward and shook his head.

"You don't seem too enthused by that." Danni shifted in her seat to study him more carefully. "Care to tell us why?"

"I've had some bad experiences with defense counsels."

"How so?" Danni's interest was piqued.

"They made me sound like I had raped the patient myself. It was a little nerve-wracking."

Hearing David mention rape made Garrett's neck hairs stand on end.

"There shouldn't be any problems in that respect." Ian looked at Garrett. "What interest would you have in a woman but as a patient?"

Garrett gave him a sidelong glance. "I guess we'll just have to wait and see what happens on Tuesday, when I appear in court."

"I'll feel better when it's over," Danni said. "What do you say we—" She stopped in mid-sentence, retrieved her vibrating pager, and looked at the message.

Garrett had received it, too. "Excuse me." Garrett produced her cell phone from a pocket and activated her speed dial. "Trivoli here." Her eyes flashed with interest as she listened. "Yes, we're both at the hospital. We can be at the helipad within five." She reached under the table with her free hand, searching for her duffel bag. "Roger that."

Garrett slipped her phone back into a pocket. "I'm sorry, but our team is needed." She stood up with her duffel bag in her hand. "Let's go, Danni. Cowboy will meet us in five."

Danni came alive. She pulled her bag into her arms, then turned to the man beside her. "I'm sorry, David, but I'm needed elsewhere." She didn't wait for a reply, and followed Garrett's lead out of the room.

Chapter 16

"There's a man pinned by something in the railway yards north of the city," Garrett said. "They say there's not much hope for survival, but they want us to come take a look."

Danni pointed toward flashing red and blue lights in the distance. "Cowboy, I think I see the accident site."

"Yep, that would be the direction. Sound off if you see the landing zone. At least we don't have to worry about power lines in the middle of a railway yard."

Garrett shifted as far as she could without unbuckling her seatbelt. "I'm not seeing any wreckage. Are you?"

"No. Everyone's gathered around those two boxcars."

"That's odd. I thought they said our patient was trapped." Garrett shrugged. "Only one way to find out. Let's land this thing. You ready?"

Danni checked her seatbelt. "Ready."

"Roger that." Cowboy turned his attention to their descent.

* * *

"I take it one of you is the surgeon." An older man with a slightly cocked helmet stood with his arms crossed over his chest.

"I'm Dr. Trivoli, the flight surgeon, and this is Nurse Bossard." Garrett's eyes narrowed as she removed her flight gloves and stowed them in a pocket. "And you are?"

"Schmidt, the scene commander," he said, speaking with an air of authority. "I'm not sure we've done the right thing by calling you here, but I figured it was worth a try."

"Where's our patient?" Danni caught up with Garrett's long strides as she stuffed her gloves into a pocket.

"Over there." He pointed to the two boxcars with a crowd of rescue workers around them and headed toward them.

Danni watched the huddle of rescuers as one of them turned and walked away. The stunned look on his face seemed out of place. He stopped short, bent over, and lost the contents of his stomach.

"Gar?" Danni pointed to the vomiting rescue worker.

"Don't worry about Dennis," Schmidt said. "He tosses his cookies all the time. He's the best rescue man I have, once you let him work on an empty stomach. Although, I will admit this victim is worse than I've ever seen." He looked directly at Garrett. "Have you ever seen anyone with a coupling through his body?"

"No, I can't say I have." Garrett glanced at him as she pulled on a pair of examination gloves.

"Figured as much," he replied. "Neither had I."

"How did it happen?" Danni edged forward.

"Best we know, the yard worker was checking the boxcars when one broke loose and trapped him. The coupling penetrated his body and locked itself into position with the other car before he could get out of the way. Someone heard him screaming and called 911." Schmidt halted until the wall of rescuers shifted in front of him. "This is what we found when we got on scene."

Before them was a surreal scene out of a horror movie: a man living on borrowed time, his body trapped between the massive metal couplings.

He had to be in horrendous pain. His frantic eyes searched from one rescuer to another, and it wasn't long before his piercing gaze fell on the flight team.

Sensing his near-hopelessness, Danni made her way over to the trapped man. She pulled on her protective gloves, then reached out for his hand.

"Is there anything I can do for you? My name is Danni Bossard. I'm a flight nurse. This is Dr. Trivoli."

"Bet you never saw nothing like this before, Doc." His forehead creased with each new wave of pain.

"Not exactly." Garrett bent over and examined the injured tissue around the coupling more closely. "How's the pain?"

"What do you think? It ain't every day you have two railroad cars coupled through your belly." His weak attempt at a smile quickly turned to a grimace.

Garrett surveyed the man's body as she took a reflex hammer from her pocket. "Let me know if this hurts." She lifted his right leg and tapped it sharply just below the knee. There was no reaction. Garrett repeated the procedure on his left leg, with the same result.

"Not good, huh?"

"I was hoping for better." Her eyes were filled with concern. "I'm sorry." Garrett addressed Danni. "Five milligrams of morphine as needed for pain."

"Thanks." He watched Garrett walk away, then turned his attention to Danni.

"What's your name?" she asked him gently.

"Paul. What's a nice girl like you doing here?"

Danni smiled as she readied the drug for injection. "Just out for a ride, Paul. Thought I'd stop in. You don't mind, do you?"

"Hell, no. You sound like my wife." He gasped as a wave of pain took his breath away. When it passed, Paul continued on a more serious note. "I know it doesn't look good for me. I just want to see her again. My wife, that is. Sounds stupid, huh?"

"Not at all." Danni struggled to keep her professional demeanor in place. "Are you allergic to anything?"

"Nothing but boxcars," he quipped weakly as Danni prepped his intravenous line for puncture.

"This is going to make you feel a little better, Paul. It will take the edge off of the pain."

"They said my wife was on the way. I don't want to be out when she gets here." Paul looked nervously at the syringe. "If I'm…" He paused, clearly trying to muster the courage to say what he was thinking. "If I'm gone before she gets here, will you tell her I love her?"

Danni's heart felt like it would break. "Don't worry, Paul, she'll be here soon. You'll be able to tell her yourself." She administered the drug, then patted his hand.

* * *

With a sigh, Garrett looked away from the yardmaster. She found herself face-to-face with the scene commander. "If there's no other way to release it, can't you cut that coupling away from the boxcars?"

"Listen, Doc, there's nothing we can do. That's case-hardened steel, and we can't cut through it with our Jaws of Life." He shook his head. "Even if we could, there's no way to transport that to any hospital short of being on a flatbed."

"Any other ideas?" Garrett turned to both men, waiting for an answer.

"Just the normal way." The yardmaster looked bleak. "It'll spring open just like it was before it clamped shut." The man used his hands to show the motion.

"And when that coupling comes apart," Schmidt added, "we all know what's going to happen."

"He's going to bleed out," Garrett said grimly.

"We hoped maybe you could do something," the yardmaster said.

Garrett's anger was evident in her facial expression. "Do what? Put a cork in it and tell him everything will be all right? You want me to tell him he'll be able to walk again even though his spine has been severed?" She kept her voice low so no one but those closest to her would hear. "I'm a surgeon, not a miracle worker."

"I know, but I had to give it a shot." The yardmaster's eyes showed his helplessness. "I'm sorry."

Garrett walked back to the patient. Even if she had a full team of surgeons, there would be little chance to save the man. Even if he survived, the disruption of organs and severance of his spine alone would be debilitating enough to devastate his quality of life. It was only a matter of time now. When the coupling was released, the life would flow out of him within a few seconds. The only thing she could do for him was try to lessen his pain enough to keep him comfortable.

"Gar, is there anything we can do for Paul?" The desperation in Garrett's eyes was all Danni needed to see. "God." She looked at the ground for a few seconds, composing her thoughts. "He said his wife was on the way. Is she here yet?"

"The police went to pick her up from work. According to the scene commander, they should be here any minute."

"Then what?"

Garrett bit her lip. "When he's ready, they'll uncouple the cars."

"Then he dies." She looked to Garrett. "Can't we do something? Anything?"

"Support and comfort him. That's about all, besides keeping his pain at bay." Movement off to the side caught Garrett's attention. "Looks like the priest is here. I think they'd like a few minutes of privacy." She turned her back to the scene and stared off into the railroad yard. "Follow me, Danni."

Garrett took off across the yard to a pair of railroad cars in the distance. Her long strides made short work of stepping over the tracks, and Danni had to hurry to keep up. When they finally arrived at their destination, her chest was heaving.

"Are you out of breath? Why didn't you tell me I was going too fast?"

"What, and make you think I can't keep up with you? Never." Danni sucked in another breath. "Now, show me this coupling thing. Maybe there's some way to unfasten it from the cars instead of in him."

Garrett moved between the two uncoupled cars. "See how the metal is shaped like a hook?"

Danni nodded.

"Now follow me to the other car. You'll see the hook is facing just the opposite. They slide into one another and mesh together in the middle." Garrett used her hands to demonstrate. "Locking them."

"Then when it went through him…" Danni's eyes widened. "Oh, God."

"Exactly." Garrett nodded grimly. "It either cut or smashed anything in its way."

Danni moved closer to get a good view of the menacing-looking mechanism. Beside the boxcar, she seemed even shorter than normal, the height of the coupling coming to just about the level of her heart. She bent over and tried to examine it from the underside.

The thought of Paul, helpless and cognizant of his impending death, overcame Danni. She closed her eyes as the first tear rolled down her cheek. A wave of compassion washed over her as she thought of what the future held for Paul and his family. She glanced at Garrett, and a giant lump came to her throat. Brushing the tears from her face, she forced herself to concentrate on the coupling device.

"Maybe if I look at them in line." Danni stood with her head at the level of the coupling, trying to see how it worked. She turned back to the closer coupling and studied it.

Garrett watched for a moment, intrigued by Danni's intense concentration. Then she leaned against the boxcar and looked back across the yard at the crowd of rescuers.

The noise level picked up as trains in other areas were being moved, and the squeaking wheels reminded Garrett of her journey to Pittsburgh. If she closed her eyes, she could almost feel the constant jiggle and hear the rhythmic clickity-clack of the cars passing over the track. It was enough to lull her into daydreaming.

Her moment of quiet ended abruptly with a jolting push and the sound of metal snapping into metal. Her first thought was of Danni, who was squatting in front of the coupling device. Pushed forward and falling, Garrett had no time to call out. Instead she lunged, launching her body in Danni's direction.

"Hey! What the—" Danni was pushed forward and pulled down all at once. It happened too fast to think, and she went with the momentum to keep from getting hurt.

"Humph!" The fall knocked the wind out of Garrett.

Danni lay on the ties with the tracks off to either side of her, the sound of metal clashing against metal directly over her head. She stared wide-eyed at the action above her. A thunderous clap accompanied the coupling latching itself together.

It took a few seconds for Garrett to catch her breath. She tried to talk, but the sting of the air expanding her lungs burned, and she grabbed her side. "Y-you okay?"

Danni took stock of her body before answering. "Everything seems to be okay. How about you?"

"Okay, now. Just..." Garrett drew in another breath. "Got the wind knocked out of me. Must have landed wrong." She worked on drawing in her next breath as she thought about what could have happened. She closed her eyes, then opened them, trying to get a fix on Danni's face.

"Hey!" A railroad worker stood with hands on his hips. "You can't lie down in the middle of the tracks like that. You want to get hurt? Can't you see we got one injured man here already? What the hell are you doing, trying to commit suicide?"

"I wanted to know how the coupling worked." Danni dusted off her pants.

"Did you get your answer, or do you want me to do it again?" He glared at her.

"Don't worry. I understand how it works now."

Garrett's temper was quick to spark. "Don't you people look before you try to kill someone?" She rose to her full height, towering above the man's head. "No wonder you have a man trapped over there." She glanced over to the scene of the entrapment. The sight of frantically waving arms spelled nothing but trouble.

"Danni, we're needed."

The railroad worker stood dumbfounded as the two women made their way across the yard.

* * *

"Doc!" A paramedic waved them down. "Paul's in a heap of pain. My protocols won't allow me to give him anything else."

Garrett could tell the medic's nerves were wearing thin. "You'd better go and distance yourself for a while."

"But I—"

"We'll take over from here."

Relieved of his duty, the medic stood, looking rather numb.

Aware of the rescuer's inability to abandon the situation, Danni put a gentle hand on his shoulder. "I'll stay with Paul." She made eye contact with the medic and held it as her words slowly sank in. "I promise, he won't be alone."

The medic stood for a long moment. Finally, he nodded, then walked off through the crowd.

"Danni." Garrett's voice recalled her attention. "Make him comfortable, whatever it takes. He doesn't need to experience any more pain."

"I know," Danni whispered.

* * *

Garrett kept her silent vigil until Paul's wife was brought through the crowd. Then she quickly explained the situation to her, making her aware of the fatal nature of the accident. The woman's grief-stricken face tugged at her heart.

Paul's concern for his wife's welfare amazed Garrett. It was as if what had happened to him was of no importance. Garrett didn't understand; his feelings seemed foreign to her. Most patients fought to cling to life, placing the emphasis on themselves and their goal to survive. Garrett had never witnessed such a love beyond self.

Danni left Paul's side when his wife arrived, affording them the privacy they needed to convey their last sentiments. It made her think of her own life, and brought home to her the importance of not waiting until it was too late to tell people they mattered. Watching them together was too emotional a scene for her tender heart to take, and tears began to run down her cheeks.

After several minutes, Paul's wife was escorted away. She told one of the rescuers that she couldn't bear to witness the inevitable. When she was far enough away, the railroad employees prepared to uncouple the cars.

Paul thanked his rescuers for trying to help. "I'm ready now," he said.

Danni clung to his hand, willing her spirit into his until the very end.

The life drained out of Paul's face as final realization set in. Danni felt it was clear from the look in his eyes that he knew these were the last things he would see of this world.

The yardmaster gave the signal with a hesitant nod, and an engine pulled one car away from the other. The sound of metal scraping on metal was drowned out by Paul's shriek of agony.

Once the cars were uncoupled, it was over in no time. The drama ended with a pool of blood soaking into the ground beneath Paul's lifeless body

Garrett knelt at Paul's side, and her fingers monitored his fading pulse. After a few moments, she looked down at her watch.

"Time of death, 2037 hours."

Chapter 17

There was no fanfare to greet the flight team's arrival back on the helipad, no crowd of caregivers eager to lend a hand. The fluorescent lighting cast its shadows on the pavement, creating an eerie black-and-white illusion of life as Danni and Garrett made their way into the building. Each woman carried a little more insight into the frailness of human beings than she had had when they left.

Garrett kept an eye on Danni. She'd been most directly involved with their patient, from beginning to end. Her compassionate nature left her vulnerable, and mindful of that, Garrett stayed vigilant. She had noticed Danni concealing her tears during the flight home, and it worried her. She cared too much about Danni to see her consumed by guilt over something neither of them had any control over.

"Do you want to talk about it?" Garrett asked.

"Talk about what? It's not like we were able to do anything."

They shared a long moment of silence. Danni spoke first. "I don't much feel like going back to the dinner. Do you? It just doesn't seem right to be having fun."

"I know what you mean." Garrett could see the effects of depression clearly written on Danni's face. She needed to be with someone she could talk to, someone she loved. "But I think we should go back to it, or what's left of it."

"I know." Danni's words were barely audible. "I'm not hungry, but we owe it to our dates."

Garrett's head jerked upward. "McCormick is not my date."

"Nobody else was picked up with a limo. Don't worry. I'm good at keeping secrets."

"But he's not my date." Garrett was utterly confused.

"It's okay. What you do outside the hospital shouldn't make a difference." Danni turned away. "We might as well stay dressed like this. I'm afraid to look at how wrinkled my suit is by now."

Garrett reflected on Danni's mood and knew what she had to do. "Let's get this night over with."

* * *

As Danni and Garrett entered the dining room, they heard the witty remarks of the emcee, which quickly flowed into an introduction. Everyone's focus centered on the man moving toward the podium.

"Come on," Garrett said. "No one will notice us with a politician speaking."

"Okay, but be quiet." Danni headed for the table they had been seated at.

"Right. I wouldn't want any more guff from Ol' Cutter."

The impassioned rhetoric of the politically motivated speech spoke of self-sacrifice and caring in the face of adversity, but did little to rouse the audience as the two women made their way through the room.

Polite clapping around them drew Danni's attention to the front of the room. "Hey, it's Dr. McMurray."

Garrett looked up. "He must be getting some kind of award."

"Maybe that's why he asked us to come." Danni saw McMurray looking straight back at her. "Uh-oh. Too late."

The sound of applause quickly drowned out Ol' Cutter's words and all eyes turned to Danni and Garrett.

"Way to go, Danni!" David boomed over the din of the crowd.

"What?" Garrett's eyes grew larger.

"Go up and get your award," Ian said, as he motioned them to the front of the room. "That's why you're here. Hell, that's why we're all here."

Danni and Garrett looked at each other. In an instant of realization, everything struck home.

"No!" The word was spoken in unison.

"Dr. Trivoli, Nurse Bossard, I'm glad you made it back in time. Please come forward." McMurray followed the pair with his eyes as they reluctantly made their way to the podium. "As you can tell," he said to the assembled group, "these dedicated women just got back from a flight. They are so committed to their cause that they wouldn't let me ground them for the night. They thought it would be unfair if someone really needed them."

Another round of applause started as Danni and Garrett stepped up onto the dais.

Ol' Cutter leaned in toward Garrett's ear. "Thought I told you to have something else on besides that suit."

"If you'd like, I could go and change right now."

"Nonsense, you're not getting off that easily. You both deserve this. Great teamwork, ladies." McMurray reached out and shook first Garrett's hand, then Danni's. Danni held onto his hand until she had his attention. "What's this all about?"

"Just a little thank-you from the lieutenant governor for the road worker's life you saved. You know, the one when you were supposed to be grounded."

"Oh, that one."

"I suggest you say something, Trivoli, before they tear the house down."

Garrett moved up to the microphone and scanned the room. "I really don't know what to say. We were only doing our jobs. It's what we've dedicated our lives to. Thank you." Garrett stepped back and Danni moved into her place.

Danni adjusted the microphone and looked out over the crowd.

"What Dr. Trivoli said is true. We are only doing our jobs. But we learn a lot from the different patients we treat. Some more so than others. Tonight, we tended to a dying man who taught me a very important lesson. He showed me that putting the welfare of others above your own gives life new meaning. In the short amount of time we spent together, he taught me that love is something to hold dear." Danni paused in an effort to strengthen her quivering voice. "He taught me to hold it so dearly that love should be our final thought when we leave this world."

The hushed silence was indicative of the crowd's profound reaction to Danni's words.

Brushing away a tear, she continued. "The patient we treated tonight found out how fragile life and love can be. His only wish was to hold the love of his life one last time. It is now, and always will be, my wish for all of you. Thank you."

Danni stepped back from the podium and shook the lieutenant governor's hand. She felt Garrett gently touch her shoulder as the audience applauded.

"You all right?"

"Yeah, I'll be okay. Just give me a minute."

A moment later, Danni was lost in the whirlwind that was David.

* * *

Garrett lay in her bed and ran the events of the evening through her mind. Something inside her had stirred during Danni's speech. All she had wanted to do was wrap her arms around Danni and never let go. Unsettled, Garrett tried to figure out her emotions.

She regretted that she'd missed her chance to ease the pained look on Danni's face. She had hoped the security of David's arms would help Danni, but it hadn't. Instead, she had looked more upset, and that bothered Garrett. David hadn't done anything wrong, so why couldn't she get used to the idea of Danni being with him?

She rolled over and squeezed her pillow in the crook of her arm. Things were so different now that David was in the picture.

"Alone was so much easier than being part of a team," Garrett mumbled, closing her eyes to sleep.

* * *

In the other bedroom, any thought of restful sleep was forgotten as thoughts of David and Garrett vied for precedence in Danni's mind. One loved her, but the other was the one she loved. She was trapped in a living nightmare. How could she tell Garrett that she loved her? In spite of Garrett's lame excuse about the limo, it was obvious she liked men.

Thoughts of Garrett in arms other than her own tormented Danni. She rolled onto her side and scrunched up her pillow, but Paul's rough whisper of "Tell her I love her" kept running through her head. Danni closed her eyes, praying for sleep to overtake her, but all she could envision was the look on Paul's face as he was about to die.

The image was simply too much. She sat bolt upright and gasped, trying to calm her racing heart.

"I need air." Danni threw back the covers and sobbed. "Damn it, I need air."

* * *

Sleep didn't last long for Garrett when the muffled sounds of crying filtered through her door. In a flash, she was up and out of bed, following the sound down the stairs. The muted whimpering was tearing at her heart. Seated on the edge of the couch was Danni, rolled up into a ball and rocking. It was obvious to Garrett that although Danni's emotions had withstood the storm of the trauma scene, they had given way in its aftermath.

"Danni." Garrett reached out to stroke her hair.

Danni welcomed the comfort of Garrett's hand. "I didn't wake you, did I?" She wiped her hands against her nightgown.

"No, I was up," Garrett lied. "I was coming down to get something to drink."

"Oh." Danni looked away.

"Are you okay?"

"I'm not sure. This whole evening has been a little emotional, even for me."

"I bet." Garrett sighed and ran her fingers through Danni's hair. "How about I give David a call? He could—"

Danni shook her head. "David doesn't understand."

"Maybe you could talk to him." Garrett sat down beside her. "Give him a chance."

"Gar, he's just… David." Tears started to stream down Danni's face.

"David shouldn't have left you alone tonight. I'm calling him. What's his number?"

"Please, Gar, don't." Danni eyes were puffy and red. "I really don't want him to know what I'm feeling right now. I'm not sure anyone would understand it." Danni lowered her gaze. "God knows, I don't."

Garrett wrapped her arm around Danni and pulled her close, her level of annoyance at David rising. She tightened her embrace. "Shh. I'm here, Danni. Come on." Garrett rubbed Danni's back in a lazy circle. "Let's get you up to bed."

Garrett helped her up from the couch and directed her toward the stairs. Each step they took together had a strange familiarity to it.

Handling Danni with utmost care, Garrett guided her as they made their way into Danni's bedroom. After she was situated in bed, Garrett pulled the covers up and tucked them neatly back into place. She brushed back blonde hair and placed a chaste kiss on Danni's forehead.

Danni grasped Garrett's arm like a drowning woman grabbing a lifeline. "Don't go." Her voice quivered.

"You need your sleep."

"I don't want to be alone. Please, stay with me."

Garrett was torn between being her old stoic self and being the caring friend she was learning to be. One look into Danni's pleading eyes and it was finished.

"Move over."

Danni was quick to comply. A long moment of silence prevailed after Garrett settled in.

"Gar?"

"Yes."

"Could you hold me?"

It was a simple request, but Garrett had no idea where or how to start. Sensing the awkwardness of the moment, Danni reached back and took hold of Garrett's arm. Garrett rolled onto her side to accommodate the move. Pleased, Danni snuggled in. Within minutes the tension in her body diminished.

"Thanks."

The whisper, though barely audible, was acknowledged by a rumbling purr from deep in Garrett's throat.

In a night filled with both sorrows and accolades, this moment was the most precious of them all.

Chapter 18

René Chabot stood at the doorway, admiring the peaceful expression on his colleague's often-troubled face. He hated to move for fear of breaking the spell. But move he must.

Feigning his first step into the room, he prepared a startled expression to aid in his deception. "Garrett, what brings you in so early?"

"I wish I knew myself, René."

"I don't understand. You looked so peaceful and happy. I thought perhaps you finally found someone. No one ever looks like you just did without thinking of a loved one, eh?"

"It's not that easy." Garrett shifted in her chair. "Someone's trying my patience. I tend to get upset when he's around. Even the sound of his name gets me going."

"Surely he wasn't the one you were thinking of when I walked in? You didn't look annoyed at all."

"Meaning?"

"Maybe your feeling of annoyance is caused by love." He watched the expression on her face turn thoughtful. "Maybe it's the possibility of love that annoys you."

"Love?" Garrett spat out the word like a bitter herb. "You think the world is filled with nothing but love. All you married people see is love." She pushed back her chair and got up to leave.

René stopped her as she went to pass by. "Love doesn't make you weak. Love can be a very powerful thing when the right two people are drawn together. It is something that can move mountains and bring calm to a troubled soul."

"If you say so. Unfortunately, I wouldn't know what love was if it were standing beside me."

"That's because you are thinking with your head and not your heart. You have to remember to open your heart, and love will come."

"René…"

"Think about it. That's all I ask." He looked at Garrett hopefully.

"Okay, okay. I'll think about it. I'm thinking about everything else, why not love?"

"Good."

Obviously alerted by its vibrations, Garrett grabbed for her pager. "The ER. If it's McCormick again, I'll—" Her eyes flashed with fire. A second later she was out the door.

"When are you going to learn, Garrett?" René's words were wasted on the empty air.

Beep-beep, beep-beep, beep-beep.

He reached for his pager and silenced it. "I guess it's time for all of us to get back to work." He, too, was through the door in the blink of an eye.

*   *   *

Danni barreled out the locker room door, almost colliding with the person on the other side.

"Oops! Sorry, Karen."

"It's all right," Karen said, catching the door with her outstretched arm. "You're here late. Garrett tied up with something?"

"I wouldn't know." Danni stepped back into the locker room. "We drove in separately."

"Did you say anything to her?"

"No. I'm still not sure what her response would be, especially after this weekend."

"What happened?"

"David happened." Danni sighed.

"David?"

"He was in town for the weekend." Danni dropped to the bench and sat. "David was my escort to the dinner on Friday night."

"So I've heard."

"When he called on Saturday and wanted to come over, I couldn't say no. I guess I sounded a little too excited on the phone when Garrett walked in. You should have seen the look on her face. Oh, God! She looked so disappointed."

"Did she say anything?"

"No, but she cleared out like the house was on fire." Danni's shoulders slumped. "It didn't get any better later on."

"David was still there?"

"Yes. He had put some music on while I got us some refreshments. I never thought one friendly little dance was going to matter."

"Let me guess, Garrett came home."

"Oh, yes."

"And?"

"I'm not sure what it was, but I'll never forget the look in her eyes."

"Maybe she was jealous."

"Get real. She probably thinks I'm in love with David."

"Don't say that too loud or it will be the hot rumor of the week," Karen said, looking over her shoulder. "What if she was jealous?"

Perplexed at first, Danni slowly turned more hopeful.

"You know," Karen said, "a lot can happen in four months."

"I wish," Danni whispered.

Karen comforted her with a pat on the shoulder. "You'll know when the time is right. Something will give you a sign. I'm sure of it."

"I hope so." Danni got up. "Did you and Rosie get subpoenaed?"

"Yeah, just what I want to do instead of sleep after working all night," Karen groused.

"Why don't we pick you up? That way you won't have to drive."

Karen studied Danni. "You're afraid to be alone with her on the long drive, aren't you?"

"I'm not afraid of Garrett." She frowned and squinted at Karen. "I just thought maybe you could see some sign."

"Sign, huh?"

"Please?"

"I have to change. Pick me up at quarter to eight outside the trauma bay doors. Remember, I can't promise I'll see anything after working all night."

"But it will be another set of eyes."

The shrill sound of Danni's beeper split the air.

"Damn!" The word came out through clenched teeth as Danni reached for her pager.

"At least you didn't get all the way home."

"It's the ER."

"Flight?"

"I'm not sure, but something's up." Danni headed for the door, "Guess I'll find out."

* * *

Long strides propelled Garrett out of the elevator and down the hallway.

"Hey! Wait up," Danni called out as she intersected Garrett's path.

"You got the page, too?"

"I wonder what's up."

"Looks like we're about to find out." Garrett motioned to the serious looking woman seated behind the monitor.

"Dr. Potter." Garrett halted at the desk.

"Dr. Trivoli, Danni." Jamie pushed her glasses higher on her nose. "There's been a huge pileup on the Parkway East. The initial report estimates seventeen cars. We're not sure how many are injured. My guess is twenty or more."

"What can we do to help?"

"I need you to do what you do best: act as a team. I'm pairing up a nurse and a physician for every two rooms. I figure we can staff at least six teams that way. I want to use the attending trauma surgeon for the first OR case, with Dr. Chabot and then you, Garrett, as backups. Until then, you can help us wade through the mess down here." Jamie looked to Garrett for approval.

"And if they need us at the scene?"

"We'll cross that bridge if we need to." Jamie said, and shrugged.

Danni gave Garrett a nudge. "Hey, Gar. You could be getting some OR time on this one."

"Now, that's always appealing to me." Garrett smiled at Jamie. "So, Dr. Potter, where do you want us?"

"Trauma Room Three. Thanks for coming to the party," Jamie called out as the flight team took off down the hall.

* * *

"Dr. Trivoli, you do remember what to do with the proper equipment and a room that doesn't lift off, eh?"

"We can fly circles around you, Chabot, even without the helicopter." Garrett gestured to herself and Danni. "Just watch us."

We? Danni's head snapped up in surprise. Her thoughts and the playfulness of the trauma fellows were cut short by the overhead announcement.

"Traumas at the back doors, traumas at the back doors. Three ambulances, more on the way."

Laughter quickly turned to somber professionalism as the teams hastened to their stations. A moment later, chaos descended on them as multiple patients were rolled in through the trauma bay doors.

* * *

Garrett watched intently as the paramedics whisked their patient into the room. "What do we have?"

"Female passenger, rear seat, driver's side. She's the least injured of the four in the car. No reported loss of consciousness, but she's covered in blood." The medic positioned his stretcher next to the one in the trauma room.

"On three." Garrett stabilized the head of the backboard the patient was strapped to. "One, two, lift."

"Sorry we couldn't get you any more info. The scene's a zoo." The medic released the board once it rested on the hospital's stretcher. "Speaking of which, I'd make it fast if I were you. There's a hell of a lot more to come."

"Thanks for the warning." Garrett surveyed the blood-soaked patient. "Ma'am, can you hear me?"

"Y-yes," the older woman said. Her eyes conveyed her fright. "What happened? Where am I? Oh, my! Am I going to die?"

"Not if we can help it." Danni reached for the patient's hand and squeezed it for a moment.

"Airway clear, and breathing on her own," Garrett announced, and continued with her examination. By the look of the blood covering the patient, she suspected an arterial bleed. Finding no active bleeding on the woman's body, Garrett focused her trained eye on the bulky dressing atop the woman's head. The coagulated blood clinging to the first dressing that she unwrapped alerted her to what she would find underneath the rest.

When the last piece of dressing was removed, a bright-red stream spurted freely into the air. Unfazed by the display, Garrett shifted to see around the crimson droplets that threatened to spatter her protective eye shield, and continued to search for the source.

"Looks like it may be the temporal artery." Garrett grabbed the sterile gauze Danni held out and pressed it on the site to stop the flow of blood.

"I'm going to die," the patient screamed. "Do something. Chris! Oh, my God! Chris!"

Danni made eye contact with the patient. "You're in good hands, ma'am. We're not going to let you die. Just hold very still, and let us do our job."

"But Chris..."

The patient's eyes bored into Danni's with such intensity it sent a chill through her. She took the woman's hand and held on. "Was Chris in the car with you?"

"Yes!" The patient cried out in desperation. "It can't end this way. We've been together too long."

"Let me check. Maybe Chris was brought in already." Danni worked her hand loose from the patient's grasp, soothing her with gentle pats. "Don't worry, I'll find out what happened to your husband."

The patient's eyes widened, then her gaze darted around the room. "There were four of us in the car. Chris, Bobby, Charlie, and me."

"I'll get the social worker to see if they're here. Let's get you taken care of first, shall we?" Danni scanned the area as she pulled a Mayo stand closer to the head of the stretcher and readied the instruments for Garrett to use.

"Ma'am, you've got an artery that needs to be sewn up to stop the bleeding. It's going to hurt a bit, but I promise you, when it's time to suture the cut, we'll be giving you some numbing medicine."

The patient closed her eyes. "Okay."

"Hold this," Garrett said to Danni, "and be ready with some fresh gauze pads. I'm going to need you to blot the blood away after I put the first suture in."

Danni responded, ready for her part in the procedure. With deft maneuvers, Garrett went through motions she had performed thousands of times. The sharp needle pierced the skin, and Garrett rolled her wrist, working the thread upon itself in a knotting effect. Each set of motions ceased only briefly while Danni wiped away the escaping blood.

"There, I think we've got it stopped." Danni blotted the site one last time as Garrett watched for leaks.

"BP ninety-six over fifty-four, heart rate one hundred and ten, and oxygen saturation at ninety-six percent."

"Give her five hundred of fluids. That will help to bring her heart rate down a bit and give us a rise in her pressure."

Danni quickly found the IV line and adjusted the control. "Lactated Ringer's running for the fluids." She softened her voice and spoke directly to the patient. "You should be feeling better in a little while."

"Thank you, but could you please see if my Chris is here?"

Garrett removed her bloody gloves and reached for another pair. "Go see if you can find Chris for her. I'll finish up here."

Danni nodded, then addressed the patient. "I'll be right back," she said and left.

"I hope Chris is all right. I don't know what I'd do without…" The patient stopped before she could finish the sentence. "Have you been working with her long?"

"It seems like forever sometimes," Garrett replied. "But we've only recently been teamed up together."

"Oh, I thought maybe…" The patient wavered. "Never mind."

* * *

Garrett stood outside the trauma room, going over the patient's films on a viewbox for a few minutes before acknowledging Danni's return. "Were you able to find her friends and husband?"

"Friends, yes. Husband…" Danni hesitated. "No."

"Maybe the next grouping of ambulances will—"

"Chris is a woman," Danni whispered.

"Why wouldn't she just tell us?"

"Consider her age. She might have been a teenager in the days of free love, but some things were still very taboo." Danni continued in a whisper, "Bobby and Charlie are both men. I would guess the four of them used each other as cover."

"Oh." Garrett returned her attention to the film on the viewbox. "Where's Chris? I'll go see how she's doing."

"I was hoping you'd say that. I used up a few favors to find her. She's on the next ambulance in."

"Okay, let's hurry and get our patient into another room for the rest of the suturing. We'll take her friend in Trauma Three."

"I'll get her moved and hooked up with someone from Plastic Surgery right away."

Garrett stripped off her gloves, gown, and mask and stuffed them into the trash while Danni wheeled the patient into the room directly across the hall.

"Okay, Chris, I'm waiting for you," Garrett said, reaching for a fresh gown.

* * *

Danni settled the stretcher into the room and applied its brake. "I'm sorry we were in such a rush to take care of you before. I don't even know your name."

"Marie. Marie Remhouse. And you are?"

"Danni Bossard. I've made arrangements for Plastic Surgery to take care of the laceration on your face."

"Thank you. Chris, is she here? Oh…" Marie pursed her lips.

"She's on the next ambulance coming in. Don't worry, I know what it's like to love someone that deeply," Danni whispered. "Dr. Trivoli and I will see that Chris is well taken care of."

"Oh, thank God." Marie looked up toward the ceiling before meeting Danni's comforting smile. "Thank you." The tears flowed freely down Marie's face.

"Our next patient is arriving."

Garrett's voice startled Danni. She took Marie's hand and nodded. "Be right there."

Marie studied Danni's face. "She's the one, isn't she?"

"That obvious, huh?"

Marie barely moved her head in a nod.

Danni mustered a weak grin. "Seems like everyone knows but her."

"Don't give up. She'll see it soon enough. It makes a world of difference to be loved."

"Thanks."

Marie squeezed Danni's hand. "You're welcome."

"I've got to go. I'll tell Chris that you're thinking of her."

"And that I'm praying for her, too."

* * *

"Trauma in the department. Trauma in the department." The sound of the overhead alert announced the next wave of incoming injured.

"Where to?" The female medic didn't slow down.

"Are you Chris?" Danni peered down at the patient as she kept pace with the stretcher.

"Yes, my name is Chris. How did you know?"

"Trauma Room Three, please," Danni directed the medics before turning her attention to the woman on the stretcher. "Marie told us you'd be coming." Danni quickly scanned over the woman's wiry body and her short, wildly curled gray hair. Then she smiled.

Danni whispered in Chris's ear, "Marie said to tell you she's okay and she's thinking about you and praying for you."

Chris nodded as best she could, being strapped onto a backboard. "That's Marie, always watching out for me."

Garrett met them at the doorway to the trauma room. "Hello Chris, I'm Dr. Trivoli. Can you tell me where you hurt?"

"My stomach hurts like hell."

The stretcher stopped, and each member of the team grabbed onto the backboard.

"On my count. One, two, lift. Airway clear, respirations good. No obvious signs of external bleeding." Garrett removed her hands from the board and reached for the stethoscope dangling around her neck. She placed the diaphragm of the stethoscope on the patient's chest. "Breathe in." She moved to the opposite chest wall and repeated the procedure. "And again."

Chris did as she was asked.

"Good. Breath sounds clear and unremarkable. We're going to be cutting your clothing off and examining you more closely. Let us know if we're hurting you at any time."

"All right." Chris winced. "But it hurts pretty bad already."

Danni used trauma shears to expose Chris's chest. She quickly placed leads and attached the monitor to them, then studied the tracing on the screen.

"Heart rate one hundred twenty-two and showing a regular rhythm." Danni turned back to Chris and placed a blood pressure cuff around her upper arm, then a clip on her finger. Once again she viewed the electronic readouts. "BP ninety-four over forty-eight, respirations twenty-eight, oxygen saturation at ninety percent."

Garrett began a systematic laying of hands. She started at Chris's head and worked down her body. Finding no signs of deformity, she concentrated on the abdominal area, first feeling for a femoral pulse in Chris's groin. It was present, but not as strong as Garrett would have liked it to be.

"Does this hurt?" Skilled fingers moved to Chris's midsection and pressed gingerly.

"Yes!" A look of intense pain distorted her face.

Garrett observed the readouts on the monitor as she moved her hands around the abdomen. All clinical indications pointed to internal injuries.

"I need chest, pelvis, and lateral cervical spine X-rays. Call Radiology for a CT scan of the abdomen and pelvis, and get another IV started. I'll draw the blood for gases and a routine trauma panel. Don't forget to add a type and cross for the blood bank."

The room became a flurry of activity as Chris's condition edged downward in a fight against time.

How would I feel if this were Danni? Garrett studied Chris as the tubes filled with blood. *Could I be as patient as her lover is, waiting to hear any word about her condition?* She thought about the woman across the hall, lying on the stretcher, draped and being sutured. *No. I'd be worse, much worse.* Garrett knew what she had to do.

"Scans are backed up at least forty-five minutes." Danni put down the phone. "Do you want to do an ultrasound or Doppler?"

"Ultrasound," Garrett said and strode out the door. Danni placed a warmed sheet on Chris as Garrett pulled the ultrasound machine into the room.

"Come on." Garrett squeezed cold gel onto Chris's abdomen. With the transducer moving over Chris's abdomen, Garrett searched the screen for answers. "There's blood in the pericolic gutter. Call the OR and tell them to get a room ready for an acute, traumatic abdomen."

Garrett's eyes conveyed the serious nature of her findings. "Chris, you've got some damage to the organs in your abdomen. I'm going to need to get in there and fix them."

"Just make it stop hurting." Chris looked at Danni, getting her attention. "Marie... you'll tell her?"

"Anything you want."

"Tell her I love her. Then, now, and forever," Chris whispered, as though it were her dying wish.

Fearing that her own voice would waver, Danni nodded. Tears started to form, but she blinked several times to halt their flow. "You'll be able to tell her all those things yourself. We're not giving up on you. Besides, you're in good hands." Danni glanced over to see Garrett studying Chris's X-rays on the viewer. "I'd trust your doctor with my own life."

"Let's package her up and get to the OR." The words were out before Garrett realized it. Adrenaline was pumping through her veins. She was going to the operating room, and this time, nobody could stop her.

Chapter 19

Fear struck deep into Marie's heart when a figure bathed in light entered her room. Marie prayed desperately that this apparition was not her lover coming to say goodbye.

"Please, God, not like this." A single tear broke through her tightly closed eyelids. "No," Marie moaned. Raising her hands to shield her ears, she pushed herself deeper into the pillow. "If I don't listen, if I don't hear..." Marie sobbed. "She can't be gone."

"Marie, it's all right. Chris has some internal injuries, and she's in surgery right now." The voice was mellow against the darkness of night where fears lurked in every shadow.

Marie opened her eyes when she felt the gentle touch on her cheek. "You're real," she gasped.

"I'd better be real." Danni let her hand linger on Marie's cheek to further establish her presence.

"I... I remember you from the emergency room. You said Chris is in surgery?"

"Yes. I hope you don't mind my stopping by to wait with you." Danni smiled. "Tears shared between two aren't as hard to bear as ones shed alone."

At first it didn't make sense, but the more Marie thought about it, it made the most sense she had ever heard. "How did someone as young as you get to be so wise?"

"Sometimes I think I'm older than dirt. Pretty good disguise, huh?"

Marie started to smile, then stopped as the movement pulled at stitches in her face. "Ow!"

"Sorry, I didn't mean to make you hurt."

"I'll get used to it."

Danni studied Marie's delicate features. Now that the bloodstains were gone, the woman's fair-skinned beauty showed through. Marie's sparkling, hazel eyes and the wisps of gray at her temples added character to her appearance.

"I thought you'd like to have someone to talk to while we wait to hear about Chris."

"Yes, I'd like that." Marie studied Danni for a moment. "Do you always dress like that?"

"This?" Danni tugged at her flight suit. "I'm part of the Trauma Flight Team. But we were paged to assist in the hospital with this disaster."

"Your doctor, I take it she's…"

"The flight surgeon. She's the one operating on Chris. Dr. Trivoli is very skilled. I've seen her do things an ordinary surgeon wouldn't even think of. Trust me when I say Chris couldn't be in better hands."

"Is Chris bad?" Marie's voice trembled. "They won't tell me anything about her."

"I'll let you know as soon as I hear anything. Do you two have a legal document, a written power of attorney?"

"No, Chris didn't want to think about those." Marie looked away before turning back to Danni. "You seem to think very highly of your surgeon. Have you known her long?"

"There are times when I think I've known Dr. Trivoli for eons, but in reality, I only met her last July. I guess living with someone, you get to know them pretty well."

"Then you two are…" Marie looked for a silent confirmation.

The smile faded from Danni's face. "No, we only share the house and our jobs until her fellowship is through."

"She's going to stay, isn't she?"

Danni shrugged. "I don't know."

"I see." Marie's mood turned somber.

"Chris asked me to tell you something for her."

"She did?"

"She said to tell you she loves you then, now, and forever."

Marie's face paled. "That's what Chris always says to me when we have to be apart from one another. When did she tell you?"

"Right before she went up to surgery."

"That's my Chris, always thinking of me."

"How long have you been together?"

"Not long enough. It's been more than thirty-five years since we first met."

"I'm curious. How did you know you were…" Danni hesitated. "I mean, that Chris was interested?"

Marie gathered her thoughts. "You know, when we were growing up, being gay wasn't as accepted as it is today. You really put yourself out on a limb if you came out."

"It's not any easier today," Danni said and sighed. "I've always known I didn't fit in with the way my mother had my life planned out. I just didn't know who it was I wanted until now."

"And that would be Dr. Trivoli?" Marie noticed the blush creeping up Danni's cheeks.

"We're friends but I'm not sure she's…"

"That way?"

Melancholy tinged Danni's response. "I don't even have a clue."

Marie reached out her hand and let it rest on top of Danni's. "How about I tell you the story of Chris and me?"

Danni looked up. "You'd do that?"

Marie nodded. "I'm not going to sleep, and if you're willing to listen…"

"I'm ready when you are." Danni pulled up a chair as Marie collected her thoughts.

"Back in the sixties, free love was all the rage if you were a heterosexual couple, but there was nothing free for us. If it became known, you paid a price, and dearly. I met Chris one day when I was taking a long walk down by the Point. I used to love standing there, watching the rivers come together." Marie grew silent as she reminisced. "I saw this skinny girl fishing off the wharf."

"Chris, right?"

"Yes," Marie said, trying to smile. "In all the times I walked down there, she hardly caught anything. But every day she would be sitting with that pole in her hands. Each day, I'd walk a little closer, until one day I was standing right next to her. It scared the daylights out of her when I asked her what she used for bait."

"Do you fish?" Danni said.

"No, but I wasn't going to tell her that. It was the only thing we had to talk about."

"I'm sorry. Please, continue."

"To make a long story short, after a month or so, Chris invited me to sit down and offered me one of her poles to use."

"I take it you did?"

"You'd better believe I did. How else could I sit by her and talk for hours on end? She wasn't too gabby when we first met, but over the years she's gotten better. Lord, she can talk your ear off now."

"So, how did you finally get together?"

"I got some bad news about a friend of mine in the army. He'd been shot in Vietnam, and I wasn't taking it too well. Chris offered to walk me home, but instead we ended up at her place because it was closer." Marie stared off into the shadows of the room. "I was a basket case by then. Charlie and me, well, we grew up together. We knew early on we were different from everybody else, but we kept it to ourselves. Our parents thought we'd grow up and marry."

Danni's brows furrowed. "But I thought…"

"We did what all the other kids were doing at the time. I guess you could say we started covering for each other, even back then." Her words trailed off.

"Marie. How did you know about Chris?"

"Some you can tell by looking at, some by the way they talk or act. With Chris, it was her touch. The first time we held hands, it was like electricity running through me. I don't know why, but I just knew."

"How did your parents take it when you told them?"

"Tell them?" Marie's voice was filled with shock. "I haven't told them yet."

"They don't live near you, then, I take it."

"On the contrary, they live two miles away." Marie motioned for Danni to come closer. "They think I'm living with Charlie, and Chris and Bobby live in the apartment upstairs."

"The four of you live together?"

"Let's just say that we all go in the same front door, with the girls on the first floor and the boys on the second."

"Charlie's the friend you were so upset about, the one who got shot?"

"Yes, he was. You might say it was his doing that brought Chris and me together at last. When we got to her place, she just held me in her arms, and I knew that I never wanted to be without her for the rest of my life. The safety and love that I felt there were undeniable."

"That's really great. You have your best friend and life partner all under the same roof."

"Yes, I've been blessed that way."

"If you don't mind my asking, how did Charlie and Bobby meet?"

"Bobby was the corpsman who took care of him when he was wounded." The older woman blushed. "It's as if that bullet acted more like Cupid's arrow, with both our names on it."

Seeing Marie lost in fond remembrances, Danni offered a silent prayer all her own. *Please, Gar, don't let anything happen to keep Marie and Chris apart.*

* * *

Garrett's nimble fingers worked at a feverish pace to find the major antagonist to her patient's wellbeing. With the blood finally suctioned out of the abdominal cavity, the nasty remnants of a shattered spleen were evident. Unable to salvage the organ, Garrett tied off the splenic artery. Unfortunately, her action did nothing to stop the nosedive the patient's blood pressure was taking. There had to be another source of blood loss.

"Damn it!" Garrett searched the glistening surface of the liver. "She's got to have an injury we can't see."

Without delay, she gently lifted a lobe of the liver and examined every side. "Where are you? I know there's another bleeder here somewhere." She leaned closer to examine the organ in her hands.

"Give me some suction here, will you?" Garrett barked out. She was not going to be the one to tell Chris's lover that she'd joined the ranks of the Lone Survivors Club. With that thought foremost in her mind, Garrett diligently resumed her search.

One by one, several small lacerations were repaired in the right lobe of the liver. Garrett turned her attention to the main source of blood for the organ, the hepatic artery. Meticulous inspection revealed a small tear in the vessel where it attached to the liver itself. Immediately, she set to suturing.

Garrett let out a long-held breath as she tied the last knot. She looked up to the electronic monitoring devices and watched the numbers as they began to stabilize.

"Hang another unit of blood." She stripped off her stained gloves and threw them into the waste bucket. "Gloves, please."

"BP seventy-eight over forty-eight, heart rate one hundred and six," the anesthesiologist rattled off the numbers on his monitor.

"Better." With a snap, Garrett released the cuff of a new glove and stepped closer to the surgical field. "Now, let's make sure we didn't miss anything."

* * *

Familiar footsteps woke Danni. She opened her eyes and saw a shadowy figure standing in the doorway of Marie's room.

"Is that you, Gar?" Danni whispered.

"Yes. Is Marie asleep?"

"Finally." Danni looked at her watch. It wasn't quite two in the morning. "How's Chris doing?"

"Holding her own, for now. We had to remove her spleen, suture some lacerations on her liver, and tend to a small leak in the hepatic artery. I came to tell Marie that Chris made it to Recovery."

"Thanks." Danni took the surgeon's hand in her own and was surprised at the energy she found there. Marie's story came to her mind. "If you want, I'll tell her when she wakes up. I'm going to stay and keep an eye on her."

Garrett nodded wearily. "I'm going to spend the rest of the night with Chris in Recovery." She let her hand linger in Danni's.

"I hope you don't mind," Danni said softly, "but I asked Rosie to stop by the house and pick us up some clothes for court in the morning."

Garrett frowned. "I forgot about that."

"I figured as much."

"Thanks." Garrett drew in a deep breath. "I'd better get back to Chris." She slipped her fingers through Danni's grip.

"I'll come find you when Rosie gets here in the morning."

Garrett nodded and left without saying another word.

Marie shifted in her bed and looked at the vanishing figure. She turned, eyes riveted to Danni. "Is she…?"

"Chris is out of surgery, Marie." Danni reached out to comfort the older woman. "She's holding her own."

"Thank God." Tears of joy rolled down Marie's face.

"She's going to need her rest tonight, and so do you." Danni patted Marie's shoulder. "I'll be here if you need me, and Garrett will be there for Chris when she wakes up."

The love and concern that filled Marie's face brought a twinge of envy to Danni.

She hoped that someday she would know a love like theirs. "Please let it be Garrett," Danni whispered.

*   *   *

Tired, but unable to sleep, Garrett sat watching the monitors recording Chris's condition. Her mind drifted from one random thought to another. She kept coming back to the moment she had held Danni's hand. It was almost as if her own hand had been trembling.

She brought her hand up from her lap and studied it, frowning. She'd never trembled before, not even in training, when she had made her very first incision. Her hands were always rock solid. So, why was she trembling now? The question plagued her until she finally gave up, closed her eyes and willed her body to sleep, even if only for a few hours.

Chapter 20

Garrett stared mindlessly out the car window. She wasn't even aware of who was driving her back to Pittsburgh. All she knew was that she couldn't get out of that courtroom fast enough. How had her testimony at a rape trial suddenly turned into questions about her own character? Through no fault of her own, Garrett had fallen right into the hands of the defense attorney. She'd been warned of the tactics he might try to get his clients off the hook, but she never thought he would resort to something so low. There were so many questions that the slick lawyer demanded answers to, half of which had no bearing on the case. He was looking for anything he could use to discredit her testimony as a material witness.

If it hadn't been for the District Attorney protesting the line of questioning, she could have been the one that damned lawyer said tried to rape the waitress. Garrett's head was spinning. The defense attorney's questions and her testimony both had given her a lot to think about.

The poignant look on Danni's face in the courtroom as she sat there, clearly trying to communicate her outrage and support, had burned a page of its own into Garrett's memory. Even in recollection, it was sending mixed emotions to the very heart of Garrett's being. She stole a look at the woman seated beside her. The furrow in Danni's brow spoke loudly of her inner dilemma, and made Garrett all the more apprehensive. The other sign of Danni's preoccupation was her quiet. She hadn't spoken a word, and that wasn't like Danni at all, especially with the likes of Rosie and Karen in the front seat.

I wonder if we will ever be that friendly again after today? Garrett's anxiety level rose. *I could understand if Danni chose not to.* She looked at the two women occupying the front seat. *Hell, I'd understand it if they all chose not to.*

Garrett rested her head against the window. She could feel a headache coming on. When did everything start to go wrong? She loved her work. She was feeling comfortable in the hospital and finally making friends. Garrett had even let Danni begin to touch her heart. No one had done that for longer than Garrett cared to remember. Now, in the matter of several minutes of courtroom interrogation, Garrett felt as though her life were draining out of her, leaving nothing but an empty shell that was hollow, cold, and withering fast.

Lost in emotional devastation, a fleeting spark of warmth caught her attention and a subtle glance confirmed it. Danni had slipped her hand into Garrett's. Silently, one woman's spirit reached out to the other, giving it sustenance.

Was that what love was really all about? To be there for someone when they were down? When there was no one else to stand by them?

A sinking feeling came over Garrett as a single thought raced through her mind. Was she in love?

Terror gripped her heart. Her eyes shifted and met Danni's. Warm and loving eyes reached deep into Garrett's soul.

Garrett looked out the window again, but her thoughts weren't on the passing scenery. Instead, she reviewed her life and her year of fellowship so far. It was turning out to be more than she had anticipated. Damn McMurray. This was all his fault.

More of the unaccustomed insecurity swept over her. In an effort to stabilize her inner turmoil, she looked toward Danni. This time when their gaze met, Garrett quickly averted her eyes. The gentle pressure Danni exerted on her hand bolstered Garrett's soul, and it was almost impossible for her not to return it. Feeling better when she pressed Danni's hand, Garrett reconsidered the subject she'd been toying with. Could she actually be falling in love?

* * *

Rosie stopped the car in the hospital parking lot, and Karen turned to the occupants of the rear seat. "Are you two going to be all right to drive home?"

"If you want, I could drop you off at your house," Rosie said.

"No, thanks." Garrett shook her head. "I have to check on a few of my patients."

"I don't care what they asked you today." Rosie met Garrett's eyes in the rearview mirror. "We're still friends, right?"

"Yeah, friends," Garrett said as she got out of the car.

Danni watched as Garrett made her way into the hospital.

"Is she going to be all right?" Rosie motioned in Garrett's direction.

"I think it's going to take some time for her to get it all together again. I'll get her home. Don't worry. Thanks, Rosie." Danni got out, closed the car door, and walked away.

There was a moment of silence before Rosie rolled her eyes and whistled a few notes slightly off key.

"Okay, Rosie," Karen said. "Spill it. What's on your mind?"

"Do you think Garrett is gay?"

"The only one who can answer that is Garrett. How about I let you be the one to ask her?"

"Me?" Rosie grabbed the steering wheel tightly and shook her head. "Doesn't make any difference to me. She's not my type."

"I didn't think you were a fool, either." Karen smirked. Either way, it didn't matter. Garrett was in good hands with Danni. She looked out the window in time to see Danni enter the building. She just hoped that Danni would get the answer she was looking for.

* * *

"Wait up!" Danni's short legs worked double-time to match Garrett's strides. "Is Chris all right?"

Garrett nodded.

"I'm sorry for what happened today. You didn't deserve to be battered by that shyster lawyer. I should have…"

"Getting yourself thrown out of court would have done nothing to stop him. I'm a survivor. Don't you know that by now?"

"What he did wasn't right."

"No, it wasn't. He had a job to do, and I was in his way." Garrett shrugged. "It doesn't matter, anyhow."

"It matters to me, and it should matter to you, too."

"It's over, Danni." Garrett stepped into the elevator and selected a floor. "Let it go."

"I thought you were going to check on Chris. Isn't she in the ICU on the fifth floor?"

"Yes, she is, but the best medicine in the world for her is on the ninth floor."

"There's no medicine there. That's the observation floor." Garrett's smile struck a spark in Danni's mind. "You're going to take Marie down to see her, aren't you?"

"I always knew you were smart." The elevator doors opened, and Garrett stepped out.

Danni looked pleased. "Mind if I tag along?"

"I was hoping you would."

Looking slightly more cheerful, Garrett stopped outside of Marie's room. "Why don't you go in and get her ready while I take care of her discharge?"

"What should I tell her?"

"You'll know what to say. You always do."

"I'm not sure Marie's going to leave with Chris still here."

Garrett pursed her lips and thought for a moment, her index finger tapping on her chin. "I have an idea. Let me go check on Chris myself. I'll meet the two of you at the ICU."

* * *

Marie fidgeted in her seat. "What's the matter, Danni, is something wrong with Chris?"

"No." Danni hung up the direct line to the ICU. "Dr. Trivoli is discharging Chris from the ICU. She wants us to wait here and then accompany them to Chris's new room."

"That's good, isn't it?"

"Very good." Danni patted Marie's shoulder.

The automatic doors sprang into action, and Marie's mouth dropped open at the sight of Garrett Trivoli spouting off orders as she moved ever forward, stopping for no one in her path. Danni tried desperately not to laugh at the sight of the unit's charge nurse running after Garrett.

"I'm moving my patient, Clarisse, whether you like it or not. It's my drug of choice, and I'm going to see that she gets what's best for her."

"What do you mean, your drug of choice?" Clarisse said. "I've got a whole list of drugs that can't be given anywhere else in this hospital but on my unit."

"I told you before," Garrett's strong voice replied, "it can't be given in your ICU and I'm taking her to someplace that it can."

"I'll... I'll..." Clarisse was showing obvious signs of being winded.

"Clarisse, you're going to have a heart attack," a co-worker called out. "It's her patient. Let her do what she wants."

"She's right. You seem to forget who the doctor here is. It's me, and I'm doing what's best for my patient. End of story. Do I make myself clear?" Garrett cast an evil eye at the nurse.

Clarisse skidded to a stop. "I understand perfectly, Dr. Trivoli." She turned around and headed back into the unit, offering an opinion in a low voice.

"I heard that," Garrett called out. "You're wrong. The 'R' for my middle initial does not stand for 'Royal-pain-in-the-ass.'"

The automatic doors closed, and a muffled scream could be heard coming from inside the unit.

Marie chuckled. "Oh my, she is a card. I'll say that for her."

Danni nodded. "That she is."

* * *

"Chris, you look so pale."

"If you start babying me, I'll get Dr. Trivoli to take me back to the ICU." Chris looked at her lover. "I understand it was your fault I got the best damned surgeon in the building to work on me." Her voice softened as she brought Marie's hand to her mouth and kissed it. "Thanks, Marie. I love you."

Marie blushed at the blatant display of affection. "Stop that. Someone will see."

"Someone already has," Chris tipped her head toward the two women standing outside the door, but her eyes never left her lover.

* * *

"Chris seems to be looking better already."

"Yes, she does. Hand-holding is the best medicine I could have ordered for her." Garrett found Danni's hand and squeezed it gently. "Provided it's with the right person, of course."

"You've got that right," Danni whispered, gently returning the gesture. "Let's give them some privacy."

"Good idea. I'll tell the nurses that if Chris needs anything else, she'll ask for it."

Danni smiled, seeing the first hint of a sense of romance coming to the surface of Garrett's demeanor.

* * *

Brie paced a little faster with each ring that went unanswered. Finally, her spirit lifted when the rhythmic noise stopped.

"Hello."

The sleepy-sounding voice set off a sense of alarm. "Danni, are you feeling all right? Are you sick?"

"Brie?"

"Who else?"

"Of course, who else," Danni said aloud. "No, I'm fine. Actually, now that I think about it, I am a little sick to my stomach, but I'm getting used to it. Why do you ask?"

"You sound hoarse."

"You mean more so than normal when I'm just waking up?"

"Yes."

"Could be that I was a little vocal in court the other day."

"Court? You were in court?"

"Brie, it's nothing for you to get worried about. Garrett and I got summoned for a rape trial."

"Rape trial?" Brie gasped. "Someone we know?"

"No, a patient we worked on."

"Thank God."

"The way the defense attorney directed his questions, you would have thought Gar was the one on trial."

"Sounds like it was hell."

"Yes, it was. It's still plaguing us, even now. That, and the lack of sleep after that disaster on the Parkway." Danni's voice trailed off. "Sis, was there a reason why you called?"

"I'm going to be in town later tonight, and I thought maybe I could meet that surgeon of yours."

"Gee, I don't know. Gar is already asleep." Danni sighed. "I'm not much better. This court thing really drained both of us."

"You are taking care of yourself, aren't you? I mean, you don't want to be losing any weight right now."

"No way, sis. I'm starting to fill out my flight suit quite nicely. Don't worry. I've been getting enough exercise to keep those few extra pounds of muscle I've picked up since I teamed up with Garrett."

Unsure of what to say, Brie contemplated that thought.

"Hey, Brie. I think I really need to rest for a while. I've been on the go for the last thirty-six hours or so."

"Go back to sleep and rest. You take care of yourself—and Garrett too, mind you."

"Sure, sis. Talk to you soon."

Even though the conversation had ended, Brie was hesitant to release the phone from her grasp. Over and over, she replayed the dialogue of the last few minutes in her head. As more of the pieces fit together, a certain air of smugness came to her face.

"Danni, Danni, Danni." Brie hung up the phone. "I've really got to let Mother know about your little situation. Otherwise, she's going to have a bird getting two grandchildren in the same year."

A devilish grin came to Brie's face. "This may go over better in person. Good thing I'm meeting Mother for lunch next week." She savored the thought as she absentmindedly rubbed her hand over her distended abdomen.

"Yes, my little one, you're going to have a bastard cousin. I can't wait to see Mother's face when she finds out her Danielle is going to give her everything she wants, but in the wrong order. I'll be your favorite for sure then, won't I, Mother?"

* * *

Startled, Garrett woke to darkness. Dreaming about her experiences in the courtroom had given her a less than restful sleep.

"Too many questions." Garrett pulled her fingers through long strands of unruly hair and set her feet in motion. "And they always come down to sex."

She moved out of her room and down the hall, stopped outside Danni's bedroom and peered through the open door. She saw Danni sprawled under the covers.

"Danni?" Garrett waited, but when no answer came, she turned away. If only there were someone she could talk to who would understand her mixed-up feelings. Garrett's mind went blank for a moment, and then an idea came to her.

* * *

The sounds of the locks clicking into place stirred Danni from her sleep. She opened her eyes and focused on the bedside clock. It was nearly midnight. She burrowed back into her pillow, only to be roused again by the rumbling of an engine. In an instant, she was out of her bed. By the time she got to the window, she could barely make out the set of taillights driving down the street.

Danni's shoulders slumped as she thought of the pain Garrett was in. "Please, keep Garrett safe and help her to weather this storm."

* * *

After donning a set of scrubs, Garrett slipped into the first empty surgical arena she could find. The aura of the room slowly seeped into her being as she thought of all her patients over the years. Building on simple procedures, Garrett had honed her skills and confidence to the point where life-and-death battles were commonplace. Now, after a few vague, inquiring questions about her life, all of that was coming undone. Garrett wondered what her patients would think of their surgeon now, if they were privy to her sentiments.

"There's one way to find out." Garrett sighed, then left in search of answers.

* * *

Chris looked up at the silhouette before greeting her visitor. "Hello, Doctor. I thought only students keep these late hours. You didn't have someone up in the OR, did you?"

"No." Garrett fiddled with the IV line. "Are you doing all right?"

"Better than expected. Thanks, Doctor. I appreciate it. But it looks to me like you've got something weighing on your mind. I guess that goes with the job, doesn't it?"

"I believe it does." Garrett motioned to Chris's abdomen. "Mind if I take a look while I'm here?"

"Why even ask? You know me inside and out. Almost as good as Marie, except she'll tell you she doesn't know me at all, sometimes." Chris's thin lips formed a smile.

"I guess that comes from living together." Garrett contemplated the thought as she moved the covers off the woman's torso. "Say, Chris, how did you and Marie ever get together?"

"I held my breath and waited her out." Chris laughed, more to herself than out loud. "I wasn't the kind to strike up a conversation. I guess she knew it, too. It took her nearly a whole month before she spoke to me."

"What did she say?"

"She asked me what I was using for bait."

"Bait?" Garrett quirked an eyebrow.

"I was sitting with a fishing pole in my hand."

"Was it love at first sight?" Garrett tried to sound nonchalant with her question.

Chris bit down on her lower lip and stared up at the ceiling. "In my heart, I knew it was love, even before we talked. Now my head, that was a different matter."

"You went with your heart, then?"

"Every time. It has a funny way of knowing what it needs."

"Then you never regretted…"

"Life's too short for regrets. Look at me. I don't regret you being here when I came in. Why should you regret something that reaches out and saves your life?"

"I'm not following you."

"Love, Doctor. Love. It can get you through the low times and help keep you grounded when the world keeps pushing you higher." Chris pointed at Marie. "She's my anchor. She keeps me from running aground in high seas, and she stands waiting for me like a homing beacon when I'm sailing off on a tangent."

Garrett focused on the incision site, and then replaced the dressing. "This seems to be healing nicely. Maybe in a day or so I can send you two home. What would you say to that?"

"Thank you, that's what I'd say. I'm truly grateful."

"Thanks, Chris. You and Marie have been wonderful patients to take care of."

"You're welcome, but it wasn't our doing to be here. But if I had to be, I'm glad it was you and that little blonde nurse taking care of us."

"Danni." Garrett smiled as she said the name.

"Yes." Chris smiled back. "Marie was telling me how you and she stood watch over us the first night. I appreciate that."

"I only do it for special patients." Garrett's eye contact conveyed her message. "Thanks for talking to me. I'm going to think about what you said."

"Don't mention it. I'm sure you'll know what's right, if you follow your heart."

"You," Garrett said and pointed at Chris, "get some sleep."

"And what are you going to do?"

"I'm going to go find a quiet place and listen to my heart."

Chapter 21

Throwing back the covers, Garrett sat up and scrubbed her face with her hands before picking up the pager that had jolted her from a sound sleep.

"What the hell?" She pushed off the bed and crossed the room to open her door. "Danni, we've got a flight."

"I'm coming, I'm coming." Danni yawned. "Why don't we just sleep in these suits, we're called out so often."

"Because they're too hard to get off to go to the bathroom, that's why." Garrett pulled on her flight suit as she exited the bathroom and headed for the stairs.

"Oh, yeah, right." Danni picked up her pace, stepping into the legs of her flight suit, then into her boots. She quickly tied the laces and dashed for the stairs. "Hey, wait for me."

* * *

"Whoa, doggies! Look at that." Cowboy's voice broke like an adolescent boy's. "Doc, Danni, look out your window. You're not going to believe this one."

Garrett craned her neck. "I can't see anything but a red glow."

"That glow is coming from all the vehicles down there. Where's the..." Danni moved, trying to see more. "Jeez, I hope they don't expect us to get to him there."

"What? Where?" Garrett stretched to see out of Danni's window.

"I don't think I'm up for this one."

"Danni." Garrett's voice showed her frustration. "Give me some idea of what we're going into."

"You've got to see this one for yourself."

"Don't you dare unbuckle that seatbelt." Cowboy glared into his rearview mirror. "We'll be on the ground in less than a minute. You can see all you want then."

Once on the ground, Danni got up from her seat as Garrett slid the door open.

"Holy shit." Garrett was dumbstruck at the rescue scene before her.

Perched precariously halfway up a huge tree was a small compact car. It looked like the vehicle had left the road at the top of the hill, gone airborne, and been skewered through both the front and rear windows by a long, thick branch.

"This is going to be one for the books." Garrett stepped out of the helicopter. "Standing here isn't getting our job done. Let's go find out who's in charge of this scene."

Danni followed Garrett's lead, her mouth still agape.

*   *   *

"Don't worry. We'll have him down any minute, Doc." The man in the white helmet stepped around them to offer more direction.

"Get that damned ladder into position," the scene commander ordered over his vehicle's loudspeaker."Bring them as close as you can, but don't let them touch." He drew the microphone away from his lips. "The last thing I want is to have two ladder trucks stuck together after this damned rescue is over." He keyed his mic. "Yeah, that's it. Work the pulley system off the lower of the two ladders. And make sure everyone climbing is secured with their own safety belts. I'm not adding to the list of trauma patients tonight."

Danni tugged at Garrett's sleeve. "Are we going to…"

"Climb up there?" Garrett finished Danni's sentence.

The scene commander spun toward them. "Don't be silly. My guys will lower him before that tree has a mind to let go. No offense, but I don't want any more weight up there than necessary. I've got my littlest monkeys climbing now." He turned and pointed to the two thin-as-a-rail rescuers clambering up the ladders. "You'll get your chance to play doctor as soon as we get them over to the triage area."

"Sounds good to me," Danni said.

"Me, too. Let's wait over there." Garrett led the way. "He's going to be full of glass. We'd better make sure we have our heavy-gauge gloves on."

"I never leave home without them," Danni said, pulling the gloves from her pockets. In the process, a small vial of solution emerged with them. Oops! She had forgotten she had that in there. Danni pushed it back into her pocket.

Within minutes, the patient was disconnected from the rope system and carried across the rough terrain. The group of rescuers didn't stop until they were well out of the danger zone and the patient was placed on the helicopter's stretcher.

The man in the lead gave his report. "He's bleeding from somewhere on his face. I can't get it to stop."

One look at the blood-soaked clothing of the rescue personnel was all that Garrett needed to see. If something weren't done to stop the bleeding soon, their patient would die.

"Get another IV line established with Ringer's running wide open."

Garrett muscled her way into the group of concerned EMS personnel. "Shine those lights on his face. Let's get a look at this wound." She lifted the pile of absorbent dressings from his face. Coagulated blood clung to the gauze. As fast as she blotted the area, more blood appeared. It seemed to be gushing out of every pore in the area around his right eye.

Danni looked up from her ministrations with the IV tubing to see several shocked faces. "What's wrong?"

Garrett made eye contact with Danni. Without saying a word, she conveyed the seriousness of the patient's injury.

The man's right eye protruded from its socket. With the massive amounts of blood being lost, the injury looked horrendous.

"Artery?"

"No, the blood keeps coming from the whole area." Garrett blotted at the raw flesh.

"The IV is in and running wide open."

"Do we have lidocaine with epinephrine in our drug bag?"

"Lidocaine with epi..." Danni thought for a moment. "We don't carry that drug. Only the plastic surgery guys use it. But I know where we can get some."

"The suturing room in the ER?" Garrett asked.

"No, a lot closer than you think." Danni reached into her pocket and produced a vial. "Would twenty milliliters be enough?"

"Yes, that just might be enough. Get me a syringe and a couple of needles. Twenty-five gauge, if you have them. We're going to use an old plastic surgery trick to stop this blood loss."

Garrett finished the last of the injections. "There, that should give us a chance to get him to the trauma center." She straightened and rolled her shoulders, trying to release the kink that was forming. "What's his pressure?"

The medic took another reading while Garrett studied the exposed eye and placed a moist gauze pad and a domed plastic shield over it for protection.

"BP is one hundred over seventy-six, heart rate is one hundred eighteen, and respirations twenty-four."

"There's nothing more we can do here." Garrett snapped off her bloodied gloves. "Okay, let's get him loaded for transport."

As fast as the words were out of her mouth, the rescuers acted on them.

"Danni, nice assist."

"Thanks." Danni's reply was little more than a whisper.

"Where did you come up with the vial?"

"Sometimes it pays to hang out in the ER when we're waiting to be paged." Danni let a smile spread across her face, content that she had everything Garrett could possibly need.

"Are you going to hang out today?"

"Somehow, I think sleep is more attractive."

"Me, too."

* * *

"That looks interesting, Mother."

"Yes, it does." Antoinette reached for her napkin and shook it delicately before placing it on her lap. "One should always entertain the eye to stimulate the palate, Breanna. I've told you that before, or was it Danielle?"

"You've taught us both a lot, Mother." Brie mimicked her mother's actions with the napkin. "It's a shame Danielle isn't here to show you how much she's learned."

"Yes." Antoinette sighed. "One day she's going to find her way in life just like you have, my dear." Her gaze dropped to her soon-to-be grandchild, and her smile grew more regal. "I'm so pleased with you. You're making a wonderful family for your father and me to enjoy." She reached over and grasped Brie's hand. "Oh, my! You'd think I'm the one expecting. You'll excuse me if I go visit the ladies' room, won't you?"

"Of course."

Antoinette placed her napkin on the table and stood up. "I promise I won't be long." The words were hardly out of her mouth, and she was already making her way through the tables.

Brie pulled her cell phone from her purse and punched in the numbers she knew by heart.

The ringing was replaced by a sleepy-sounding "H-hel-lo."

"It's nearly one in the afternoon and you're still sleeping? I thought you didn't work the night shift anymore."

"Don't. I'm with Gar, sleeping."

"Are you feeling all right? You're not sick, are you?"

"No. I haven't had a queasy stomach since the last time we spoke."

"And you're still in bed because..."

Danni laughed softly. "Gar and I were up and down so many times last night, I thought I'd never get any sleep."

"Is that good right now?" Brie couldn't hide the concern on her face when she saw her mother coming back to their table. The inquiring exchange of looks lasted only a moment before the young woman put a finger to her lips.

"Yeah, they said the calls to action would increase before they leveled off. Everybody tells us to enjoy it while we can."

Brie thought of her own sex drive during her pregnancies. "I've got to admit it, they're right." Brie's brows furrowed. "Is that snoring I hear?"

"Gar's snoring, to be exact."

Brie glanced cautiously over to her mother and grimaced. "Are you happy with this?"

"I'm liking it more and more. You might say I can't seem to get enough of it. I think it's wearing Garrett out, which is really surprising me, because Garrett can usually go all night long without a problem."

"You could kick back a little." Brie gulped, her eyes growing bigger as her right hand began to rub the side of her abdomen. "You don't have to go all the way every time."

"Are you kidding me? That little signal goes off, and I know Gar will be coming in a minute, banging on my door trying to get me up and ready for action. I guess we're getting more physical than Gar is used to, just standing around in that operating room all day."

Brie eyes grew bigger. "I-I don't know what to say. I've never found myself in that position." She grimaced again, this time moving forward in an attempt to ease the cramping she felt.

"I can tell you what I'm going to do. I'm going to grin and bear it." Danni's soft laughter floated over the phone. "Hey, Brie, I'm really tired right now. If you just called to chat, can we do it later? I'd like to get some more rest before we're up and at 'em again."

"Bye." Brie pulled the phone away from her ear and stared at it, refraining from looking across the table at the tight-lipped face waiting for more information.

"With whom were you conversing, Breanna?"

"I thought I'd give Danni a call to find out how she was doing."

"And how is Danielle?"

"She didn't really say much."

"What was her excuse? Was she too busy working again?"

Brie gathered her composure. "She wasn't working, Mother."

"Finally, the girl has come to her senses. I've told her time and time again to do more than work all the time."

"Actually," Brie said, trying to sound as nonchalant as possible, "she was sleeping after being with that surgeon of hers."

"What's his name?"

"Garrett." Brie glanced over to see if her mother had heard her. "It seems the man is tiring her out."

"I thought she was off that dreadful night shift. What could possibly bring her to the point of exhaustion and snoring into the phone when you're trying to talk to her? You did say you heard snoring didn't you?"

"Yes, I did, but it wasn't Danni snoring."

"I don't understand. Who else would be there?" Antoinette watched as the smile grew on Brie's face.

"Danni told me it was Garrett. Now do you believe me, Mother?" Brie savored the startled look on her mother's face. "First the morning sickness at Christmas time, and now the unbridled sexual urges."

"Sex?" Antoinette's eyes grew bigger. "I can't believe…"

"Danni's pregnant," Brie said triumphantly. "I'd say she's right in step with her second trimester, according to my pregnancy book."

Antoinette took a moment to gather her senses. "Where did I go wrong? She knows my wishes. First, she was to find a doctor, get married, and then have children." The matriarch wiped her mouth with the napkin then tossed it down on the table. "Get the check, Breanna. We're going to Pittsburgh. I want to see it for myself."

"Mother." Brie reached out and caught her hand, stopping her from getting up. "I'm not sure that would be prudent right now. I mean, they didn't sound like they were receiving company anytime soon. Besides, if Danni is pregnant, you don't really want to upset her, do you? Think of the child—your newest grandchild."

The anger building up in Antoinette rivaled the power of an atomic bomb, but somehow she kept the explosion from triggering.

"You're right. My Danielle would never be the one responsible for this. I'll take my anger out on the real culprit, Dr. Garrett Trivoli." Her eyes glowed with fury. "Who does he think he is, to turn my eldest into a little trollop? I'll not accept any bastards in this family, I tell you. He'll marry her. Alive or posthumously," she seethed through gritted teeth, "and it won't make a bit of difference to me which way he chooses."

She worked hard to calm her outraged emotions. "I have a meeting in Pittsburgh next week. I'll just stop in at Danielle's hospital and talk to him when my daughter isn't around. We'll see who'll have the last laugh here." She pushed herself up from the table. "Come, Breanna, we have things to take care of."

As Brie watched her mother walk away, a self-righteous smile slowly painted itself across her face. "Danni, you can have all the fun you want with your surgeon, but I'm the matriarch-in-training now."

*   *   *

Garrett opened her eyes and took in her surroundings. The table lamps and recliner chair seemed out of place. Obviously she'd never made it to her bedroom, but had fallen asleep on the sofa.

She rubbed her eyes and stifled a yawn. Only then did she feel the strange sensation of movement, as something stirred against her body. Lifting her weary head, she saw blonde hair. The sight of Danni's body cuddled up to her own melted her heart. Garrett rested her head on the back of the couch, and her fingers gravitated toward silky tresses.

Danni nestled in, enjoying the closeness.

Chapter 22

The first thing to catch Danni's eye after opening her front door was the blinking light on the phone.

"More messages." She shook the water from her slicker before stepping inside. "I'll be glad when the April showers have ended." She sighed, knowing another month had slipped by. "Might as well get this over with." She hit the button.

"You have seventeen new messages. First message."

Beep!

"Hey, Danni. It's me, David. I'm returning your call. Guess I've missed you. I'll keep trying."

"That's what I'm afraid of, David. You'll keep trying," Danni said, as the next message started.

"I'll be leaving the hospital as soon as I check on a few things. I've got my pager with me, so if it goes off…"

"And you know it will," Danni quickly inserted.

"I'll meet you on the helipad. Oh, guess I should have said who this is. It's me, Gar."

Danni closed her eyes as a subtle smile graced her face.

Beep!

"Danni, it's me, David. I guess you're still not home."

Beep!

"Me again, David. Maybe we should just e-mail each other."

Beep!

"Danni, it's Brie. Great. You're not there, as usual. Well, I'm either in labor or I'm…" There was a distinct sound of a sharp intake of air on the tape, followed by a rapid exhalation. "Ow! That one was sharp. I sure hope this is one of those Braxton-Hicks things, or you're going to be an aunt sooner than we thought. I'll call you later and leave another message when I know for sure."

Danni massaged her temples. "That's my sister for you, Drama Queen to the very end."

Beep!

"David here, but I guess you're not. I'll try again."

Beep!

"It's David."

Danni stopped the messages. A quick scroll through her Caller ID log told her the rest of the calls were all David's. "Playing phone tag isn't going to do it. What I've got to tell you, I need to say face-to-face, just like I'll have to with Garrett."

Garrett seemed more contemplative now than ever before. Perhaps she was considering what to do after her fellowship, or where to go with her career. Danni prayed that somehow, in some way, she would be a part of it.

She picked up a pile of unopened letters addressed to Garrett and fanned through them. "I guess when you're as good as she is, you get recruited. I wonder what it would take to make her stay?" In her heart, Danni knew what she was willing to offer. The question was, would it make Garrett stay, or would it make her run like hell to get away? Like the woman who was bounding up the walk, the answer would come soon enough. For now, Danni chose to enjoy each moment she had with Garrett.

She placed the mail back on the table. "Are you ready to go shopping?"

"I'm not sure I'm ready, but I'm willing to drive." Garrett dangled the keys to her Blazer.

"Oh, good! More room to bring things home in."

Garrett rolled her eyes. "Why do I think this may not be a good thing?"

* * *

"It's going to be another one of those nights." Karen met the stretcher coming through the door. "Medic Four, knee injury, right?"

"Minor fender bender and no seat belt. His knee hit the dashboard. Nothing else hurts, and his vitals are fine."

"Okay, let's see..." Karen spun around and looked at the board. "Take him into Room Ten. I'll have the doctor see him in a minute or two." She looked around for an available nurse. "Rosie, can you take this one?"

"Not really. We just got a report of two more coming in, a Level One from an MVA, and the other patient is one of the rescuers."

"Come on." Karen motioned for the medic to follow her. "I'll take you myself."

"Looks like it's going to be a busy one." Rosie passed by on her way to the trauma rooms. "What I wouldn't give to be working with Danni tonight."

* * *

"Traumas in the department. Traumas in the department."

Dr. René Chabot rounded the corner into the trauma room. "Okay, everybody ready, eh?" He looked over his team, then grabbed a lead apron to put on. "Dr. Kreger, I'll take the Level One. You've got the second patient. I understand it's one of the rescuers."

The chief resident nodded and moved out into the hallway. "Anybody know what happened?"

"They didn't say. Can't be too bad, though. They were both coming in the same ambulance." Rosie looked up, surprised to see Danni, dressed in jeans and a pullover sweater. "Ooh, I like that."

"Fifty-two-year-old male, unrestrained driver of a single car into a utility pole. We initially found him unresponsive." Danni rattled on as they transferred the man from one stretcher to another. "Loss of consciousness lasted approximately two minutes. Heart rate is at fifty, showing some PVCs on the monitor, with occasional runs of irregular heartbeats lasting for a minute or so. His BP is one hundred and ten over seventy-two and respirations at a rate of sixteen."

"Thank you." René looked questioningly at Danni. "New uniform?"

"No, we were shopping when we saw the accident happen."

"We?" René peered out into the hall.

"She'll be coming." Danni hid a grin at the sounds of commotion coming down the hall. "Speak of the devil. Here she comes now."

"I told you I don't need this," Garrett seethed. "I can walk perfectly well."

"Sure you can, Doc. Just humor me, okay?"

"Humor you? You want me to humor you? How about you humoring me and letting me out of this damned thing?" Garrett batted the arm of the wheelchair.

Danni grinned. "They always say doctors make the worst patients. Sounds like I'm needed elsewhere." She turned just in time to see a sopping-wet, jean-clad Garrett Trivoli being whisked past her.

Rosie shook her head vehemently. "I'm sure glad I'm not the one to get her out of those clothes."

A round of subdued snickers circulated through the room. "Okay, everyone." René cleared his throat. "Let's get to our jobs, eh?"

* * *

"Son of a bitch! What kind of idiot would put a goddamned hole in the middle of the fucking street?"

Karen stuck her head into the room. "Is there anything that I can do to…" Her eyes bugged out at the sight of Garrett tugging at wet denim. "Dr. Trivoli?"

"What?" The irritated voice was matched with a set of equally menacing eyes. "Can't you see I'm busy?"

"Could you stop cussing out the world? Think of the example you're setting for the rest of the patients." Karen's hands were on her hips, her right foot tapping. "Who's your nurse?"

"You call that perverted little man back here, and I'll send him on another wild-goose chase. I'm not letting him cut my jeans off."

Karen snickered. "Come on, let me give you a hand. I bet Danni would just love to help you out of these. Where is she, anyway?"

"Over there, filling out the report with the medics."

The nurse looked at Garrett's swollen ankle. "What the heck did you do to this? Use it to kick some fool lawyer when no one was looking?"

"No, but I think that would have been more to my liking."

"Cut out that pouting," Karen scolded Garrett. "Now tell me what really happened, and watch your language, young lady."

"I was going over to the accident scene after parking the Blazer. All of a sudden, I was knee deep in a blasted puddle."

"Welcome to Pittsburgh, Garrett. You've just been sucked into one of our famous potholes."

"Pothole? It felt like I stepped into a crater in a minefield."

"We've been known to have small cars swallowed whole in them." Karen suppressed a grin.

"Why would they let them get that big? Doesn't anybody see them when they start?" Garrett winced as Karen gently eased the clinging denim over the injured limb.

"You know, Doc, not everyone sees things the same way. For example, it takes a little feeling or emotion to let some people know things are different, while others are oblivious to the activity going on around them. Take the way you and Danni have become friends over the last few months. Most people would think you two are very close friends."

"Of course we're close." Garrett bristled. "You work with a person long enough, you get to know them."

"I don't mean in that way. There's something different about the relationship the two of you have."

Garrett looked down at her discolored ankle, not one bit happy with its appearance. "That's because we live together, too. We both know what's going on in the other's life."

"Or think you do," Karen said. "Sometimes, I think you need to be hit with a railroad tie to wake up and see what's going on." She laid the jeans over the foot of the stretcher. "Doc, you can be so observant of the tiniest imperfection in someone's anatomy, but you don't see the amount of good that you being here does for her. I don't get it. Then again, maybe I just don't get you." Karen pulled the sheet up, covering the surgeon to her waist, but leaving the injured ankle visible. "You'd better start thinking about what's going to happen when this year is over. I swear, Garrett Trivoli, if you just leave without so much as a goodbye, I'll..." Karen hesitated. "I just don't. I don't know what she sees in you. But then again, who does when they're in—" Karen stopped abruptly at the sound of footsteps outside of the room.

"In what?" Garrett looked at Karen. "In here?"

Danni stuck her head into the room. She gave a pained expression at the sight of Garrett's ankle. "Ouch."

"Yeah, too bad her ankle isn't as thick as her head. She'd be just fine, then." Karen bustled out of the room. "I'll go get an attending to come look at that."

Danni stepped aside as Karen hustled out the door. "What's up with her?"

"I'm not sure. She was telling me about the car-swallowing potholes and then started to talk about friends and saying..." Garrett stopped short of finishing her thought out loud.

"What?"

"Nothing." Garrett shrugged it off, letting her attention gravitate back to her injury. "She thought my ankle looked bad."

"It does look nasty. Can you walk on it?"

Garrett tried to move her ankle, but every attempt was met with pain. Grudgingly, she pulled out her cell phone and handed it to Danni. "Here, you'd better call the Command Desk and notify them that we'll be out of service for a while."

* * *

"That's the fastest emergency room visit I've ever seen," Danni said as she headed for the exit doors. "Do you think we have a chance for the world record?"

"Yeah, right alongside the craters you Pittsburghers grow. Using these crutches is worse than walking. Now my armpits are starting to hurt." Garrett halted her forward motion after clearing the door. "Hey, how'd you get my Blazer here?"

"The medics dropped me off when you were in Radiology. I thought it was better than taking a bus."

"Oh, that would have been fun." Garrett's reply was droll.

"Exactly. I figured you were in way over your head on the fun things today." Seeing no reaction, Danni pushed on. "Okay, let's get you home."

A puff of air ruffled Garrett's bangs. "I guess you're driving."

"I'd say so, and I've got the written orders signed by both Dr. Kreger and Dr. Potter to prove it."

"Traitors."

"They're just treating you like any other patient who walks into that emergency room."

"There you have it, the true nature of the beast. I didn't walk in. I was pushed in, and against my will, I might add."

"Be honest. Do you really think you could have walked?"

"I got myself out of that crater and over to the accident scene, didn't I?"

"True, but it took you the entire time the rest of us were working to extricate the patient from his vehicle."

A low-pitched growl came from Garrett's throat. "You try to walk in wet jeans, and we'll see how fast you move."

"Right. I talked to Dr. McMurray about your injur—I mean, your incapacitation—for a few days, and he suggested that I take some time off, too. You know, to relax a little."

"And keep an eye on me."

Danni crossed her arms over her chest. "Contrary to popular belief, I'm not a private duty nurse. Now, get into the Blazer before I have John come and help you in."

Garrett scowled. "I'm going." After maneuvering her body into the passenger seat, she started chuckling.

"Something funny?" Danni turned the key in the ignition. "Go ahead, spit it out."

"You know, there's something I've always wanted to say."

"What's that?" Danni asked apprehensively.

Garrett looked out the windshield, reining in the hint of a smile that threatened to blow her whole delivery. "Home, James."

* * *

By the next day, it was obvious that Garrett was in need of some space of her own. Being coddled wasn't her style. With Garrett's best interests in mind, Danni decided this was the perfect time to talk to David face-to-face.

"I didn't hear you come down the stairs."

"I'm getting better on these crutches than I'd like to admit." Garrett motioned toward the stove. "What are you making?"

"Pancakes and sausage. I thought I'd make you a good breakfast, since I'll be gone for the rest of the day." She hesitated before looking up to see Garrett's reaction.

"Oh." Garrett became more somber. "I guess I'm getting on your nerves."

"Don't be silly. I thought I'd give you some time to yourself and take care of a few things I've been putting off."

"Anything special?"

"I thought I'd visit Brie and my new niece, Katerina."

"New niece? When did that happen?"

"Last night, when you were dozing on the couch."

"You should have gone then."

"Didn't have to. Mark and my mother were at the hospital, and that's all Brie needed. Besides, I had more important things to worry about."

Garrett looked confused. "What?"

"You and that ankle of yours."

"Oh." Garrett took a deep breath and let it out. "Take all the time you need visiting with them. I'm doing pretty well. I haven't even taken any Percocet today." She looked away and mumbled. "Don't intend to, either, no matter how much it hurts."

"There is something else I wanted to take care of today."

"Just because I'm limited, that doesn't mean you have to be. Please, enjoy your time off. I'll feel worse if you don't."

"Okay."

Garrett played with her crutches. "So, what are you going to do?"

"I thought I'd drive down and see David. We've been playing phone tag a little too much lately."

A wave of regret filled Garrett. "Oh."

Danni picked up on Garrett's shifting mood and jumped to another subject. "You should do some reading."

"Yeah." Garrett's words were clipped. "Reading." She nodded, then moved toward her seat at the table.

"Gar…"

"Have a good time. Don't worry about me."

"Will you be all right?"

"I can't get into too much trouble with my leg up and a magazine in my hand, can I? You go ahead, I'll be fine. Maybe I'll spend some time planning a few activities for the Lone Survivors." Garrett picked up her utensils and started to cut her food. "When were you thinking of leaving?"

"Soon. I thought I'd throw a few things into a bag and leave after I clean up the breakfast dishes."

"Bag?" Garrett froze.

"You know, change of clothes, toiletries. I may not be home until late, or possibly not until tomorrow sometime."

Garrett didn't move a muscle.

"Gar?"

"Yes?" Garrett stared at the food on her plate.

"I know that you like figuring out puzzles. Why don't I give you my journal to read? Maybe you can make some sense out of the pieces of dreams I've written down."

Garrett shrugged. "I can give it a try."

"I'll bring it down for you before I leave." Danni was relieved to know that a small part of her would still be keeping Garrett company.

* * *

"Damn!" Danni smacked her hand on the steering wheel. "I forgot to bring my journal down for Garrett." She looked at her surroundings. "Too late now. Another couple of miles and I'll be at David's hospital."

Her thoughts shifted to David. For months she'd been toying with an idea, and she was finally doing something about it.

"God, I hope he understands. It wouldn't be right to say anything to Gar before I talk to him." The image of the surgeon came to Danni's mind. "It's the only way she'll know what I want."

And what exactly was it that Danni wanted? One word loomed in the front of her mind. Right or wrong, she wanted Garrett's love. Danni only hoped David would understand that love wasn't something that could be turned on or off. Garrett Trivoli was the only one who could make her emotions come alive, and Garrett would forever hold Danni's heart in the palm of her skilled hand.

* * *

Garrett laid down her magazine and rubbed her eyes. On the table to her right were a bottle of water and a bowl of fruit. "You always know what I need, don't you, Danni?"

She picked up an orange and peeled it, letting its fragrance fill her nose. Then she broke off a piece and divided it into smaller segments. With each division, her mind drifted to how much like the orange she and Danni were. Each of them was a part of the whole, Each was an individual, yet both came together as though they were meant to be that way for life.

"What the hell am I thinking? It's obvious she's in love with David. Why else would she be headed down to meet him? I should be happy for her." Garrett shifted, uncomfortable with the thought, and reached for another magazine.

Chapter 23

"Hello. I was wondering if you might be able to help me. I'm a friend of Dr. David Beckman. Could you let him know that Danni Bossard is here to see him?"

"I'll let Dr. Beckman know."

"Thank you." Danni turned away from the receptionist to view the hospital lobby. The warm colors of the homespun fabrics took the edge off an otherwise impersonal area.

Now she knew why David wanted to practice here. He never had seemed to relish the big-city atmosphere. Danni noticed the motioning hand of the receptionist in her direction.

"Yes?"

"Dr. Beckman is in surgery, but he's asked that you be directed to his office. He'd like you to wait for him there."

"Thank you."

* * *

Garrett gingerly lowered her leg, letting it hover just off the floor as she positioned the crutches for support. Standing up, she worked the kink out of her back and winced.

"Damn, how long was I sitting there?" She looked at the clock on the hallstand. "It's only 1400, now what do I do? Maybe there's a book I can—" Garrett remembered her promise. "Danni's dream journal."

Garrett searched, but it was nowhere to be found. "I'll bet she forgot to bring it downstairs. I guess it's time for a bathroom break." Garrett headed toward the stairs. "Who knows, a change of scenery may even help my mood."

* * *

David's heart started racing when he saw Danni. How peaceful she looked, dozing in his office.

Without a word, he moved to her side and kissed her hair.

"Gar?"

The name took David by surprise.

"Sorry, David. I didn't mean to doze off."

"I'm sorry, too. My surgery took a little longer than I anticipated."

"That's okay, I'm used to it." Danni pushed herself up on her elbow. "Nothing is ever predictable once you start a procedure."

"Always the understanding one, aren't you?"

Danni looked up into his eyes, as if searching the man's very soul. "All we can do is try to be understanding of one another."

Unsettled, he looked away before moving to his desk. He flipped open his daily planner and studied it. "Why don't I make up for it with dinner tonight? I'll take you out to the best restaurant in town. We could even do a little dancing to start the night off. What do you say?"

"David, I didn't come here to go out."

"You don't have to be anywhere, do you?"

"No."

"Good." David took her hand and held it. "If you don't want to go dancing, we could take in a movie, or have a long, leisurely dinner filled with candlelight and conversation. Anything you want, Danni, just name it."

"Thanks for the offer." Danni bit at her lip.

He cast a wary eye in Danni's direction. "But...?"

"I came to talk."

"Then we'll do it over dinner."

"I don't think dinner would be a good idea." She searched his face for any semblance of understanding. "I was hoping you might be..."

"Hiring?" David's eyes lit up. "Are you thinking about coming here to work?" He spun around, took a few steps toward the door, then stopped and faced her again. "Have you seen our ER? I could show it to you right now."

"David, I'm not interested in leaving Pittsburgh. I've made a commitment to the Trauma Flight Team until the end of June."

"The end of the staff year."

"Yes."

"You know Trivoli won't stay. Someone of her caliber will have offers."

He was right, and Danni knew it. Garrett could go anywhere she wanted, moving on in her career and her life. In a matter of weeks, Danni could lose the one person she had truly come to love.

David studied Danni's sad expression. "Why don't you come here and team up with me in July? We could see more of each other then, like before. Who knows, we might even find out we like each other as more than friends."

"Thanks for the offer, but no thanks. We have so much going on with the flight team and the Lone Survivors group that we started this year. I don't know how..." She stopped talking and looked at David. "I don't want Garrett to go." Danni's voice was full of emotion. "I can't force her to stay, but I know she would if she realized how much it means to me. Or rather, how much *she* means to me." Danni looked away.

In all the years he'd known her, David had never seen Danni so emotional about anyone. Seeing her on the edge of breaking down brought tears to his eyes, and he reached out and wrapped his arms around her.

"It's all right, Danni." He rocked her gently, speaking in hushed tones. He had realized what she was trying to tell him. "You love her, don't you?"

"Yes." Danni averted her gaze. "She's touched my heart and my soul like no one ever has before. I'm sorry. I know that you thought we..."

"What I thought and what is are two totally different things. You have to choose what's right for you. No one else can."

"I've never had feelings of love for anyone in my life. Friends and friendships yes, but love?" Danni shook her head. "I never dreamed I'd feel that for another woman." She turned toward him cautiously. "I hope you're not angry."

David weighed his discomfort against the pain on Danni's face. In a split-second decision, he set aside his aching heart and searched for the right words.

"I had a friend in college who realized she was gay. It's not something you wake up one day and decide to do. It's something that takes time and a lot of work to come to terms with. I know you only speak what's in your heart." He tightened his arms around her. "How could I be angry because you didn't choose me?"

"Really?"

"Maybe a little bit. You know, I had this godawful crush on you the whole time I was in medical school, and all through my residency."

Danni looked into his eyes. "I'm sorry," she whispered. "I never realized."

"All I ever wanted was for you to be happy. If Garrett Trivoli makes you happy, then that's all I can ask for."

"If I told you I want to have her in my world for the rest of my life, loving her and sharing myself with her, that wouldn't upset you?"

"No, I'm just sorry it couldn't have been me."

"Thanks for being so understanding, David. I'd hate to lose you as a friend."

"Then what do you say I take you out to dinner?" He caught the glimmer of trepidation in her eyes and quickly countered. "As friends, Danni, strictly as friends. I'd like to hear all about the person who's captured your heart."

Seeing the sincerity in his eyes, Danni accepted the invitation. "All right, over dinner."

"Thanks."

* * *

Danni pushed open the door and let her eyes adjust to the light inside the bedroom. There was Garrett, the comforter pulled across her body, sleeping in Danni's bed. Danni couldn't help but smile. She ventured in for a closer look and found herself wondering what could have brought such a relaxed, peaceful look to Garrett's face.

Closing her eyes, she sent off a silent prayer. *Please, let it be me she's dreaming of.* Taking the journal from Garrett's loose grip, she placed it on the nightstand.

"Good night, my love," Danni whispered, brushing back a wayward wisp of hair from Garrett's face. Retreating in silence to the hallway, she closed the door and pondered her options. She looked from one end of the hall to the other. The couch, or Garrett's bed? It wasn't hard to choose.

* * *

Sleepy eyes popped open. "Danni?" Garrett raised her head, setting off a cascade of dark hair across the pillow she held firmly in her arms. She drew in a breath filled with Danni's scent, and her thoughts turned to the last thing she remembered before falling asleep.

"The journal." Garrett swept the hair out of her face. "Damn. I must have fallen asleep." Looking around, she spied the journal on the nightstand, but didn't remember putting it there She threw back the comforter and sat up, fumbling for her crutches. She slipped out of Danni's room and headed toward her own.

Bracing herself at the door, Garrett reached for the light switch. Like a scene out of Goldilocks and The Three Bears, a blonde was asleep in her bed. There was a peaceful expression on Danni's face, and she was wrapped around one of Garrett's pillows.

"Still hanging on to David, I see." Garrett gripped her crutches with white-knuckled fingers as a twinge of jealousy gnawed at her. "Wait a minute. It couldn't be David, otherwise, she'd have stayed with him." A smile slowly surfaced.

Danni pushed back tousled hair and focused on the woman in the doorway. "Gar?"

"That's who I was last time I checked." Garrett watched as a blush rose from Danni's neck, clear into her hairline.

"I-I..." Danni withdrew from the pillow and folded the covers back. She rubbed her arms to stave off the shivers as she slid out of the warm bed into the cool night air. "It was late when I got home, and you were already asleep in my bed. I didn't think you'd mind if I used yours." Danni looked at the disheveled bed, then back at Garrett. "I'm sorry."

Garrett's eyes were fixed on Danni's chest.

Danni looked down, startled to see protruding peaks, veiled only in cotton. "Oh!" She hastily folded her arms over her chest. Embarrassed, she glanced at Garrett in time to see a dark eyebrow edging upward. Danni set a course for the door. "Excuse me, please."

Like twins in a mirror, each woman inadvertently matched the moves of the other, first stepping to one side, then the other. After their third attempt, Danni stopped and glared, sending a silent but direct message.

Garrett turned sideways, filling up half of the doorway, and waited for Danni to move. Halfway through, Danni's hardened nipples grazed ever so slightly against Garrett's body. Something stirred inside Danni, and the ache that followed caught her completely off guard. She hurried past and nearly ran to her bedroom.

Garrett looked at the recently vacated bed, then down the hall to Danni's bedroom door. "What the hell?"

Chapter 24

"Whoa! Close that door, young lady." Danni glared at her human cargo. "Can't you wait until I park?"

Obediently, Garrett closed the door, and nervous laughter bubbled out around her reply. "Sorry, I guess I should wait. I sure don't want to get hurt again."

"I didn't think so." Danni maneuvered the Blazer into a parking space.

"You handle this vehicle pretty well for someone who's used to driving little cars."

"I'll consider that a thank-you, by the way." Danni smiled and applied the brake.

"Sorry. I didn't realize how much I missed being at the hospital until René called last night. You can only read so much about new surgical procedures without wanting to get back into the action."

"I know how badly you want to be here, but remember I'm only working a half-shift in the ER today. When I'm done, we're both going home."

"Yes, Mother. I have my pager, just in case you feel the need to track me down and make sure I'm being good." Garrett grinned cheekily and opened the door.

"You're a brat." Danni gave Garrett a wry smile as she watched her slide out of the seat, then reach for her crutches. "Remember, if you're a good girl maybe I'll bring you again tomorrow."

"What?" Garrett's head snapped up.

"You heard me. I volunteered to help again tomorrow. I thought maybe you'd like to come and hang out again for a while. So take it easy."

"I will." Garrett leaned on one crutch and reached into the back seat with her free hand.

"What are you looking for?"

"René asked me to bring my flight suit today."

"And he needs your flight suit for what?" Danni looked suspicious. "I think you have plans for that suit."

"Not other than letting him try it on, I don't. He wants to see if he feels comfortable working in it, that's all. He's thinking of staying on after his fellowship and being part of the team." Garrett crossed her heart. "I swear."

"I don't know. You were pretty antsy the last day or two at home." Danni regarded her. "How can I be sure?"

"Look, no boots. Okay?" Garrett held up the folded flight suit, then shoved it under her arm. "You know the rules. Steel-toed boots are part of the uniform. I couldn't get that boot on if I tried." Danni's doubtful look prompted Garrett to continue. "Okay, I did get it on, but I couldn't get the laces tied."

Danni tried not to laugh. "All right, I trust you. Now, go have yourself some fun with René. Just don't forget about going home."

"I won't." Garrett stepped back from the door then looked at Danni for a long moment. "Danni?"

"Yes?"

"Thanks."

"You're welcome." Danni shooed her away with a flick of her hand.

* * *

"Good morning, Dr. Potter."

"Good morning, Danni." Jamie shuffled through the charts in her hands. "How is tall, dark, and dumped-by-a-pothole doing? Is she still mad at me, the pothole, and Pittsburgh in general?"

"If I were you, I wouldn't let her hear you call her that. She's still pretty angry at the pothole, not to mention at you for grounding her on crutches."

Jamie rolled her eyes. "If only that was my only problem in life."

"Yeah, right." Danni gave her a knowing look. "Actually, she's doing better. The discoloration is pretty much gone, but the swelling is still there. I keep telling her to give it time."

"Don't worry, Garrett will be good as new and wreaking havoc before we know it."

"Isn't that the truth."

"Are you here to visit or work?"

"Work. Where do you need me?"

Jamie turned to the assignment board. "Looks like Nan has you covering Trauma Room One."

"Imagine that." Danni's voice hinted at sarcasm. "Let me guess, there's one coming in."

"One a minute for the next four hours. Why don't you get ready?"

"Gee thanks, Jamie. You always know how to make me feel right at home." Danni returned Jamie's smile with one of her own and headed down the hall.

*　*　*

Garrett felt a comfortable ease settle over her as she stepped into her office for the first time in days. All was right with her world as soon as she looked at the picture of her brother.

She placed her crutches off to the side and sat down at the desk. Immediately, her mind began churning with the events of the last few days. Her thoughts were cut off, however, when the door opened.

"Dr. Trivoli, I presume? The rumors of your death have been greatly exaggerated."

"Cut it out, René. I'm stir-crazy from being at home with my foot up on pillows for the last week or more. Don't put me in a pine box, too." Garrett's initial glare softened and her mouth turned up into a smile.

"See?" he said, pointing. "I knew I could get you to smile."

"Yes, you did. So, what makes you so full of life today?"

He clutched at his heart with both hands. "My wife and babies! They come home today from Canada." His face became somber as he eyed Garrett. "Let me tell you, my friend, you have never appreciated love until you don't have it at your fingertips anymore. Being away from someone you love makes you want them all the more."

Garrett's eyes drifted to the photograph of her brother, but Danni's image filled her mind. Stunned, Garrett didn't know what to think. "I... ah..." She sighed. "René."

"Yes."

"Here's that flight suit for you to try on."

"Thanks." He held the suit up. "Would you mind if I wore it for a little while? To see if I like the feel?"

"Sure, go ahead. Just don't go home with it."

"You are my friend, eh, are you not?"

"You're really thinking of doing some flying, huh?"

"It's an option I'm considering." René held the suit up against his long frame. "How about you? Have you decided where you'll be practicing next year?"

Garrett's face became an emotionless blank. "No, I haven't."

"Surely you've had offers."

"Lots of them."

"Well? Which hospital has made the best offer?"

"I wouldn't know what any of them have offered." She looked away. "I haven't opened them yet."

"Garrett, Garrett, Garrett." René shook his head. "Our fellowship year is almost over."

"I know. I've been busy."

The silence in the room weighed heavily on her, and the pensive look on René's face added to the seriousness of the moment. Finally, she couldn't stand it another second. "Okay, I'll start thinking about it." She gave him the barest hint of a smile as she motioned to the flight suit in his hands. "Now, go try it on."

"All right. Thanks."

"Don't mention it. I think I'll go scare a few nurses." She pushed herself up from the chair, grabbed her crutches, and headed for the door. "I'll see you up in the unit for rounds."

*　*　*

Antoinette Bossard slipped her car keys into her handbag and shouldered it. No surgeon was going to slap her in the face by encouraging her daughter's moral turpitude. Danni had always bucked the guidance she was offered in the past, but this time was going to be different. The Bossard matriarch was going to make things right again.

She crossed the street and started down the walkway toward the hospital. Eager to find her man, Antoinette stopped the first medical-looking person she could find.

"Excuse me. Could you tell me where I might find Dr. Garrett Trivoli?"

The woman in blue scrubs and a lab coat looked directly at her. "That one's nothing but trouble, lady. Do yourself a favor and find somebody else."

The snide reply didn't faze Antoinette. She asked again, intent on getting an answer. "Dr. Trivoli, please."

"Try the helipad. Trivoli's the only surgeon I know who operates in a flight suit." With that said, the embittered woman continued on her way.

"Trouble, hmm?" Antoinette fumed to herself. "You have no idea." She altered her course and headed for the helipad.

* * *

It seemed pretty poor planning to have a helicopter approaching while one was still on the pad. Danni's concern grew as each second ticked by, until the familiar sound of long strides and metal taps came from around the corner.

"Hey, Cowboy." Danni greeted the pilot with a hug.

"There's my Danni." Cowboy wrapped his long arms around her. "Oops. Sorry about the helmet."

"That's okay."

Playfully, he tugged at her paper trauma gown. His smile grew bigger with each catch of the breeze that made the gown expand around Danni's small frame. "I can see why you don't wear these around a helicopter. You could hide a small army in there."

"You should see Garrett in one."

"No, thanks. I'd rather see the two of you in those flight suits and back in my helicopter." His expression turned somber. "When are you coming back?"

Danni reached out and pulled him down to her height. "Soon. We'll be back real soon." She placed a kiss on his cheek.

A blush crept up Cowboy's face. "I don't deserve that."

"I just wanted to let you know we miss you, too. Although, I'm sure Gar would have just shaken your hand."

Cowboy snorted. "Someday, that woman's going to wake up and surprise us all with the size of her heart."

"I'm praying for that more than anything." Danni lowered her gaze. "I hope it happens soon."

Cowboy lifted her chin with his finger until they made eye contact. "Trust me, it will." Cowboy looked away. "I'd better get this bird up in the air if you want that pad for a trauma. I'll talk to you later." He walked toward the hospital.

"Hey!" Danni called. "I thought you were going to move the helicopter."

"I'll be right back. I have to let that last coffee out."

* * *

"Why, I never..." Antoinette was shocked by the obvious public display of affection. "Were they never taught manners? Don't they realize that some things should be left to the privacy of their own homes?" She looked away, appalled at the continued display. A second later, her eyes returned to the couple, and she found herself staring as she ventured closer.

"Oh, my God! Is that Danielle?" Antoinette scanned over her daughter's full form. "Breanna was right, she is pregnant." She focused on the man in the flight suit who was entering the building. "I've got you now, Dr. Trivoli."

With renewed purpose, she doubled back toward the main entrance. It was time to put an end to this, once and for all.

* * *

When Rob Kreger caught sight of the flight-suited figure headed his way, he squinted, not believing what he was seeing. "Dr. Trivoli? Is that you?"

"And who else would I be?" Chabot made his French-Canadian accent heavier than usual.

Rob rubbed the back of his neck. "You sure don't look like René Chabot, not dressed like that."

René squared his shoulders and stroked the sleeves of the flight suit. "Don't you think I do the suit more justice than she does?"

"I think she fills it out better in certain places."

A matronly, well-dressed woman was coming down the hallway. Rob smiled at her, but she didn't seem to take note of his greeting. He watched her for a moment before she turned away. "Speaking of which, does she know you're wearing it?"

Chabot laughed. "Hey, it's with her blessing. I'm not sure she'll ever let anyone into her pants again, though."

Dr. Kreger shuddered. "I don't want to go there."

"Speaking of going, I've got to get back to the OR." He paused. "Remember, you're assisting me tomorrow morning. I'll see you then, no?"

"I won't forget." Kreger watched his colleague head for the elevators.

"Hey, Rob."

"Huh?" Rob spun around. "Danni, hi."

"Have you seen Garrett?"

"Not lately, but René did say something about meeting Garrett in the OR."

"Thanks."

* * *

Hearing her daughter's voice stopped Antoinette dead in her tracks. Recovering, she hurried along the hall to the elevators.

"The cad. I can't believe he was joking with a colleague about 'getting into her pants'—with Danielle only a few steps away! I swear that man has no couth, and obviously no morals." She strode into the empty elevator and pushed the button marked for the operating rooms. "I can't believe that friend of his, outright lying to my daughter."

She could feel her raging temper getting the best of her and fought to control it.

"Garrett Trivoli sounds just like my father-in-law, the French-Canadian peasant. And after I've fought so long and hard to have everyone think of us as simply French."

* * *

Rob looked toward the elevators. "Hey, Danni, did you see that older lady hanging out in the hall?"

"Not really, why?"

"Nothing." He thought for a moment. "You know, if I were a gambling man, I'd bet she was up to no good."

"Should I give Security a call?"

"No, I'm probably reading too much into it."

Danni replayed the brief glimpse of the woman she had seen getting on the elevator. She reminded her of her mother, but that couldn't be right. What would her mother be doing in Pittsburgh? Danni reconsidered the possibilities. *No, I'm sure she's with Brie and the baby.*

"Come on, Rob. The next trauma's going to be landing soon. We might as well meet it at the door."

"Yeah, might as well," he said. "It's better than standing around here being paranoid."

* * *

Antoinette bustled off the elevator and looked at the sign. "'Operating Room, Authorized Personnel Only.' Damn it!" Undeterred by this obstacle, she addressed the first hospital employee she saw. "You, there. I need to find Dr. Trivoli."

"If it's about a family member, perhaps I could—"

She glared at the woman. "Of course it's about a family member. Now, where can I find Dr. Trivoli?"

"I saw Dr. Trivoli and Dr. Chabot outside the doctor's lounge just a moment ago."

"Which way to that lounge?"

"Down the hall and to your left. But you can't go in there," she called after Antoinette, who was already stalking away.

* * *

"There you are," René said. "I've been looking for you all over. I thought we were going to do rounds together."

"What, no greeting?" Garrett leaned on her crutches with her back against the wall outside the doctor's lounge. She gave René a casual glance. "You want to get right down to business, don't you?"

He took her hand and kissed it. "Oh, but you are so lovely this fine day."

"You never give up, do you? What would your wife say if she saw that?"

"But how could she see it, if she is nowhere around?" René wiggled his eyebrows. "Wife? Do I have a wife?"

"Whatever you want to call her, then."

"Ah, yes. The mistress of my nights." His eyes grew wide. "At least, when I'm not on call for someone else."

"You're never going to change, are you?"

"And why should I, eh? I'm having way too much fun." He leaned against the wall next to Garrett and draped one arm around her shoulder. "If you would listen to me, you'd be having some fun, too. No?" René glanced at Garrett's chest. "Open your heart and let love find you. That's what I do."

"I know, you keep telling me that." Garrett looked away. "So, any idea when the babies are coming?"

"Very soon. Let me tell you, it will be so good to have my twins. I can't wait to see them. They're growing every day, getting bigger and bigger. Why, just the other day, one kicked me while we were playing." René scratched his head in thought. "What is that game? Hard to get?" Seeing the confused look on his colleague's face, he thought again. "No, hide and seek."

Garrett opened her mouth to speak, but stopped at the sound of a commotion down the hall. She motioned to a matronly-looking woman being attended to by several staff physicians and nurses. "I wonder what's up"

Dr. Chabot studied the scene. "Maybe she got some news she weren't prepared for. Come on, let's go to the office and I'll give you this suit back." With a flourish, he motioned for her to lead the way. "After you."

The two colleagues made their way past the group of people attending to the dazed woman. Her belongings were scattered across the hall, and René stopped and gathered them up. He smiled politely when his gaze met that of the older woman. The next thing he knew her eyes had rolled back, and she fainted.

Garrett waited for René to return to her side. "Anything we can do to help?"

"It doesn't look like anything surgical for us to worry about. She keeps passing out. Maybe she has a bad heart."

Garrett looked back at the crowd of caregivers attending to the woman. "You could be right. I guess we'll never know."

Chapter 25

Shock registered on Brie's face. "Twins?"

"Shh!" The shrill outburst was quickly contained by Antoinette's experienced hand. "Now maybe you can see why I had that fainting spell." Her voice took on an air of indignant superiority. "With just this pregnancy alone, Danielle will have doubled the number of my grandchildren."

"Are you sure, Mother? I mean, really sure?"

"I heard it with my own ears. He was joking about getting his twins like it was an everyday occurrence." The expression on her face soured. "Arrogant, that's what he was, laughing and talking about his affairs, and with Danielle not fifty feet down the hall." She turned away and stared into the distance. "I even heard him flirting with another woman. I believe she was a doctor." She turned toward her daughter and focused. "I remember seeing her photograph in that hospital paper Danielle left at Christmas time. René, I think her name was. She's probably just another hussy on his long list of—"

"Mother!" Brie feigned a shocked face.

"It's true. I know what I saw."

"Saw what, Mother?" Matt stood in the doorway with a bouquet of flowers in his hand.

Brie turned at the sound of her brother's voice. "It's about time you showed up. You're late for Mother's Day."

"Better late than never," Matt said, brushing past her and heading for his mother. "Besides, I called, didn't I, Mother?"

"Yes, you did. Was your trip out of town beneficial, Matthew?"

"Very," he said and beamed. "The partners at the law firm were so pleased with my handling of the matter that I hear talk there might be a junior partnership headed my way."

Mrs. Bossard tipped her head in approval. "Very nice. Now if I could just get your sister on track with her life."

"Brie? What's wrong with her?" He eyed his sibling. "She looks healthy, even if she did just deliver a few weeks ago. And a belated happy Mother's Day to you, sis."

"Thanks." Brie glared at him. "It's your other sister you should be asking about."

"Danni?" His eyebrows knitted together. "What's wrong with her?" He presented the flowers in his hand to his mother. "Happy belated Mother's Day." He kissed her cheek.

Brie snickered. "That's one way to put it."

"Huh?" Matt looked confused. "Is there something going on that I'm not aware of?" He directed his question to their mother. "Tell me Danni didn't even send you a card or gift of any kind this year."

"Oh, she got Mother a gift all right. You might even say she got her two."

"And twice the shame." Antoinette lowered her eyes.

"Two gifts?" Matt looked from Brie to his mother. "Shame? What are you talking about?"

"Our sister, Little Miss I'm-Too-Good-For-Anyone, has gotten herself—"

Antoinette interrupted her youngest child. "Has found herself in a family way."

Matt froze. "Wh-what?" He stumbled over the word when it finally left his mouth. "Danni is—"

"Pregnant," Brie snapped, a satisfied smile on her face.

Matt thought back to the discussion he'd had with Danni over Christmas. She'd mentioned the possibility of bringing someone home next year, and it made him wonder if this child was the person she meant.

"And with twins, no less." Brie watched with triumphant satisfaction as Matt processed the information. "Two little bastards."

"Now, that's a good one. You finally got me, Brie." Matt started to laugh. "I almost believed you until you said twins."

"She's not joking, Matthew, and neither am I, when I tell you that I'll not have a bastard in the family, let alone two." Antoinette's stern look conveyed her anger. "That man will marry your sister whether he wants to or not. I'll see to it."

"Whoa." Matt reached out to calm his mother. "You can't force someone to…" He stopped when his mother's glare almost burned a hole right through him. Seeing her conviction, he softened his approach. "Why don't you let me talk to this man? Perhaps I can use a little legal persuasion to help him come to an understanding where Danni and the... ah... the babies are concerned." Matt waited for his mother's gaze to meet his. "Do you even know who the father is? I mean, presuming Danni really is pregnant."

"Always the lawyer, aren't you?" Brie said. "I'm surprised Danni hasn't told you already. You've always been thick as thieves with her."

"Only when it came to raiding the cookie jar, sis." Matt's face was devoid of emotion as he stared Brie down. When she'd finally averted her eyes, he turned back to his mother. "Does Father know about any of your presumptions?"

"Presumptions, hell!" Brie gloated. "I saw all the signs. I knew Danni was pregnant by the way she was acting over Christmas. She took naps in the middle of the day, and she refused her favorite wine with dinner. And when did you ever know her not to have breakfast on Christmas morning?" Brie bristled at his reluctance to accept her observations. "Come on, Matt. She had morning sickness. Think about it a little, and you'll come to the same conclusion I have. Danni's pregnant with twins," Brie said, a smile tickling her lips again.

Matt glanced at his mother for confirmation.

"The signs are all there. As for your father, he knows nothing as of yet. It would kill him to think Danielle would disgrace the family in such a manner. I know, because it's killing me. I'll not have him struck such a humbling blow. Not only to him, as her father, but to his family name, as well."

"It all boils down to the family name again." Matt sighed.

Antoinette puffed out her chest and sat rigidly straight. "Of course it does. Family names are everything. They are our heritage. Our name may be Bossard," she enunciated it with the best French-sounding accent possible, "but we will not be known for bastards."

The circumstantial evidence was piling up fast, and it was definitely not in Danni's favor. "Let me handle this," Matt said. "Tell me who you think the father is."

"Think? I know. I heard it with my own ears at the hospital. It's that surgeon your sister is working with." Her eyes turned menacing. "The one who bought her with a leather jacket. Dr. Garrett Trivoli."

* * *

Garrett winced. She had pushed her ankle a little too far. "That pothole got you good, just like Danni did. Damn! Why did you have to go make friends anyway?" Garrett closed her eyes for a fleeting moment and regrouped. "Time to get serious. It's nearly the end of May, and you still haven't given any consideration to a single offer." She picked up an envelope from the top of the pile and read the return address. "Charleston, South Carolina. Warm, on the eastern seaboard." She ticked off the obvious points. "I wonder what the trauma ratio is?" Garrett opened the envelope and started reading. It wasn't long before she burst into laughter.

"They've got to be kidding. Who offers computer dating arrangements as an enticement to work?" Garrett tossed the letter aside, wondering if they knew something she didn't.

The ache in her ankle gnawed at her, much like the puzzle she was trying to fit together ate at her peace of mind. In a manner of speaking, her life seemed to be constantly up in the air, as did the people who surrounded her. People like Danni. How often had she seen that hopeful look in her eyes lately? And on numerous occasions, she'd caught Danni distracted, or daydreaming. Garrett found this a little unsettling, to say the least, coming from a woman she considered a true professional. Her heart went out to Danni, but she wasn't quite sure what Danni wanted from her. She was trying hard at this friendship thing, but perhaps there was something more, something Garrett just wasn't getting.

Come to think of it, Garrett was finding that her own responses to some situations were up in the air, too. In one instance, Danni's touch could send her mentally tumbling, and in another, it would take her breath away. No one's touch had ever affected her that way before. Why now, and why Danni? Garrett wondered if there wasn't some plan being put into motion that she didn't know about.

"Fate." Garrett picked up the pile of letters. "It all comes down to fate. Maybe I should cast my fate to the wind. What do you think?"

Danni, coming down the stairs, heard Garrett's question. In a split second, a million thoughts came rushing through her mind, all of them dealing with Garrett. Riding out her inner storm, Danni pulled herself together before she spoke. "I'd rather you let your heart rule your fate than the wind."

"Damn it, Danni! Don't scare me like that."

"I'm sorry."

Garrett shifted uncomfortably in her seat. "I wasn't really expecting anyone to answer me."

"I thought you asked a question. I didn't mean to disturb you." Disconcerted by her reception, Danni headed for the kitchen without saying another word.

Garrett's gaze followed Danni's gently swaying hips as they moved from the room. She closed her eyes, savoring the moment. Without warning she could feel her pulse quickening. Could she deny the attraction?

She had to face facts. That defense attorney might have been right. Maybe she was gay. Why else would she have tested those waters in college? But what would Danni think about having a lesbian for a friend?

"Now what do I do?" Garrett sighed and ran her hand through her hair. She envisaged several different scenarios, in which Danni shifted from denial, to rejection, to flat out avoidance of the issue altogether. And what if she didn't deny it? Would Danni even consider a relationship if it meant placing her career and family ties in jeopardy?

Garrett weighed the choices. They all led her back to the job offers in her hand. "Then again, I could always run."

She toyed with the idea until the beeping of her hospital pager put an end to her thoughts. Pulling her cell phone from her pocket, she pressed the speed-dial number and waited for the connection to go through.

"Garrett Trivoli here. You paged me?"

* * *

The sounds of metal striking metal only emphasized Danni's bad mood. It didn't get any better as she moved from one side of the kitchen to the other, putting together a makeshift breakfast.

"Why don't you just pack her bags for her and have them at the door, come the end of June? Who'd want to stay with a moody bitch like you?" She plopped her cup and spoon down on the counter, then reached for the whistling teakettle. "Sure, you want her to stay, but would she if she knew why you want her to?" Danni poured the water into her cup and tossed in the tea bag, sending it to the bottom with a jab of her spoon.

"And what happens when you find out for sure?" Already Danni could feel her emotions working into a full frenzy as she pulled open the refrigerator door, then reached in. "By God, if I keep this up I'm going to lose it for sure." She looked down at the juice in one hand and the fruit muffin in the other. "Or weigh a ton."

Danni saw Garrett standing in the doorway and quickly averted her gaze. "Sorry, I was talking to myself."

"We should drive in separately this morning,"

"I'm not mad at you."

"Dr. McMurray has plans for me today. I don't know what, the Command Desk only said he wanted me to make sure you had a way home tonight."

"Sounds like you're going to be there longer than usual." Danni stared at her cup of tea before looking back at Garrett. "You don't think something happened to Nathan or René, do you?"

"They didn't say. They just told me to report to McMurray's office as soon as I can get in."

"You'll be leaving soon?"

"Yes." Garrett motioned toward the front door. "I'd better get going."

"You'll let me know what's up, won't you?"

Garrett's response was an abbreviated nod, and then she was on her way.

Danni let her breath out in an explosive sigh. "Great, just great. I couldn't push her out any faster if I tried."

* * *

"I see you're admiring my work."

The voice startled Garrett as she stood in the reception room. "Dr. McMurray, I didn't hear you come in."

"Doesn't matter." Ol' Cutter brushed the comment aside and eyed the photograph Garrett had been examining. "I was fresh out of my transitional year and ready to take on the world of surgery. I had two dollars in my pocket and a shiny new scalpel in my bag." He leaned in toward Garrett and chuckled. "Back then, we still carried bags. You would have thought I was a king." McMurray straightened, giving a tiny groan. "Do you see anything out of place in that picture? Go ahead, take a good look at it."

Garrett stepped closer and studied the row of proud young surgeons standing for their graduation class photograph. In the background, off to one side, was a small group of nurses. "Isn't that your wife in the background?"

"Technically, no. I hadn't even met her yet, let alone married her. Mary happened to be there in my shadow, like she was in all of the rest of these. It was as though fate had dictated that we would meet and spend the rest of our lives together." He looked at Garrett. "Do you believe in fate, Dr. Trivoli?"

Garrett thought about it as visions of blue scrubs and blonde hair came to mind. "I'm beginning to think I might, sir. Why do you ask?"

"I think our fates are planned for us, even before we exist. They write our story in the sands of time, and it's our obligation to live them out."

"Excuse me, Dr. McMurray," Stella interrupted him. "You have the Board meeting at eight o'clock. You asked me to keep you on time."

"Yes, the Board," he replied. "Thank you for reminding me." His voice became more businesslike. "Come into the office." He ushered Garrett in, then rounded the desk and sat down, resting his elbows on the desktop. "I won't beat around the bush, Trivoli. I have a favor to ask of you."

"Anything, sir."

"Good, I was hoping you'd say that." McMurray waved a hand at her injury. "Are you having any trouble with that ankle? I mean, you're able to stand on it for a while, aren't you?"

"I think I could manage a round or two of surgery a day. Of course, that's without jumping up and down or throwing any tantrums. They told me to save those for next week's physical therapy."

"Good." McMurray leaned back into his chair. "It seems our former chief resident is in a bind and needs some surgical bailout. Some of his colleagues were delayed returning from a conference, and just yesterday, the other surgeon on his service fell and broke his arm." McMurray looked at Garrett. "You wouldn't mind doing a few emergency appendectomies or anything like that, would you?" He looked nonchalant as he swiveled his chair to the side. "If you did, I could always send somebody else. René or Nathan, perhaps."

"Me, mind a few appys? Never. Who do I report to?"

"I believe you know him. Dr. David Beckman." McMurray watched the expression on her face turn cold. "Is something wrong, Trivoli? Some problem I'm not aware of?"

"No, sir. No problem professionally."

"Personally, then?"

"No, it's nothing, really." Garrett forced a confident smile and met her mentor's questioning eyes. "I assure you, nothing will get in the way of my treating the patients."

McMurray studied her for a few seconds more, then nodded. "All right. I've made arrangements for you to stay at his hospital. You'll get your own call room, and while you're there, all of your meals will be covered."

"Fine. When do I start?"

"I told him you'd be there by noon. Stella has directions for you and anything else you might need. Who knows? Maybe this is something the fates have had in store for you all along. It'll give you some time to think about where you want to be after you're done with your fellowship. Or have you already made up your mind?"

"I haven't given it much thought." Garrett felt a little uncomfortable under his constant scrutiny. "If that's all, I'll pack a few things and be on my way." She turned and crossed the room in several long strides.

"Trivoli."

Garrett looked back. "Yes?"

"Thanks."

"You're welcome, sir."

* * *

Danni thought about the way her life was spinning out of control. "My mother's going to have a fit when I tell her I'm gay. I can just hear it now." Danni shook her head and continued to sort through the mail. "She'll disown me and throw me right out of the family. As if I'm not almost there already."

Familiar handwriting caught Danni's eye, and she fumbled to open the envelope. Her eyes got bigger the farther down the page she read.

"What the hell is Mother talking about, 'take care of my grandbabies'?" Danni turned the page over and looked at the back of it. It was blank. She picked up the envelope and reread the name on it. Ms. Danielle Bossard. It was definitely hers. Danni rolled the words over in her mind then raised her shirt to view her flat stomach in utter disbelief. "I'm pregnant?"

Garrett froze in mid-step at the moment of Danni's disclosure.

She's pregnant? The words echoed in Garrett's mind, and she looked at Danni's normally taut abdomen. Her anger grew when she realized who the contributing male must have been. It was David. If she had personal issues with the man before, this put the icing on the cake.

And you thought everything was fine when you found her asleep in your bed, didn't you? I guess it didn't take all night to give her that little present. Garrett took a deep breath, trying to calm her nerves. There was no question now. It was blatantly evident that Danni preferred men. Make that a man—namely, one Dr. David Beckman.

Danni released her shirt as she saw Garrett and shoved the letter into her pocket. "Gar? What are you doing home?"

"I came back to pack."

"What do you mean, pack?"

"McMurray is sending me to another hospital."

"Where? How long?" Danni searched Garrett's face for answers. When none came, she shifted gears. "I guess I'd better get packing, too."

"He didn't say anything about you, Danni." She saw the hurt in Danni's eyes. "I could call him and see if it was an oversight on his part." Garrett slipped her phone from her pocket and hit the speed dial.

"Stella, is Dr. McMurray still in the office?" She paused then nodded. "Thanks, I just wanted to ask him a quick question."

Danni stepped closer to Garrett and held her breath.

"Oh, good. I caught you before you left. I don't remember you saying anything about Nurse Bossard going with me. What do I tell her?" Garrett listened while Danni strained to hear.

"Thank you for your time, sir. I'm sorry if I bothered you." Garrett terminated the call. "He's disbanding the team for now. You're to stay here and work in the ER."

Tears welled in Danni's eyes, and she hurried from the room.

Disappointment colored Garrett's mood. Unconsciously, she had assumed Danni would be going with her, but now it looked as if David Beckman and John McMurray had teamed up to separate her from the one person she had come to rely on: Danni.

Chapter 26

Garrett surveyed the front of the rural hospital. It definitely wasn't a cutting-edge institution. The whole facility took up little more space than that occupied by a single wing of the hospital in Pittsburgh.

"At least I'll get some OR time. Here goes nothing." Garrett tightened her grip on her duffel and headed for the information desk.

"I'm Dr. Trivoli. Could you page Dr. Beckman for me?"

"Yes, Doctor. I'll do that right away."

Garrett examined the room. The homespun décor brought Danni's unselfish nature to her mind. She could see Danni sacrificing herself for the good of the baby and David's career. Could Garrett ever be like that, giving up everything for someone else's sake? Then it came to her. She was already giving up any chance of a relationship with Danni because she thought Danni wanted something—no, make that someone—else.

Anger roiled inside her. She would go tell David exactly what she thought of him, if not for her promise to McMurray.

Engrossed in her thoughts, Garrett didn't hear her name being called until everyone else in the lobby was staring at her. Only then did she realize the woman behind the desk was talking to her.

"I'm sorry," she said. "I wasn't paying attention."

"Dr. Beckman will meet you on the second floor, right outside the operating suite."

"Thank you," Garrett said, pulling her mask of stoicism into place.

* * *

"I'm glad to see you're keeping busy without a certain surgeon to look after."

Danni turned on her heels, ready to meet the challenge, and saw the Chief of Trauma Services. "Ah... good morning, sir." Her voice had a bit of an edge to it.

McMurray eyed her. "I see you're mad at me for breaking up the team."

"You're the boss."

"That's right, and I have to do what's best for everyone here. I was glad when Dr. Beckman called me with the request. Trivoli needs a little time to herself."

"Did he ask for Dr. Trivoli specifically?"

"Not in so many words. He asked for a surgeon to help him out in a sticky situation."

The sound of the bell for the elevator grabbed their attention.

"That's for me," McMurray said. "Are you going up?"

Danni shook her head. "Down, actually."

"All right then." McMurray's next comment coincided with the closing of the doors. "Don't worry, Nurse Bossard. She'll be home before you know it."

"Home before I know it?" Danni smiled tentatively. "Now, if I only knew what David was going to do." She sighed. "As if I don't already know."

* * *

Garrett played with the change in her pocket as she waited outside the surgical suite. She relished the thought of performing surgery, but everywhere she looked she saw fleeting images of Danni, and David was lurking not far behind. Closing her eyes tightly, Garrett tried to will the images away. When she reopened them, David was emerging from the doorway.

"Dr. Trivoli, I see you made it, and early, too."

David's voice brought the taste of bile into her mouth. Garrett swallowed, hoping it would stay down. "Yes, it seems to be my fate today. I hope you don't mind."

"Not at all. I'll be able to show you around."

Garrett reached for her duffel bag and shouldered it. "Lead on."

"First, let's get you settled in." After a few quick turns down the hallway, they stood in front of a door. "This is my call room. You can sleep here when you get the chance. I'll use my office the nights I'm on call." He opened the door and then held out the key for her to take.

"Thanks." Garrett slipped the key into her pocket, her eyes transfixed on the single bed. *I wonder if this was where...* Garrett fought the image forming in her mind. She didn't want to go there.

"It's bigger than it looks," David said as she stared at the unmade bed. "I'll have one of the housekeepers make it up for you."

"Don't bother, I won't be using it." Garrett set her bag down on the chair. "Now, how about showing me to the Emergency Department? That's what you want me to cover, right?"

"Sure. Let's go." He motioned for Garrett to start down the hallway ahead of him. He closed the door, and the lock clicked as it set into place.

Garrett slowed her pace and waited for David to catch up. "I'll need to see the emergency, operating, and recovery rooms. Maybe the cafeteria, too."

"I can do that, but I didn't think you were as big an eater as Danni is."

At the mention of Danni's name, Garrett's expression softened.

"I'm not. I'm just asking."

"Danni grows on you after a while, doesn't she?"

An image of a very pregnant Danni appeared in Garrett's mind. She bit her tongue to keep from disclosing any information. It wasn't her place to tell David that he was going to be a father. That was strictly between Danni and him.

They rounded the corner and came to a stairwell.

"We're headed down to the first floor, right outside ER One. The hospital provides services on a Level Three Trauma Accreditation. We only receive and keep traumas between seven in the morning and seven at night, when the full complement of services are available."

"And the other twelve hours? What happens to those traumatized patients?"

"We stabilize and transport to a Level One facility, like the one that loaned you to us." David flashed her a smile.

Garrett wasn't sure she liked that concept, but she would have to live with it, if only for a few days.

As they reached the bottom of the steps, David's pager went off. "Level One trauma page. Inbound male victim with a single gunshot to the chest. Agonal breathing noted. ETA, two minutes. This is a Level One trauma page."

"Mind if I assist you, Doctor? I'd like to see firsthand how your department runs."

"Right this way, Dr. Trivoli. I'll be happy to have a second pair of hands."

* * *

Garrett noted intermittent and labored breathing sounds as the stretcher passed by her. The patient's complexion was pasty-white, and even through her glove, Garrett could tell that his skin was cool and clammy.

"Someone page Anesthesia, stat." Garrett's voice rose above the din of the room. She caught sight of a small pool of blood on the left side of the stretcher. "We'll need to preserve the left side of the shirt for the police. Cut his shirt off on the right side of his body and across the left shoulder and sleeve."

David pressed the tip of his thumb deep into the patient's nail bed, then released it. Poor blood return caused the whitened nail to remain that way far longer than David would have liked it to.

"Let's hang two units of blood." He looked up at the heart monitor. The slowing complexes signified a dying man. "He might be in PEA. Check for pulses."

Both surgeons reached for the pulse point closest to them, Garrett at the neck and David at the patient's groin. Seconds later their gazes met in confirmation of what had to be done.

"Set up a thoracotomy tray. We're cracking his chest." Garrett reached for a bottle of Betadine and sprayed the patient's bared chest.

Seeing the determination on Garrett's face confirmed David's confidence in her. "Get a dose of epinephrine on board and stand by with the atropine. Let's get a chest tube set ready."

Immediately, the staff pulled in a crash cart and broke the protective seal. The nurse's expertise belied her youthful appearance as she pulled out drawers filled with the drugs needed to work a cardiac arrest. Calmly, she readied the pre-filled syringes as requested, then called out her actions. "Epi in."

A flurry of footsteps sounded down the hall and a new person entered the room. "Anesthesiologist here. What do you have?"

"Gunshot wound to the chest. Care to intubate?" Garrett kept her eyes on her patient.

"Let me through. I'll need a curved blade on the laryngoscope and a size eight endotracheal tube." The anesthesiologist grabbed a set of gloves from his pocket and prepared to intubate the patient.

"Suction! He's got vomit blocking the airway."

A suction catheter was shoved into his hand. After several passes to remove the obstruction, he said, "I see the vocal cords. Steady." He slipped the tube into place. "I'm in." He retracted the laryngoscope and tossed it aside. The respiratory therapist connected the Ambu bag to the tube and started manually filling the patient's lungs with air.

Both sides of the patient's chest rose as oxygen was squeezed into the lungs. With the tube properly positioned, the anesthesiologist secured it in place. "We're good to go. What's the plan?"

"We're getting ready to crack his chest." David looked across to Garrett, who stood poised and ready with a scalpel in her hand. "You're on, Dr. Trivoli."

"Here we go." Garrett made an incision down the length of the ribcage, cutting swiftly through the tissue to bring the contents of the chest cavity into view.

"Rib spreaders." David held out his hand.

A nurse behind him picked up the sterile sealed bag and opened it. Once free of the covering, the instrument no longer kept its form. The nurse held up the completely independent pieces, horror in her eyes. "They're broken, Doctor."

David looked back and saw the pieces in her hand. "Shit." The word slipped out under his breath. "Get me another one."

The unfortunate finding didn't faze Garrett. "You, and you." She pinned the nurses on either side of her with a penetrating glare. "Grab a rib and separate them. There's no time to wait for another spreader."

The two nurses jumped at the command, while an aide took off down the hall in search of another set of rib spreaders. When they had retracted the ribs sufficiently, Garrett gently pushed aside the expanding lobes of lung, revealing the inner contents of the cavity.

David adjusted the surgical spotlight and looked to see the extent of the damage caused by the bullet.

"I'm not seeing"—Garrett moved her hand a little deeper into the chest cavity—"or feeling any fragments. From the size of the hole, I'm guessing he was shot with a small-caliber weapon."

"Twenty-two caliber?" David peered into the cavity and repositioned the light.

"Maybe. It may not be lethal initially, but it can leave a lot of damage in its trail. Pull back a little more, if you can." Garrett evacuated a few small clots, sending them slithering onto the floor.

The aide dashed back into the room. "I have the rib spreaders." She handed them to a nurse who tore open the sterile packaging and presented them to Dr. Beckman.

Taking the intact spreaders, David slid them in place. "You can let go now, thanks." The gloved hands of the nurses withdrew, leaving Garrett unencumbered.

"Let's get an abdominal X-ray. There's hardly any blood in his chest cavity." Garrett held the patient's heart in her hands. Instead of a full, well-rounded, beating organ, it was a contracted and barely-moving mass.

Her decision was immediate. "We've got to expand his volume. Give him two more units of blood and open up the other lines with Lactated Ringer's." She began to gently massage the heart muscle, trying to get the chambers to open. The tension in the room grew with each minute. Slowly the heart began to respond, and Garrett withdrew her hands.

"X-ray! Clear the abdomen," the technician bellowed, then exposed the lower half of the man's torso to the beam. A few seconds later, the film plate was gone, and the activity around the patient resumed.

David saw it first. "Here! There's a hole in the diaphragm."

"Suture, please. Call the OR and tell them we need a room. We're coming up." The words rolled out of Garrett's mouth before she realized what she was saying. She glanced at David. "Don't you think, Dr. Beckman?"

"Definitely." David hurried to assist her with the suturing. "We'll need to explore his abdomen for injury." He looked over to the recording nurse. "Get us an elevator to the OR." He threw the surgical scissors down onto a pile of used instruments and draped a sterile blue towel over the patient's exposed chest. "Pack up, we're moving."

David stepped back. The nursing staff attached the patient to a portable monitor and gathered the bags of intravenous fluids hanging on the pole of the blood infuser. Every person in the room did his or her part to prepare for the trip to the operating theater.

"The elevator's here," someone in the hall announced.

"Lead on. I'll be right behind you." Garrett ripped off her gloves and grabbed a fresh pair as the stretcher was wheeled from the room. She stopped momentarily in front of the viewer as the radiograph of the patient's abdomen was being hung. She knew the worst of the patient's injuries lay within that area, and took a moment to search for signs of metal in the abdomen. She then

234

pulled the film from the box and took off for the elevator at the end of the hall.

In a new hospital for less than an hour, and she was already heading to the operating room with a trauma. Garrett shook her head in wonderment and made a mental note to tell Danni of her adventure.

The mask covering her face hid her wry expression. *Better learn to squelch that now before it becomes a habit, Trivoli. Danni's more interested in David's stories now.*

*   *   *

Tight-lipped and calculating, Antoinette waited for her son to return her phone call. It had taken her a full week to come to terms with the idea of her older daughter being pregnant with bastard twins. Now she was ready to deal with it, and who better to help her than her son, the lawyer?

She settled back into her comfortable chair, pleased with herself for pushing Matthew in the right direction. His part of her blueprint for her children's lives seemed to be working as planned, much like Breanna's role as a wife and mother. Now, if she could only get Danielle on track, life would be good.

When the phone finally rang, she reached for it. "Hello, Mrs. Bossard speaking," she said with an air of aristocratic elegance.

"Hello, Mother."

Antoinette relished her son's rich, deep-toned voice. "Matthew, I've been waiting for your call. Have you taken care of our problem yet?"

"I've been in court all week. You can't expect me to ask the judge for a recess to take care of some family business."

"Humph," she snorted in disgust. "I bet if that judge's family name was in jeopardy, he'd find the time."

"I'll be done with this case in the next few days. I can look into it then. I'm sorry if it's not fast enough for you, but some things take time."

"Matthew, your sister is in trouble, and I need you to take care of it."

"In our country, a man is considered innocent until proven guilty." Matt sighed. "At least let me get all the facts we need before I confront Dr. Trivoli."

"Facts? I've given you the facts. What more do you want? I was at the hospital. I saw your sister and she's..." She stopped to clear her throat. "She's quite full with child. Two, to be exact," she added. "I heard Trivoli boasting of it with my own ears. I tell you, the man is a cad. He needs to be brought to terms. I want the name on those birth certificates to be Trivoli, not Bossard. Do I make myself understood?"

"Yes, perfectly." There was a pause. "Listen, I have to get going. I'm almost back at the office, and I think the battery in my phone is about to give out."

"The sooner you start, the better, Matthew. Now, get on it. I'm the law here," Antoinette said flatly, then hung up the phone.

* * *

It was nearly evening when Danni ventured into her living room. In Garrett's absence, the usually cheery environment lacked the energy it once held. For the first time, Danni knew what loneliness really was.

Her mood ruined, she pulled out her mother's letter and read it again.

"What the hell are you talking about, Mother? Does she know about me?" Danni muttered as she wrestled with her thoughts. "How could she, when I don't even know for sure myself?"

Trapped between night's approaching shadows and the emptiness she felt inside, she lowered her head and started to cry. Answers eluded her, but there was one thing Danni knew for sure: her pain wouldn't ease until Garrett came home.

* * *

Garrett was crumpled into a ball in an armchair that stood in the recovery room. She had spent a long afternoon in surgery, and an even longer night by her patient's bedside. Garrett yawned, then stretched her legs, trying to get some life back into them before attempting to stand. Wiping the sleep from her eyes, she focused on her patient for a few seconds before she spoke, her groggy, sleep-filled voice breaking the silence in the room. "Any change since the last report?"

"No, he's holding his own," the nurse at the patient's bedside answered. "Can I get you some coffee, Doctor?"

"Thanks." She worked a kink out of her neck. "What time is it?"

"It's almost change of shift. Ten minutes to seven, to be exact."

"Damn!" Garrett rubbed the back of her neck and winced. "One down," she said, more to herself than to anyone else.

"Pardon me, Doctor?"

"Nothing." Garrett dragged her hand through her hair, letting the strands fall where they may as she walked out of the room. "I wonder what today will bring?"

Chapter 27

R-r-r-ring! R-r-r-ring!

Danni jumped to answer the phone. "Gar?" She immediately chastised herself for the slip.

"No, I'm sorry. It's your brother."

"Matt, I wasn't expecting you."

"Obviously. I take it Garrett's not with you?"

"No. Why do you ask?"

"I was hoping to talk with you both."

"I'm not sure when that will happen. They've loaned Garrett out to another hospital."

"I'm really sorry to hear that."

"Me, too." Danni's response was less than enthusiastic.

"How about I come by on Friday after work, and we have dinner together? Do you think Garrett might be home by then?"

"I'm not sure."

"Hey, the worst case scenario is that I get to see my sister and order in a pizza. What do you say?"

"Okay, you win."

"Great."

"I'll keep my fingers crossed that Garrett will be here, too."

"Would you mind if I asked you something?"

"You're my brother. Why would I mind?"

"Are you taking care of yourself?"

She heard the concern wrapped in his question. "Why do you ask?"

"Mother mentioned that you were in court."

"Only to give testimony. That defense attorney really put Gar through the wringer." There was a moment of silence. "You're not like that, are you, li'l brother?"

"Let's just say that I try to do my job, and leave it at that."

"Okay, I'll let you off the hook."

"Thanks. Remember, I'll see you on Friday."
"Yeah. See you Friday, Matt. Bye."

* * *

"Damn!" Garrett came to an abrupt stop when she found David seated in the doctor's lounge.

He looked up and greeted her. "Dr. Trivoli, could I have a word with you in my office?" He stood.

"Now?"

"I think it would be best." He started walking.

She waited for the door to close after David. "Son of a bitch! All I wanted was to be left alone."

David poked his head back in the room. "You coming?"

Reluctantly, Garrett nodded. "Yes, I'm coming."

As soon as Garrett entered the hall, David started with his idle chatter. "Are you enjoying your stay with us?"

His question took her by surprise. "Yes, as well as can be expected."

"Good. I'm glad I finally got the chance to see what all the fuss is about. You've even impressed Danni."

"I do my job," Garrett said dryly.

"Well, now I see why Danni picked you as her surgeon." David fumbled with his key, then opened his office door.

Once inside, Garrett faced him. "What do you mean, picked me? I know for a fact the Board of Directors put us together."

"I can see where you might believe that."

His words left her dumbfounded.

"Have a seat." He waved her toward a chair, but she remained standing as he seated himself behind the desk. There was an uneasy silence between them as they studied one another.

"You know Danni is smitten with you, don't you?"

"Right." Garrett stifled a laugh. "I suppose that's why she's been calling and seeing you."

"We've dated, I'll grant you that, but I wouldn't call it anything serious."

"You're a pompous ass if you don't think she needs you."

David tried to keep a straight face. "Pompous ass?"

"Why do you think I had Rosie invite you up for the ski weekend, or suggest that you come to Pittsburgh later in March? It wasn't to keep me company." Garrett glared across the desk.

"You were trying to set us up?"

"Somebody had to take the bull by the horns." Garrett looked away. "I'm just sorry I didn't stay out of it. I'm the one feeling responsible, now that she's—" Garrett bit her tongue.

David looked at her suspiciously. "Now that Danni's what?"

"I just think you should start taking some responsibility."

"Responsibility for what?" David's voice turned harsh. "What did I do?"

"As if you don't know. My God, man, you're a doctor."

"What?" His brows knitted together in utter confusion. "All I did was take her dancing and show her some good times."

Garrett clamped her hands down on the edge of his desk and leaned over it. With each breath she took, her nostrils flared and her expression grew more menacing. "Exactly. So, what are you going to do about it?"

He moved his chair back and stood up. "What the hell are you talking about?"

"I can't believe you're the one who got her in that condition and you don't even have a clue."

David leaned in over his desk. "If you ask me, I think you're the one without a clue."

Garrett leaned closer yet. "She's pregnant."

"She's what?"

"You heard me. Danni's pregnant." Garrett swallowed hard. "She doesn't know that I found out. I heard her say it myself, yesterday, before I left to come here."

"How could that be?" David's face lost all its color. His eyes roamed aimlessly around the room. "You don't think that I..."

"You said yourself that you showed her some good times." Garrett's gaze nearly drilled a hole into his flesh.

"I kissed her, but I never pushed. How could I be the one who... She told me she was..."

"What, on birth control?"

"No, that she was in love with—"

Garrett punched him in the face, then stood there in total silence, shocked. A moment later, her knuckles stung like crazy, but she didn't mind. She had done what needed to be done.

David wasn't sure what had hit him: a Mack truck, or Garrett Trivoli. He wiped the sleeve of his lab coat over his nose, smearing a trail of blood across his face.

"Trivoli, you're a fool." He sniffed, coughed a time or two, and then continued. "Frankly, I don't know what Danni ever saw in you. Why she loves you is beyond me."

"What did you say?" Garrett focused directly on David. "What do you mean, she loves me?"

"You heard me." David wiped his nose on his sleeve again and looked at it. "She confided in me."

"When?"

"The other week, when she came down to visit." David shook his head. "You really are dense, aren't you? You don't even believe it when it's told right to your face."

"She couldn't be. You're trying to confuse the issue. She's..." Garrett's words began to slow. "Why, she's..."

"She's in love with you. Head over heels, I might add." David's voice grew calmer. "If you don't believe me, maybe you should ask her yourself."

Garrett opened her mouth to speak, but nothing came out. She stood, looking helpless, as it all began to sink in.

"Surely you must have had some inkling of how she felt."

Slowly Garrett's breathing became less ragged. "I thought... I knew how she felt about you."

"Trust me," David said, his demeanor serious, "I'd be the happiest man alive if Danni were carrying my child, but she's not."

"Then who?"

"If it's true, I haven't a clue."

Garrett looked to David for answers, but found her attention drawn to the evidence of her temper. Telltale rings of discoloration were becoming pronounced on his face.

"You'd better get some ice on that." Garrett pointed vaguely to his face. "Maybe get it checked out with a CT scan or some X-rays."

At a loss for anything more to say, she looked at David for a quiet moment. "I'm sorry," she whispered. "I don't know why I snapped like that. I'm sorry." She turned and walked out of the office.

"Oh, but I know." David gingerly touched the side of his face and winced. "That'll teach me to be Cupid's little helper."

* * *

She'd been there only a few minutes, but already the walls of the call room were closing in on Garrett. The closer they came, the more her heart pounded. She hurriedly changed her clothes, shoved her belongings into her bag, and bolted through the hospital until she was outside in the fresh air. Finally, she could breathe. She inhaled deeply, and headed for her Blazer. It was stuffy inside the vehicle, and she reached for the control to open her window. Frustration set in when nothing happened.

"Damn it! Isn't *anybody* listening to me?"

She jammed the key into the ignition and turned it until the motor started. This time when she jabbed at the control, the window responded. Garrett sank down into the seat and rested her head on the window ledge. Aimlessly, she stared up into the night.

"If it all boils down to fate, why was I sent here?"

Perhaps she was merely a pawn in the game. Garrett sat up and fastened her seatbelt. With one hand gripped tightly on the steering wheel, she shifted into gear, and pushed down on the accelerator. The engine roared to life, sending the Blazer into a lurching start as she took off out of the parking lot.

* * *

Sensing the presence of another person, Danni struggled to awaken. A shadowy figure appeared out of her sleepy haze, revealing sculpted curves and the gentle swell of full breasts. Danni gasped.

"Gar, you're home."

"I've been home since the first day I met you."

The softly spoken declaration sent Danni's heart racing. Before she could respond, strong arms encircled her and warm breath tickled her ear.

"I love you."

Danni closed her eyes. The scent of leather and spice filled her nose, and soft kisses peppered her cheek. Danni held her breath in anticipation as she waited to feel of Garrett's lips on her own. Tentative at first, the kiss soon escalated as lips parted and tongues began to explore. Danni's passions were sparked as she melted into the kiss. The thought that Garrett was loving her consumed Danni's being. She was starving for more than breath alone when the kiss ended.

"Garrett."

Another kiss silenced her.

"There's been too much talking already. It's time to feel."

Strong thighs straddled Danni, pinning her to the bed. Worshiping hands roamed over satiny skin while taut muscles quivered below. The mounting ache grew until it was driving her wild with desire. One by one, delicate kisses edged down Danni's torso, brushing over her hips and onto her thighs. Surrendering to the heady aroma of her own arousal, Danni silently pleaded to be taken. Before she knew it, her pelvis rocked in a steady rhythm, and moisture gathered between her legs.

All at once, Danni's inner world burst into fireworks, and she was sure she could hear bells tolling off in the distance. But the pounding in her ears was nothing compared to her wildly beating heart. Her time had come. Giving it all up in one final release, Danni cried out, "I love you, Garrett!"

No words of love were returned to embrace her. The only sound she heard was a ringing in her ears. Conditioned from many nights on call, Danni reached for the phone. Too out of breath to speak, she just listened. It didn't take long to figure out that the raspy-sounding breaths were not her own, but those of an obscene phone caller. Her body still pulsating, Danni gathered her senses. It wasn't a long, lean body that held her onto the bed, but her covers, twisted tightly around her.

Angered and on the verge of tears, Danni shifted her rage to the receiver in her hand.

"Like I really needed this. Let me tell you, buddy, you're way too late. I was already there ahead of you." She slammed the receiver down.

"Damn it! I need you, Garrett. I need you." Danni sobbed and clutched her pillow, crying herself to sleep.

* * *

The blur of white lines and asphalt hypnotized Garrett so strongly that she had to rub her eyes to keep them focused. After three hours of driving, she still had no destination in mind, and she needed coffee. She took the next exit, and the neon lights of an all-night coffee shop directed her from there.

"Coffee, please."

The waitress snapped her gum. "Have a seat and I'll bring it over."

"Thanks." Garrett picked a booth and slid into it, laying her key ring and a stack of envelopes on the table.

"Here ya go. Best coffee in town." The waitress flashed a smile as she set the cup down and filled it to the brim. "I made it myself. I reckon you'll want it black. Most people do this time of the night. Or morning, whatever you want to call it."

Garrett glanced down to her watch. "0100. I guess it's morning."

"Military time, huh? I hear it a lot when the kids come home on leave. You in the military?"

"Sort of."

"Driving home to your sweetie, are you?" The waitress seemed completely unaware of the puzzled look on Garrett's face as she arranged the condiments on the table. "Doesn't matter what brings you. In the middle of the night, there's not a better place to be than right here. Lordy, listen to me! You'd think you had nothing better to do than to hear me jabbering. I'll let you get to your coffee." She started to walk away, the carafe in her hand. "We're the home of the bottomless cup, so yell when you need more."

"Thanks." Garrett raised the cup to her lips and sipped. "Mmm, this is good." She settled into the booth and studied the cup in her hand.

What a quagmire she'd gotten herself into. The evening's events came rushing back, paired with Danni's revelation of the previous morning. Garrett wished she could deny it all. Things would be so simple, then. How could she approach Danni with the offer of any kind of relationship when only a few weeks were left to her fellowship? It wouldn't be fair to either of them. Then there was the question of the baby. Would it be fair if Danni's child were taken away from its father?

And who would that be? Garrett sighed as every male staff member came under suspicion. Some, like John, were no sooner considered before being rejected, while others brought long moments of consternation to Garrett's face. Time and again, her mind came back to one pairing. Garrett drank more coffee. The more she considered it, the more sense it made. It had to be David, even though he denied it. Garret was sure he was only trying to confuse the issue. Why was this all about Garrett, as if she were the key?

"Key," Garrett said quietly, looking at the set on the table. "Like what I do makes a difference." She looked at the stack of mail, and a thought struck her. Perhaps it did. She reached for the envelopes and sorted through them. One stood out, and she plucked it from the group.

"Arizona is as good as anywhere. That should be far enough away to take me out of the picture. Maybe then everyone's fate will be decided."

Garrett raised the cup to her lips and drained it. Staring at the bottom of the empty cup, she tried to work things out in her mind. *Danni will forget me after I'm gone. The question is, will I ever forget her?*

Blonde hair and green eyes clouded Garrett's vision, and deep in her heart, she knew the answer. Never. Not for as long as she breathed would she forget the kindness of Danni's soul.

Garrett emerged from the diner with a new outlook on life. Things were going to be different, but there were a few things she still needed to do. First, she'd finish her assignment. Second, she would cherish the rest of her time in Pittsburgh with Danni. Then she would step out of the picture. Now that the plan was set, all she had to do was follow it.

Standing next to her Blazer, Garrett looked up into the night sky. The trail of stars above her seemed more like a road map than a mystery, now. Her eyes following one particular shooting star, Garrett made a silent wish.

Please let me keep her in my heart.

Chapter 28

"I heard a drunk punched him last night in the ER," the redheaded nurse casually informed anyone within earshot of the nursing station. "Knocked him out cold on the floor."

"That's what I heard. It's the talk of the housekeeping staff," another nurse said as she passed through.

"You've got it all wrong. I heard Dr. Beckman..."

At the sound of David's name, Garrett looked up from the chart she was writing in.

The heavyset nurse leaned back in her chair and looked around before motioning her co-workers closer. "I heard Dr. Beckman got what he deserved and right here in his office," she said. He was cold-cocked by a jealous husband."

"No!" Another nurse gasped.

"Yes." She crossed her arms over ample breasts with an air of superiority. "Didn't you see the shiner he was sporting this morning at rounds? I haven't seen one like that since Rocky Three."

"I bet that hurt."

Boy, did it ever! Garrett flexed swollen knuckles before shoving her hand into her pocket. *Next time, I have to remember to lead with the left.*

"He seems so quiet, though." A young nurse shook her head. "I mean, he's never made a pass at me."

"Consider yourself lucky." A brunette came into the conversation. "I heard he's a real lady-killer."

"And next you'll be telling me he's Dr. Jekyll and Mr. Hyde," the redhead snapped. "I think the story I heard is more credible. Drunks are always taking swings at the staff."

"All I have to say is—" The nurse stopped abruptly when a new presence arrived at the nursing station. "Good afternoon, Dr. Beckman."

Garrett fought to keep her jaw from dropping when she saw the bruises on David's face.

"Afternoon, Rhonda. Fine day for gossip, isn't it?" David pinned her with a look before making eye contact with each person at the desk in turn. "Now that I've gotten everyone's attention, let me tell you what really happened."

Garrett's stoic mask slipped into place as she waited to hear his story. Her grip tightened on the chart, and she braced for the attention to be shifted in her direction.

"I was making my rounds last night and startled a feverish patient. She hauled off and caught me in the eye with a well-placed punch." David touched his discolored skin gingerly. A gamut of emotions was displayed on the faces of the staff: disappointment, disbelief, and on one face in particular, confusion. "I assure you, it looks a lot worse than it is, and that's the truth."

"Humph! I told you my story was closer to the truth." The redhead glanced over to David. "Sorry, Doc. Maybe you shouldn't get so close when you're trying to wake somebody up."

A bittersweet smile formed on David's face. "Good advice, Suzanne. I'll try to remember that. So, what do you say we all get back to work?"

The nurses went about their business, scattering to different areas. Soon, only the two surgeons were left standing at the unit desk. Unsure of what to do or say, Garrett stared at David. He had shown her the grace and charm a well-schooled host would offer his guest. It would have been easy for him to turn on her with anger, but he hadn't.

"So, Dr. Trivoli, as I asked you yesterday, are you enjoying your stay with us?"

Garrett weighed her options. "It's always a pleasure to do surgery."

"I'm glad." David picked up a chart and perused it. "Thanks for coming back this morning. I know it was a difficult decision."

"I never let personal issues get in the way of doing my job." Garrett closed the chart and slid it back into the rack. "Excuse me, but I have patients to see."

"Garrett." David bit his lip.

"Yes?" Her eyes narrowed.

"I don't suppose we could lure you into working here permanently?"

Garrett knew her surprise registered on her face.

"I didn't think so." David sighed. "Where will you be going, if you don't mind me asking?"

"Arizona." Garrett sounded detached. "I cut the deal between my cases this morning."

"You what?"

"Don't worry. I used my cell phone to make the call."

"That's not what I was concerned about. I was thinking about—"

"Getting back to work." Garrett finished his sentence and changed the subject all at the same time.

"Speaking of which," David said, "the rest of the surgeons will be returning in time for rounds tomorrow morning."

"Then I'll hand off to them and be on my way. Thanks for letting me know."

"No problem, Dr. Trivoli. Thanks for helping out." David offered his hand. "I have a lengthy OR case in the morning, so I won't be around to say goodbye."

"Thanks for your spin on that story," Garrett said quietly, shaking his hand. "I'll tell Danni you asked about her." She watched him for a reaction. Seeing none, she released his hand.

"I really do want what's best for Danni." David turned and walked away.

Garrett stood watching until David was out of view. Although her time in this rural community hospital had been short, she had learned a valuable lesson. Friendships come in all different shapes, some you didn't even know existed until they were almost over.

"Chalk up another one for Dr. McMurray," she said, reaching for the vibrating pager on her waistband.

*   *   *

"Nurse Bossard."

Danni turned. "Dr. McMurray, hi."

"I thought that was you. I was just heading for the ER. Figured I'd kill two birds with one stone, so to speak."

"If you're talking about Dr. Trivoli, she's not back from her assignment."

"I was sure David said she would be finished this morning." He waved his hand as if to dismiss the thought. "No matter. I'll let you relay the news."

"News?" Danni perked up. "What news?"

"I've had her cleared for flight. Your team is back together as of six in the morning tomorrow. That should give you both a good night's sleep."

"Thank you, sir. I haven't slept well since..." Danni's voice trailed off, and her mood became subdued "Sorry, I just haven't slept well lately. Thanks."

"You're welcome. Tell Dr. Trivoli that I got a very good report on her from David. It seems she handled herself so well, they tried to lure her away from us." McMurray quickly said, "Don't worry, she didn't accept it."

"Thank God."

"My sentiments exactly. Have a pleasant evening, Nurse Bossard."

"I will." Danni watched as Dr. McMurray started to walk away. "And thank you again," she called out before turning back to the elevator, her smile beaming from ear to ear.

*   *   *

As she got out of her car, Danni scoured the street in front of her home for a familiar black Blazer. It wasn't there. She hoped her disappointment would be short-lived.

Think positive. Gar probably stopped for dinner. Danni gathered her belongings and headed for the house, picking up the mail as she passed by. Reflexively, she sorted through it as soon as she walked inside. "Me, me, me, Gar." Danni looked at the envelope curiously. "I've seen this logo before. Arizona, huh?" Danni tapped the envelope on the palm of her hand. "Same-day delivery. They must be in a hurry to entice her." Distracted by the sound of someone outside her door, she laid the letter on Garrett's side of the desk and sprinted for the entrance.

"Gar!" Danni pulled the door open. The person standing there wasn't who she had expected. "Matt?"

"Hi, sis. Nice to see you, too." His sarcasm was evident.

"I'm sorry, I forgot you were coming. Come on in." Danni stepped back from the door and took one last look, searching for her elusive roommate before she closed the door.

"Can I get you something to drink? Water, juice, beer, wine?" Danni walked toward the kitchen and Matt followed her.

"A beer would be fine."

"What's so important that you needed to come see me?" Danni opened the refrigerator, pulled out a bottle, and offered it to her brother.

"Thanks." He took the bottle and twisted off the cap. "Mother wanted me to check out your friend."

"Garrett?"

Matt gave his sister the once-over while he swallowed. "That, and other things," he said. "You know, make sure you were being well taken care of." His eyes lingered ever-so-slightly on Danni's abdomen. "So, how have you been feeling lately? No reason to see any doctors, right?"

"Get real. I see lots of doctors all the time." Danni laughed. "I live with a doctor, for heaven's sake."

"Besides that, I mean." Matt followed her back into the living room.

Danni sat on the couch and laced her fingers around her knee. She nailed Matt with her stare. "It's just the two of us here. What the hell is this all about?"

Matt took another drink. "Mother seems to think that you're being played for a fool."

"A fool? How so? Does mother think that Garrett isn't paying a fair share of the expenses?"

"Actually, she thinks Garrett is leading you on and has gotten you..." Matt grimaced. "You aren't... I mean, you didn't..."

"Didn't what?" Danni eyed her brother curiously.

"Lose them."

"Them?"

His attention focused on Danni's abdomen. "Them," Matt repeated, with a little quirk to his brow.

Danni followed her brother's line of sight. Her brow furrowed as she thought. "Unless you mean virtue or virginity, I'm at a loss as to what you're talking about." She stared at her brother. "Please enlighten me."

"Babies," Matt said. "Mother says you're pregnant."

"By whom?"

"Garrett, of course."

Danni burst out laughing. "Me? Pregnant?"

"With twins," he added.

"Now I know Mother's delusional. Matt, trust me, I'm still a virgin." Danni started to blush.

"You know Mother. It only takes one thing to get her going off on a tangent."

"And that one thing had to be Brie."

"You did give a few of us the idea with your behavior this Christmas."

"How?"

"You refused your favorite wine at dinner, you took naps with Gunny, and you were queasy when breakfast rolled around the next morning." He shrugged. "Even I gave it some consideration, based on that one thing alone. Face it, sis, you've never given up being first in the food line before."

Danni had to admit that Matt was right; it wasn't like her at all. "No wonder Brie packed me ginger ale and crackers for the trip home. Why didn't you just ask me? I would have told you."

"Hey, it was a holiday." He held up his hands. "Do I have to be a lawyer all the time?"

"So, why are you investigating this now?"

"Well, according to Mother and Brie, your phone conversations have been rather explicit as to what you and Garrett are doing... together."

"Huh?" Danni studied his face curiously. "They asked me what was going on, and I told them about our flights."

Matt looked perplexed. "Flights?"

"Our job. I told them about work."

"On the helicopter." A brief laugh spurted out of Matt. "Okay, it's making more sense. Spinning tail rotors... I get it now."

The implication struck Danni. "Oh, God. Mother thought I was talking about..." She covered her face with her hands, then peeked out between her fingers. "Sex?" Danni watched as Matt's smile broadened. "Stop it!"

"I'm sorry. I think it's funny, you having twins."

"But why does Mother think that?"

"She was at the hospital, and apparently she heard Garrett talking about twins."

"Why would Garrett be talking about twins? The only twins we know are..." Danni stopped dead. "Oh, good God. If Mother was at the hospital, she must have heard Dr. Chabot talking about his twins."

"Don't you think it's kind of funny?" Matt quirked a grin and quickly amended his words. "In an odd sort of way, I mean."

"Yes." The room filled first with giggles, then with all out laughter as Danni and her brother lost their composure entirely. "Especially since Garrett's—"

"Garrett's what?"

Danni stopped laughing. "Do you believe everyone has someone out there for them?"

"I sure hope so." His laughter slowed to a chuckle. "Why? Have you found your someone?"

Love radiated from Danni's expression. "I think I might have."

"It's Garrett, isn't it?"

She bit at her lip for a moment, trying to find her courage. "Matt, Garrett is…"

"The prodigal surgeon has returned home. Is anybody going to welcome me?"

Danni jumped up from the couch as Garrett came in the door. "You're home." She scurried to reach for Garrett's hand as soon as the duffel bag was set down. "I want you to meet someone."

Garrett tensed. "Someone?" A dark eyebrow arched high on her forehead, and her stare turned icy.

"Cut it out. He doesn't bite." Danni pulled Garrett behind her. "Matt, I'd like you to meet Garrett Trivoli. Gar, this is my brother, Matt." Danni beamed with pride.

Garrett was caught off guard. "Hi. It's nice to meet you." She gave a lopsided smile as her eyes moved between the two siblings.

Matt offered his hand. "Same here, Dr. Trivoli."

"Please, call me Garrett," she said, shaking his hand.

"Garrett, then. So, you and my sister are friends. I'm glad you're keeping an eye on her here in the big city."

"Someone has to." Garrett looked at Danni. "Although, I think it's been more like her keeping an eye on me."

"Have not," Danni said, smiling.

"Have, too. Who else makes sure I eat regularly?" Garrett teased.

Matt started to laugh.

"Stop it," Danni chastised him, then turned to Garrett. "Both of you." Her heart filled with happiness as these two people she loved seemed to be getting along so well.

"All right, I'll stop," Matt said, "but only if you let me take care of dinner." He looked from one woman to the other. "My treat. That way we can all concentrate on having a good time."

"Pizza!" The word burst from both women simultaneously.

"Pizza it is," Matt declared.

*   *   *

Stuffed with pizza and lighthearted from all the laughter, Matt stood at his car and looked back at Danni's house. He pulled out his cell phone, and waited patiently as the answering machine droned on.

"Mother, it's Matt. I've talked at great length with Garrett Trivoli and have cleared up that situation with Danni. Trust me, the surgeon has nothing but the best at heart for your daughter." He pulled the phone away from his face and stared at it for a moment before terminating the call.

"There you go, Danni. That should give you more than enough time to reel in your surgeon." Matt got into his car, pleased with what he'd done. "Next Christmas is sure going to be interesting," he said through an ever-widening smile.

Chapter 29

Danni's urge to reach out and touch Garrett was overwhelming. Even while running through their checklist before a flight, her mind often strayed. Ever since their time apart, there seemed to always be a reason to touch or look at one another. In an odd sort of way, Garrett seemed friendlier than before. Maybe they both had come to some kind of inner awareness. Reluctantly, Danni brought her mind back to the task at hand.

As if they were taking turns looking at one another, Garrett ventured a glance toward Danni. When their gazes met, Garrett quickly averted her eyes to the case in her hands.

"Are you ready?" Danni asked.

Garrett nodded and strapped the case down. "It's simply a meet and greet for me. You're the one with the speaking part." A smile crossed Garrett's face. "Nice idea by the way, showing teens what really happens if they don't give their full attention to driving."

"I'd rather meet young drivers this way, than wrapped in crumpled metal with the smell of blood heavy in the air."

"Not to mention alcohol."

"You're right. The two do travel in close company. I'm happy McMurray and the Board agreed to let us do it."

"They know a good PR idea when they see it." Garrett patted Danni on the shoulder. "Congratulations. I'm sure it's only the first of many fine ideas you'll offer them in the years to come."

Danni blushed. "Thanks, but I'd save the congratulations until after we're done. I've got butterflies on top of butterflies fluttering in my stomach."

"So, ladies." Cowboy looked at his passengers. "What's the verdict?"

Danni turned to the pilot and gave him a thumbs up. Garrett responded in a similar fashion.

Cowboy returned their sign. "Now that's what I like to see. My team's back at work. What do you say we go enlighten some young minds?"

* * *

The prearranged drill was a simple one, with the local Fire and EMS Departments providing the rescue scenario reenactment. The flight team landed, accepted handoff of the patient, then took off for a brief spin around the athletic field. Then the helicopter landed, allowing the mock patient to get back to his everyday life. The young man emerged triumphantly, the hero of his school.

"Richie! Richie! Richie!" The chant went up from the crowd as the teen bowed and waved, making his way into the stands. As the revelry in the stands rose to a crescendo, the procession of nurse, surgeon, and pilot—all in flight suits—made its way to the small stage constructed on the field. When the cheering diminished, a man with tousled hair stepped up to the microphone.

"All right…" He waved his hand in a quelling motion. "Now, if everyone will take their seats, I'd like to introduce you to some of our guests." He looked at the flight crew and smiled. "As you can see, they are all very different from each other. Some are medically trained, while others take care of their safe delivery. Together, they work as a team to give their patients the very best care. It's just another example of how people in all walks of life can make a difference." He looked down at the note card in his hand. "Let me introduce to you the gentleman who gets them here, there, and wherever they need to go, Pilot L. T. Ferriman."

Cowboy stepped forward and waved to the crowd, his aviator sunglasses reflecting the bright afternoon sun.

Danni leaned toward Garrett. "What do you think the L. T. stands for?"

"Last Trip, maybe." Garrett chuckled. Seeing the skeptical look on Danni's face, Garrett shrugged. "I haven't a clue."

Danni glared back, trying to suppress a smile. "Don't look now, but I think you're up next." She giggled when the tip of Garrett's tongue peeked out at her.

"Next in our lineup is Flight Surgeon Garrett Trivoli." He paused while Garrett slipped off her flight helmet and shook her hair loose. "Let's give her a real welcome."

The applause thundered in response.

"Nice touch, Gar. You're going to be every schoolboy's fantasy tonight."

"Oh, please. Let me get them in a trauma room, and those fantasies will quickly turn into nightmares. Ask any medical student." Garrett gave Danni a meaningful look. "They'll tell you."

"And last, but not least," the man at the microphone said, "we have Flight Nurse Danni Bossard, who is going to say a few words about staying safe this summer." He started to clap, as did the rest of the audience.

Danni moved forward and waved to the stands. She stepped up to the microphone, removed her helmet, and played to the crowd.

"Whew! You can sure get hot wearing one of these." Danni tossed her helmet to Garrett. "Thank you," she said softly, already feeling her hands starting to perspire. She made light of the applause with a hasty glance at her team members, then used the crowd's enthusiasm as a springboard into her talk.

"We all have hidden qualities, and every day they are called upon to make a difference in not only our lives, but in other lives, as well. For us, our actions—or lack thereof—can make a dramatic difference in our patients' lives. You, on the other hand, have the ability to impact your own lives, and the lives of your families and friends, by the simple act of getting behind the wheel of a motor vehicle. Whether it be a motorcycle, car, truck, SUV, or van..."

Garrett looked out over the field. As if it were yesterday, her mind flooded with memories of her youth. Days just like this one, sunny and clear, spent playing sports, with her family in the stands cheering her on. *God, what I wouldn't give for just one more day with them.* She lingered on that thought before turning her attention back to Danni, unaware of the pilot leaning in to speak with her.

"I wonder what she's looking at?" Cowboy caught Garrett's eye and motioned toward Danni.

Garrett studied Danni's concerned expression and searched the stands for its source. Sudden action to the left of the seats caught her attention. Before she could react, Danni's calm voice was turning over the microphone to the next speaker.

"And now our pilot will tell you a little about his part in our mission to serve and treat the injured. Let's all give a big hand to Cowboy."

"Hey, that's not part of the routine."

"Sorry," Danni said as she brushed past the pilot on her way off of the stage.

256

"But I… you…" Cowboy protested as he watched both of his team members break into a run. Defeated, but willing to do his part, Cowboy gathered his wits to pull a story from his extensive experiences as a helicopter pilot. He hoped he could keep the crowd interested and out of his crew's way. "Here goes nothing." Cowboy stepped up to the microphone.

* * *

"Everybody, step back please. Give us some room to work." Garrett surveyed the scene. The angle of the boy's arm and the spattering of blood on the ground around his head were enough for Garrett to assess the severity of the fall.

"Danni, you've got his head until someone from EMS gets here." Garrett glanced at her patient's chest. "Good. He's still breathing on his own."

"Has someone called EMS?" Danni immobilized the patient's head.

"Yes, I sent one of the students over to the ambulance." An older female instructor edged nervously forward. "Is Richie going to be all right?"

A glance between the flight team decided who would take the lead. Danni spoke calmly. "We're going to do the best we can for him."

"Coming through. Excuse me, coming through." The lead medic picked his way around the crowd. Seeing the flight crew already in attendance, he slowed his steps and called out. "Forget the flight team, they're already here." He turned his attention back to the accident site. "What do you need, Doc?"

"Collar, board, and an IV line on the uninjured arm. Don't forget to do a quick splint on his deformed arm while you're at it."

"Gotcha. We'll get right on it." He swung around and started directing his crew. "Jerry, Sue, you're on the collar. As soon as you're done, one of you run back and get the long board and some belts. Marty, get a line set up, and then work on getting that arm splinted. Let's go. Move it, people, we've got a job to do, and this time it's for real. Pardon my back, young lady." He slid in next to Danni, giving her a smile. "I'll start the IV as soon as I hook him up to the monitor."

"No problem." Danni smiled back, keeping Richie's head stabilized as everyone around her went into action.

After the patient was strapped onto the board, Garrett did one last round of neuro checks. Clapping her hands together in front of the patient's face, she called out his name.

"Richie! Richie, can you hear me?" Seeing no reaction, Garrett moved on. With her thumb, she found the small notch in his supraorbital rim. Pushing on it, she waited for a reaction to the painful stimuli.

"Come on, blink," Garrett willed the teen. "Open up your eyes." Nothing happened.

"His breathing is becoming a bit labored," Danni said.

Garrett nodded and continued her tests, placing her fingers in his uninjured hand. "Richie, squeeze my fingers if you can hear me." Garrett repeated her command, but again, there was no response. Frustration set in. "Damn it! Move something, Richie."

Making a fist, Garrett roughly ran her knuckles up and down the teen's sternum. The teen lay motionless through it all.

"How's his breathing, Danni?"

"Becoming more labored as we speak." She assessed the monitor. "His heart rate is up in the one-twenties. He's cool and clammy to the touch."

"Neurogenic shock." Garrett looked at the EMS providers. "Do you have intubation equipment?"

"Yes. Right here." The woman held up a bag.

"Good. Let's get him intubated before we load." Garrett walked to the head of the stretcher and accepted the offered equipment. "Danni, can you give me a little pressure over the cricoid, please?" She opened the laryngoscope and slid the blunt, straight blade into the patient's mouth. The tiny, bright bulb on the end of the instrument lit her way as she searched for landmarks.

"Press a little harder. That's it, I see the vocal cords. Tube." The endotracheal tube was slapped into Garrett's outstretched hand. She inserted it through the cords and situated it in the teen's trachea. Her goal reached, Garrett removed the blade, then slipped out the stylet. She held onto the tube while Danni inflated the small retention cuff.

"Okay, let's bag him. Danni, listen for his breath sounds."

One of the EMS providers produced a roll of tape and hastily secured the tube. Danni adjusted the earpieces of her stethoscope and positioned its bell on Richie's chest. Listening for a moment, she moved the instrument from one side of the teen's chest to the other.

"Lungs sound good. They're equal and clear, bilaterally." She pulled back from the patient. "Finish the securing—"

"And we're ready to go," Garrett said. She held the tube with one hand and squeezed the Ambu bag with the other.

Danni saw Garrett looking directly at her.

"Run ahead and have Cowboy get the ride ready. Tell him he's done a good job so far." Garrett motioned to the EMS crew. "We'll start out to the helicopter."

"Will do." Danni took off on her mission, knowing that time was of the essence. It wouldn't be long until they were once more in the air and speeding toward the hospital. Only this time, the patient was real, and his situation critical.

* * *

Only a few minutes after the patient was handed off to the trauma team, the X-ray images appeared on the viewer. Garrett studied them. The bones in Richie's neck were not in perfect alignment. That alone could have caused his lack of movement and labored breathing. But until she saw the CT scan of his head, Garrett wouldn't bet her paycheck on a single injury being the cause of all his problems.

Sensing a presence behind her, she turned, catching Danni in her view.

"Great job with that speech. I'm sure no one outside of the area knew there was a real emergency going on when you handed it off to Cowboy. Nice idea to get him involved."

"Thanks. We're a team, remember?"

"I'm going to miss that."

Seeing Danni's confused expression, a bittersweet smile came to Garrett's face. She turned her attention back to the viewer. "I've accepted a position in Arizona. I'll be working there starting next month." Garrett closed her eyes tightly in an attempt to hold in the pain. Then she reopened them. "I'm sorry I didn't mention it sooner."

Danni's heart plummeted. "Oh." The word fell out of her mouth in a whisper. "I... I'd better replace the supplies we used." She turned and walked away.

Garrett sighed. *That wasn't so hard. Yeah, right.* It didn't make her feel any better, but deep inside she knew she was doing the right thing for all the parties concerned.

Chapter 30

The crisp morning air was typical for early June, and it brought the promise of good weather for the rest of the day. That made one less thing to worry about for a picnic the size of a family reunion. None of the participants would be related. They were tied together by bonds of another sort—the shared loss of loved ones. The upcoming day was meant to nurture their souls and strengthen those ties. Satisfied with her preparations, Garrett waited patiently at the loading dock. Danni, on the other hand, was a ball of nerves.

"People can get awfully hungry out in the fresh air, Gar. You think they're going to give us enough food for the group?"

Garrett looked over the top of her sunglasses. "And you're saying this because?"

"I'm concerned, that's all. How many picnics have you planned?"

"None."

"I thought so," Danni said. "Face it, you're not the partying type."

"Ah, but I am the commanding type." Garrett turned her attention to the line of dietary staff headed toward them. She surveyed the numerous boxes they carried. "Mission accomplished, I see. You can load it into the Blazer." Garrett saw an older woman at the end of the line holding a bakery box protectively in her hands. "Mrs. Wainright, you remembered my little package."

"How could I forget it, Dr. Trivoli?" The gray-haired woman placed the box into Garrett's hands. "You know, most of the staff never ask my opinion. It was a welcome change working with someone who knows her limitations."

"That I do," Garrett said gracefully. "I wouldn't expect you to do my job, so why would anyone even consider doing yours? According to the grapevine, you're the master."

The sound of Danni's chortle drew a raised eyebrow. "Mrs. Wainright, have you met my team member, Nurse Danni Bossard?"

"No, I can't say that I have."

Danni stepped forward. "It's a pleasure to meet you, Mrs. Wainright."

"Likewise, Nurse Bossard. I've heard a lot about you."

"You have?"

"Yes, thanks to Dr. Trivoli."

"Just spreading a little PR around like the Board wants." Garrett smiled cheekily.

"And when did you start listening to them?" Danni delivered a mock punch to Garrett's arm. The fake look of shock on Garrett's face took her by surprise.

Garrett spoke again to Mrs. Wainright. "I'll make sure the Board knows what a fine job you did for this picnic."

"Thanks, but don't give them any more ideas." Mrs. Wainright saw Danni starting to rummage through a box. "Is the food going to be safe?"

Garrett gave the box she held a little shake. "That's what these are for."

"You're the boss, Doctor." Mrs. Wainright started to turn, then stopped to look over her shoulder. "If you run out of anything, just give me a call. I'll be here all day."

"I'm sure there's a store close to the park. Don't even worry about it. Besides, they'll be too busy boating, biking, or playing games to think about it. Thanks again for all your help."

"Anytime," Mrs. Wainright said, before following the last kitchen worker back into the building.

Garrett shifted her attention to Danni's perusing efforts. "Finding everything to your liking?"

"Huh?" Danni asked.

"In the boxes."

"Oh, yeah. Looks good so far." She eyed the box in Garrett's hands. "What's in there?"

"Something I had them throw in at the last minute."

Danni closed the tailgate and followed Garrett around the side of the Blazer. "Wait a minute. I smell... No, it couldn't be."

Garrett opened the door and slid into the driver's seat. "You're going to be sorry if you don't hurry up and get in."

"Oh, my God." Danni's face lit up. "You got them, didn't you?" The sound of the ignition turning over spurred Danni into action. She ran to Garrett's window and tapped on it anxiously. "You got them to give us those little muffins, didn't you?"

Garrett laughed. "You'd better get in, or I'll have to eat them all myself."

Danni scrambled to the passenger seat and climbed in.

"I figured I'd have to take care of the morning crew."

"But the picnic doesn't start until noon."

"I know. Care for one?"

Danni dug in. "Who said you didn't know how to plan a picnic?"

* * *

Garrett looked around, trying to get her bearings as she pulled into the parking lot.

"Are we lost?" Danni said.

"No, I think we're here."

"We're in the park, that's for sure. What's the name of our grove?"

"We don't have a grove. We have a building."

"A building?" Wide-eyed, she turned to Garrett. "You planned this picnic when?"

"Last month."

"I can't believe you got a building."

"What's not to believe? I've got the permit right here." Garrett produced the envelope from the center console. "We have the Boat House." Garrett eyed the sign off to her right and smiled. "See, we're here."

"Here? People would kill to have an event here." She viewed Garrett with mock suspicion. "You didn't, did you?"

"No."

"Then how?"

"Timing, I guess." A slow smile surfaced. "Apparently someone cancelled right before I called. The only groves open were up on the hillsides, so the choice was easy. I hope the group likes it."

"Like it? They're going to love it." Danni looked around. "There's so much to do here. Boating and fishing on the lake, and with all this level area around the building, we can have…"

"Three-legged races, egg and balloon tosses, and lawn bowling," Garrett said.

"Not to mention tennis, for anyone so inclined." Danni indicated the sign pointing to the nearby courts. "There's even a sandbox and a swing set here for the kids to use."

"And a place to rent tandem bicycles."

Danni was in awe.

"I saw the sign at the last intersection."

"You really have surprised me, Gar. I thought you had this all planned out before we got here. Now I see you can be spontaneous, too." Danni grew quiet, fighting the urge to touch the woman next to her.

Sensing the intimacy of the moment, Garrett turned off the ignition and focused on the lake. "Guilty as charged."

"I like that," Danni whispered.

"Good."

Their eyes met, and time seemed to stand still. Danni's heart began to beat with wild abandon. Instinctively, she wet her lips and leaned in.

In the blink of an eye, Garrett shoved her door open and jumped out. "Come on, help me set the place up," she called out, walking to the rear of the vehicle.

The words jolted Danni into clenched-fist frustration. *God, that was close. More like wishful thinking. Maybe I should be spontaneous, too.* A spark of adolescence lit up in Danni, and she took off for the set of swings.

"Hey! Where are you running off to?" Garrett called out, then chased after her.

"Swinging. Care to join me?"

It wasn't long before both women were flying back and forth through the air in pendulum arcs. Like two children, laughter enveloped them.

"Did you ever have a really good friend when you were growing up? I mean, besides your brother?"

"No. Why?"

Danni shrugged, letting the swing's momentum carry her. "I was just wondering."

Garrett's swing moved opposite Danni's, her body leaning back until she was almost upside down. "How about you?"

"Mother would never allow it. Why don't we make believe we're kids again? You know, do all the things we missed out on growing up." *Please, Gar. Let me remember you as that close friend.*

Garrett slowed her momentum until she hung still at the end of the chains, pondering an idea. It wasn't long before a shy smile tugged at Garrett's lips. "I…"

Danni caught the ground with her feet and stopped swinging. She turned and studied Garrett intently. "You what?"

"I think I'd like that." Garrett's eyes twinkled mischievously, and a flash of white teeth blossomed into a smile. "Race you to see who gets the highest first." Garrett's long legs pushed off the ground, setting her swing into motion.

Caught off guard, Danni was slow to start. "Sure, pick something to do with heights." She watched as Garrett's long, lean form whooshed by her. "I'm not giving up, Gar. I'm right behind you." Filled with determination, Danni leaned back and pushed off, setting her swing in motion.

* * *

With the waning afternoon sun at her back, Danni surveyed the picnic grounds. Smiling, happy faces were everywhere, including those that gathered in small groups along the fringes of the activity. "Looks like everyone's have a good time, Gar. You've done a great job."

"Who'd have thought?"

"You *are* something more than a cut up."

Garrett bowed. "Dr. Garrett Trivoli, Trauma Surgeon, Picnic Planner, Group Organizer, at your service."

"You forgot one or two," Danni said.

"What, lowly woman and Ian's little girl?"

"Oh God, no!" Danni stifled a laugh. "I was thinking more along the lines of winner of the three-legged race and friend."

"Shh." Garrett looked around to see who was within earshot. "I'll lose my hard-ass rating if that gets out. You know how rumors spread at hospital functions."

"I suppose. Well, I don't know about you, but I'm getting hungry. Do you think we have enough food for seconds?"

"More than enough." Garrett followed Danni's lead.

"Look, there's Diana Morgan," Danni said. "She seems to be adjusting well after losing her family."

Garrett eyed the girl. "Sometimes denial has a way of covering up your innermost feelings. In any case, I'm glad she came."

"Me, too." Danni stepped into line behind the teen. "Diana, are you enjoying the picnic?"

The teen spun around. "I'm having a blast. I was out on the paddle boats for the longest time."

"Good to hear. We'll have to give that a try after we eat. What do you think, Gar?"

"It looks pretty easy to me. I'm game for a race."

"You're always game." Danni nudged Garrett.

Without warning, Diana asked the question neither woman wanted to think of, let alone answer.

"Dr. Trivoli, will you be staying with us after your fellowship?"

Garrett's expression became serious, and she shook her head.

"Oh, I see." Diana's mood became more subdued. "I'm glad you're with us today."

"Me, too."

Danni paled and walked away, looking like tears were threatening to spring forth. "I left something in the car. I'll be right back."

"Dr. Trivoli?" Diana said. "I was wondering, since you and I are kind of alike, could I... um..."

"Yes, Diana?"

"Could I call you sometime, if I really need to talk about something important?"

Knowing the young girl's situation was similar to her own, Garrett couldn't refuse. "Anytime you need to, you call me."

"But I don't have your number."

"You will. I've included my cell phone number in the handout everyone will be taking home with them today."

"We did that at my dad's family reunion last year." The girl's words slowed as her memory kicked in.

"We're all family now, Diana. Think of me as your big sister, if you like. I'll be there to listen anytime you need me—provided I'm not in surgery or with a patient, of course." Garrett watched a spark of hope light up in the girl's eyes.

"You wouldn't mind?"

"No, I wouldn't mind at all." Garrett's mind drifted, as did her gaze. "Besides, you can keep me up-to-date on what the members of the group are doing."

*   *   *

"Damn it!" Tears flowed down Danni's cheeks, and the ache in her chest threatened to overwhelm her.

"I'm not going to do it. Not on the one day I have the chance to be carefree. I won't ruin it. Gar's here now, and I'll make the most of it until she's gone." Danni wiped her eyes and prayed she could do it.

She stood on the edge of a grassy knoll and focused on the lake. Its calming effects rippled through her until she was nudged from her reclusive moment by a familiar voice.

"I hope you like burgers."

Danni braced herself. "You know I do." She wiped her eyes, then turned around.

"Good, because I brought you one." Garrett offered a plate. "Did you find what you came out here for?"

"Yeah, I've got everything I need right here." She glanced at the plate and its contents. "How about you?"

"I'm good. For now."

Chapter 31

Karen noticed Danni's mood the moment she walked into the ER locker room. She gathered her stethoscope and pens from her locker. "I didn't think I'd see you here when I came in at eleven. What's up? Bad day in trauma?"

Danni shook her head. "It's just a bad day, period."

"How so?"

"I start my vacation tomorrow," Danni said glumly.

"This should be a good day, then. I know how much you love going up to the cottage. You are going there, aren't you?"

"That was my plan, but now I'm not so sure."

"You take the last two weeks of June for vacation every year. What's different now?"

Danni didn't say a word; with her eyes lackluster and pathetic looking, she merely stared at Karen,

"Oh, I see," Karen said. "It's your last day with Garrett."

Danni nodded and glanced at her watch. "It's almost over."

"So that's why you're in this mood."

"Part of it." Danni produced a small box from her locker. "Here, you might as well take this. I won't have any use for it."

"What is it?"

"It's a pendant. I bought it a while ago."

Karen opened the box. "Oh. But didn't you buy it for—"

"Yes."

"Still not sure?"

"I haven't a clue." Danni slammed her locker shut in frustration. "It's too late now to even consider it. Her mind's obviously set on leaving. You keep it."

"It looks expensive, and it wasn't meant for me. I can't take it."

"Trust me, it's not worth the heartache I'd feel seeing it lying here in my locker."

Karen opened her mouth to protest further, but the sound of Danni's beeper stopped her.

"MVA with multiple victims..." was all Danni read out loud before she set her feet in motion. "Got to go."

The door to the locker room closed, leaving Karen still holding the box. "What am I supposed to do with this?" She shoved it into her locker and closed the door before heading out to start her shift.

* * *

The flyby over the accident scene showed the severity of the crash, the result of drunken driving at its worst. One vehicle had impacted a utility pole and split in two. On the other side of the road, another vehicle sat teetering on its roof, the front end smashed beyond recognition.

"Looks like we have our work cut out for us." Garrett took a moment to prepare herself mentally for the role she'd have to play, deciding who would have a chance at life and who was beyond help. "Are more choppers being sent to this scene?"

"That's an affirmative, Doc." Cowboy glanced into the rear compartment. "Are we doing a load-and-go?"

"No. We'll triage and take the last one out."

"I'll park us in the farthest slot." He turned his eyes back to the ground. "What do you think, wedding limo?"

"My guess is a prom." Danni's voice was filled with emotion. "They were probably having the time of their lives."

"Get us down there, Cowboy," Garrett said. "Let's see what we can do."

* * *

Bodies lay haphazardly, evidence that none of them had been wearing seatbelts. There were six patients from the rear compartment, only two of whom had been immobilized. That was where the first round of triage would begin. Garrett set to the task without delay.

Soon, the sound of more helicopters filled the air, pushing Danni into the role of expeditor, directing patient flow out of the scene as Garrett continued evaluating them. Within minutes, two packaged patients were loaded into helicopters and on their way to definitive care. Danni scanned the scene for the other red-helmeted figure in a flight suit. Finding Garrett in the mix of fire, EMS, and police personnel, she walked toward her with determined steps.

Garrett was standing over the young woman who had been closest to the point of impact. The patient's shallow, gasping breaths were a sure sign of fractured ribs. Given the mechanism of injury, there was a major concern of spinal involvement, too.

"Rib fractures, pneumothorax, among other things. This one goes next." Garrett jotted a few words on the triage tag and affixed it to the patient, then moved on.

"Roger that." Danni kept her patient shielded from the wash of a helicopter descent as she listened to lung sounds with her stethoscope.

"Gar! Her breathing is getting worse on the left. I'm not hearing any movement at all. I think she needs a chest tube."

Garrett looked up from the patient she was getting ready to intubate. "I'm already committed to this patient. You'll have to needle it and use the tip of a glove for a flutter valve."

"But I've never…"

"You've watched me do it a number of times. I'll talk you through it. You'll do just fine."

"I'll try."

"You'll do it," Garrett said in no uncertain terms. "Get an eighteen-gauge needle and cut the finger off a sterile glove. Insert the needle down through the tip you just cut from the glove."

Hurriedly, Danni followed the instructions. "Okay, done."

"Good. Now find the fourth intercostal space on the affected side." Garrett paused. "Give me some suction here. You got that tube ready?" she asked the ambulance member who was assisting her in the intubation. "Did you find it, Danni?" she called out, her eyes never straying from her patient's oral cavity.

"Yeah, I found it."

"Clean the area with alcohol, then pass the needle just over the top of the rib and insert it into the chest wall at the midline, parallel with the nipple. You'll know you're deep enough when you hear the trapped air escaping through the flutter valve. Once you've got it in place, tape it down."

Danni did what she was told. A rush of air escaped with a fluttering sound for a few seconds, then stopped. She breathed a sigh of relief. "Got it, Gar."

"I knew you could do it."

Danni beamed with renewed confidence.

"I'm in," Garrett stated, referring to her patient's intubation. "Now secure it. Give her a minute, and she should be breathing easier." She watched the patient's chest rise and fall evenly, then filled out another triage tag. "Get these patients transported next. EMS will bag this one while I see to the last few."

"You've got it," Danni said. "It won't be long, they're landing now." A fleeting glance between team members was all that time allowed before Garrett took off in search of her next patient.

* * *

At first glance, their injuries weren't devastating, but it was evident that the drama they had witnessed was taking its toll. It tore at Danni's heart to see the emotional trauma one young man was experiencing. His wild-eyed, frenzied look told her that this night would be forever locked in his memory, haunting him when he would least expect it. Danni sat next to him and held his hand, using her soothing voice to comfort him.

Five feet away, Garrett was being plagued by the nonstop questions of the teenager in her care.

"What happened? Where's Julie?"

"You were in a car accident," Garrett answered. "And as I told you before..." Feeling the touch of a hand on her shoulder, Garrett turned to see Danni.

"I'll take care of him. Why don't you go check out the one in the van?" Danni motioned to the overturned vehicle the rescue personnel were working on.

"Thanks. I take it your patient has been lifted out?"

"No, I sent him by ground. I didn't think he was a good candidate for a helicopter ride. Go on, I'll stay with this one."

"He's got a head injury."

"I know."

"What happened? Wh-Where's Julie?" The teen kept asking.

"You were in a car accident, and Julie's at the hospital. You'll see her very soon." Danni waved to the incoming helicopter crew. "This one's next."

Garrett marveled at the endless patience Danni seemed to possess. The ephemeral moment passed all too quickly. Turning to the opposite side of the street, Garrett moved toward the body being removed from the overturned van. A quick look at the unnatural bend of the man's neck and the large area of impact on his head revealed the seriousness of his injuries. Garrett reached for a pulse point but none could be found. She glanced at her watch, then made the somber announcement.

"Time of death, 0138 hours."

"Hey, Doc!" A rescuer waved his arms wildly and yelled above the din of hydraulic tools and diesel engines. "We got the last one out."

Garrett swung around to find Danni. "Tell Cowboy to saddle up. The last patient is about to be ready."

* * *

Relieved of their patient obligations, Danni and Garrett left the ER to deposit their helmets and restock supplies and equipment for the next flight.

Cowboy waited until Danni and Garrett had finished before he approached. He extended his hand to Garrett. "Doc, it's been a pleasure flying with you. Anytime you want, I'd be honored to have you as a team member."

"Thanks, Cowboy. You made it easy for us." The next thing Garrett knew she was being gathered up in a hug. His strong arms reminded Garrett of her father's, and it nearly brought her to tears. Hesitantly, she melted into the embrace.

Danni grew misty and closed her eyes, silently sobbing until a firm hand on her shoulder guided her into a group hug. She didn't know whether to curse Cowboy or thank him. Unable to express their emotions, the women remained silent, taking comfort in the shelter of Cowboy's arms.

* * *

Garrett watched Danni put a stack of clothing into her suitcase and then take it out again. "Something wrong?"

"Not really," Danni said, her attention still on the pile of clothing. "I can't decide what to take. It can get pretty chilly in the evenings with nothing to keep you warm." She smiled bleakly.

Garrett thought for a moment. "I've got the perfect thing." She disappeared out of the room.

"God, Gar, I wish you were going with me," Danni whispered.

"It doesn't look like much, but it's one of the warmest shirts I have," Garrett called from her bedroom.

Danni closed her eyes for a brief moment. *Oh God, why can't it be you?*

"Found it." Garrett entered the room carrying a well-worn USC sweatshirt. She held it out to Danni. "Here, take it. That way, if I ever come back, I'll, ah... I'll have something to wear." The words seemed to stick in Garrett's throat.

"I can't take this."

"Yes, you can. I insist." She pushed the sweatshirt into Danni's hands. "I'll never wear it in Arizona. It's a favorite of mine—took me quite a while to get it all broken in and soft. See?" Garrett took the sleeve and rubbed it against Danni's cheek. "I'd rather you were wearing it than have it collect dust in a storage container."

A moment of bittersweet agony engulfed Danni as she held the garment next to her heart. "Thanks, Gar. I'll take good care of it." She packed the sweatshirt into the suitcase, then looked up and saw a hint of longing on Garrett's face. "It'll be here if you ever need it."

An uncomfortable silence came over them, and Danni felt compelled to end it.

"I made some coffee. Would you like a cup?"

"Sure, why not? I'll just grab the empty cup from my room," Garrett said as she crossed the hall.

Control. Danni chastised herself. *If she doesn't want to stay on her own, you can't hold her here.*

Familiar beeps resounded through the second floor, and Garrett emerged from her bedroom with pager in hand.

"Forget the coffee. That was the hospital. They need another surgeon for a trauma patient." Garrett paused in the hall until Danni's eyes met hers. "Thanks for everything this past year."

Fearing a total loss of control, Danni entered the hallway and wrapped her arms around Garrett. "Anytime, Gar." *I'd do it all over again in a heartbeat.* Danni buried her face into a broad shoulder and tightened her grip.

"I guess you'll be gone by the time I get back home."

Danni nodded, too choked up to speak.

"I thought so." Garrett kissed the top of Danni's head. "I'll send you my address when I get settled." She held Danni out at arm's length and drank in the sight of her, committing it to memory. The second Danni released her, Garrett bounded down the steps and headed for the door.

"Goodbye," Danni whispered. Numb to everything but the ache in her heart, she stood motionless. At the sound of screeching tires, her knees buckled and an empty feeling washed over her. Panic threatened to overtake her as realization set in. Garrett was gone.

Tears flowed freely down her face as she made her way down the stairs and over to the desk. After gathering pen and writing paper, she poured her heart out onto the page. Finished, she tucked the letter into an envelope and sealed it with a kiss. With a deep sigh, she slid her letter into the stack of Garrett's mail.

There would be no need to stall her packing any longer. The day Danni had dreaded for so many months had arrived. It was now time for healing, and to move on with her life. If she could.

Chapter 32

Dr. McMurray got up from his desk and paced around his office, wondering how to approach Dr. Trivoli with what was on his mind. "They always look out for one another, take on the other's battles as if they were their own."

He stared down at his wife's picture and sighed. "I see it in their eyes when they look at one another. It's just like the way you look at me. I don't know why Trivoli wants to leave." He shook his head in dismay and moved to his window. "It's almost like she's leaving for another reason. But what?"

He searched the Pittsburgh skyline until his thoughts were disrupted by a knock at his door.

"Come in," he called out, his eyes remaining focused out the window.

"You wanted to see me, sir?"

"Dr. Trivoli, have you ever felt like you were caught between a rock and a hard place?"

Garrett's eyes narrowed. "Yes, sir, I have. I've found you're damned if you do, or damned if you don't. Sometimes, you just have to pick the damning you can live with and still do your job."

McMurray nodded. "You're really set on heading to Arizona, aren't you?"

"It met my needs."

He looked dubious. "I suppose they offered you everything under the sun and then some."

She stared at him, a slight smile on her lips. "I won't be hurting." *Like hell I won't.*

"In four or five years, I'll be looking for someone to take my place as Chief. We could've groomed you during that time, making you one of the most renowned authorities on trauma. No one would have disputed your ability when the time came. That is, if you had chosen to stay here under me."

"I've been a little preoccupied lately. I hadn't really considered staying."

"I see." McMurray studied her as he formulated his plan of action. "Does the object of your affection know how you feel, or are you keeping it all to yourself?"

His question startled her. "What?"

"You know what I'm talking about." Ol' Cutter sniffed as he searched her face for an answer. "Humph! I can see you haven't even discussed it with yourself, let alone the person who's so important to you." He eyed her with disapproval.

"It's not that easy."

"I see. You think you know what's best."

"There are a lot of things to consider before I—"

"Before you what? Let love pass you by?" McMurray gestured at the photos on his desk. "Sometimes you only come upon an opportunity once in your life, and then the world takes you in another direction." He looked directly at Garrett. "Don't live the rest of your life wondering what it would have been like. Take it from someone who knows. Thank God, I came to my senses after only a year of heartache."

Silence fell over the room as Garrett contemplated her mentor's words.

"You're repressing your feelings, aren't you?"

Garrett tried desperately to hold on to her resolve. "You're correct, sir. I'm not sure my feelings would be well received, anyway." *I don't have the right. She belongs with the father of her—*

"This person isn't already married, by any chance?"

"No."

"All right, then." McMurray abruptly turned back to the window to give himself a chance to think. "Things are viewed a lot differently today than they were in my day," he said in a mellow tone.

Garrett's eyes grew big. "I can't believe it wouldn't be an issue—an obstacle…"

"Dr. Trivoli, let me remind you that when injured patients come seeking help, they don't care whether you are a left-handed surgeon or a right-handed one. All they care about is that you are able to help become as whole as possible once again. Why do you think it will matter who is at your side when you head for home?"

"I know how some people are. They wouldn't understand."

"Since when did you start caring what people think?"

Their gazes locked, each one weighing the validity of the other's statement.

"With HIV running rampant, I'm sure anybody you operated on would rather know that their surgeon is engaged in a monogamous relationship—no matter who the relationship is with. Hell, you'd have to be a fool to take chances on someone who wasn't. Now, don't think I feel every patient needs to know your private life. They don't," McMurray said. "But at least you could answer that question if it were ever an issue. You'd be able to assure them of your complete and undeniable dedication to your partner, putting their minds at ease."

Garrett's mouth dropped open at her mentor's candor. "I never thought—"

"Then you'd better start." His stare pinned her in place tighter than if he had used a hammer and nails. "I'd think about letting the other person know what's in your heart, or you'll lose her for sure. I can't understand how you can be such a damned good trauma surgeon and not be able to take control of your own life. I thought you'd learned more while you were here with us. I guess I was wrong." Ol' Cutter waved a hand in frustration. "May I suggest you be woman enough to talk with her and see where she stands before you throw it all away?" He walked to the window again. "Now, go. You've got a lot of things to consider before you move on with your life."

Garrett left the office. She was riddled with doubt, but still determined to do what she thought best.

* * *

Bleary-eyed from doing more thinking than sleeping the previous night, Garrett glanced up at the clock as she reached for the last set of folders. It was nearly 1600. She opened the first folder, then the second, and her smile grew broader.

"What a nice way to end the day." Garrett looked up and saw the last of her clinic patients walk into the room. She smiled as she recognized the two women from a car accident. "Marie, Chris. I'm glad to see you."

"Why if it isn't Dr. Trivoli," Marie said in her calm, elegant manner.

Garrett motioned to the examination table. "Hop up, Chris, and let me take a look at how well that incision is doing."

"Sure, Doc." Chris pulled up her shirt and did what was asked of her. "I think it's looking pretty good."

Garrett pulled on gloves and gently probed the site. "Looking very good. Are you experiencing any problems, or tightness of the skin?"

"Heck, no. You did a good job of patching me up. Marie told me how you bent the rules to bring her to see me, and I appreciate it."

"Yes," Marie chimed in. "Thank you for not following what somebody else dictated as policy."

"I'd like to think I do what is best for the patient, not just follow the rules," Garrett said.

"You do. I hope you do it for yourself, too, Doc."

"Some things don't always happen like you want them to."

"Doctor, isn't that nurse here with you? You know, the cute blonde one?" Chris grinned.

A smile lifted the corners of Garrett's mouth. "Danni."

"Yeah, that's it."

"She's on vacation."

"But she's coming back, right?" Marie sounded tentative.

"She'll be back shortly after I'm gone." Seeing the shocked looks on their faces, Garrett continued. "I've accepted a position in Arizona. I'll be leaving tomorrow."

"Are you sure you want to do something like that?" Chris asked. "Move all that way across the country?"

"It's a great job offer. I'd be a fool to pass it up."

"Does Danni know about this? I'm sure she wouldn't—" Marie stopped abruptly. "We'll miss you, Doctor."

"Thanks." Garrett drew the material of Chris's shirt down again. "Keep up the good work. Now, let me take a look at your face, Marie." Garrett replaced her gloves with a new pair and turned to study the fading scars. "Your plastic surgeon did a good job. A little more healing time, and you'll hardly see any traces."

Now, if only the scar Danni left on my heart would heal as well.

* * *

Garrett opened her office door, surprised to find Dr. Chabot stretched out, his feet resting on the edge of the desktop.

"Taking over the whole office, eh?"

"I thought it was going to be a little bigger with you gone. I can see now that I was wrong." He watched as Garrett reached for her only possession.

"This will add to the feeling of it being your room." Garrett plucked the framed photo of her brother off of the desk. "The office is all yours."

René turned serious. "You really are going to Arizona, aren't you?"

"Are you going to miss me?" Garrett studied his face intently.

"I will."

"I'll miss you, too." Garrett broke eye contact with him. "It was nice working with you, even if you are Canadian."

"Hey! Do you want to start an international incident, or what?"

"No, of course not," Garrett said with the tiniest bit of laughter. "I enjoyed our talks. They always made me think."

"That's what they were supposed to do, but I'm not sure they did everything I wanted them to."

"They did. Believe me, they did."

René stood and offered his hand. "Perhaps our paths will cross again."

She shook his hand, both as a colleague and as a friend. "You never know what the fates have in store for us."

"Goodbye, Garrett." René hugged her.

"Kiss those little ones for me, will you?"

"I will." He let her slip from his embrace and watched her leave for the last time.

The office felt very empty. René considered the impact Garrett's leaving would have on those who had worked with her. Other than the elation of the nurses in the operating room, there would be little if any celebrating going on, especially among those who had worked closely with her.

"What is Danni going to do without you?" René mused. "Even more important, what are you going to do without her?"

* * *

"Hi, Stella," Garrett said as she approached McMurray's secretary. "I believe I'm supposed to drop these off with you." Garrett held out her office key, two pagers, and her hospital I.D.

Stella accepted the items. "Thank you, Dr. Trivoli. If you would, just sign here and you'll be free to go."

Garrett scribbled her signature one last time for hospital records. She looked at the wall to the left of the door. "New pictures coming?" She pointed to the empty hooks.

"Yes. I'm surprised Dr. McMurray didn't tell you." Stella produced several framed photographs from behind her desk.

Garrett was surprised to see pictures of herself and Danni. The larger of the two was the PR shot for the flight team. The smaller was a black–and–white photo from the softball game last July.

"This is the last one." Stella held up another frame, which held a photograph of four people clustered on a podium.

Garrett gasped. "When was that one taken?"

"You should know. You were there, Dr. Trivoli."

"I guess I was."

"Don't you think it's a good likeness of you?"

"It's good." Her focus drifted from her own image to that of the person next to her. "In fact, it's great." *And I thought I was doing the right thing by leaving. Danni will see me every time she walks through this reception area to McMurray's office. Damn that awards dinner!* Garrett bit her lip nervously. "I've got to go," she said, and bolted for the door.

"You sure know how to pick them, Mary." Stella brushed a piece of lint from the glass over Mary's photo. "Don't want anything to cloud your vision, sister dear. Just like that Ol' Cutter of yours, I'm sure Dr. Trivoli will be back once she figures out what she left behind."

She looked at the photograph of the four people: Dr. and Mrs. McMurray, Dr. Trivoli, and Danni Bossard. "I guess it's going to take some time."

* * *

"God, I'm going to miss coming in here." Garrett made her way through the ER for the last time.

"Hey, Dr. Trivoli." Jamie Potter tried to wave her over. "Can I get you to take a look at a belly for me?"

Garrett shook her head. "Sorry, Dr. Potter, but I no longer have OR privileges here."

"Jeez! I forgot you were leaving." Jamie grabbed a chart. "I guess you won't be playing on our softball team this year, will you?"

"Hardly. I'll be in Arizona."

"Good luck, and take care. It was nice working with you."

"Same here, Dr. Potter." Garrett watched as Jamie moved on about her business. "That wasn't too bad." She turned and sought out the next person on her list.

* * *

Karen saw Garrett making a beeline for her. She caught her with open arms and hugged her. "I'm going to miss you, you Amazon." When Garrett stepped back, Karen wiped a tear from her eye. "You'd think I'd get used to my kids leaving home." She made a face. "Never."

"You should try it from this side, sometime. It's not much better."

"Hey, Doc." Rosie came through a door. "Are you stopping by to help out, or to say bye-bye as you get out?"

"Getting out, Rosie. I just came by to say thanks for all the good times this past year."

"Trauma is in the department. Trauma is in the department."

The overhead paging system spurred Rosie into action. She gave Garrett a quick hug. "Sorry, Doc, I have to go."

"Bye." Garrett watched as the nurse took off for the trauma rooms.

"You know something, Doc? I never thought I'd see Rosie hug you after what happened the first day you came through those doors." Karen shook her head. "She was ready to hunt you down and throttle you."

"Why didn't she?"

"Danni promised to make you more nurse-friendly."

"And that she did," Garrett said.

"Speaking of Danni, she gave me something for you. Let me get it." Karen took off before Garrett could react. It wasn't long before she was bustling back down the hallway, holding a small box. "Here, open it."

"What's in it?"

"Beats me," Karen lied.

Garrett opened the box and revealed a small, free-floating gold heart on a necklace. Startled, she looked at Karen.

Karen acted surprised. "When Danni loves, she loves with all of her heart."

Garrett leaned over and hugged her. "I have to go." She held up the box. "Thanks for everything." She turned and walked out the ER doors.

* * *

Garrett was losing hope of getting any sleep at all. Dr. McMurray's words weighed heavily on her mind, and images of Danni popped up in every corner. At one point, she even imagined a tow-headed child running down the hallway, with a very pregnant Danni giving chase. The image was so real it brought an amused smile to her face. It faded quickly when the shadowy figure of a man came into the picture. Garrett shivered.

Feelings of regret overtaking her thoughts, she sought something to keep her mind occupied. She pushed herself up from the couch and grabbed an empty box. "If I'm going to be up all night, I might as well finish packing."

Soon, the few things she had accumulated while living in Pittsburgh were boxed. Garrett stood up and wiped the side of her face with her shoulder. She stretched her body to its full height and felt the bones of her spine ease back into place. A good hot shower would do wonders.

She started for the stairs. When the phone began to ring, she looked at it curiously and waited for the answering machine to click on.

"Hi. I'm not here. Leave a message. I'll get back to you." Garrett closed her eyes and savored the sound of Danni's voice. A male voice jolted her back to reality.

"Danni, I hope you don't mind, but I've acted in your behalf where Mother is concerned. I've made her aware that you're not pregnant, and never have been. Perhaps this will settle things between the two of you. See you later, sis. Oh, and I almost forgot to tell you it's me, Matt."

Garrett stared at the machine. "David was right. He never… Danni's not…" She closed her eyes and fought back tears. "I was a fool." Garrett's fist slammed down onto the hallstand, sending a shockwave of noise throughout the house. "Damn it!"

Resigned to her fate, Garrett set her course for the shower.

* * *

Once the suitcases were stowed into the rear of her vehicle, Garrett made a last sweep of the house. She pulled her mail from the slot and shuffled through it. An odd piece of stationery caught her eye, and she shoved it into the pocket of her jeans. She tossed the rest into the wastebasket.

Garrett turned to view the house one last time. She picked up her jacket and took the house key from its pocket. Hesitantly, she placed it next to Danni's stack of mail.

"Goodbye, Danni," she said to the empty house.

She crossed to the door and pulled it open. Halfway out, Garrett stopped and took one last look. With a bittersweet smile, she pulled the door closed on another chapter of her life.

Chapter 33

The morning sun felt warm on Danni's face. Seven days had passed since she'd come to her grandfather's favorite retreat. She'd hoped to refresh her tattered soul, but little progress had been made. Her heart still ached.

"I wish you were still alive, Grandfather," she said to the open sky. "You'd know how to help me over this."

Her thoughts drifted, and soon a somber expression settled on her face. "You'd tell me to go for a long walk and let nature be my guide. If only things were as simple now as they were when I was a child. All I had to do then was go to school and follow Mother's wishes."

Danni walked a little farther, until she came to a fork in the path. "I wonder if my life would have been any different if I'd known a woman would capture my heart?" Danni sighed. "Mother would have had me marry the first man she could find, just to set me straight. Then where would I have been? Stuck in a loveless marriage and living a lie."

Danni chose a fork to take at random. "Maybe it's good that I didn't know my sexual orientation back then."

The farther down the path she walked, the more tears ran down her face. Dropping her chin to her chest, she wiped the moisture away, clearing her vision. The upside down USC on her chest came into view. Immediately she was slapped with an image of Garrett, and it took her breath away.

"Oh, God. It hurts so much," Danni rasped, closing her eyes and hugging the shirt tightly to her chest. She opened her eyes to see fleeting images of dark hair and blue eyes. They seemed to be everywhere. Danni shook her head, half-wanting to dispel the image, and half-afraid that if she did, her memory of Garrett would be gone forever. "Gar only spent a weekend here with me, and she's everywhere I look. How am I going to deal with it when I get back home?"

Tormented even more, Danni wondered if the pain would ever stop. Out of the blue, a thought struck her. If the pain stopped, did that mean Garrett no longer held her heart?

Scared beyond belief at what the answer might be, Danni hugged her chest even tighter and hurried back to the safety of the cabin.

* * *

Garrett pushed to put as many miles behind her as possible, and it was midday before she turned off the highway.

She slowed her car to a stop at the end of the turnpike ramp and turned into the parking lot. She got out and stretched as she looked around. "Mabel's Home Cooking," she read from the sign. "Sounds good to me." She headed for the door of the diner. She picked a booth away from the crowd and slid in.

"Potluck's good today, if you're in the mood."

Garrett saw a flash of golden hair, and instantaneously, Danni came to mind.

"Are you ready to order, or do you need a little more time?"

Distracted, Garrett forced herself to look at the menu.

"Better make it fast. We run out of things quick around here." The waitress's laugh carried into the next sentence. "Have you made your mind up yet?"

"Burger and fries." Garrett glanced up and saw the pencil in motion. "I'll take a milkshake, too." She closed the menu and set it back in its holder. "No, better make that coffee. Black."

"Are you a Steelers fan? I just love watching them play football."

"Huh?" The question took Garrett by surprise.

"You know, black and gold." She motioned to Garrett's necklace. "Black coffee, gold heart. Sounds like a fan to me."

Garrett glanced down self-consciously.

"So, are you a fan?"

"Me? Not really, but I do know one."

"Steeler or fan?" Her smile was an obvious flirt.

"Fan." The image of Danni dressed up on game days in her black and gold danced through Garrett's mind. She hoped it would linger forever.

"Hold that thought, sweetie, I'll be back in two shakes of a lamb's tail with your dinner."

Black and gold, huh? The image of the PR photo of the flight team fluttered through her mind. *How appropriate, if only for our hair colors.* Somber, Garrett looked for a distraction. She reached into her back pocket and dug out Danni's note. Unfolding it, she started to read.

My dearest Garrett,

This past year has been a wonderful experience I wouldn't trade for the world. Your friendship and understanding have touched my heart in a way I cannot describe. I wish we had more time together. My only regret is never having told you in person how very much you mean to me. I have no past relationship to compare this friendship to. Even if I had, I'm sure it would pale beside the love I have for you.

Thanks for all the confidence you had in me, especially when I didn't have any in myself. Your support and understanding sustained me and spurred me on to better things as a part of your team. You only walked out the door moments ago, and already I can feel the void growing in my heart. With more time together, you would have cured me completely of all my insecurities. Perhaps then I could have told you in person exactly how I feel. I love you, Gar. There, I've said it, and I hope you're not offended by it. You will always have a home in my heart.

Always,
Danni

Garrett stared at the letter, Danni's words echoing in her head. There it was, in black and white. Danni loved her. How could she deny it now?

"Hey, hon. Are you all right?"

The waitress startled Garrett. "Yeah, I'm fine."

"You could have fooled me. You don't look fine."

"I need to make a call." She reached for her phone, but she had returned it. "Do you have a phone here?"

The waitress drew back under Garrett's intense stare. "Sure, it's over there by the restroom." She pointed, but Garrett was already in motion.

After spending a short time on the phone, Garrett came back to her table with an air of determination. She nibbled on a few fries while digging into her pocket, then tossed a ten dollar bill on the table and scooped up her burger.

"Hey," the waitress yelled from behind the counter. "Don't you want any dessert? I've got some great cherry pie for you to taste." She flashed a sultry smile.

"No, thanks. I've got a taste for something else."

Chapter 34

Another day was coming to an end, and with the evening came the dismal prospect of being alone. Preoccupied, Danni strolled around the edge of the lake, ignoring the approaching sunset. The water—still, quiet, and all-consuming—beckoned to her. Before long, she stood at the edge of the pier and stared into the pond.

"I should have said something, anything to her." First one tear fell, then another, each causing a small ripple in the water.

"What I wouldn't give to have you here with me now." The words slipped out of her mouth before her mind could register them. Danni closed her eyes, trying not cry. The ache in her chest was so painful, she thought her heart was breaking in two. She opened her eyes and saw Garrett's image floating on the surface of the water.

Now I know why people contemplate suicide. First, it's her image, next, I'll hear Garrett calling my—

"Danni."

Danni gasped and spun around before taking a tentative step toward the mirage. Boldly, she reached out to embrace her fears. Touching a physical presence startled her, and she jerked her hand back.

"You're real."

"Of course I'm real."

"Gar?"

"Who else?"

"It's really you. I thought I was seeing things again." Tears rolled down Danni's cheeks as she flung herself at Garrett and embraced her.

Absorbing the shock of the full body hug, Garrett sought a way to lighten the moment. "Hey, what's this, tears of joy to see me?"

"They are now." Embarrassed, Danni looked away.

A delicate touch on her chin guided Danni's gaze back to Garrett's face. Their silent exchange lengthened and their anticipation grew. Garrett edged closer until their lips met. Like a wisp of smoke on the horizon, the kiss lingered, soft and tender. As the contact faded, both women savored the moment.

Once their breathing returned to normal, Danni looked up into Garrett's blue eyes and waited.

"I love you," Garrett said.

The utterance of those three little words brought Danni's heart to life. "I've waited so long to hear those words."

"Really?"

"Yeah, really. I love you, too." A smile of happiness completed Danni's answer.

"Oh." Garrett leaned in again. Lips touched, then parted, and soon tongues were entangled. All logical thought stopped, and emotions soared. Neither woman moved to end the kiss until it was absolutely necessary. Breathless, they stood with their foreheads touching as they struggled to regain their equilibrium.

Self-conscious, nervous giggles erupted when the sputtering engine of a boat broke the spell. Their bodies separated, but their entwined fingers held them together while the threat of interference faded into an insignificant spot on the horizon.

Danni's curiosity got the better of her. "Aren't you supposed to be on your way to Arizona?"

"I'm not taking the position."

"But I thought it was a done deal."

"It was."

"I could go with you." Danni held her breath.

"And leave all the things and people you love? I couldn't ask you to do that." Garrett looked away, focusing on the lake. "The truth is, my heart isn't in making the move. I finally came to realize that no matter where I went, my heart would always be here with you."

Danni was mesmerized by Garrett's words. "I feel the same way."

"I know. I read your letter. It brought me here." Garrett fingered the pendant she wore. "Thanks, by the way, for this necklace."

"Necklace?" Seeing the floating heart displayed on Garrett's chest, Danni sighed.

"Karen said you wanted me to have it. You did, didn't you?" Garrett searched Danni's face.

"Yes, but I wasn't sure how you'd receive it."

The corners of Garrett's mouth turned upward. "Could we..." Her voiced trailed off. "Could you give me a second chance?"

Danni turned toward the resplendent sunset on the lake's horizon. "Do you see that sunset, Gar?"

"Yes."

"Rumor has it there'll be another one tomorrow, possibly even more spellbinding than today's." Feeling Garrett stiffen, Danni turned back and held onto her even tighter. "I'd like to see it with you. Yes, I'll give us a second chance, if you will."

"Thanks, I was hoping you would." The distance between them dwindled, and another kiss ensued.

"Now," Garrett said, "let's watch our sunset together."

"The first in a long line of sunsets." Danni reveled in the sensation of Garrett's arms wrapped around her and the warmth of Garrett's breath on her skin. They basked in the waning glow, until the last burnt-orange glimmer of sun faded from the sky.

"Gar?"

"Hmm?"

"What are you going to do now?"

"I'm not sure." Garrett took her time answering. "I thought I'd talk to McMurray at the end of the week." Hearing the hitch in Danni's breathing brought a smile to Garrett's lips. "I'm afraid a position in surgery might be a little up in the air. I'll have to wait and see."

Danni closed her eyes and cherished the feeling of love enveloping her. "Why did you want to leave in the first place? Was it because you weren't sure of my feelings?"

"I thought you were pregnant."

Danni's eyes shot open. "What?"

"Let me explain."

"Please do."

"I thought you and David—"

"David and I?" Danni looked surprised. "Whatever gave you that idea? David is a friend. I'd never—"

"I know. He told me." Garrett paused long enough to collect her thoughts. "I thought you were in love with someone. I assumed it was him."

"But why would you think I was pregnant?"

"The day McMurray sent me to David's hospital, I heard you say you were pregnant."

"Say what?"

"I have to admit, it caught me off guard."

"Me, too." Danni shook her head. "Mother strikes again."

"What?"

"Thanks to the overactive mind of my sister, Brie, Mother was led to believe that I was having a wild, torrid love affair with a staff member at the hospital."

"Who?" Garrett sounded jealous.

"The tall, dark, and always-on-the-prowl-for-new-meat trauma fellow," Danni replied, pausing for dramatic effect, "Garrett Trivoli."

"Me? I don't understand."

"Mother was at the hospital one day and overheard René talking about expecting his twins soon. She thought René was you."

"Why would your mother think he was me, or that I was him?" Frustrated, Garrett shook her head. "You know what I mean."

"I have an idea. I told my sister that you moved in with me."

"Okay." The tentative-sounding reply matched the cautious look on Garrett's face.

"I guess one thing led to another, and seeing René in your flight suit made Mother think that he was Dr. G. Trivoli, as the nametag read. Thus, in her mind, I was pregnant with his twins."

"I bet my parents never realized how much trouble my name was going to be."

Danni tugged at Garrett's hand. "I don't want any more misunderstandings or miscommunications between us."

"I agree. Let's do our best to be open and honest with each other." Garrett looked deep into Danni's eyes. "I'm sorry I didn't do that earlier."

"You're not the only one at fault. I hid my feelings, too. We'll take it nice and slow."

"Agreed."

"We'll talk things out instead of jumping to our own conclusions."

"Talk, huh?"

"Communicate. You know, exchange words." Danni traced her finger over Garrett's lips.

"I might be able to do that, among other things." A grin spread across Garrett's face. "Let me start by saying I've got a lot to learn about love. It's not something I've had in my life, at least not in the last twenty years."

"Neither have I, at least not in the physical sense." The hint of a blush colored her face. "I've never..."

"Shh." Garrett placed a gentle kiss on her forehead. "We're a team, remember? We don't rush into anything until we're both ready for it. Understand?"

"I understand."

They walked toward the cabin hand in hand until Garrett stopped short.

"Danni, I was just thinking."

"About what?"

"Nothing." Garrett shrugged. "Everything." She waited until their eyes met. The kiss that followed was soft and tender. Garrett was the first to break contact, only to reestablish it with fervor. Finally, when neither woman could last a moment longer without a breath of air, their connection ended.

"Whoa! I like how you think."

"Me, too." Garrett rested her forehead on Danni's and looked crossed-eyed at her.

Danni giggled. "Stop that, or you'll be seeing double."

"You mean like twins?" Garrett stifled a laugh.

"Only if my mother's around. Then we'll really have some tales of two."

* * *

Snug in bed and content to do nothing more than hold Danni in her arms, Garrett reflected on the past year. Her fellowship had honed her skills as a trauma surgeon and had also taught her many lessons. The two most important ones had more effect on her life than on her job. First, she'd been shown how to open her heart to love. Second, that through doing so, she no longer felt alone.

Danni was her family now. The nurse with a heart of gold meant more to Garrett than performing surgery ever would.

Danni's embrace tightened around her, sending a chill down her spine.

"My family now," Garrett said with a sigh, nestling closer to the woman she loved. As she drifted off to sleep, she realized that in more ways than one, that's exactly what Danni was.

© K Darblyne, 2007

About the Author

Deeply rooted in the Western Pennsylvania area, **K. Darblyne** has spent years observing people, both on and off the job. Her schooling in the physical sciences may be the foundation for her analytical thinking, but it's her time spent in the fields of EMS, firefighting, and health care that give life to her stories.

Trauma is second nature to her after having been involved in all aspects of the human emotions that a crisis evokes. It is with this commitment to the spirit of survival, for both victim and rescuer alike, that she writes from the heart.

Four small feet connected to a tail and a bark, along with the belief that soul mates are real, vie for the rest of her time when she's not poised over a keyboard working on her next story. The house and yard, on the other hand, will be there long after you're done calling them home.

Blue Feather Books is proud to offer this
excerpt from Karen Badger's debut novel,

ON A WING AND A
PRAYER

Available now, only from

Bluefeatherbooks
L I M I T E D

www.bluefeatherbooks.com

Forty-five minutes later, Cass had just finished showering off the sweat from her workout. She stood in the den with a towel around her middle, rubbing a second towel through her hair as she booted up her computer and waited for her wallpaper to appear—a smiling picture of Rox she had scanned from the back cover of *Stargazer II*.

"Damn, that woman is gorgeous," she commented as she sat down and accessed her e-mail program. Her inbox opened, indicating two pieces of new mail. The first message was from the airline, indicating that her flight to Durango that Monday was being rescheduled to depart an hour earlier than usual, which wasn't an uncommon occurrence with international flights and foreign airports. The second was from Rox. Scanning the contents of the note gave Cass a very uneasy feeling. *This is a very unhappy woman, E. God, I wish I could take her away from it all.*

"Why can't you?" Enforcer asked.

What do you mean, 'why can't I?'

"Why can't you? What's stopping you?"

Well, for one, I don't even know that she's into women. Like you said during chat, she said she loved me for caring, not that she loved me, remember? Her friends Nikki and Jerri are obviously a lesbian couple, but that doesn't make her gay. It's possible that all she wants from this relationship is someone she can be emotionally intimate with, but not on a romantic level. Anyway, she made it perfectly clear that she had to stay in her current relationship until her father was gone. What chance do I have?

"Well, you could always knock her father off, get it over with. Whaddaya think?" Enforcer suggested.

Cass clapped her palms to her forehead and shook her head in disgust at where her mind was taking her. *Damn it, Cass, just answer the note.*

She sat back for several moments, then scanned Rox's note once more before composing a reply.

My dearest Rox,

I feel so privileged to be allowed a glimpse of your soul. Thank you so much for sending your journal. Yes, I would very much like to continue receiving daily entries. I feel like you are showing me a secret part of yourself, a part reserved only for those you hold dear. Thank you for trusting me.

Rox, you have posed many valid questions. You have the mind of a philosopher and the soul of an angel. I wish I had answers for you, but I don't. Nevertheless, here are my thoughts.

Why do people need contact? I don't know. I suppose we need contact to measure our impact on others, and maybe even to validate our own self-worth. You know- -the more people we physically touch and the more people we have who voluntarily touch us, the greater our sense of worth. That's one theory. I think we draw comfort from touching... we seek refuge in it.

That's why we need contact even more when we are ill. We all want to be taken care of, in one respect or another. Too many of us are the caretakers, never receiving anything in return. Yes, even something as simple as a touch to reward our efforts... a kiss, a hug, a hand cupping your cheek. That type of touch validates us, and tells us that the world is a better place with us in it. I don't know, Rox. These are only my thoughts. They're not based on fact, or on psychological doctrine, they're just my thoughts.

I'm glad to hear that you're making progress with your new book. I'm afraid the cast on your hand will hinder you, though, unless you can get some help. Nikki seemed to do a very good job typing for you last night... maybe she would be willing to help?

Rox, like Nikki, I'm worried about your relationship with Chris. I want so badly to rescue you from his brutality. Say the word, and I will be on the next flight to Maine. Please feel free to call my home whenever you need me. I've already given you the number, but here it is again: 408-555-1080. My pager number is 408-555-0046.

Please don't let Chris hurt you again, Rox. Please call me, and I will do whatever is in my power to stop it. Nikki is right to be worried about you. What if Chris does return? What then? I am so glad Nikki and Jerri are staying with you. They sound like wonderful friends.

Rox, I feel a closeness to you I never thought I would feel again after Patti died. In the three years since her death, I've held a small sliver of my heart in reserve, saving it only for Patti's memory. I find you invading that sliver, as you have invaded the rest of my heart. I can't stop thinking of you, Rox. I don't want to stop. Please promise that you will call me if you need me. I don't care what time of the day or night it is. If you can't reach me at home, please call my pager. If you need me, Rox, I promise I will find a way to get to you.

Enough said; I'll let you go for now. I'm so looking forward to your next note.

Lovingly yours,
Cass

Happy with her note, Cass sent the message and watched it disappear from her screen.

* * *

Rox waited patiently as the server retrieved her messages. Her eyes brightened when she saw the message from Cass, and she opened the note. She scanned it quickly, then took her time rereading it. Rox stopped when she saw the phone number. *Do I dare?* she thought, looking at the clock. *Let's see, It's nearly one p.m. here, so it's ten a.m. there. He must be out of bed by now.*

* * *

Cass dressed and waited for Angie to pick her up for a much-needed shopping trip. She hated shopping, but at their last meeting, she'd had to grudgingly admit that she needed some new underclothes and a pair of running shoes. Angie had immediately volunteered to drag her through the mall.

Soon after she'd finished getting ready, Cass heard a car horn and stepped out onto her small balcony, which overlooked the parking lot. *Precisely ten a.m.; Angie's right on time.* Groaning loudly, she grabbed her wallet, went back inside and headed for the door, only to hear the telephone ringing.

Cass stopped dead at the door, turned around and looked at the phone hopefully. *Maybe it's work calling. Maybe I can get out of this stupid shopping trip.* She walked the few steps from the door to the end table and picked up the receiver.

"Hello?" There was only silence on the line.

"Hello?" Cass said again, a little louder, and an audible click was the response.

She looked at the receiver questioningly, her brow furrowed, then shrugged. "Crank callers." Cass hung up the phone and went out to meet Angie.

* * *

Rox slammed down the receiver.

"Oh, my God," she said. "A woman answered the phone."

"Huh? Did you say something, hon?" Nikki asked from the kitchen doorway as she wiped the last dish.

Rox was still looking at the receiver. "I said, 'A woman answered the phone,'" she replied, partially in a daze.

"A woman answered whose phone? Roxie, honey, maybe you should take that nap now," Nikki suggested, going into the living room to feel her friend's forehead.

Rox brushed her hand away. "Nik, I'm all right. A woman answered Cass's phone. He gave me his phone number in his last message. I called and a woman answered his phone!" she said in an agitated voice.

Nikki raised her eyebrows as she wiped her hands on the dishtowel. "I see."

"What do you think it means?"

"It means he had a woman in his apartment. Maybe it was his mother or his sister," Nikki suggested.

"Or his girlfriend," Rox added. "Nik, what do I really know about this guy? He could be some wacko!"

"Rox, he's an airplane pilot, not a wacko," Nikki said, trying to soothe her.

"Are you saying airplane pilots can't be wackos, Nik?" Rox challenged.

"No, I'm not saying that. Look, Rox," Nikki said, exasperated. "Why don't you skip your e-mail for this afternoon and get some sleep? It'll still be here when you get up. Okay?"

When a yawn gave away her true fatigue level, Rox reluctantly agreed.

"You go on up… slowly, and hold on to the railing. I'll power down the computer then come tuck you in, okay? Hell, I may even join you," As Rox turned and headed toward the stairs, Nikki watched the computer shut down and thought, *If you're messing with my friend, you're a dead man, Cass Conway.*

Find this and other exciting Blue Feather Books
at

www.bluefeatherbooks.com

or ask for us at your local bookstore.

Blue Feather Books, Ltd.
P.O. Box 5867
Atlanta, GA 31107-5967

Tel/Fax: (678) 318-1426

Printed in the United States
82014LV00005B/22-36